THE FLYING CROSS RANCH
THE COMPLETE SERIES

SHANAE JOHNSON

THOSE JOHNSON GIRLS

Copyright © 2023, Ines Johnson. All rights reserved.

This novel is a work of fiction. All characters, places, and incidents described in this publication are used fictitiously, or are entirely fictional. No part of this publication may be reproduced or transmitted, in any form or by any means, except by an authorized retailer, or with written permission of the author.

VOW TO LOVE

A FLYING CROSS RANCH ROMANCE 1

There was nothing like country air. Charlie Matthews took a deep inhale, filling his lungs with an abundance of the oxygen offered to him in this wide-open space. The sweet tang of honeysuckle tickled his nostrils. The musk of hay and horses clung to his upper lip. He gulped down more of the intangible substance until the smells left his lungs and permeated his heart.

Charlie was so used to breathing the processed air inside a cockpit. Up in the clouds, the sparse oxygen was clean, pure. It didn't smell like it belonged to anybody. Down here on earth, on the Flying Cross Ranch, it smelled like home. Because this was home.

He was home.

Charlie inhaled again, opening his mouth to take in even more of the scents of the ranch he'd spent much of his life on. The tang of manure touched his tongue. The perfume of wildflowers was a cloud around his nose. And best of all, the savory scents of a dozen casseroles stuffed into the fridge made his belly grumble.

By his inability to shut the fridge door without force, Charlie could easily estimate that everyone in Honor Valley had brought over a dish. All of his father's neighbors wanted to make sure that Haran Matthews had everything that he needed. Which was a change.

Not the notion of folks being neighborly. This was still a small town, after all. It was a change because, once upon a time, the community had been leery of the Matthews boys.

Just a decade ago, anytime a car would kick up gravel on its way down the drive of the Flying Cross Ranch, Charlie and his brothers would run into the woods and hide. Even if whatever damage had been done to whatever discarded piece of property, or ruffian's jaw, or pretty girl's misguided heart, wasn't their fault. Because if it was any one of their faults, then it was all of their faults. Their parents believed in group punishment as a deterrence.

It never worked. The singular thing that actually deterred the six sons of Haran and Tessa Matthews from their wicked ways and childish games was the day their beloved mother took ill and passed away far too suddenly for the boys to catch their breaths and process their loss.

"That's enough now, son," said Haran Matthews.

Charlie's father was propped up on the living room couch that overlooked the hundreds of acres of the family's land. The pillows Father Matthews's wife had sewn surrounded him, like plush soldiers flanking his every side. Charlie had been in the process of adding one more pillow to his father's back when the old man shooed away his intentions.

"I'm fine here," said Father Matthews. "Why don't you go out and see some of your old friends."

In this town, the only friends the Matthews boys had had been themselves. Well, that and the Silver sisters on the ranch next door, who were also social pariahs in this town. Charlie knew his father wasn't referring to his other sons or their next-door neighbors.

By old friends, Charlie knew exactly which friend his father meant. Seeing her was on his agenda soon. But not today.

Charlie reached out and covered his father with a blanket that his mother had knit. The light blue fabric was in stark contrast against his father's brown skin. Charlie's pale hand was in contrast as well as he tucked the edges.

Father Matthews's hands were what Charlie loved best about his father. Those large, callused hands were what Charlie had noticed when he became Father Matthews's son twenty years ago. The man who would become his father had reached his hand out to Charlie, open-handed like they did on television shows where men dressed in suits and clasped hands.

The eight-year-old boy that Charlie had been had hesitated. He'd never shaken another person's hand before. He wasn't sure how to do it. Even before that, he wasn't used to any adult being kind to him. Somehow, he'd willed up enough courage to do that new and unknown thing. Taking Father Matthews's hand had been the best decision in his life.

"Don't the two of you have some pact where you have to be the first person each other sees when you're both back in town at the same time?"

The two of them did have that pact. This was the first time that Charlie would be breaking that promise to her. When she learned why, he knew she would forgive him.

She probably would forgive him.

She maybe would forgive him.

Hopefully, she would forgive him.

They'd made that pact when they were kids. They were adults now. Like him, she had grown used to adults breaking their promises over the years. This would be the one and only time he would break his promise to her.

His father had had a heart attack only a few days ago. Charlie had to take care of family first. Even though she had been his family before the Matthews had come in to rescue him from foster care.

That day had been the first time that Charlie had left her behind. It hadn't been the first time that she'd left him. Nor would it be the last.

For two decades, they'd been ships passing in the night. Docking a few days here and there. Rarely in the same port for too long. Today, Charlie was casting his anchor.

Which was entirely the wrong metaphor since, as an Air Force Pilot, he had hung up his wings before coming home. He was setting down his anchor, parking his boat, and mixing all the metaphors. The point was, Charlie Matthews was home to stay.

He took in another deep breath. This time breathing in the scent of his father.

Fresh pine.

Sweaty tack.

Safety.

Love.

"Just go and see her," said his father. "I'm just going to rest here."

For a man of the cloth, his father was actually a decent liar. Father Matthews uttered the bold-faced untruth with the peaceful air he'd use in a sermon. The problem was that Charlie had already caught him outside in the stables the other night. His father might not want to be babysat, but it's exactly what he needed.

"Nice try, old man. But I'm taking you in for your checkup today," said Charlie. "I have the rest of my life to spend with Savy."

Charlie thumbed the plastic ring he wore on a chain around his neck. He'd be seeing Savy soon. He'd be seeing her every day for the rest of his life after he got his father back on his feet.

CHAPTER TWO

It was times like these that Savy James felt like Cinderella. Here in this old, cluttered house, she scrubbed the floors and tended to the pots of food cooking on the stove. There weren't rats scuttling about in the walls, but a few ants had made their way inside since technically she lived in the wild. Unfortunately, unlike her girl Cindy, none of the wild creatures taking up space in and around Savy's home raised their voices in song or picked up a broom to help her clean.

Savy supposed that was fair. Her voice wasn't the delicate soprano of the Disney princess. She was an alto. Her voice was rich and full with a hint of smoke, though she'd never had a single cigarette. Still, she supposed with a voice slightly deeper than Ursula in *The Little Mermaid*, the mice and woodland creatures might think her a villain rather than the heroine.

They weren't the only ones.

"Yo, give it back. It's mine. 'Fore I drop you like a dime."

"You are so lame. You'll never make it as a rapper, not even for a candy bar."

"We gone see who be lame, when my records brings me fame."

"Ms. Savy's stupid rule says it's communal property, so it's not yours."

The shouted words were followed by a loud crash. The crash was the splintering of wood, not the break of bones. Savy had learned to distinguish those sounds at a young age. So, she didn't rush to the other room.

They were expecting an important guest soon, and the house was still in disarray. But she supposed it would look bad if she was mopping up blood when their visitor arrived. So, Savy decided to pick her battles. She rested the broom against the kitchen counter and walked calmly into the other room.

"Ashton, Denny," she said, raising her alto voice.

The commotion immediately stopped. It was always jarring to others when Savy used the bass in her voice. She was technically a contra-alto, the lowest register for a female singer along the lines of Cher, Tina Turner, and Billie Holiday. However, if someone made her mad enough, she could reach the heavy tenor of Luciano Pavarotti. Most of the time, she had the smokey voice of the actress Kathleen Turner.

"If one of you kills the other, not only will that person have to clean up the blood, but I'll make you dispose of the body all by yourself. Do you hear me?"

The loud ruckus stopped abruptly, followed by two sulky, "Yes, Ms. Savy."

Had this been a Disney movie, she and the kids would've broken into a song and dance about cooperation and sharing. Savy could've pulled off the song. Not the dance. It wouldn't have mattered anyway because the two young boys scurried off in opposite directions.

The kids at the Bright Horizons foster home all hated chores. Which was entirely normal. All kids hated chores, especially if they involved a rag and a broom.

Not Savy.

Chores had been one of the few consistencies in her life. As a young girl surrounded by the chaos of narcissistic and addicted parents, she'd clung to any routine and sense of normalcy. So, although Savy gave each of her charges daily chores at the foster home, she still went behind their work with a rag and a broom each night. It was the only way her mind settled enough for her to go to sleep.

Savy headed back to the kitchen to retrieve her broom as well as her zen, when another crash from a different room shook the walls. Once again, Savy let go of her trusty broom and went in search to see which hellion in her charge was trying to let loose the Devil in this house.

"Daria, what are you doing?"

That sopranic voice belonged to Savy's youngest sister. Along with her high-pitched voice, Foxy could've physically passed for a Disney princess with her wide eyes, button nose, and heart-shaped mouth. She most resembled Princess Jasmine with her golden tanned skin and raven braid hanging over her shoulder. All she needed was a tiara to complete the look. A tiara and a washcloth with lots of soap.

Foxy was bent over, looking up into the fireplace. She was covered from head to toe in soot, like she was the little Cinder girl instead of a runaway princess off on a magic carpet ride.

"What's going on?" said Savy.

"Daria climbed up the chimney," said Foxy.

"Oh, no," Savy groaned. "Not another superhero stunt."

"Remember that kid Neil who was here last year," came a disembodied voice from the chimney.

"Daria, get down from there," said Savy.

"He stole money and hid it somewhere in the house," said Daria. "But no one ever found it. I saw him in here, and he looked suspicious."

"Neil always looked suspicious," said Foxy. "Because he was always doing something he shouldn't."

"Which is why they took him to juvie after he stole from the library and tried to sell the books at the school book fair," said Savy.

"He was not the smartest," sighed Foxy, wiping the soot from her cheek, only to replace it with more streaks.

"Exactly," called down Daria. "I thought he hid the money he earned in the chimney."

Savy wanted to argue that money gained from thievery wasn't earned, but she had to keep her priorities straight. Once again, she picked her battles. "Daria, get down from there. You'll hurt yourself."

There was a sharp intake of breath that echoed down the chimney. Then a puff of soot. No child emerged.

"But, Ms. Savy, if I find the money, then we can buy the foster home from the government, and they can't take us away. We can all stay together."

If Neil had stashed money in the chimney, it wouldn't be enough. Because this house wasn't for sale. The land was being taken over by the government in favor of the protected wildlife in the valley. The herd of mustangs had tugged on the heartstrings of the community more than the wildlife inside the foster home. And now, they were the ones who had to fend for themselves.

"Daria, I need you to get down here now," said Savy, putting bass in her voice. "The representative from the government will be here any minute, and you're supposed to be in a dress with a clean face."

"A dress?"

There was another plume of soot. Along with a scuffling sound. Daria was likely climbing higher, more likely over the threat of a dress than a clean face.

"You'll need to get that, sis," said Foxy, canting her head toward the front hall.

Savy didn't ask for clarification. Foxy fancied herself a bit of a psychic. Their Creole grandmother had had the touch. Every once in a while, Foxy got a prediction right. When it came to expected visitors, her clairvoyant sister was batting a thousand.

As if on cue, the doorbell rang.

"I'll stall," said Savy. "You get her out of there. And then clean both of your faces."

Savy headed to the front door, but Ashton was already there. The kid wore a faded T-shirt with the explicit lyrics of a rap song that were blacked out. But the gist of the song was still easy to get by filling in the blanks. Savy believed in allowing the kids to express their personalities. She just wished she'd censored Ashton before he'd gotten to the door.

"What you at my door for? When you don't know the score?"

The brown-skinned man in a dollar store suit stepped back. He looked at the address, which was crazy, as this was the only house on the road. Then he looked again at the pint-sized wanna-be rapper with blond cornrows.

Savy had talked with Ashton—who insisted on being called Ashtray—about manners, opening the door to strangers, and misappropriating other people's cultures. What Ashtray spat back was the notion that he had freedom of speech. And yes, he spat it all in rhyme. The kid walked around with a thesaurus and rhyming dictionary. Which was a boon to his education. So, Savy decided not to pick that battle.

The government official took one look at Ashtray, then Savy, then the mess left in the hall, and began to jot down some notes. This was not going well. She knew that if she didn't win this battle, then she might lose the entire war.

"Mr. Davidson, hi. I'm Savy James."

Savy gave the man her most winning smile. His facial features didn't crack as he regarded her. Before he could take her hand, a scream came from the other room. Then a thud. Followed by a plume of soot.

"I think I broke my arm," sobbed Daria.

Savy looked outside at the deserted road. A white horse ran in the distance, wild and free. There was no rider on its back. Even as she thumbed at the plastic ring she wore around her neck, she knew better than to wish for a prince to ride in and save her.

She knew Prince Charming existed. She'd found her prince when she was a little girl. The problem was he never showed up at the right time, and he always left too soon. Forever was off in the future for her and Charlie Matthews. Forever definitely wasn't today when she needed him most.

CHAPTER THREE

"I can drive my own car, son."

"So I've heard. I hear you can fly a plane, too. But even the best pilots still need to be cleared for duty before they get back in the cockpit or behind a wheel."

Father Matthews didn't argue with his son. The man never argued. Just like always, he sat back and allowed his sons to experience the boons or consequences of their decisions.

When Charlie had wanted to speed on a country road, after Father Matthews said it was against the rules, the old man sat back and didn't say a word when the State Trooper pulled them over and gave Charlie a $150 speeding ticket. Neither did he give his son a penny toward the fine.

When Charlie decided he wanted to follow in his father's footsteps and go into the Air Force, his father sat back and smiled peacefully. He said nothing about the practical jokes that often cost Charlie clean underwear or the callout challenges that left him with a bloody nose that were hazing rituals of Basic Training.

To this day, Charlie obeyed speed limits on the road. Though he had broken the sound barrier in the air. He'd also earned the Flying Cross medal along with the respect of his fellow airmen. He took the lessons and the licks, just as his father taught him.

That was Haran Matthews's way. And Charlie loved the man for it.

Father Matthews had somehow known that his boys wouldn't take to a hovering parent. But not one of them balked at having him as their copilot.

Charlie was in the driver's seat now as he pulled into the hospital parking lot. When he climbed out of the truck, his father followed suit. Father Matthews walked a bit slower, his shoulders a little slumped, but he managed to get into the hospital on his own power. All the while, Charlie hovered over him.

"Charlie Matthews, you're back."

Charlie looked up as one of the nurses broke from the reception desk and circumvented the line formed there to come over to him. She was blonde with porcelain skin that looked like it would burn if she got too close to the windows.

"It's me; Tina Billings. I was two years behind you at Honor Valley High."

"Right. Tina. Hey, long time." Charlie flashed a quick smile at the woman who he had no clue of ever meeting before. Certainly not ten years ago when he was consumed with thoughts of and stolen moments with Savy. "We're here for my father's appointment."

"Look at you, all grown up."

That threw Charlie off guard. Didn't she just say she was younger than he was? "Thanks, Tia. You, too. About my dad—"

"It's Tina." She wrapped her fingers around his biceps and squeezed. "You filled out in all the right places, didn't you?"

Charlie glanced over at his father. Of course, Haran Matthews said nothing. He simply stood to the side, barely hiding a grin at his son's discomfort.

"Is this your father?" Tina raised her voice and enunciated as she turned to Father Matthews. "Hello, Mr. Matthews. How are you today?"

Turnabout was fair play. Charlie grinned widely, saying nothing as Nurse Nia treated his dad like he was an invalid. For his part, Father Matthews looked over the woman's shoulder, like he was playing the senile role she'd cast for him.

"You're such a good son, Charlie." The nurse fixed her sights back on the younger Matthews. "You're going to make a good father."

"Yeah, probably because I was raised by a good man. The one standing here who just had a heart attack a couple of days ago. You think we can get him a wheelchair?"

"I don't need a wheelchair, son. I see Dr. Nelson down the hall. I can get to his office all by myself. Why don't you stay here and talk with your old friend."

Grin restored, Father Matthews whistled as he made his way down the hallway. Charlie would've cursed the man if he didn't know for sure that God was on Father Matthews's side. Watching his father, Charlie couldn't help but wonder if his steps weren't as sure as they'd always been? Did his shoulders droop a bit? Was that a hunch in his back?

The guilt that Charlie had been harboring since learning of his father's condition while he was hundreds of miles away washed over him again. He'd been gone for such a long time this time. But it couldn't be helped. There had been orders. If his father had taught him anything, it was that a soldier should excel at his orders.

So Charlie had. And with each mission accomplished, he'd been given another. And then another.

Now his flying days were over. This was his new mission. His final mission. To get his family's house in order. That would start with his father, and it would end with the woman he loved.

"So, what do you think?"

Charlie blinked. He looked down to see that Nurse Telia had a hand on his chest and another snaking around his neck. He'd missed the entire thread of the one-sided conversation she'd been having with him. Likely because he'd forgotten she was even there. Because there was only one woman Charlie Matthews had ever been interested in for his whole life.

And there she was.

Like he'd called her to him, Savy James came in through the sliding glass doors of the hospital. Like every single time Charlie had seen the woman, beginning all the way back when she'd been an eight-year-old girl with ashy knees, dirt under her fingernails, and a mean purse to her lips, she took his breath away.

Her tan skin that reminded him of spun gold. Her raven curls that no comb could ever tame. Those long legs that outpaced him when they were young had mesmerized him as he grew up. Even with her long legs, she wasn't a tall woman. Savy came up to Charlie's chest, right where his heart beat. It kicked into high gear at the sight of the first person to ever make it race.

He'd planned to go to Bright Horizon's in the morning. Probably later tonight, after he'd made sure his father was snug in bed. Now he wouldn't have to wait. She was here. In front of him. Within his reach.

Charlie took a step toward her. He didn't get far. Something was holding him back. Something was holding onto him.

Charlie couldn't tear his gaze away from Savy to find out what. Those charcoal-gray eyes landed on him. Even from across the room, he felt the electricity zap between them. Above, the fluorescent light flickered. Outside, the sun broke through clouds.

Savy held him still with her gaze. Or maybe the world held still around him. Charlie didn't know. He didn't care.

What he did care about was the frown on Savy's face. Why was her gaze narrowing? Why were her lips pursing?

Charlie knew every look and quirk of this woman's face. She was upset with him. But he hadn't done anything. He hadn't even said a word. It was far too soon in their reunion for her to be angry with him.

There was usually the breathless moment when they came back into each other's presence. Followed by a moment of awkwardness. Then there was kissing.

Oh, he wanted to skip straight to the kissing. It was his favorite thing to do in the world. Flying was a distant second to the weightless joy he found against Savy's lips.

Charlie wanted to take flight. But something was holding him down. Finally, he looked over and remembered the excess baggage hanging off his bicep.

CHAPTER FOUR

There was a saying in the South. It was a saying about how women clutched their pearls when they were shocked. Savy wasn't a fan of pearls. They were the guts of an oyster. She'd never taken to the idea of wearing an animal's innards on her body.

Still, when she saw Charlie Matthews embracing Tina Billings, her hand immediately went to her throat. There weren't any pearls there. Just the thin gold chain with a piece of plastic dangling from the end.

It was the plastic that was priceless. A prize won from a Cracker Jack box years ago. A promise given to her with sugary fingers and a sweet smile.

Savy clung to that pact as she watched the impossible play out right before her eyes.

Charlie Matthews was home. He was back in Honor Valley.

That wasn't the impossible part. He always came back. He just never stayed. Not since he'd enlisted in the Air Force. He was always being called away on a mission.

Which she supposed she should be pleased about. It meant he was good at his job. It meant he was indispensable to their country. He was indispensable to her, too, and he'd enlisted his services to her first. Surprisingly, the U.S. Government did not respect the dibs of an eight-year-old girl.

But he was home right now. Which baffled Savy because she hadn't been the first person to know about his return. She was always the first to know. It was part of their pact.

The pact that started after the first time her mother, who had abandoned them months before that, snatched Savy, Foxy, and Tricksy out of the foster home to go on the road with her as backup singers. When her mom overdosed after a show in Vegas, the girls had been taken and returned to the foster care home. Charlie had snuck into their room and held her hand tight until the morning when he'd been found and confined to his room during free time. They'd lost those three days apart, but they were back together again. Until her mom got clean and came back to reclaim them for a show in L.A.

From that point on, it was a series of hits and misses with the two of them. Her mom would go on a bender, and Savy would return to Honor Valley, only to find that Charlie was away at summer camp. Or Charlie would be home on leave, only to come home and find that she was back on the road singing with her sisters.

The stars had trouble aligning for Savy James and Charlie Matthews. Looking at him now, as he stood under the fluorescent lights of the hospital, the impossible glared back at Savy. Charlie Matthews—her Charlie Matthews—was embracing another woman. A woman who wasn't her.

"Back again, Savy?"

Savy broke her gaze from the impossible scene on display down the hall and focused on the intake nurse. The gray-haired woman reminded Savy of her second-grade teacher. All the kids swore Mrs. September was actually the witch in Hansel and Gretel. Nurse Ruddell had the same grimace on her wrinkled face when she glared down at Daria.

"What was it this time, Daria? Trying to fly? Trying to walk through walls? Or proving you're impervious to pain by putting your hand in a fire?"

Mr. Davidson raised both eyebrows to his hairline. The fingers of his right hand twitched as though he wanted to jot down some more incriminating notes about Savy's foster kids. Luckily, he couldn't reach for his pen and notepad. His hands had a Daria-sized bundle in them.

Daria held her upper lip stiffly. Her red cape hung limp at her back, covered in soot. She was always surprised when she bled, bruised, or broke a bone like a normal human.

"This has happened before?" asked Mr. Davidson.

"That child's in here every other week," supplied Nurse Ruddell. "She thinks she's a superhero. She's got a medical record like a rap sheet. If I hadn't seen her antics firsthand, I would've called CPS."

Nurse Ruddell chucked her head to the side to indicate Savy. Little did Nurse Ruddell know, Mr. Davidson was worse than Child Protective Services. A few more unfavorable notes written down about Savy and her kids, and these children would be let loose in the wild. Wrangling the wild horses running in the valley would be simpler than trying to tame them.

"I encourage my charges to develop a healthy imagination," Savy said.

"One that requires stitches and casts," Nurse Ruddell said as she placed the hospital intake band around Daria's arm. She hadn't even bothered to hand Savy any intake forms. They were in here so much that the nurses knew the kid's details by heart.

"I'm okay, Ms. Savy," Daria said as Mr. Davidson deposited her into the wheelchair offered by Nurse Ruddell. "I'm sorry I didn't find the money in the chimney."

"You told this child to go looking for money in a chimney?" Mr. Davidson turned to Savy in horror.

"No, I di—"

He was already scribbling more notes down on his pad now that his hands were free. Nurse Ruddell was wheeling Daria down the hall for an x-ray. Savy stood in the middle of the reception area, flustered and defeated.

She couldn't lose these kids. She was all they had. No one else wanted them. Savy knew because she'd tried to place each of them in a permanent home. One by one, they came back to her, returned to sender. Two families quit fostering after taking in Denny and Daria.

Savy had promised the kids would always have a home at Bright Horizons. It had been the one place that was constant in her life. Which was why when she retired from singing at the ripe old age of twenty-two, she'd taken over Bright Horizons. And now it, along with the children, was in danger of being taken from her.

She hadn't felt this alone since the first time she returned to Honor Valley, and Charlie was overseas, entirely beyond her reach.

Then warm arms were around her. Followed by a warm, familiar smell. Those strong arms fit her snug and tight. That smell brought about instant peace and calm. Then came the voice she heard every night in her dreams.

"Hey."

It was just one word. Just one syllable. It meant nothing. It meant everything.

Savy had been holding herself so tightly wound these last few days. She couldn't break. Everyone needed her to be strong.

Not him.

He was the strong one. In his arms was the only place she could show her weaknesses. He was the soft place that absorbed her harsh edges. His was the gentle voice that softened her tenor.

Savy slumped into Charlie's body. Her feet left the ground as she allowed him to whisk her away like her very own Prince Charming. When she opened her eyes, they were alone in an exam room.

A gurney with ripped paper covering the hard cushion. A heart monitor that showed a flat line. A tissue on the floor that had missed the waste disposal bin.

And Charlie.

Her Charlie.

Here. With her. As it should be.

Savy pulled his head down to hers, and she was kissing him. He was kissing her. They were kissing one another.

The only time her world made sense was in this man's arms. When she was gazing into his eyes. When he was whispering in her ear how much he adored her. Those few moments in her lifetime that the stars aligned and everything else fell away.

The overhead fluorescent light made a buzzing noise, interrupting the soundtrack of soft sighs that accompanied this reunion. The light blinked out and in, like a fading star. When it flicked back on, shining its full force, Savy broke the kiss.

"You're dating Tina Billings?"

"Who?"

"The woman who had her hands all over you."

"What woman?"

Charlie asked the question, likely more out of the politeness hammered into him by his adoptive parents. He clearly wasn't interested in the answer. Because he was kissing Savy again.

That kiss told Savy loud and clear everything she needed to know about what she thought she'd seen. There had been nothing between Charlie and Tina. Savy knew there had never been anything between Charlie and any other woman that wasn't her.

She didn't doubt his fidelity. He didn't doubt hers. The first time they'd laid eyes on each other, both their hearts had shouted *this one.*

They'd both been eight when they met. They'd been thirteen when they'd shared their first kiss. They'd been sixteen the first time Charlie proposed to her.

Saying yes to Charlie Matthews wasn't the problem. Being with him was.

"You're here," Savy said, placing her hand on his chest. She felt the same thin chain and the same plastic ring that she wore around her neck.

"I am." Charlie grinned that devastating grin that kept her heart locked down from every man who came near.

"How long?" She hated to ask it, but she had to know. She had to get her expectations set. She had to know how long she could rest in heaven before she was flung back down to earth when he left. "How long?" she repeated.

"Forever."

There had been soft sighs coming from her mouth only a second ago. With that single word, a gush of hot air burst from her chest and out of her mouth. Her nostrils flared but not with desire. Savy pressed her hands against Charlie's chest, ignoring his racing heart, and shoved him away from her. Hard.

CHAPTER FIVE

harlie didn't budge when Savy pushed him away. Oh, his girl was strong. He'd made sure of that. Racing with her through the woods when they were kids. Challenging her to push up and pull up contests when they were teens. And teaching her self-defense moves when they were new adults.

There was no way he was leaving her unprotected in this world. Not with what they'd seen growing up in the system. Especially not with her addict of a mother dragging the girls off to seedy concert halls and dives.

If he hadn't been sure that Savy could hold her own, Charlie doubted he would've been able to be away from her for such long stretches. He also knew this weak display of her power had to do more with emotion than an actual desire to send him away.

So he held on. He had too many years of practice holding on to this woman to let such a flimsy shove push him away. Now that he was here to stay, he was not letting her go.

"This is because I broke our pact?" He squeezed her tighter. "Because I didn't come to you first."

"I didn't expect you to come to me first, you big oaf." She stopped her ineffectual shoving and splayed her hand over his heart. "Your dad had a heart attack. Of course, you would go straight to him."

"Right." Charlie pressed a kiss to her temple, breathing in the scent of her. Cinnamon and bleach and Savy. "So, what are you mad about?"

"You said forever."

Her voice was a whisper. A shaky whisper. A shaky whisper that rattled through him and tucked in behind his chest.

"It's never forever with the two of us," she continued on in that whisper, as though she was afraid of being overheard. "It's always for a short time. And that's fine."

Her voice trembled on the word fine. It sounded as though her teeth chattered as they pressed against her bottom lip to make the F sound. The rest of the word came out as though it was made of smoke.

It was not fine.

It was forever.

Charlie had said forever. He'd said forever to her since he'd looked the word up in a dictionary and decided it applied to the two of them. And now, he could finally live up to that definition.

"It's true," said Charlie. "I'm out."

"Out?"

"Out of the Air Force and back home. For good."

"What do you mean *for good*?"

He meant forever. But she'd already shoved at him with that word, so he couldn't repeat it. Instead, Charlie pressed more kisses to her temple as though he were anointing his queen with a crown of affection.

"It means exactly what it sounds like, Sav. I hung up my wings."

Charlie pulled back from Savy, then he pulled the chain that hung beneath his shirt out. He traced the links until he came to the ring attached. There were two rings on there. The first one was the plastic ring that mirrored hers. The second had a real diamond.

"I wanted to do this in front of our families, but now's a good a time as ever."

"Charlie—" Savy choked. Her lips stayed parted, but no other words came out of her mouth. Even better, she kept her hands to herself.

Charlie sank down to one knee. This was his favorite view of her. Looking up at Savy as she loomed large over him. This woman had always loomed large over him.

She was his moonlight, his sunshine. If it had been ancient times, he would've been one of the idolators who worshipped the sun or moon goddess. He was entirely certain that God had put Savy on this earth as a brag about how perfect His craftsmanship truly was.

"Savy James, I have loved you since before I knew what the word meant."

Savy's hands reached down to cup Charlie's face. She tilted his head back so that she could peer directly into his eyes. He grinned at her machinations, having no trouble staring right back at the woman he loved and baring his soul to her.

Savy's charcoal-gray eyes glistened with unshed tears. She shook her head slowly from side to side. Charlie knew she wasn't denying him. She'd already said yes the first time he'd proposed when they were sixteen. This was just a formality.

"Would you do me the honor of—"

"No!" Savy snatched her hands away from his head and planted them on her hips. It was her matronly pose, the one she used when her sisters or any of the Matthews boys got out of line. She'd never used it on Charlie.

Charlie's head jerked to the side to get a different view of her. "Beg your pardon?"

"I said no."

"Sav, I'm asking you to marry me."

"I know."

Charlie stood then. He took in a deep inhale, letting the air settle past his chest and down into his gut. "You're saying no?"

"I am."

Why would she say no to him? They were destined to be married, to be together for the rest of their lives.

He reached for her again. She hesitated, but it was only perfunctory. She put up no resistance when he wrapped her in his embrace, their lips less than an inch apart.

"I don't get it?" said Charlie.

Savy pursed her lips in the universal language of *I'm about to explain it to you*. She didn't get a chance to explain anything because the door to the exam room opened up.

"There you are, Ms. James."

A dark-skinned man in an ill-fitting suit poked his head in the door. He took one look at Savy and frowned. Then his glance turned to Charlie, which only served to deepen the frown.

"The child is asking for you," he sneered. "And I find you making out in a closet with a man."

"We weren't making out," said Savy.

"We were making out," said Charlie.

"He was just asking me to marry him again," Savy said dismissively. Then, once again, she shoved at Charlie's chest in a weak attempt to break free. "Charlie, not now."

Savy shoved again, this time with real force, as though she was actually trying to get away from him. What was going on?

"You're engaged to this man?" asked the suit.

"Yes," said Charlie.

"No," said Savy.

The man ignored Savy and eyed Charlie. "Well, that does change things a bit."

"Excuse me?" said Savy.

"Change what?" said Charlie.

The man jotted notes down on a pad as he spoke. "What those children need is a man's firm hand in the home."

Charlie wasn't exactly sure what was going on. But he was pretty good at math. Adding up the man's ill-fitting suit told Charlie that this was clearly a government employee. Plus the note-taking on a yellow legal pad? Definitely a bureaucrat. Altogether, this pointed to something happening at the foster home.

"That's me," said Charlie. "I have a firm hand. And I plan to be in the home."

This must be Savy's hesitation. He knew she'd do anything for the kids under her care. She'd been the same way when they were kids, taking each new foster kid under her wing. She'd tried to do that to Charlie when he'd arrived at Bright Horizons. But they both soon learned that his wingspan was broader than hers.

So, this official was doing a report on the foster home. Well, Charlie would be happy to move in there after he and Savy got married. It would allow him to be with the woman he loved, help the kids, and take care of his father.

It was perfect.

"I'll take your engagement under advisement and put it in my report."

The bureaucrat gave Charlie a nod. Charlie held out his hand to the man and shook. It was a weak handshake, which told Charlie everything else he needed to know about the man.

"I'll see you back at the foster home," said the weak-handed man with a sour glance at Savy. He turned on his heel and walked out the door.

When Charlie turned back to Savy, her glance at him was sour.

"What?" he asked. "This is perfect. We'll get married and live in the foster home. Meanwhile, I'll be within driving distance to help my dad on the ranch every day."

"The foster home is being demolished."

"What?"

"Bright Horizon's isn't going to be here in the valley anymore. They're moving it across the state."

CHAPTER SIX

"They're moving the foster home?" Charlie leaned back against the door. He crossed his arms over his broad chest.

Savy had spent cool afternoons in the sun basking in the comfort of that chest. He'd wrapped those strong biceps around her as they lay out on a blanket, staring at the clouds. The memory of Tina Billings hanging off Charlie's arm was a distant wisp of the past. That space at Charlie's heart, that nook between his neck and his shoulder, that spot at the underside of his chin, all those places belonged to Savy.

Right now, she desperately wanted back inside those arms. The day had been trying enough with Daria and Mr. Davidson. And then this fool had to go and propose to her.

"Why are they moving Bright Horizons?" Charlie asked.

"Tilly."

It was a one-word answer. A name that anyone in Honor Valley would understand and need no more explanation for.

"Of course." Charlie pinched the bridge of his nose. It was a common move seen whenever anyone in the valley came up against that particular Silver sister. "Let me guess; one of Tilly's petitions to save the wildlife?"

Charlie let go of his nose. His hand didn't go back to his side. It went to hers. His fingertips grazed the waistband of her pants.

He didn't tug. He didn't need to. The two of them were magnets. They always found one another.

So, of course, Savy took a step toward him. "Tilly filed a petition to have the wild horses of the valley protected by the government. She did it back in high school. Ten years later, and it's reared up to bite us."

Charlie's arms were around her now. Savy's head found her way to the space at his heart. It beat loud and strong, just as it had when they were little kids. Charlie Matthews had always had a big heart, and he always saved the most space for her.

"Now that the land is protected for the horses, they're moving the foster home," said Charlie. It wasn't a question. The words were said without inflection. As though they were just meant to fill the silence. Or perhaps to distract her.

She had somewhere to be. But for the life of her, she couldn't remember where. Savy shifted from the center of Charlie's heart to the nook between his neck and shoulder.

"I'm trying to stay with the kids, to keep them together." Savy's lips brushed the underside of Charlie's chin and held there. She'd missed the smell of him. Irish Spring soap, salt, and her Charlie.

"And The Suit's in charge of that decision?"

Savy giggled at that nickname. "He does wear an awful suit."

"Doesn't suit him."

She giggled again, raising her head to glance up at Charlie. She had forgotten how devastatingly handsome the man she loved was. Even with tons of pictures in albums and on her phone, not a single one of them did the man's actual beauty justice.

Dark hair that had grown just a little too long for military regulation. Dark eyes with that ring of hazel that always made her feel he was shining a light on her when he gazed at her. Those lips that always rested in a half-smile.

Those lips.

That smile.

Those lips.

Charlie smiled fully, stretching his lips until his white teeth flashed at her. "God, you're beautiful. I forget how beautiful you are in the flesh. When I see you in my mind, it's a pale comparison. Even the pictures I have of you don't do you any real justice."

That was all it took. Savy snaked her hand into his curls. She gripped hard as she tugged his head down. Charlie came willingly. His lips crashed down on hers.

The impact was powerful enough to destroy them. Instead, it set Savy soaring. Kissing Charlie Matthews had always made her feel weightless and carefree.

Except she couldn't be carefree. She couldn't fly away. Not now. There would be collateral damage left on the ground.

"The kids," she breathed when she broke the kiss.

"Everything is going to be fine, Sav."

Charlie took her hands in his. She felt something cold and metallic against her palm and then over her finger. Looking down, she saw the diamond ring. It felt heavy on her hand.

Savy had dreamed of Charlie proposing to her. He'd done it before. Those other times they'd been kids, not fully in charge of their living situations.

Now they were adults. He was out of the military. She was no longer on the road touring as a singer with her sisters. But she wasn't free to fly away with him.

The kids.

Savy had to go where these kids went. She was all they had. She couldn't let them break the siblings up. She and her sisters had fought so hard to stick together when they were that age. Who knew what would've happened to them if they got split up.

She knew Charlie understood that. The only reason his brothers had made it to adulthood in one piece and not behind bars was because they'd been able to stick together. That, and they had the Matthews as foster parents.

"I came home to marry you," said Charlie.

"You can't marry me."

"I am going to marry you."

"Charlie—"

"Isn't it a part of your job description to make kids believe they can be anything when they grow up?"

"We're not kids anymore, Charlie."

"You're right. We're grown up. This is exactly what I wanted to be when I grew up. Now I'm all grown up. I came home to finally be with you."

"I'm leaving Honor Valley."

"Then I'm coming with you."

"Really?"

"Really."

"Truly?"

"Yes, Sav."

"How's your dad?"

That stopped him short. Father Matthews needed his son's help. Savy had seen the man just days before the heart attack, and he hadn't looked as spry then. Haran Matthews was getting on in his years. He couldn't move around the ranch the way he had a decade ago.

He needed his family. He needed his sons. He needed Charlie.

Once again, forever took another step into the future for her and Charlie. It wasn't going to happen today.

"Sav," Charlie reached for her.

Savy moved out of his reach, out of the one place in the world that always made her feel safe, even if only for the short bursts of time they had together.

"It's not our time," she said.

How many times had they said that to each other over the years? When would it be time for them to be in the same place at the same time? Would it ever happen?

"Sav."

"Your dad needs you, and those kids need me."

"I need you."

Savy shook her head. "I have to go."

Charlie pulled her back to him. She let him, too tired to fight it. She rested another second at the space at his heart and listened to his heartbeat. She turned her head into the nook between his neck and shoulder and inhaled the scent of him. She lifted her lips to the spot at the underside of his chin and gave him a kiss farewell.

"I love you forever," she whispered.

"I love you always."

He didn't fight her when she backed away. This part was as familiar as the kissing. It was familiar as his scent. They always had to say goodbye sooner or later.

CHAPTER SEVEN

Charlie watched Savy walk away. He was tired of that sight. He wanted the sight of her coming into his arms. Of her looking comfortable and secure because he'd taken her worries away. Savy's shoulders slumped as she moved down the hall.

This was all wrong. Today was supposed to be the start of their forever. Instead, it felt like they were even further apart than yesterday.

Charlie knew he needed to give Savy space. She didn't do well when pressured. He also knew there was no way he was letting the woman of his dreams get away from him.

Against his better judgment, he took a step toward her. However, instead of flying off toward his only destination, he felt a heavy weight tethering him in place.

"Charlie Matthews, you naughty boy. You disappeared on me."

Charlie turned to see Nurse Tia hanging off his bicep. The situation looked vaguely familiar. Then he realized that this was the woman Savy had been referring to earlier.

Was the nurse coming onto him? Charlie wasn't sure. He'd never been able to read the cues correctly because he'd never paid attention to any woman who wasn't Savy.

When he looked back in the direction Savy had walked off, she was gone. Fine. He'd let her slip away today. He'd be back in fighting form tomorrow.

"Where's my father?"

"He's nearly done with his checkup." Nurse Nina snaked her hands from his bicep to his chest. "I was coming to find you."

Charlie stepped out of her embrace and around her. She was a petite little thing, but she had arms everywhere. "Just point me to his room."

"This is his prescription." She held up a small square of a paper with a doctor's illegible chicken scratch on it. "And this is my number." She held up a pink Post-it note with unmistakable clear block letters and numbers.

"What for?"

"Wow, you have been gone for a long time." She sidled back up to him, cornering Charlie against the door where he and Savy had shared their all-too-brief reunion. "When a girl gives you her phone number, she wants you to call her to take her out on a date."

"I don't date."

"It's easy. I'll show you how."

"I've never been interested in learning how."

Finally, it looked like he was getting somewhere with her. Nurse Telia leaned away from him, her features crinkled. "Are you… gay?"

"Engaged. Since I was about sixteen." And he would be getting married soon. He'd managed to slip a diamond ring on Savy's finger, so he'd say that was progress.

"Ha, that's funny," singsonged the nurse.

Hadn't she said they went to school together? If they had, then she would know that Charlie Matthews had been completely, totally, and solely head over heels in love with Savy James since, well, forever.

"Where did you say my father was?"

"Right here, son."

Another nurse wheeled his father down the corridor in a wheelchair. This nurse was doing her job, fussing over Father Matthews instead of flirting with his son. The man who had been the hero of Charlie's life looked older, frailer sitting in the rolling chair.

When Charlie had left home for the service, Father Matthews had still been strong. He'd had his other sons to help him on the ranch. For the last five years, his father had been all alone with all that land. In the state he was in now, he definitely couldn't manage the ranch alone.

Charlie looked back toward the hall where Savy had disappeared. The urge to follow her was still strong. It always would be. But he couldn't leave his father behind. Not now.

Savy and Charlie's forever would just have to wait a little while longer to begin.

Father Matthews was looking down at his pocket watch. Charlie didn't need to come closer to know what picture was inside of the watch. It was his wife.

Haran and Tessa Matthews had had a love so bright that Charlie and his brothers had had to hide their eyes the first few months they lived at Flying Cross. It had been gross the way the two carried on, stealing kisses, always smiling when the other came in the room, saying crazy things like *I Love You.*

Charlie got over the grossness of it before his other brothers did. Because Charlie recognized that the way his foster father looked at his foster mother was the way he felt when he looked at Savy.

Charlie came over and put an arm around his father as he rose from the wheelchair. Thankfully, the older man didn't protest.

"What took you so long?" Father Matthews asked.

"I was talking to Savy."

"Savy's here?" His father perked up. "Oh wait, don't tell me? Is it the little superhero again?"

"Superhero?"

Father Matthews's eyes crinkled the way they did when one of his sons made him laugh. "One of her kids thinks she's a superhero. She's in and out of the emergency room every month. Worse than your brother, Joe."

Joe had loved comics growing up. He'd gone into the military to be a hero. He'd never seen a day of combat in his role once there. Now he was setting his sights on politics. He didn't like it when Charlie pointed out that many of the villains in the comics were politicians.

"How'd things go with you and Savy?" Father asked as they stepped out of the hospital's sliding glass door.

"Same as usual."

"That bad?"

Father Matthews clapped Charlie on the back. Charlie jerked forward. His father's heart might've faltered a few days ago, but he still had the same strength in his hands.

"She said they're moving the foster home across the state."

"Oh." Father Matthews's hand splayed on Charlie's back. Just as his father's strength was still there, so was the instant comfort that spread from his fingers and into Charlie's chest.

"She's trying to make sure she and her sisters stay on at the home."

Father Matthews nodded as the two men crossed into the street, walking side by side. "Savy's been with those kids for the last five years. Foxy joined her just last year. I think Tricksy is still out on the road singing, but she makes it back to the valley from time to time."

"Savy's the best man for the job."

His father nodded at that pronouncement.

When he and his brothers were kids, everyone lined up behind Charlie. Charlie always lined up behind Savy. Because he followed her everywhere. He would follow her across the state if he had to. He just had to get his father back on his feet first. Of course, that's when the old man stumbled.

"Dad." Charlie flung out his hands, but his father had already righted himself.

They both looked down to see what had caused the stumble. It was a skateboard. A sulking kid was walking toward them.

"Watch it," Charlie shouted. "You could hurt somebody."

The kid narrowed his eyes at Charlie, his body tense as though ready to put up a fight. The little pipsqueak couldn't have been more than five feet and a hundred pounds to Charlie's over six feet and two-hundred pounds. But when the kid's eyes reached his father, the rascal's look softened.

"Sorry, Father Matthews."

"What are you doing out here, Denny?"

Denny stepped on the edge of the skateboard. The board flipped up and landed in his open palm. "I was looking for my sister."

"I don't see the foster van," said Father Matthews as he looked around.

Charlie gave the kid a second glance. He did have all the hallmarks of a foster kid. Scuffed shoes, frayed edges at the neck of his shirt, and shifty eyes that said he didn't trust any adult.

Denny glared at Charlie. Charlie glared right back. From his years in the system, he knew he had to establish dominance quickly, and size and age didn't matter.

"I think you may have missed Ms. Savy and your sister," said Father Matthews when his gaze returned to the kid. "We'll give you a ride home, won't we, son?"

That question had an easy answer. Charlie would use any reason to see Savy. Even if it meant dragging this little thug along for the ride.

By the time Savy put the van in park back at Bright Horizons, the sun was starting to set. It had been a long day. A long week. A long lifetime. And she was tired.

Charlie Matthews was home. For good. And because their timing was epically awful, she was the one leaving this time.

The only thing she wanted to do was curl up inside a set of strong arms, lay her head against a strong chest with a heart that beat just for her, and steal kisses at the underside of a chin with a five o'clock shadow. Too bad she just walked away from the only man who met all those descriptors.

For the first part of their lives, it had always been her leaving. Not that she'd had any choice. Her mother would inevitably get herself clean, get a gig featuring her and her daughters as backup singers, and scoop them out of foster care. After a month or two—the longest stretch being a full year—Fanny James would just as inevitably relapse, lose the gig, and get her kids taken from her again.

The cycle continued until Savy's eighteenth birthday. Ten years of instability. No child should've survived that. But she and her sisters did.

Many of the kids she now fostered had had similar beginnings in their lives. Ashton was born an addict. His mom was still out on the street making money on her back. LaTisha had spent the first six months of her life in the Neonatal unit because of the drugs in her mother's system. Denny and Daria had never actually slept on a bed until they came to the foster home. Miguel had been from a loving family, but his family had wanted more for him, and so they'd sent him to the border at the tender age of five in search of that better life.

In some ways, her kids had had it worse than Savy had. But Savy was determined to give them the best that she could. She was going to lose the house; she accepted that. What she would not accept was having those five kids taken from her. They could find another house and make it their home, as long as they stuck together.

The door to the van flew open, and a small body whizzed out, a cape flying behind her.

"Daria, slow down!"

"Yes, Ms. Savy," called the kid, whose pace slowed only a fraction.

Daria still moved as fast as a little rabbit, even with the ankle brace. Her foot wasn't broken, only a sprain. It would likely be broken by the morning if the child kept up that pace.

"We have a problem, sis."

Four out of five of those were Savy's least favorite words. She decided to focus on her favorite word, sis.

Savy loved being a sister. Even more, she loved being a big sister. Managing Foxy and Tricksy from such a young age had cemented what Savy was going to do with her life. Though she had a voice that could bring down an auditorium, it was best used at wrangling underaged hellions.

Foxy had certainly been a hellion in her youth. She'd only calmed down over the last couple of years. She was an invaluable addition to the foster home staff and came to love the kids as much as Savy did.

"Denny's missing."

Why couldn't Foxy have said the pipes had burst? That would've been an easier situation to deal with on the day a government official came a' knocking. Or better yet, that the house was on fire. That would've been a far more manageable problem at the moment.

Where Daria wanted to fly, her older brother wanted to disappear. They had trouble with Denny sneaking off. But he always came back. This was the worst time for him to pull a stunt.

"You check all the usual places?" asked Savy, getting out of the van.

"I did. He's not outside on the land. I called around to a couple of stores, but Mr. Finke hung up on me, and Mrs. Rhule said she'd call the police if she saw him."

There was a tension headache brewing at Savy's temples. This was just what she needed. A hospital visit, followed by picking up a kid at the police station while her fitness as a foster mom was under scrutiny.

Foxy reached up and gave Savy's temples a rub, bless her soul. "I know, sis, it's the last thing we need right now when Mr. Clicky Pen is here. But it could be worse. He could've seen one of us making out with some random guy."

Savy whipped her head out of her sister's hold. Foxy wasn't looking at her. Had she been joking? Did she know that Charlie was back? That was the only man Savy had ever kissed.

Tricksy was the only James sister that had had more than one boyfriend. Was Tricksy back? Her middle sister returning at this point in time was only slightly better than a house fire.

"Ms. James," called Mr. Davidson as he jogged down the steps, click pen in hand. "I have nearly everything I need to start my report. I just need to interview the fifth child, Dennis."

"He won't answer to that," called Daria. "His name is Denny."

Mr. Davidson ignored the little girl and focused on Savy. "Where is the child?"

Savy swallowed. This was it. She was going to lose these kids. They'd been counting on her, and she was about to let them all down.

She opened her mouth, but before she could get a single word out, she choked. Dust from a truck kicking up rocks on the gravel drive pulled up to them. Savy immediately recognized the old beat-up truck. She'd spent many an evening on the flatbed of that truck making out with Charlie.

Charlie sat in the driver's seat now. His father in the passenger seat. And... was that Denny in the back?

Charlie climbed out first. Savy had the instinct to run to the man. To fling herself into his arms and bury her face in his chest. But this was not the time for that. Charlie had provided her with an out, and she grabbed for it.

"I'm sorry, Mr. Davidson," she said. "I forgot to tell you that Denny was out with my fiancé."

Foxy looked from Charlie and back to her sister. Savy sent her daggers to hold her tongue. It wasn't a lie. She and Charlie had always planned to get married. Some day. Though some day never turned out to be today.

For his part, Charlie came up and put an arm around her. Savy's body sagged into his chest. She couldn't help it. It was exactly what she needed. So was the kiss he placed at her temple.

Her tension headache disappeared with the press of his lips. Savy let out a low sigh. She couldn't help it. Whenever she was in Charlie's arms, all of her cares went away.

"I don't believe we were formally introduced," said Charlie. "Captain Charles Matthews. And this is my father, Captain Haran Matthews. I believe you were looking for Denny. Sorry, we were just having some man-to-man time."

"Why weren't we invited?" came Miguel's voice.

"Yo, that's unfair," rapped Ashton. "That time shoulda been shared."

There was that headache knocking at Savy's right temple. Charlie squeezed her tighter, resting his chin at the top of her head. The pain dissipated like a whisper.

Mr. Davidson clicked his pen and jotted down more notes. "Military men; that's what these kids need. A strong hand to guide them. It's good to know these kids will have a strong hand guiding them when we move you across the state."

Savy sank deeper into Charlie's chest. Just when she thought she might skate by, it was all about to be taken away from her again.

She could have Charlie if she left the kids. Or better yet, she could have Charlie and keep the kids if Charlie came with them. Neither of those situations was tenable. The reason why spoke up to confirm it.

"There's been a misunderstanding," said Father Matthews. "My son isn't moving across the state. He and his future wife will be moving their family onto our ranch."

"The ranch?" both Savy and Charlie said in unison. The surprise was loud in each of their voices.

For his part, Mr. Davidson clicked his pen so that the point retracted. It looked like he was done taking notes. Instead, Mr. Davidson nodded, as though Father Matthews's statement made it all a done deal.

CHAPTER NINE

The children eyed Charlie curiously. Well, the two girls did. The one with the cape—Daria, he'd learned her name was—and ankle brace cocked her head to the right and then to the left, eyes squinting like Christopher Reeve used to do in the Superman movies when he was using his laser vision. Charlie rubbed a hand just under his chin where it felt a little hot.

The other girl, who was slightly taller than the shero, had her lips pressed in a thin line. Braids encircled her brown head, making her look like an African princess. He'd learned her name was LaTisha.

LaTisha tapped the thumb of her right hand to the tip of each finger. *Tap-tap-tap-tap.* Then she started again at her index finger. *Tap-tap-tap-tap.*

It was a tic Charlie had seen in the highest ranks of leadership, on down to some of the meanest prisoners of war. The repetitive motion was most often brought on by anxiety, either a need to control a situation or the fear that came with a loss of control.

Charlie wanted to sink down to his haunches and tell LaTisha that things were about to change. For the better. He wanted to tell Daria that he wasn't the villain in this story. He was the hero come to rescue them all.

He wouldn't have made it to the girls if he tried. Three boys stood in the path between Charlie and the girls. The three male foster kids all stood perfectly still with their arms crossed over their small chests as they frowned at him.

Denny, the skateboarding runaway, glared at Charlie with clear suspicion. Even after Charlie had given the kid a ride across town and didn't rat him out to Savy. Charlie understood that glare. He'd given it to Father Matthews when he'd come to him as a foster kid. Denny was clearly the big man on campus. Now that Charlie was on the scene, Denny's power was in question.

The boy standing next to Denny had been introduced to Charlie as Miguel. Miguel wore a shirt a size too small for his round belly and pants held up by a belt stretching against the last hole in the loop. Miguel tried to glare, though his gaze would dart away anytime Charlie tried to catch it.

The last child, who had cornrows like LaTisha, even though his hair was blond had Charlie's full attention. Ashton, or Ashtray as the boy had corrected, wore a Snoop Dog t-shirt and low-slung jeans with no belt. Charlie was a fan of hip hop himself—Wu Tang For Life. But there was a fine line between fandom and faking it, and Ashtray was on the wrong side of that line. Charlie would just have to have a heart-to-heart with the kid.

He'd have a heart-to-heart with all of the kids, just like his father had done with him and his brothers. By the end of the day, they would all be one big, happy family.

"Charlie?"

Charlie turned to the sound of Savy's voice. She beckoned him into the office of the foster home. Charlie followed her. He'd follow the woman anywhere. Luckily, with his father's solution, it would be Savy that would follow him home this time. She'd follow him home and stay forever.

It was time—finally time for their forever. After all these years of waiting. After all the missed opportunities. It was here.

"We can't," she said the moment the door to the office was closed.

Charlie had been reaching for her, pulling her into his embrace and aiming his lips for her. "We can't what? I can't kiss you? We're going to be married."

"We're not getting married." Savy shoved at his chest. It was another of the ineffectual shoves, so Charlie held tight.

"Why not?" he said, tightening his embrace and resting his nose in the strands of her hair.

When no answer was forthcoming, Charlie peered down at the woman he loved. Savy tried to answer, but her lips only open and closed. No words came out. What did was a huge sigh that sounded like surrender.

"Charlie, this is crazy."

"What's crazy?" he asked as he nuzzled the space behind her ear. It was her soft spot and how he got her to agree to most things.

"I can't bring these kids to the ranch," she said after letting loose a shuddery breath.

"It's the perfect solution. I'm only sorry I didn't think of it myself. There's plenty of space for each kid and the two of us."

They were so close. So close to finally having everything they both had dreamed of since they were kids in this room, hiding from the cruel realities of their world.

"This is it, Sav. This is our someday. Our start to forever. It's here."

Savy leaned into him. She rested her cheek against his chest, right where his heart beat for her. She tilted her head up until her nose was just under his chin. She exhaled, and Charlie felt the entire world stop.

"I came back for you," he said. "Let me take you home with me."

He'd been flying at top speeds for years. Always racing forward to get closer to her. The ride had been bumpy, but this was the smooth landing he'd always imagined.

A crash permeated the air with turbulence. The change in pressure forced Charlie and Savy apart. The disturbance of the children's voices rose until that was all that could be heard. Charlie took a step toward the door, but Savy held him back.

"I can't bring this pack of wild animals to Flying Cross," she said. "They'll destroy it."

"Flying Cross withstood the six of us," said Charlie. "A skater boy, Vanilla Ice, and that little daredevil you got out there won't stand a chance."

She cracked a smile at his characterizations of her kids. Savy's smile was everything. There was no way he was taking off in any direction without her. Never again.

Charlie wrapped her back up in his embrace. "They'll also have you and me. Together. We withstood the six Matthews boys and the three James sisters. We're unstoppable."

"Yeah," she grinned. "We do make a great team when it comes to wayward misfits."

"So, is that a yes?" he asked.

"A yes to moving in with you?"

"I'm not that kind of man. You'll need to make an honest Matthews out of me."

Savy snorted at that. Her laughter and amusement weren't enough. He wanted the right to be by her side forever. He wanted her to take his last name. He wanted to stand before his father and his God and proclaim this woman as his, and he as hers.

"I want to marry you, Sav. I'll take everything that comes with you. Say yes."

Savy closed her eyes. When she opened them, Charlie knew he had the answer he wanted. He sank down to his knee.

"Savy James, will you marry me?"

"Yes, Charlie. Yes, I will."

The diamond ring was still on her finger. He pressed a kiss to it. Then he stood and pressed a kiss to her. The moment his lips met hers, another crash sounded, and the door banged open.

In the doorway stood the three little thugs who would now be Charlie's responsibility to guide. Each kid looked feral and ready for a fight. Charlie wasn't going to fight any of these kids. He knew what they needed. A firm hand to guide them on the right path. Luckily for them, he had both a firm hand, and he knew of a well-tread path.

"We're not moving to a farm."

"I'm scared of horses."

"This is slave labor. Not only is that against the law. It's bad behavior."

Oh, man. Someone needed to get little Ashtray a rhyming dictionary. Charlie's ears would be bleeding by the end of the week unless the kid came up with better verses.

"Ms. Savy," said Daria, the Daredevil, as she squeezed past the boys, "I don't want to move to a stable with horses. I want to sleep on a bed, not in hay."

CHAPTER TEN

"That," Daria pointed to the tall, wooden structure that loomed large in the afternoon sunlight, "is a barn."

Technically, she was right. The two-story wood structure was indeed a barn. Though Savy knew firsthand, there were no horses inside. She knew that there were six separate bedrooms, three on the bottom floor and three on the top floor. She also knew that the oak tree around the back led to the second-floor bedroom on the back right. Furthermore, she knew that same tree was sturdy enough to handle the weight of a young girl and young boy as they stole quiet moments away from prying eyes.

A small smile played at Savy's lips as she allowed those memories to swirl around her head along with the light breeze of the day. She caught sight of Charlie in the distance walking toward her. His gaze followed the trajectory of her eyes, and she knew he was remembering those stolen moments of their youth as well.

"You said we wouldn't be sleeping in a barn, Ms. Savy," said Daria.

"It's against code to put kids in a barn," said Denny.

"I like horses," said LaTisha. "I'd be okay sleeping on a horse."

"Oh, wait!" Daria's cape billowed in the wind as she whipped around. "Can I sleep on a horse? That would be totally different, especially if the horse was my animal familiar."

"You're not sleeping in a barn or with the horses," said Savy. "You'll each have your own bedroom, as per DFACS code."

Both Daria and LaTisha pouted. Denny narrowed his gaze, clearly looking around for something else to complain about. Miguel and Ashton maintained dubious expressions.

"But there are horses here, right?" said Daria. "The Amazonians rode horses in Themyscira. Diana rode one in *Wonder Woman 1984* when she was just a kid. Can I ride one, Ms. Savy, please? Please?"

"Didn't Diana fall off that horse?" said LaTisha.

Daria threw the older girl a scowl. "She did, but she got back on and nearly won the whole tournament against all the older women. You always have to get back up and try again. Right, Ms. Savy?"

"Yeah," said LaTisha. "But Diana lost the tournament because she took a shortcut. You can't win in life if you take shortcuts. Right, Ms. Savy?"

Savy had not been paying attention to the film. She'd been paying attention to the hottie Chris Pine who played Wonder Woman's back-from-the-dead-boyfriend, Steve Trevor. Steve was a pilot that had the same smolder in his eyes as Charlie.

Charlie was almost to her. Even from this distance, Savy could see the burning flame in his hazel eyes that brought out the gold flecks. Her Charlie, whose lips were raised in a smirk as he took her in. Savy had kissed that smirk yesterday. She would get to kiss it again today. Then tomorrow, and on and on for the rest of their lives because now—unlike poor dead Steve from the movie—Charlie was here to stay. Forever.

When he reached her, Charlie wrapped an arm around her waist and pulled her to him. His smiling lips pressed into Savy's temple, making her think thoughts that definitely were not PG rated. He pulled away, his eyes burning into hers, so bright she felt hot in the tank top she wore this afternoon.

"I'll teach you to ride," Charlie said when he turned to the kids. "But first, you have to learn how to take care of the horses."

"Will you teach me to shoot a bow and arrow from a horse?" asked Daria. "It would really help my superhero cred."

"Super heroine," corrected LaTisha.

"I can teach you to shoot a bow and arrow, too," said Charlie. "But not while on a horse. One thing at a time."

Ashton and LaTisha perked up at that. Miguel looked horrified. Daria looked up at Charlie as if he were Superman in the flesh.

Denny took one look at his sister's clear admiration. Then he turned to Charlie. Charlie grinned at Denny. Denny's gaze narrowed, just as Christopher Reeve's did when he shot lasers from his eyes. Being that Charlie had never been interested in superheroes, the kid's death glare skated right by him.

Savy wasn't so sure about the list of activities Charlie had planned. She encouraged more academic and artistic activities. She was a proponent of physical activities, but more along the lines of bowling with the kiddie guard rail up.

"It smells like horse sh—"

Both Savy and Charlie turned glares on Denny. They might not be on the same page activity-wise, but they were in synch when it came to language and manners.

"Get used to that smell," said Charlie. "One of your chores will be to shovel it."

"So we're slave labor," said Denny.

"Slaves didn't have a choice," said Savy. "You do. You either live here in warmth and comfort, with three square meals, with people who care about you, and you do your chores. Or you get put back into the system where you roll the dice on the next home you end up in."

Denny glanced at his sister. They all knew that that roll of dice would almost certainly mean they'd be pulled apart.

"I'll shovel for you, Denny," said Daria in a whisper loud enough for everyone to hear. "I'll use my super strength."

Daria wrapped a spindly arm around her brother. Her cape flapped at Denny's knees in the light breeze. Her older brother's glare softened for just a second as he peered down at her.

"You look super strong," said Charlie. "Why don't you come meet my favorite horse. I think he'll like you."

Daria dropped the arm she had around her brother. The edge of her cape lifted as she reached for Charlie's hand. Denny's hands tightened into fists as he watched the two walk off.

LaTisha grabbed at Charlie's other hand. Ashton took ginger steps in the dirt as though any speck would end up on his polished sneakers. He pulled his cap low on the cornrows Foxy had braided into his hair this morning. Miguel hung back alongside Denny.

Savy knew the young boy wasn't standing in solidarity with Denny.

Miguel was not a fan of any creature on four legs, be they horses or mice or anything in between. Denny and Miguel were temporary allies.

Most foster kids didn't believe in permanency, especially when it came to adults. How could they when their own parents weren't in their lives to stick up for them? To complicate matters more, a series of strangers all insisted they had the children's backs. Those adults were often on a conveyor belt that never stopped until the kids were legal.

Savy knew all of this firsthand. Her own parents had been in and out of her life since she was Daria's age. By the time she'd reached Denny's age, she knew better than to depend on her mother. Or any adult, for that matter.

Denny and Daria had been with her for months, but they both still lived out of their backpacks, ready at any moment to leave and be moved away. Savy needed them to understand that she wasn't about to let them go. The truth was, she couldn't make that promise. Not when she was at the mercy of the state, just as they were.

"Denny, this is a good thing. I promise you're going to like it here if you give it a chance."

Denny shrugged. "I've only got four more years before I'm eighteen and can get me and my sister out of this. I can hold my nose for that long. Or however long you stick around."

CHAPTER ELEVEN

"Great job, Daria. You're a regular Amazonian."

The girl in the cape preened at Charlie as she bounced atop the horse like they were on a Merry Go Round. Her spindly legs tried to kick the horse like she was a jockey in a race. Luckily, Duff was the most docile horse on the ranch and ignored her antics as he walked on with his energetic charge.

That was now, but back when Charlie was a rough and tumble adolescent, Duff had been known to pull on the lead and buck at the slightest provocation. Charlie and his brothers had provided a lot of provocation. Mainly with each other. Though the horses had sensed the turbulence within them, too. Back then, when they were all young and easily riled up, Duff would pin his ears to his head whenever one of them came near in a clear sign of agitation. His eyes would widen, and his nostrils would flare in nervous anxiety.

It was a wonder that none of the Matthews boys had gotten a hoof in their bellies or broken their necks from being thrown. Just as the wild stallion had had to go through his paces with the young humans, the boys had had a lot of lessons to learn from the animals, from the work on the farm, from their foster parents who had had the patience of saints as they worked with the six wild animals they'd brought into their home. In comparison to his brothers, these five kids would be a walk in the park.

"Faster, Mr. Charlie. Faster."

Charlie continued his slow strides, leading Duff around the pen in a leisurely walk. The horse's eyes were half-closed as Daria bounced in the saddle. The aged stallion likely couldn't even feel the girl's slight weight.

"Not yet," said Charlie. "You gotta learn to walk before you can fly, Wonder Woman."

"Wonder Person," called LaTisha from her place, sitting on the fence. "Heroes should be non-binary."

"Right," said Charlie, not truly understanding what that meant. But he couldn't let a ten-year-old see that she knew something he didn't.

The kids had finished all of the chores he'd set out for them today. That had mainly been learning to muck out the stalls and organizing the tack walls. They'd done a fair job of it. Even Miguel, who had stayed at the stall closest to the exit. He'd perked up a bit when he got to help place down new hay and water for the horses. The kid liked helping with how the food went in, not how it came out.

The oldest kid, Denny, had made a mess of the mess left by the horses. Then the delinquent screwed his features into a helpless pout and let the pitchfork clatter to the ground.

It was the old screw up the chore so that the adult won't ask you to do it again tactic. Charlie had tried the same tactic when he was young. Father Matthews had simply nodded his head as though in commiseration. Then he'd shrugged and said, *Try again*. When Charlie had proceeded to make an even bigger mess, he was met with the same result from his foster father. By the time Charlie learned his lesson, it was the dead of night and his dinner was cold.

Denny was still learning that lesson while the younger kids were reaping their reward of riding one of the horses they'd just cared for. By the time Denny came out of the stall with sweat beading his brow, the others had already gone off to explore the ranch before dinner.

"Do I need to triple check your work, son?" Charlie asked.

Denny's jaw ticked. Charlie was almost certain it had nothing to do with checking behind the kid. The first time Father Matthews had called him *son*, Charlie had balked, too. Until he'd come to love the endearment.

"You know slave labor is against foster care rules," said Denny. "I could have you reported."

Charlie had said the exact same thing to Father Matthews. Yeah, he and this kid were on the road to a sappy After School Special happy ending real soon.

"These are chores, Denny. We all do them as a family to keep this place running."

The baby fat that still clung to the kid's cheeks hardened. He bit at his lip as though trying to hold his tongue. At his sides, his fists clenched.

Yeah, this was definitely a moment for wise words that would open the kid's heart and bring him closer to Charlie's side. Only a step or two closer, though. Charlie estimated it would take him a good couple of months before he won the kid over completely.

"We're going to learn to work together as a team, as a family. This is your home now, for as long as you want it to be."

Something sparked in the kid's eyes. Not like a fire that burned off hard edges. More like a light coming on in a dark room.

"You know what, Charlie—"

"It's Mr. Charlie, to you."

"I might've judged you too harshly." Denny pressed his lips together, then opened them to let out a sigh. "I'm not used to people believing in me."

Maybe Charlie would have to revise his heart melting estimate. Looked like that Afterschool Special ending would happen sooner rather than later.

"Truce?" Denny opened his arms.

Charlie wasn't certain of protocol. Was he allowed to give a foster kid a hug? He certainly didn't want to reject the kid now that he was making some leeway.

In the end, Charlie decided to throw caution to the wind. They were standing out in a wide-open field. He wrapped his arms around the kid's back. Denny was nothing but skin and bones. That would all change soon as he worked the fields alongside Charlie.

"Thank you for this chance, Mr. Charlie," said Denny. He mimicked Charlie's motions, patting him on the back.

Charlie watched Denny walk off toward the barn house. Visions of teaching the kid catch and advising him about girls flitted through Charlie's mind. He'd always known he wanted to be a father. He knew he'd be good at it, too, with the example Father Matthews had set. Now he would get his chance sooner than later.

With a pep in his own step, Charlie went in search of his fiancée. He found her standing in one of the bedrooms of the guest house, looking at the made-up bed. Charlie scooped Savy into his arms from behind.

"Hurry, Joe. We don't have much time. Charlie will be back any second."

Charlie squeezed Savy until she giggled uncontrollably. "Trying to incite fratricide?"

"Yeah, I'm still mad at your brother for eating all the Jolly Ranchers that one Halloween."

"That was over fifteen years ago."

She turned in his arms, grinning up at him. "I still can't believe this is really happening."

"It is, Savy. It's happening. I'm going to marry you."

"I'm gonna marry you right back."

He dipped his head to hers. Her lips were sweeter than all the Halloween candy he'd ever had all put together. Charlie would never tire of kissing this woman, and now he could do it year-round instead of stealing moments while he was home for a holiday.

"Will you two get a room," said Foxy from the doorway.

"This is my room," said Savy.

"Not for long," said Foxy as she headed into the second bedroom. "Joe's coming home in a couple of days."

Charlie frowned at that prediction. As far as he knew, Joe was still in the thick of boring military legalese in his role as a Judge Advocate General or JAG. But he knew Foxy's foresight had a fifty-fifty chance of being right as being wrong.

"Great," Savy sighed dramatically. "So now I'll have to juggle two brothers."

Charlie ignored the love of his life's antics. Mainly because he knew his younger brother had always had a crush on Foxy. A crush Foxy had always been oblivious to, even though she claimed to be psychic.

"Wait a minute?" Savy tried to pull away from Charlie, but he didn't let her go. "If you're here, and Foxy's here, who's minding the kids?"

"I let them roam."

Savy's pull became a jerk. It was no matter. Charlie still held her tight to him.

"You let five city kids roam on a ranch?"

"City kids?" Charlie scoffed. "They lived at Bright Horizons, which was surrounded by forests and wildlife. They're fine. I told them to keep the ranch house in view and not to go to the Silvers because those women eat little children."

"Charlie," Savy sighed in exasperation. "Who knows what trouble they'll get into?"

"Sav, relax. I'm making great headway with them. Denny even gave me a hug."

Savy went slack in his arms. Her jaw tensed as her gaze widened. "Denny hugged you?"

"Yeah." Charlie grinned, entirely pleased with himself and his progress. Though he wondered why Savy wasn't singing his praises? Instead, she patted down his pockets. "What are you doing?"

"Did you have your phone on you during this *hug?*" She said *hug* as though she were making finger air quotes around the word. As though the word *hug* didn't at all mean what it should mean.

"Yeah, it's…" Charlie patted down his back pocket. His empty back pocket. "That little… I can't believe I just got taken by a fourteen-year-old punk. I have real-world experience leading troops into danger zones. Heck, I have years of combat from living with my brothers."

Charlie turned on his heel, marching toward the door. Before he got to the handle, a knock sounded from the other side. Charlie pulled it open to find Denny standing there.

"I think you dropped these, Mr. Charlie." The kid held up his phone and wallet.

Charlie shuffled back a step. He tipped his head to the side as he regarded the kid. Denny could've taken his phone and wallet and wreaked a bit of havoc with them. Instead, here he was, handing the lost items back to Charlie.

Oh, yeah. He definitely was getting through to this kid.

Charlie wanted to go in for another hug. The kid deserved it with all the progress he'd made today. But that might be way too touchy-feely. So instead, he held out his hand.

"Thanks, Denny."

"Sure thing."

Denny gave Charlie's hand a shake. It was a little weak, but they'd work on that later. A man's first impression was in his handshake.

"Good talk earlier."

"Glad you think so, son."

Denny's eye twitched. But it was almost imperceptible. They'd work on that too. The kid nodded and turned on his heel.

"See that?" Charlie said to Savy, who stood watching the interaction from over his shoulder. "I'm getting to him."

"I don't know." Savy scrunched her nose and sucked at her teeth. "He's up to something."

"If he is, he won't outsmart us. Not the dynamic duo."

Savy opened her mouth to say more, but Charlie silenced her with a kiss. The shock of her sweetness never got old. It never would. The two of them were forces to be reckoned with apart. Together, they would be unstoppable. Especially when faced with a fourteen-year-old kid who simply wanted to belong.

Charlie would teach Denny that, too. He'd teach them all about the joy of belonging not just to someone but to a family.

"Hey," he said when he broke the kiss. "I'm going to marry you."

"So I heard." She grinned up at him before bringing his head down to hers for even more kisses.

CHAPTER TWELVE

*S*avy felt a tickle move up her calf. She bit her lip but was unable to hide the giggle that escaped her mouth. She was too old to be playing footsie. But here she was seated at the Matthews's dinner table, tangling her bare feet with Charlie Matthews's boot.

Charlie was the only horseman she knew in town who'd never taken to cowboy boots. Even at a young age, Charlie had known he was going into the military to follow in Father Matthews's footsteps. So it was Charlie's combat boot that snaked around Savy's ankle to lift up her heel and rest her instep on his laces.

"I see someone wasn't playing around this afternoon," said Father Matthews.

Charlie's foot landed with a thud on the floor. Savy snapped her foot back under her own chair. When they looked up, the older man wasn't looking at either of them.

"This looks delightful, Miguel," said Father Matthews. "You truly know your way around a kitchen."

"It's fusion," said Miguel as he served up the steaming dish that smelled of onion and tomatoes and peppers.

Instead of tortillas, there were mashed potatoes beneath the salsa. The dish should not have worked. The watering of Savy's mouth and the grumbling of her belly reminded her how well the Midwest potatoes and the Mexican dishes fused.

"Miguel is going to be a chef when he grows up," said Foxy.

"I'm working on my knife skills," said Miguel as he placed a bowl of shredded cheese at the center of the table. "You'll notice how the cut of the onion and peppers are uniform because I julienned them. That's different from dicing, which is when you make them smaller and more square than rectangle."

"You should set another plate," said Foxy. "We're missing someone."

Savy's heart gave a little jump as she looked around the table. But all five children were accounted for. Sometimes her sister made predictions that came true. Sometimes, Foxy just said things that made no sense.

"I don't like vegetables," said Daria.

"You won't know they're there because they're so small," said Savy.

"Miguel just told me they're there." Daria turned to Father Matthews. "Vegetables are my kryptonite."

Father Matthews nodded sagely. "That's too bad. Spinach is what made my childhood hero Popeye, The Sailorman, grow strong."

"Who's Popeye? Was he your father? Are you going to be my grandpa?"

Father Matthews smiled indulgently at the child. Savy couldn't take her eyes off that smile. She'd often imagined him smiling at her like that when she became his daughter. That hadn't happened when she was just a little girl. He and his wife had only picked the boys from the foster home to come and live with them.

Father Matthews had never been anything but kind to her and her sisters. His wife, too, when she'd been alive. Tessa Matthews had been something out of a Disney fairy godmother lineup, the guardian angel every child would've loved having at their back.

Savy had told the woman that she would be marrying her son when she was just twelve years old. But then her own mother had swept in and carried Savy and her sisters away again. By the time Savy was able to come back to the Flying Cross Ranch, Tessa Matthews had flown up to be with the other angels.

Back here on earth, Tessa's husband still kept Savy at a distance. Which was confusing to Savy because he knew—everyone knew—that she was head over heels in love with his son. The same son who was back to rubbing his booted calf against hers and grinning at her from across the table.

Charlie had that look in his eyes. That look that told her she was going to be kissed senseless the moment he got her alone. Under the heat of that smolder, Savy forgot about the older Matthews and focused exclusively on the younger man.

"Who would like to say grace?" asked Father Matthews.

All around the square table, the five children looked up in confusion. Forks were in hands. Mouths were open, ready to shovel in Miguel's fusion feast. Gazes were wide as they tried to decipher this foreign word.

"We didn't say grace at the foster home," said Savy. "The children often came from different religious and cultural backgrounds. So I thought it best that each child practice the customs they were taught, or that they gravitated toward."

When she looked across the table, she noted that Charlie winced.

Father Matthews pursed his lips. He didn't frown. The man never frowned, but it was clear that he wasn't pleased with her chosen protocol.

"It's not that I don't believe in a higher power," Savy tried to backtrack. "I just think that children should find their own path to the Creator."

"Or Creatress," said LaTisha.

"How will you know the path to the Creator-" Father Matthews offered the child a glowing smile. "Or Creatress, if you don't have a guide?"

The kids all turned their gazes to Savy. The forks squeezed in their hands, which still hovered over the bounty before them.

Savy pasted on the smile she gave government officials, hospital staff, and public school teachers when they questioned her methods. "Children are born smart. We have to let them make mistakes so that they can grow up."

Father Matthews nodded. He didn't verbally disagree with her, but his smile faded at the corners.

"I'll say grace," said Charlie. "The kids can listen and determine if it resonates with them."

Charlie offered his father a placating smile. He offered Savy a wink.

Savy was grateful for Charlie's interference. She didn't want to offend Father Matthews. Not when he'd opened up his home to the lot of them. Not when she wanted his blessing to marry his son. Not when she still craved the fatherly affection she'd never gotten from him.

"Father God, we thank you for—"

"Why did you say Father God?" asked LaTisha. "It makes most sense to me that God is a woman. It's women that give birth. Not men."

Inwardly, Savy wanted to give the little girl a high five for the logical question. This is what happened when adults let kids think for themselves instead of telling them what to think.

"Is love male or female?" Father Matthews asked in his patient voice.

LaTisha screwed her button nose to think this over. "I don't think love is a person."

"But you can feel it? Can't you?"

LaTisha nodded slowly.

"Love isn't something you can prove. You can only feel it. Doesn't matter if you're loved by a male or a female. When you're loved, you're simply loved. God is love."

There was a peaceful hum hovering in the room at this pronouncement. Each child looked at Father Matthews with thoughtful gazes. Even Savy felt her heart expand at the explanation.

"I'm hungry," Daria said into the quiet moment. "Dear God, can we just eat already?"

"Amen," said Denny.

Forks dug into plates. Lips smacked in appreciation. Savy's own fork was only an inch from her mouth when the doorbell rang. She looked up at Foxy, who shrugged as if to say, *I told you so.*

When Father Matthews made a motion to rise, Savy held out her hand to stop him. "I'll get it," she said, rising from her chair.

She took one glance at the fragrant, steaming plate of food before heading into the main room. When she opened the door, she found an unwanted visitor there. She'd curse her sister for not warning her about exactly who this guest was.

"Are you here to see Father Matthews?" asked Savy. Although she knew that couldn't be the case. Not when Tina Billings wasn't here in her nurse's scrubs. Instead, she was standing in a slinky black dress that looked like it would slip off her with a slight wind.

"No," Tina smirked. "I have a date with Charlie."

Savy slow blinked. Then her eyelids fluttered in quick succession. She'd expected something along those lines with how the woman was dressed. Still, it was a shock to actually hear her gumption.

Really? Was dating so hard in Honor Valley that a woman had to show up on the doorstep of an engaged man? A man who'd been engaged since he was a kid.

"He texted me to pick him up here."

Tina held up her cellphone. Savy barely glanced at it. But in the flash that she saw, the sequence of numbers was familiar to her. Those were Charlie's digits. In exactly the order that would ring his phone.

But no. That couldn't be right. Charlie had never been on a date that didn't include her. Putting that most important fact aside, Charlie would never ask a girl to pick him up. He was far too much of a gentleman not to pick a woman up at her place. The most wrong thing about this whole scenario was the text. Charlie hated typing with his thumbs.

Savy stepped aside to let Tina in. Really, it was the only decent thing to do. It was chilly in the air tonight, and the woman was barely dressed.

Tina didn't wait for a formal invitation. She walked into the house like she owned the place. Either she followed her nose to the dining room, or she had acute senses that were tuned into bachelors.

"Who's this?" asked Charlie when the two women appeared in the dining room.

"Your date," said Savy.

"My what?" Charlie's fork clattered down to his now empty plate.

Savy took one more look at her cooling dinner before she turned to the culprit in this scenario. If she weren't so hungry, she might've found the whole deal a little funny. But her stomach was grumbling, so she was cranky when she said, "Let's ask Denny."

CHAPTER THIRTEEN

Charlie shut Tina's car door with a decisive thunk. The naughty nurse in a scrub of a dress gave him one last pouty look before putting the car into reverse and heading down the driveway.

With that bit of business done, Charlie engaged the locking feature on his cell phone. That was a first. He spent a few minutes pressing his thumb to the device, ensuring that only he would have access to it from now on. Then he crumpled the small piece of paper with Tina's number on it that he'd completely forgotten was in his wallet.

He let the scrap flit out of his hand on the night's breeze. It bumped along the hay strewn over the ground. Charlie didn't consider tossing the refuse as littering, not when the horses would likely eat it in the morning. That is, if a night critter didn't grab it to use in its bedding.

He didn't care what became of it. It hadn't caused him any trouble, just a slight annoyance that he'd had to get up from the dinner table before being served seconds. By the sassy look Savy had given him when she'd picked up her knife and fork, he knew there wouldn't be anything left of Miguel's dish when he came back inside.

Turning, Charlie was met with a youthful face full of defiance. Pinched cheeks that couldn't pull off a hallowed look because of the lingering baby fat. Spindly arms crossed over a chest that would barrel out in a few years. Scowling eyes filled with mistrust and wariness.

Man, that had been him a decade ago. So ready to defy any type of authority, no matter if it hurt him in the process. After a slew of foster homes, it was only Father Matthews that had gotten through Charlie's distrust of the world. The man had done that without raising his voice in anger.

"So, you're trying to get rid of me," Charlie said calmly in his best imitation of his adoptive father.

"Very good, Sherlock." Denny's head cocked to the side as he glared at Charlie.

"You know, I tried that with every foster parent I came in contact with when I was your age."

"Bet that was easy. Them getting rid of you, I mean. Easy to get lost in dinosaur caves."

"Funny. You're funny." Charlie bent down so that he was eye level with the kid. Hazel eyes, like his own, stared back at him, unflinching. That was fine because Charlie didn't flinch either. This next part was the most important part for this kid to understand. "Here's what you need to know about me, Denny. I will never, ever, leave that woman."

Denny glanced down the road where Nurse Tina's car was now out of sight. However, the kid seemed to think better of whatever crack he was about to make that put Charlie with the other woman. A mischievous glint lit up the golden flecks of his eyes.

"Really?" Denny smirked. "Because I've been with Savy for months, and I've never seen or heard of you."

"I've been in the Air Force." Charlie straightened to his full height. "And it's Ms. Savy to you."

"Not Mrs. Matthews, because as a pilot, you don't walk away. You fly away. Got it."

"Look here, you little—"

Charlie had taken a step toward the kid. He stopped abruptly. Not only had he raised his voice, he felt anger coursing through him.

For his part, Denny smirked again. The look on the little demon spawn's face hollered, *gotcha*.

The little cretin had gotten Charlie. Denny had gotten him. And now Denny was stuck with him.

Because Charlie saw it. Charlie saw behind that raised chin and those red cheeks. Charlie saw the kid in those eyes that had seen too much. That crooked grin that was a twitch away from wobbling in a sob. Those balled fists that had had to defend himself when there was no adult around to do it for him.

Charlie saw it all. Because Charlie had lived every second of it himself. But he'd forgotten.

He'd been so long inside a home where he didn't have to guard against anything but his brothers' good-natured roughhousing. He'd been so long on a team that would lift his head for him at any disappointment. He'd been so long standing back-to-back alongside men who would throw a punch at anyone who dared raise a fist to him.

Charlie had started this life on empty. Now, his cup overflowed. Not just from his family but from the love of his life.

When he'd left the Air Force, all he could think about was getting back here to Savy. To finally start their lives together. She had left her singing career years ago to answer the call to the foster care system, to save kids like them.

There was a ringing in Charlie's ears. Much like when he was at high altitudes. Looking down at Denny, Charlie realized he was being called. Not just to a life with Savy. He was being called to save these kids.

"Crap," he sighed.

"Excellent language to use in front of a minor, Captain," said the smart-mouthed minor.

"I'm not gonna be as good at this as Savy."

"Could've fooled me."

Charlie ignored Denny as the realizations kept rolling in. "I'm not gonna be as good as my father, either. You and I are going to butt heads. We're probably not going to get along for a while. You already don't like me. I'm trying hard to warm to you."

It wasn't the most ooey-gooey as motivational speeches went. But Charlie wasn't an Afterschool Special. He wasn't a Disney Prince. He wasn't even sure if he qualified for the Hallmark Channel?

But he was real.

He'd grown up around boys. Rough boys that didn't talk about their feelings. He still wasn't sure his brother, Topher, had actual feelings? What the Matthews boys did do was tell the truth, work hard, and take care of family.

"The other thing you need to know about me is that I don't give up. Ever. I waited my whole life to be with that woman. I love her. She loves you. And so, we are going to get along."

Charlie didn't know what he expected from the kid. A tear at the corner of his eye before he broke down and admitted all he'd ever wanted was to be loved. A sigh of resignation before he flung his arms wide open and clung to Charlie. Whatever Charlie expected was mute because what he got was a snort.

"Whatever, man. I'll be outta here in a couple years."

"That's true," Charlie agreed. And that should've been the end of it. They could simply tolerate each other for a few years. "Or this could be your home base, a place you can always come back to no matter how old you are or how far you go."

Denny took a step back. Then another. His arms were now straight down at his sides, hands locked into fists. Clearly, Charlie was not breaking through the kid's defenses. But he wasn't ready to give up. The whistling of the night's wind was far too close to a harp melody that would be played during a family sitcom at the time after the kid finally owned up to their mistake and the lovable, dopey dad got down on one knee to impart the life lesson for that week.

Charlie didn't get down on one knee, but he did take a step closer to the kid. "I came from Bright Horizons too. Father Matthews took me and my brothers in. We all made something of ourselves. You could do it on your own, but it's easier to do it with a family."

"I don't see anyone else around here."

"Not yet. Not now. But we always come back. Because this is my forever home. It can be your forever home, too. For you and your sister."

That got a response out of him. That tough veneer slipped for just a quick second at the mention of Daria.

"There's no guarantee you'll stay together outside of here. If you decide to stay here, no one will ever take you from this place. I promise."

Charlie held out his hand. Palm up. He waited a full sixty seconds while Denny mulled the offer over. Finally, a limp hand barely touched his.

"I'm not calling you dad."

Charlie perked up at the word dad. He let it go the second Denny dropped his hand. It was a start. And Charlie planned for them to go the distance.

CHAPTER FOURTEEN

"Good work today, Super Daria." Savy gave Daria's cape a shake. The piece of cloth was filthy. But Savy knew better than to secret it away for a wash while the girl was still awake. She'd have to sneak back in the middle of the night to run it through the wash. And just like always, when the kid woke up, she'd believe her pristine cape came to her by way of magic.

"That's a pretty lame superhero name, Ms. Savy," said Daria. "For one, it reveals my secret identity."

"Ah, good point." Savy came and sat on the edge of the bed. The quilt was hand sewn, likely the work of Tessa Matthews. Charlie had shown Savy the quilt his foster mother had made for him when he'd first come to Flying Cross Ranch. She'd made each of her boys one to keep him warm at night.

"You can give me a hug if you want," Daria said.

There was faux annoyance in her tone. Many foster kids weren't used to, or interested in, physical forms of affection. Especially those that were abandoned by their birth parents. Many kids in the system were never hugged by their parents or shown any affection. It often took weeks, or even months, for them to stand any form of care, be it verbal or physical.

Savy always trod very carefully in this part of her work. She'd found the best tactic was to make affection a choice that the child was in charge of. "Are you sure it's okay? I know it's been a physically demanding day for you and your powers."

"No, it's fine. I have a little bit of energy left. And you did a good job today, so you probably need a hug."

Daria opened her arms. Savy leaned down and scooped the girl's small body into her chest. She wanted to squeeze tightly, to show Daria how much she cared. She wanted her to know that her love was real and lasting. But she couldn't make those kinds of promises as a foster parent.

Any of these kids could be taken from her at any moment. Which was why Savy worked so hard to keep her reputation as a foster parent pristine. She knew no one else would love these kids like she did.

"Did you know that Clark Kent grew up on a farm?" Daria asked as she snuggled deep into the quilt. "So did Captain Kirk and Luke Skywalker. I think this place will be good for my backstory."

Savy grinned down at the little imp. This place would be good for Daria to grow big and strong. It'd be good for Miguel to learn about fresh foods and how they're grown. LaTisha would find a ton of reading nooks out here in the woods. Unfortunately, the ranch would completely ruin Ashton's street cred, being that there were no paved streets or corners he could hang on to try to become a rap star.

Denny was the one Savy worried about. But she had faith in Charlie. If anyone could turn that kid around, it would be him.

The two males were so much alike.

Which meant they would butt heads before they would ever hug it out.

But together, she and Charlie would save that kid from himself, just like they saved each other.

She and Charlie. Savy couldn't believe that sentence was finally here in reality. She and Charlie were going to raise these kids together. She and Charlie were going to get married. She and Charlie were finally starting their forever. Her dream had come true.

Peeking into each room of the bunkhouse, Savy saw that her kids were all tucked safely in bed. Each beneath one of Tessa's quilts. All lost in dreams of their own.

A sense of peace washed over Savy as she stepped out into the cool night breeze. The air smelled different on the ranch, cleaner even though she was surrounded by farm animals heeding the call to nature. This was now her home. This was now her life.

The creaking of wood against wood brought Savy's attention round to the big house. Father Matthews sat on the porch, rocking idly back and forth in an aged rocking chair. The moon kissed his weathered skin, making him look like a wise old man from epic fantasy lore.

"Long day?" he asked when Savy reached the porch.

"It was actually pretty peaceful. No one had to go to the hospital."

The old man chuckled. His eyes reflecting some of the moon's glow as though that celestial body was radiating from within him. Savy wouldn't have trouble believing that to be true. The Matthews boys all believed wholeheartedly that their father had a direct line to the Man Upstairs.

"You've done a good job with those kids," said Father Matthews. "You were gifted with the voice of an angel, but I believe you were born for this kind of work."

Savy leaned against the railing and looked out at the ranch. The land teemed with life, but all was silent now at this moment. "I didn't thank you personally for what you've done for us."

"It was purely selfish on my part," he said. "It's been too quiet here all these years."

Savy knew that wasn't entirely true. Father Matthews lived next door to a gaggle of Silvers. Those girls were just as much of a handful as the Matthews. Even before General Silver had passed away, the Silvers had always come to their neighbor for advice, problem-solving, and peacekeeping amongst them. Between the Matthews boys, the Silver sisters, and a few visits from the James girls, the Flying Cross Ranch was never quiet.

"You've already paid your dues raising your six boys," she said.

"Parenting never stops," he grinned, "meaning that bill is always accruing."

"For those kids in there," Savy inclined her head toward the bunkhouse, "parenting never started."

It had never started for her, either. She and her sisters were either an inconvenience to their mother, who wanted to be on the stage. Or they were a temporary act when she needed backup singers. Savy often wondered who she would've been if she'd been parented full time by Tessa and Haran Matthews.

"You are exactly the parent they need. I don't think I've ever told you personally how proud I am of the woman you've become."

The corners of Savy's eyes burned. She wasn't a crier. Tears were dangerous in the foster system. But she wasn't in a foster home any longer. She was in the safest place on earth. So when Haran Matthews opened his arms to her, Savy and her tears didn't hesitate to fall into him.

Savy had always dreamed of the Matthews adopting her and her sisters. But her mother would never terminate her parental rights. After each one of her slip-ups, as she called them, the state would take her girls. She would do just enough to keep the tether strings tight.

It wasn't until Fanny James overdosed when Foxy was nineteen that the strings had been permanently severed. By then, Savy had gained custody of both her sisters and was grinding hard to keep a roof over their heads and food in their bellies. Father Matthews helped out as much as she would allow him to. Money wasn't hard to come by. But funds weren't what Savy was starving for.

Father Matthews squeezed her tight. He pressed his palm into her spine, and she swore it flipped a switch, turning her from a strong, superwoman with a stiff upper lip to a little girl lost in need of saving. Savy clung to the warmth that radiated from his heart. She filled her nostrils with the familiar, comforting, earthy scent of him.

"Like I said, purely selfish motives."

With another press of his palm, the switch flipped again. Savy felt like a gas tank being filled to the brim. Not the regular unleaded fuel either. She had super diesel in her veins. By the time she pulled away from Father Matthews, she felt charged and ready to take on the world.

"Really? My own father is moving in on my girl?"

Charlie stood eying them from the porch steps. Moonlight bounced off his dark hair. The rays caught in his hazel eyes, making them sparkle. Savy took the few steps to the bottom of the porch to land in his arms.

She was overflowing with affection, and warmth, and energy, and love. She never imagined she could be this happy. But here she was, in the home she'd dreamed of living in as a girl, with the man she'd dreamed of every night.

Distantly, she heard Father Matthews excuse himself and head into the house. Savy sank into Charlie's arms. Neither said anything. They just held onto each other under the moonlight.

"They're a handful," he said, finally.

"You want out?"

His hold tightened around her. "I want you."

"Me and the kids are a packaged deal."

"So were you and your sisters. If Tricksy didn't scare me away, nothing will."

Savy pulled back to look at him. "We're really doing this?"

Charlie brushed a strand of hair across her temple and tucked it back behind her ear. "We're really doing this."

They were really doing this. Savy waited for surprise to wash over her. It never came. Instead, the peace of the night rang quietly in her ears… until a shout rang out in the night.

Charlie jerked away from her. His feet were already in motion toward the bunkhouse. Savy tugged on his arm, holding him back.

"Nope, let them figure it out," said Savy.

"They sound like they're going to kill each other."

"If they do, then we won't have to settle the argument." Savy shrugged, wrapping her arms around his neck.

He chuckled, pressing his hand into the small of her back. "You sound exactly like Mother Matthews."

Savy's breath caught at the comparison. As silence once again washed over the night, that sense of rightness settled around her. All the parts of her life were coming together, like a quilt made just for her.

CHAPTER FIFTEEN

Charlie rolled over in his bed. He reached his hand out, but there were no warm curves to greet him. No sweet-scented hair to burrow his nose into. No heated flesh to brush his lips against.

Because Savy was not yet his wife. So, she was not allowed in his bed. A rule his father put his foot down on. Instead of holding onto Savy in real life, Charlie had spent the night dreaming of her.

Waking up was the last thing Charlie wanted to do this morning. Not when his dream was so good. He'd run his hands through his dream girl's thick curls. His vision of love had pressed her palms against his chest. All night long, he'd drowned in the smokey-sweetness that was his fantasy.

Charlie's heart raced even as the dream faded into the bright light of the morning. His body felt tasked, like he had spent the night holding tight to the woman who was his entire world. His lips felt bruised, like he had actually tussled with Savy's mouth into the wee hours. His arms felt heavy, like they had been locked around her form, fulfilling his promise of never letting her go.

His arms were empty now as he cracked one lid open. With the rays of the new day prying his eyes open, a thought ran through his head. It was that thought that yanked him out of sleep and into alert wakefulness.

In this shiny new day, Charlie could, in fact, spend his time with his arms wrapped tight around Savy. He could laze the day, exploring the fullness of her mouth. He could get lost in the curls of her hair.

What was he doing still in bed when the woman of his adolescent, teenage, and adult fantasies was just on the other side of the fence? He could be at the guest house in under five minutes if—

The sound of something tumbling down in his closet brought Charlie up to a sitting position. Someone was in there. If he had any doubts after the small thud of something falling, he knew it for certain by the gasp. That was a person, not a thing, that made that sound.

Was it Savy? Had she beaten him to a tryst? Was she defying Father Matthews's no fraternization until they'd put a ring on it edict? His naughty dream girl.

Charlie tossed off the sheets. The cool morning breeze hit his bare chest. He padded on bare feet to his closet. When he pulled the closet door open, he wasn't met with the tall, shapely love of his life. Instead, there was a short, gangly little girl in a cape and ill-fitting mask.

"Daria?"

The little girl sighed dramatically, looking entirely put out by Charlie's discovery of her. "I'm not Daria. She's a child. I'm Ultra Girl, a superhero on a secret mission."

"A secret mission in my closet?"

"I'm not stealing anything. Superheroes aren't thieves." She held up her hands, palms open. Only her palms weren't empty.

Daria stood to her full four-foot height, closing her hands and putting them on her not-yet-there hips. Her right hand balled into a fist to conceal what rested in her palm.

"Hand it over." Charlie held out his hand in a silent demand.

"I was just looking at it. I wasn't going to take it."

Daria opened her hand again to reveal a bronze medal hanging from a chain. The medal was in the shape of a cross. Instead of T-shapes, the ends of the cross were rounded like the blades of an airplane. Behind the blades were sharper blades jutting outward, like the rays of the sun.

"LaTisha looked you up on the internet," Daria said, stepping past him and out of the closet. "It said you were a hero and that you won a medal. Is this it?"

Charlie had been awarded the Flying Cross medal two years ago for an act of heroism during flight. The medal felt heavy in his palm now. Stepping away from the closet, he pulled out the chair at his old desk and slumped down into it.

Daria leaned on his thigh. She unfurled his fingers from around the medal so that it lay flat in his palm. Her round face peered down at it in awe.

"Did you get the bad guys?" she asked. "Is that why they gave you this?"

"Being a hero isn't always about getting the bad guys. I got this," he held the medal between his thumb and index finger, "because I saved some of the good guys."

The pink tip of Daria's tongue sneaked out of her mouth as she peered at the medal. Her eyes were big in her small face, as though she was transfixed by the medallion. "I want to be a superhero when I grow up."

"Soldiers are superheroes."

"Can girls be soldiers?"

"Of course," said Charlie. "Some of the best soldiers I know are women."

"Do soldiers ride horses?"

"Some do. I was a pilot, so I got to fly."

She considered that. Then she reached behind her head and undid the tie holding her flimsy mask in place.

"Oh!" Charlie widened his eyes and opened his mouth into a rounded O. "It's you, Daria. I had no clue you were Ultra Girl."

Daria giggled. "I decided I could let you in on my secret identity since you're going to be a part of the family."

Charlie looked down at the little superhero. She still leaned against his thigh. Her weight was insignificant, but her words hit him hard. He'd assumed he was bringing these kids into his family. The truth was, he had to find a place in their tight-knit community.

Denny might not be his biggest fan. In fact, the kid definitely looked at Charlie as though he was the villain. But now Charlie had at least one ally on his side.

"You know the name Ultra Girl is already taken?" he said. "She's one of Captain Marvel's sidekicks."

"Ugh." Daria placed a knee on Charlie's thigh and hefted herself into his lap. "Who knew the hardest thing about becoming a superhero was choosing a name."

Charlie suppressed a chuckle. He looked again at her cape. It was a mix of white, orange, brown, and gold. Though Charlie suspected the brown wasn't permanent and would come out in the next wash.

"How about Jupiter Girl?" he said, thinking about the gas giant that had always looked like swirling sand in a glass jar to him.

Daria wrapped her spindly arms around his neck. The contact surprised Charlie. It wasn't like when her brother had given him a fake hug. This was real.

"Hmmm, maybe," was her reply.

The little superhero rested her cheek against his chest for a second. When she pulled away, Charlie was sure she took a piece of his heart with her.

"Really, Charlie? I sneak in here to find you with another woman?"

Savy stood in the doorway to his bedroom. This superwoman presented a very different picture with her hand cocked on her hip than the little superhero. The grin on Savy's face melted his heart. The gaze she fixed on him was enough to bring him to his knees.

"Relax, Ms. Savy. It's just me, Daria." Daria held up the mask cloth.

"Daria?" Savy pulled on a mask of fake surprise. "You let him in on your secret identity?"

"Yeah," Daria nodded with a grin. "I trust him. He's a hero too, you know."

"I know." Savy nodded, her gaze sparkling with love as she looked at him. "He's been my hero for a long time."

CHAPTER SIXTEEN

"You missed a couple of strands."

Foxy wasn't even looking at Savy as she said it. So she also missed the glare as Savy tucked the loose pieces of hair that hadn't made it into her hastily redone ponytail.

"I don't need to be psychic to know what you were up to."

"Shut up." Savy bumped her sister's shoulder. All that got out of the annoying little fortune teller was a snort and a smirk.

Some mystic she was. Of course, if you put two long-lost loves within the same vicinity, kissing was definitely going to occur. Which would easily lead to a few strands of hair going astray.

Duh!

"What you need to be focusing your energies on is your certification," Savy said.

"No worries," Foxy shrugged. "I have a real good feeling about that."

"Fox, we need more than a feeling if we want to get the certification for elevated care."

Traditional foster care was hard on both kids and families. When a child who had faced trauma was tossed into that mix, it was a recipe that rarely worked out in the kid's favor. That's where elevated care workers came in.

Foxy had the temperament for it. Over the year she'd been working in the system, Foxy had gotten through to kids who'd had very troubled paths. Unfortunately, those kids couldn't come and stay at Bright Horizon's because Foxy's knack for getting through to troubled youth remained on a volunteer basis and not an official one.

"Relax," coo'd Savy's baby sister. "It's all going to work out by the end of the month. Trust me."

Savy wasn't one for predictions. Mainly because Foxy got as many of her foretelling right as she did wrong. The main fortune Foxy had misjudged? That the three James sisters would finally be together now that they were no longer a singing trio. That trio had turned into one solo act. Savy had never been sure if it was meant to be a duo.

"Fox, are you sure this is what you want?"

Foxy turned to her sister with a quizzical look. Her screwed features were funny to Savy. Hadn't Foxy seen this question coming?

"I can sing whenever and wherever I want, Sav. These kids need me here."

Okay, so this was one of those times her sister's psychic abilities were eerily correct.

"Tricksy will be home soon," Foxy continued. "We're all going to be one big happy family. Soon. Not yet, but soon."

"Ms. Savy!"

Savy turned her attention to Miguel. The kid had a forklift in his hands and hay in his hair.

"I feel like this is slave labor," Miguel grumped.

Denny shoveled a forkful of hay that only narrowly missed Miguel. "No, it's more like indentured labor because we only have to do it for a certain amount of years before we gain our freedom at age eighteen."

"That's a very good distinction, Denny," said Savy. "And what era did indentured servitude happen in history?"

The chores were character building, but she also had to get the school lessons in where she could during these summer months. Denny narrowed his eyes at her as he scooped up another pitchfork of hay. The kid was smart enough to aim the hay into a pile instead of at her feet.

"Indentured servitude didn't end until the early twentieth century," said Miguel. "But don't indentures need to sign a contract? We didn't sign a contract."

"You can't legally sign a contract until you're eighteen." That came from Charlie.

Even though she'd just left him, the sight of him swaggering up to her made Savy's breath catch. The man was just too beautiful for words. And he was all hers.

"These are your chores," said Charlie. "You do them because this family is a team."

"This isn't a family," said Denny.

Charlie didn't bother responding to the kid. Neither did Savy. She knew it would take some time for Denny to warm up. He was still warming up to her. Not all foster kids came around to trusting their foster parents. But that was okay. Savy would keep the kid safe and prepare him for the world so long as he was in her care. And now Denny had the perfect male role model to look up to.

"Mr. Charlie, can we visit with Duff now that you're here?" said Daria.

The girl stood at the entrance to the pen. LaTisha stood by her side, already fumbling with the latch.

"You finished your chores?"

"Yes, sir," said both girls, bobbing their heads.

"You girls can sit on the fence while he eats," said Charlie. "I'll show you how to brush his mane in a minute."

Daria and LaTisha scrambled up onto the fence nearest the horse. They made clucking noises at the horse while he ate. Duff swished his tail in response, a clear sign of annoyance. Savy didn't blame the animal. He likely wanted to eat his breakfast in peace.

The sound of tires broke the peace of the morning into even more little pieces. A dark sedan ambled to a stop at the front of the house. A man in an ill-fitting suit climbed out of the driver's side with a manilla envelope in his hands and started toward them. When he got closer, Savy recognized him.

"What's he doing here?" said Daria from her place on the fence. "He's a villain. He can't be in our secret lair."

"He's not a villain," said Savy.

At least she hoped Mr. Davidson wasn't a villain. She and the government official were on the same side. They each wanted what was best for these children. Hopefully, what the man carried in that manilla envelope would prove he was an ally.

"I've brought the provisional license," said Mr. Davidson, holding up the envelope.

Savy pressed her hands to her heart. She hadn't realized it was beating so wildly until she felt the kick of the organ against the palms of her hands.

"We got it?" Savy's words were a question, an exclamation, and a prayer of gratitude all in one.

Charlie pulled her into his side and kissed the top of her head. It was all happening. She was going to keep these kids together. She was going to have a forever home here at the Flying Cross Ranch. And she was going to marry the man beside her. It all made her heart beat impossibly faster.

"Since the Flying Cross Ranch was approved in the past as a care facility," said Mr. Davidson, "it made the way forward easier."

Savy's fingers shook as she took the manilla envelope from Mr. Davidson. The documents inside made it all real. It made it official.

"But wait," Savy looked closer at the last page. "There's a mistake. The provisional license is only for four kids. We have five."

Mr. Davidson sighed. He raised his head and looked pointedly at something over Savy's shoulder. Not something. Someone.

Savy's heart stopped. It was a painful feeling going from one hundred miles a second to zero. She knew without it being said what was about to happen.

"After reviewing her medical records, we think Daria Myers will do better in a rehabilitation foster home with elevated care."

For a full sixty seconds, the only sound that could be heard was Duff's chewing and the *swish swish* of his tail. Then the soft thud of a pitchfork being thrown against the ground.

"You're not taking my sister away."

Denny marched purposefully toward Mr. Davidson. His normally pinched features filled with outrage. Before Savy could grab him, Charlie had a hold of the boy.

"Wait, Denny," Charlie said. "We're going to figure this out."

"There's nothing to figure out," said Denny, trying to dodge Charlie's hold. "You said this could be our forever home. You're a liar. You're both liars like all the rest of them."

The accusation must have stung Charlie because Denny dodged and broke free of Charlie's hold. Before the kid could get to Mr. Davidson, or whatever he'd intended, a scream came from behind them.

They all turned in time to see Daria leap from the fence, cape flying and mask on, onto the back of Duff. The startled horse reared up on his hind legs with the child on his back. Everything in the whole entire world stopped.

CHAPTER SEVENTEEN

Standing out in the wide-open space of the ranch with the cool country air flowing all around him, Charlie could not breathe. The sweet scent of honeysuckle was cloying to his tongue. The smell of hay and horses burned his nostrils. He gulped, but there was not enough air to fill his lungs.

Charlie's heart beat an erratic pattern as Daria's little body sailed up a couple of feet into the air. Her cape billowed around her torso as though it would save her from the fall. It wouldn't. It couldn't. It was only fabric, too thin to cushion the blow.

The shouts that came from Denny's throat were deep and panicked. It cracked the boy's veneer, exposing the softness beneath his tough exterior.

Savy's scream pierced Charlie's heart. His first instinct for as long as he could remember had always been to run directly to her, to shield his love from any pain that dared come near her. Not this time.

By the time Daria had raised up on the fencing and prepared to leap, Charlie had been in motion. He'd vaulted over the fence just as she'd landed on Duff's bare back. When the horse reared, tossing her off his back, Charlie had been a step behind.

Daria landed on the solid earth with a thud that was louder than her brother's and Savy's cries. The little girl landed a yard away from him.

The only thing Charlie could do was to put himself between her and the horse.

To his left, Duff walked off to the opposite end of the pen. His tail swished as though fighting off an annoying gnat. He ducked his head for another bite of hay. His wide eyes went half closed as he relaxed back into his morning meal.

Charlie stepped to his right, where Daria lay curled into a ball. He had to fight his instincts to scoop the girl up to his chest lest she was severely injured. His chest constricted as he knelt down to her, still unable to take in enough air.

Daria's lips parted. She opened her mouth wide and sucked in the lungful of air that eluded Charlie. Her eyes popped open, and she stared at Charlie, a tear forming at the corner of each eye.

"Daria, what on earth were you doing?" Savy's voice was shaky as she came up behind them. "You could've killed yourself."

"I was trying to fly away, like Mr. Charlie," said Daria. "So that villain wouldn't kidnap me."

Daria sat up. There was no wincing or constriction in her movements. Just a bruise on her shin where she'd met with a rock. It was a miracle the girl was unharmed.

"I've seen enough," said Mr. Davidson. He'd pulled out a notepad from his suit jacket and was furiously scratching on the yellow paper. "I thought you'd be a positive influence, Captain Matthews, but I can see I was wrong. She's coming with me."

"You're not taking my sister." Denny started toward the government official.

It was the second beast to rear up today. Luckily, this time, Charlie made it to the kid before any damage could be done. He caught Denny around the waist and hauled him against his chest. The kid struggled like Charlie was the enemy. His arms and legs flailing to get at his target.

"Don't make it worse," Charlie whispered in Denny's ear. "I got this."

Denny took a deep breath. His small chest expanded. When he exhaled, there was a modicum of calm, but his features were still screwed up in mutiny.

Charlie chanced letting him go. When he did, the kid held still. Though Charlie was certain he was on borrowed time.

Savy held Daria in her arms, checking every inch of her flesh and joints. The other kids were on the other side of the fence with Foxy, holding as still as insects under inspection, fear and uncertainty shining brightly in their eyes.

Charlie turned his attention to the government official. "Mr. Davidson, the kids are still learning the rules of the ranch. You can't let one mistake inform your entire judgment."

"It's not just one mistake," the man said. "My job is to do what's in the best interest of these kids. Daria is going to need more specialized care that I don't believe you can give her."

"If you take her, you're taking me too," said Denny.

Charlie stepped in front of Denny before he could make it worse. He spread his hands in the universal language of Stop, hoping it would allow calm to enter the scene. Or at least give him a few moments to stall and come up with a plan.

"Let's just all take a breath here," said Charlie. "There's nowhere for you to place her tonight. Since you're closing the only foster home in the city. The nearest one is at least a hundred miles away. Let her stay the night, and we'll talk again in the morning."

Mr. Davidson looked from Charlie, who had his hands spread to Denny, who looked ready to murder him, to Daria, who was sniffling as she clung to Savy.

There was a brief moment where Charlie saw a light of compassion in the man's eyes. But then Mr. Davidson looked down at his notepad. A glance at the words written there dissolved his empathy.

"One more night," he said. "Say your goodbyes. I'll be back in the morning with help."

With that edict, Mr. Davidson stuffed his notepad back inside his ill-fitting jacket. He turned on his heel and marched to his car.

"You're a liar."

Charlie turned to face off against Denny. The boy looked at him with betrayal.

"You said this was a forever home, but you're going to let them take my sister."

"Denny, we're going to figure this out."

The kid wasn't listening. Denny stormed off in the direction of the woods. Charlie decided to let him go blow off some steam. There was an even bigger storm brewing in the dark gray of Savy's eyes.

CHAPTER EIGHTEEN

It was silent. Silence in a foster home did not bode well.

Savy kept her eye on the bunkhouse, watching for any movement. So far, all she saw was stillness. All she heard was silence. She wasn't the psychic sister in the James clan. Still, she knew something bad was about to happen.

The reality was that something bad had already happened. The tracks of Mr. Davidson's tires were still visible from the porch, even though the sun had set. Savy had the urge to go and kick rocks until the dirt covered the pattern.

It wouldn't matter. Mr. Davidson was still coming back in the morning to take Daria away. And there was nothing Savy could do about it.

"We're not letting this happen."

The sound of Charlie's voice in her ear was once the most comforting thing to Savy. Over a phone crackling with static. In a letter as she imagined him speaking the words. Directly into her ear as he whispered his undying love to her when they were together.

They were together now. Charlie stood behind her as though he would catch her if she fell. She was the one standing sturdy while the world crashed around her.

"They can't just do that, can they?" Charlie asked.

"She's not ours." The words felt like acid on her tongue. "These kids are wards of the state. I just take care of them."

"You do more than that." Charlie turned her to face him. "You teach them. You care for them. You have their best interests at heart. No one could possibly do this better than you."

He was right. Except Savy didn't just care for these kids. She loved each and every one of them with every fiber of her being.

She hadn't thought she could love another soul apart from her sisters and the man now holding her close in this way. She'd been wrong. Her heart seemed to have no boundaries.

It was only the government who did. The government could come take one of her charges away. Because they were only hers in her heart, not legally.

"We're not letting them take Daria. I promised Denny this was their forever home."

Savy reared back from Charlie. Reflexively, he didn't let her go. He held tight.

"You did what?" she demanded.

"In my heart-to-heart with Denny. I told him this was his forever home. That no matter where he was in his life or the world, he could always come back here."

"You had no right to do that, Charlie. You can't promise these kids forever. They're not ours."

Even as she said those last words, the acid in her stomach burned through her chest.

"We promised each other forever," said Charlie.

"We were kids. Now we're adults. Adults can't make that promise. Not in the foster system."

Charlie opened his mouth. Then closed it. His eyes never left Savy's. They screamed that he did not agree with her assessment. But the words to back him up never came.

The quiet that had permeated the night settled between them. It grew louder and louder until it itched at her skin.

"I'm going to go and check on them," Savy said.

Charlie reached for her as she took a step past him. Then appeared to think better of it. He brought his hands back to himself and shoved them into his pockets.

The love of her life was standing right by her. There were just inches between them. But it was as though he was miles away.

Savy hated it. But she knew that even though she was arguing with Charlie, and she was angry with him, she knew he would be there in the morning. She could not say the same about Daria. And so Savy trudged into the bunkhouse on her own.

The quiet that greeted her scratched at the acid that had started in her gut, climbed into her chest, and was now making its way up her throat. She wanted to speak, to call out to the kids. The quiet told her to listen carefully.

The quiet broke with the squeaking of a sneaker against the polished hardwood floors.

"Ms. Savy!" Ashton appeared in the doorway, blocking her entry. "I wanted you to listen to this dope rhyme I came up with."

That didn't rhyme. It was another warning.

As Savy sidestepped him, Miguel stepped in. "Ms. Savy, Father Matthews gave me this old cookbook. But I'm not sure what some of these ingredients are. Can you help me?"

Miguel knew Savy couldn't cook. It was the reason he'd picked up his first cookbook. The warning bells were getting louder.

Savy stepped around the young chef, only to be confronted with LaTisha. The girl tugged at the rounded tip of her nose. She'd never been one for lies. Not after Savy had read *Pinocchio* to her.

"They're gone," said LaTisha.

Savy already knew. It was the quiet. That old adage was true when it came to kids.

Silence is golden... unless you have kids, then the silence is just suspicious.

The three kids were silent. Savy didn't even need to look in Denny or Daria's rooms to know that they had run away.

CHAPTER NINETEEN

"There has to be something else I can do." Charlie gripped the steering wheel as he spoke into the phone.

Montana was not a hands-free state, and Charlie didn't have time to feel guilt over multitasking. There were lives at stake. And so he clutched his ancient cellphone to his cheek as he peered out the passenger window at the sidewalks and into the dark alleys.

He had to find them.

"Sorry, bro, but I don't see what else is to be done?" said his brother Joe from the other end of the line. "From the records I can see, it looks like the kid is in serious trouble."

Charlie heard the *tap tapping* of keys through his earpiece. He could imagine his brother hunched over a large conference table as he bent the red tape of government software to his will. Unlike Charlie, Joe had seen less field combat and more battles in military war rooms.

Tap, tap, tap. "Multiple instances of running away." *Tap, tap.* "And, wow, have you looked at her medical records?"

"Joe, focus. Can't you find some case precedence where Savy gets to keep her?"

"You know the system doesn't work like that. Savy's not the biological parent or even a relative. It would be easier if she was. It's hard to take kids from their parents. Though I see here, the mother's parental rights have been terminated. There's no mention of the father."

That's why it had been easy for the Matthews to foster and then adopt him and his brothers. They were all lost boys. Lost to deceased parents, terminated rights, or a blank on the birth certificate.

"Look, bro, I gotta go, but I'll keep looking. I suppose I'll be staying in the guest house since my room in the bunkhouse has been commandeered."

Foxy had been right about Joe's coming home in a few days. Apparently, he was leaving his position in the JAG Corp for one closer to home. Though he was quiet about exactly what that was.

"Savy and Foxy are staying in there right now," said Charlie.

There was a clatter on the line like the phone had been dropped onto Joe's keyboard. "Foxy? Foxy James is staying in the guest house?"

"Yeah, she'll be living there when we move them all in starting next week."

"And Foxy is staying in the guest house?"

"Yeah, you got a problem with that? You two have known each other since you were kids."

Joe made a humming noise on the phone. His fingers tapped on the keys but in a pattern that didn't sound like he was typing recognizable words. "Exactly where am I supposed to sleep?"

"There's plenty of room in the big house."

"Along with my father and my newlywed brother? No, thank you."

"Then stay in the guest house with Foxy."

There went that humming and tapping noise again. "It won't be a good look for me. The council is considering appointing me to the vacant District Attorney post after my separation from the military. It won't look good for me to stay with an unmarried woman."

"Look, I don't care where you sleep. Just find legal ground for us to get Daria back."

"You gotta find the kid first."

"I'm looking."

Charlie took a sharp left turn. Just like the last street, he was met with nothing but darkness, not a single soul. It was nearing midnight. They couldn't have gotten far and certainly, would be getting tired. They'd also skipped dinner and would likely be hungry.

"You check the pizza parlor?" asked Joe. "Best place to go for scraps."

It was a good idea. Charlie ended the call. He used both hands to navigate back to Main Street and to one of two pizza parlors in the town. Parking the car in front of the closed shop, Charlie got out and went around back.

It was quiet. Too quiet. No bugs or rodents made a peep. Because there were bigger predators out.

"Daria, keep quiet."

"But I like Mr. Charlie. I want to stay with him. Plus, he'll know it's me since I already told him my secret identity."

Daria appeared from behind a large green dumpster. Her cape hung limply around her small shoulders. Her mask was askew. There was red pizza sauce on her chin.

"Hey, Ultra Girl," said Charlie.

"I decided on Jupiter Girl, like you said."

Daria took a few tentative steps toward him. Then she broke out in a run. Charlie held still, too afraid that the wrong move would send the child running again. When she was within his arm span, he scooped her up and crushed her to his chest.

"You okay? You hurt?"

"No, I'm indestructible."

Her spirit might be indestructible, but not her frail body. There were goosebumps on her arms, and she shivered a bit in his hold.

"You gonna turn us in?" said Denny. He still held back, standing closer to the trash bin. "We'll just run again."

"I believe you," said Charlie. He did not let Daria out of his embrace. Instead, he shifted her to his hip as though she were just a baby. "But look how easy it was for me to find you."

"That's why I keep telling him he needs a secret identity," said Daria, leaning into Charlie with all the trust in the world. Which is why it broke Charlie's heart to say the next thing.

Charlie's gaze locked with Denny's. By the scowl the kid gave him, Charlie knew that Denny knew the words he was about to say. When Charlie turned to Daria, the little girl was completely guileless.

"They're going to take you away tomorrow," said Charlie.

Daria's little lip quivered. The slight weight of her multiplied in his arms. But he did not let her go. He had to be strong for his family.

Denny stormed up to them. "I'm not letting them take my sister. She's the only family I got."

"What if she wasn't?" said Charlie.

He wanted to reach out to the boy, to include him in the embrace, but Charlie knew there were too many layers of hurt and distrust coating the kid's exterior. That was okay. Charlie was determined to break through. And once he did, Denny would see that Charlie would never hurt him or give him a reason to doubt. They just had to let Daria go for a moment before she could come back and be with them forever.

"I have an idea. But I need you to trust me."

"I trust you, Mr. Charlie," said Daria.

They both looked to Denny. Denny's eyes were hard as they glared at Charlie, but they softened when he looked at his sister.

CHAPTER TWENTY

*S*avy came into wakefulness with a jolt. There was a warm blanket around her body. Her aching body was curled awkwardly on the living room couch.

She must have fallen asleep here sometime in the night while she waited for word from Charlie. Her phone lay on the coffee table. There wasn't a single alert of a missed call or new text.

Where was he? Where were the children? Her gut tightened into knots to think that Denny and Daria were still out there on the streets alone.

"Relax, my dear. Everything is as it should be."

Father Matthews sat across the room in an old rocking chair. His booted feet were entirely on the ground as he gave himself a little heave to rock forward and back. In his hand was an old bible. His smile was the same pleasant peacefulness Savy had come to know since she was a girl.

Savy had always wondered how he kept that smile in the face of the six little hellions he'd taken into his home. Sure, she'd seen him not smiling many times with a thin line across his features. A handful of times, she'd even seen him cross, his mustached mouth turned upside down. Those looks never lasted long. It was as if the frown was too heavy for him to hold on to.

"The kids are back," said that smiling, peaceful face. "Charlie found them and put them to bed. He told me not to wake you. Said you needed the rest."

Savy sat up and uncurled her legs. They creaked and groaned in protest. She had needed the rest. What she needed more was to pull Daria close to her heart and see with her own eyes that Denny was alright.

But something weighed her down. A question she'd always wanted the answer to but was afraid to ask. "Why didn't you take us?"

Father Matthews's legs were straight, heaving the rocking chair all the way back. He bent his knees, and the chair came to rest forward. The peaceful smile straightened as he regarded Savy.

"Me and my sisters? Why didn't you offer to adopt us, too?"

Father Matthews's mouth turned down into a frown. There was no anger there, just a heavy weight. It lifted before he spoke.

"You know, my wife and I couldn't have kids of our own. You girls had parents. We would never imagine taking kids from their parents."

"They were bad parents; awful parents."

"They tried."

"They failed."

"No, they didn't." His smile was sad, but there was a certainty to the weight of it. "As I told you before, you turned out just as you were meant to be. A siren who calls wounded souls to them. You are a strong, compassionate woman whose life work is to care for the kids that society doesn't know what to do with. You won't fail these kids because you know what it means to be failed."

He was right, but… "I still think I could've learned that lesson while on this ranch."

Father Matthews chuckled, his legs straightening as he began to rock once more. "My boys were broken when they came to me. They were each like wild horses untrusting of humankind. Much like your young Denny."

Savy looked out the window. Standing in front of the porch, she saw Charlie and Denny talking. Denny didn't look as though he hated Charlie completely. What had he done to the boy?

"Besides," Father Matthews continued, "I always knew you were destined to be my daughter. One of the first things my son said to me was that he'd vowed to love you until his dying day."

Savy's legs didn't creak as she straightened. She walked over to

Father Matthews on sure legs. He ceased his rocking so that she could reach down and give him a strong hug.

When she pulled away, he was grinning at her as though the two were in on a secret. Savy was certain there was nothing this man didn't already know. Had he known she would one day be in this spot? Watching over her as she slept? Holding her tight as she let go her worries? Bringing to him the next generation of troubled youth whom he would have a hand in healing and raising? His sons always said he had a direct line to The Man Upstairs.

Turning back to the front door, Savy made her way outside to the love of her life and the child she wanted to care for. Charlie's head was still bent with Denny's.

Denny looked up at her. Then the kid looked back at Charlie. With a huff, the teen said, "Fine."

He turned and sauntered off. Hands in his pockets. Shoulders hunched as if Charlie had asked him to do chores on a Sunday.

"What was that?" said Savy.

"We've come to an understanding." Charlie caught her in an embrace and pulled her close. "How are you feeling? Rested?"

She didn't have a chance to answer. She didn't even have a chance to ask about Daria. The sound of gravel being kicked up by tires turned her attention to the road where Mr. Davidson's sleek sedan was winding its way toward them.

Savy broke from Charlie's embrace, and for once, he let her go. Savy took a step toward the parking car, but her attention was dragged to the bunkhouse. Daria and Denny were walking hand in hand from the bunkhouse, followed by the other kids. Daria had a backpack strapped to her shoulders as though she was preparing to go to school or camp since it was summer.

Mr. Davidson stepped out of the car with what she could only describe as a goon. A goon who was going to take Daria away. Savy couldn't let that happen. Daria had only just started giving her unsolicited hugs. It would take weeks, maybe even months, for the child to be comfortable enough to give that affection to another person.

But no one was fighting it. LaTisha, Ashton, and Miguel all stopped a few feet away. Denny let go of his sister's hand and let her continue on. Even Charlie had backed up to make a clear way for Daria to go with the goon.

What was going on?

"I'm sorry I was bad, Ms. Savy," Daria said as she wrapped her arms around Savy's middle. "I'll be good while I'm away."

Away? Who said she was going away? Weren't they going to fight?

Daria gave a tug as though she were ready to pull away from Savy. Mr. Davidson and the goon looked on expectantly. Instead of letting her go, Savy locked her arms around Daria and scooped her into her arms. She turned, giving the government men her back, preparing to run. But she was stopped by the most unexpected person.

"Sav," said Charlie. "We have to let her go, but it's not forever."

Forever. There was that word again. Hadn't Charlie promised her forever.

"We're going to get her back. I promise."

Savy wanted to rail that he couldn't promise that to these kids. They weren't hers, not legally. They were in every other way that mattered.

"Trust me, Sav."

Savy's mind and heart were whirling. It was a tornado of emotion. But one thing rang true. She trusted this man with her life. These kids were her life, and so she would trust Charlie with their fate as well.

And so Savy took Charlie's hand, and they faced Mr. Davidson and his goon together.

CHAPTER TWENTY-ONE

harlie hated the pain in Savy's eyes. What he was about to do was going to hurt her. It was unavoidable, but it wouldn't be forever.

"We have to let her go," he said.

Savy didn't say the word. She didn't have to. Her whole body radiated the word no. But she didn't pull away from Charlie. She leaned into him as though it was only his strength that held her up.

He would be strong for both of them. He would be strong for all of them. Because the thought of Daria leaving them hurt him, too.

Charlie wiped the tear from Savy's eye before turning and going down on one knee. He came level to Daria. The little superhero wasn't wearing her mask. She stood as her true self, and she had a tear in her eye as well.

Charlie collected it in his thumb along with Savy's. "You remember the plan?"

Daria opened her mouth to respond. Her lip wobbled. Instead of speaking, she nodded solemnly.

Charlie reached into his pocket and retrieved the medal of honor he'd received. He unclasped the chain and brought it around Daria's tiny neck. The medal hung well below her heart, closer to her gut, where bravery was said to live.

"Now, you remember what I told you?"

"It's not always about the bad guys," said Daria. "Sometimes, you have to focus on saving the good guys."

"That's my girl." He squeezed her shoulder, trying to infuse all the bravery he had into her little body. "We're going to save you."

Daria clutched the Flying Cross medal in her palm. One of the blades peaked out between her thumb and index finger. "I know you will."

"It's time for her to go," said Mr. Davidson.

Charlie straightened to face off with the man. He wanted nothing more than to rail against the unfairness of it all. But as Joe had told him, that wasn't the way. Instead, he was going to do it the government's way. With that in mind, Charlie handed the government official a packet of papers.

"What's this?"

"Petition for adoption," said Charlie.

"You can't adopt her."

"Not Daria. Her brother. We've already started the process to make Dennis Myers a Matthews."

Denny took a deep inhale and let it out slowly. He glanced at his sister and her stiff upper lip. He glanced at Savy and her teary eyes. Then he turned that stone-faced glare on Mr. Davidson and nodded as though conferring his agreement with Charlie.

It was the best Charlie could hope for. Right now. In a matter of weeks, he was certain he and the rebel youth would be off on a fishing trip, or playing catch, or having a heart to heart around a pit fire.

Okay, maybe a couple of months.

"After we adopt Denny, we'll legally be his family. No judge will deny us trying to keep the siblings together when we want Daria to be ours."

Mr. Davidson pursed his lips. A small sigh broke through. It was clear the man wanted what was best for these kids. But he had to follow protocol.

That was fine. They would all bide their time until the paperwork and the protocol tipped in their favor.

With one final longing look, Daria turned to hop in the backseat of the sedan. Her cape billowed behind her as she took a seat. Then the door was closed, the car started, and they were pulling off.

"Adoption?"

Charlie turned to face Savy. Her eyes were still watery, but those tears didn't look sad. They looked surprised.

"It was all that I could come up with on short notice," he said. "I figured you'd be okay with it? But now I'm thinking it might be too much. First marriage, then moving, and now having two kids all at the same—"

Charlie didn't get to finish his statement. Savy leaped into his arms. He caught her at the first instance, not the last moment. She wrapped her arms around him and kissed him. Hard.

"Ew gross," said Miguel.

"I don't think that's appropriate for kids to see," said LaTisha.

"Yeah, they're using tongue, see," said Ash. "Definitely not PG."

No, the short-term plans Charlie had for his long-time fiancée were definitely not PG. Luckily, there was plenty of work they could send these kids off to do that didn't require parental guidance. Pretty soon, he and Savy would need to start the adoption paperwork for each one of them. But first thing was first.

"Hey," said Charlie when he broke the kiss.

"Hey," said Savy, chasing his lips and not letting him get too far.

"You're here."

"I am."

"How long?"

"Forever."

EPILOGUE

"This is your time, Joe. You're definitely the man for the job, and the Board of Commissioners will see it that way."

Captain Joe Matthews swiveled around in his chair. It was a base chair, so it creaked and wobbled. The government spent top dollar on weapons for the men and women who protected their interests. Not so much on ergonomic office furniture.

"This is the first step in what you always wanted." Richard, Joe's soon-to-be campaign manager's voice crackled as it came over the satellite phone line.

Joe had wrapped up his time as a JAG officer in the Armed Forces. He'd spent the last three years serving as legal advisor to one of the military's top commanders. He'd done good work. But this wasn't the work he wanted to do for the rest of his life.

He wanted to continue to serve the people of this great nation. Especially little people like he and his brothers had been. When Charlie had called him a few days ago asking for help with a foster kid, some old spark in Joe's belly had ignited.

This was the reason he'd gone into the law. He'd spent the first years of his life not having a say in his own life. Now that he was grown and had a command of the law, he would never be put in that position again. He could help others in need to find their own voices.

The perfect platform to do that would be as the District Attorney for his county. And maybe, someday, the State Attorney. And then, later in life, something more…

"So, that's the plan," said Richard. "You head home, and we start the schmoozing campaign with the Board of Commissioners."

"I'm headed back home," Joe confirmed. "But when I get there, I first need to help my family with a legal matter."

"What legal matter?"

"Just some help with a foster kid they want to adopt."

"That's…" There was a bit of static over the phone, and a few of Richard's words were lost to the ether. "… great on your resume. It'll definitely convince Commissioner Benson that you're the man for the job."

"I thought you said they all see me as a fit to fill the District Attorney position."

"Yeah, well," Richard hedged as the phone line crackled. "A few need convincing. A good deed like that will convince them. That and you finding the right hometown girl to propose to."

"Propose?" There must've been a disconnect or interference with the line. Joe couldn't have possibly heard that correctly.

"Can't have a bachelor in line for U.S. State Attorney for Montana."

Joe heard that loud and clear. That was his ultimate goal. But marriage?

"I'll work on finding you the right girl," Richard was saying, his voice coming across loud and clear on the phone line. "We just can't have any scandals in the meantime."

"Right. No scandals."

"I'll also have a realtor looking into a condo for you."

"A condo?" asked Joe. "Why would I stay in a condo when my family has a two thousand acre ranch?"

"Didn't you say there were people staying there?"

"Yeah," Joe said, then added. "Just some foster kids." He hesitated another moment and then conceded. "And my brother's fiancée… and…"

The line crackled again. Joe waited for the interference to die down. It didn't. The connection snapped before Joe could finish his sentence.

What Joe didn't mention was that there was another adult guest staying there as well. But what happened between him and Foxy James was years ago. No reason they couldn't be on the same ranch. In the same guest house.

None at all.

———

You've met Foxy.
So you know her and her psychic abilities are a scandal waiting to happen for Joe.
Wonder if Foxy will predict what will happen when Joe returns?
Find out in *His Vow to Treasure,*
Book Two in the Flying Cross Ranch Romances!

VOW TO TREASURE

A FLYING CROSS RANCH ROMANCE 2

CHAPTER ONE

There was a *bump bump* as the plane came in for a landing. That was Joe Matthews's first indication that the road ahead of him would not be a smooth one. Whenever he was in the cockpit and he brought the craft back to earth, there was never a bump. Because Joe Matthews was precise, level-headed, and even-handed.

The swerve to the left, and then the hitch to the right as the pilot put on the brakes indicated that they were none of those things. Joe sat straight in his seat as many others braced themselves and tilted forward. During his time in the Air Force, he'd been in much hairier situations. Though it was his time in boardrooms and courtrooms negotiating and advising as a JAG officer that had been the most combat-laden.

As the commercial airliner slowed to taxi to the gate, a sense of calm came over Joe. Finally, he was back home. And home for good this time. His service in the Judge Advocate General Corp was finally done. What wasn't over was his need to serve. Though that need would be filled, as he took a different path on a different battlefield.

"Ladies and Gentlemen, the fasten your seat belts sign has been turned off, and it is now safe to move about the cabin. Thank you for flying with us today, and we wish you well on your next journey."

Joe stepped off the plane. It was a small puddle jumper aircraft that had flown him from the major airport in Yellowstone to his neck of the woods, which was still a ninety-minute car ride to his small hometown. So when he stepped off the plane, he stepped onto the tarmac and into fresh Montana air. With his lungs full, he looked up at the mountains, knowing he had a hard climb ahead as he prepared to step forward into his next journey in life.

Captain Joe Matthews was out of the war business. He was embarking on far more treacherous territory; the world of politics.

"There he is."

A smoke-filled, whiskey-laced voice broke through the soft rustle of wind of the day. That was the voice of Joe's campaign manager, soon to be chief of staff, Richard Wilson. The two men had gone to undergrad together. Where Joe finished his degree early and gone into the service, Rich had taken a more scenic route on his path through education and had finally graduated three years ago with a handful of half majors and a bucketful of minors that were cobbled together into a completed B.S.

Rich could've graduated at any time with parents that paid an endowment to the school. He just enjoyed campus life too much. Aside from the degree, Rich had collected people. He knew everyone that was worthy of knowing in the state of Montana.

"Ladies and Gentlemen, Cowboys and Ranch hands, may I present to you the next United States Attorney for the great state of Montana."

Rich spread his arms wide and made a sound at the back of his throat meant to mimic a roaring crowd. His antics were met with a couple of stares, some eye rolls, but mostly huffs of annoyance as passengers tried to wheel their way around the two men stopped in the middle of the tarmac.

"I don't think they share your enthusiasm, Rich," said Joe as he retrieved his bag from the plane-side cart.

"That's just because they don't know this golden boy yet." Rich clapped him on the shoulder as they headed into the terminal. "They'll learn you're a hometown boy who done good. An underdog from foster care who rose through the ranks of the military to become a top JAG officer. Man, they'd eat this stuff up if we took it to Hollywood. Which reminds me, we have a meeting with a producer at the end of the month."

At some point, they'd picked up their pace. Joe only realized that because he was trying to catch his breath. He was still in top form, but Rich could be a whirlwind that would eat up lesser men and women and spit them out whole with his big dreams. The man talked a big game. Joe had realized over the past year that his old college bum of a friend could deliver.

"You have a lot of meetings this week," Rich continued, pulling out a handheld device that looked like it could launch missiles. "We're going to have a party announcing your interest in just a few days. All of the council members will be in attendance. Then I've got community events scheduled and—"

"Rich, I just got back. I'd like to at least go home and see my dad."

"Yeah, sure, sure. Which reminds me, we need to get a photo op with you and the old man. A preacher father? That is going to do great with the religious demographics."

Joe didn't even bother to sigh out loud. This was Rich. Everything was staged with him and used to an advantage.

Joe wouldn't let that happen to his father. Haran Matthews had had a heart attack not too long ago. The man needed rest. Joe still felt guilty that he and his brothers hadn't been here for their father in his time of need. The man had been there for each of them at all the important parts in their lives. Seeing his dad was priority number one.

"Commissioner Benson is available for dinner tomorrow night. He's the one that's still on the fence about you as acting D.A."

The last District Attorney had retired suddenly because of health reasons. The board of commissioners had the right to appoint an acting D.A. in her absence. With his credentials, Joe was the top candidate for the post.

"Like most of the commissioners, Benson is very traditional," Rich went on. "He doesn't trust a man that isn't leg-shackled. I have the perfect woman for you for that. I've set that up for later this afternoon."

Now Joe did sigh out loud. He hadn't been on board with this idea of a fake fiancée the first time Rich had brought it up. Joe wasn't good at faking anything. Most soldiers weren't unless it came to pain tolerance and torture. Faking a relationship certainly sounded like torture. Especially when his heart had decided long ago that it belonged to one woman.

"You'll like Charlotte," Rich was saying. "She's a lawyer, like you. Not military, but she's definitely active. Man, wait till you see the legs on her."

"Rich, I'm not going to pretend I'm in love with a woman to get a job."

"Who said anything about love? It's a business arrangement. Isn't that what marriage is?"

Not for Joe. For years he'd tried to convince his heart that it was illogical to pine for Foxy James. She was the most impractical, irrational, incongruous, beautiful, bold, bright—

Joe gave his head a shake. He'd entirely lost his train of thought. What were they talking about?

"She's exactly the type of woman a District Attorney would have as a wife," Rich was saying.

Those words brought Joe back to reality. Foxy James—even her name—was not political wife material. Foxy was a mess of curly hair that never behaved. Her skirts were too short. She also had a penchant for wearing sparkly colored sneakers that mismatched those short skirts. And then there was the other matter... she believed she was psychic.

"If you want to achieve your goal of someday soon becoming the US Attorney for this state, then the least you can do is meet her for lunch later today."

Meet her? Not Foxy. The woman who was a perfect political wife. The woman who would help Joe achieve his goal of serving at a higher office where he could help keep the scales of justice balanced.

That was his chosen purpose in life. That was his dream. That's what would be his legacy after a rough start in life, where the scales were tipped out of his favor. He'd achieved balance, and he wanted to do that for others. With the right partner, one who was his equal, he could make that dream come true.

"Joe!"

Joe looked up at the sound of that familiar voice. His grin split wide as he saw his brother. Charlie's and Joe's smiles matched, as did their hazel eyes. Charlie held out his tanned hand. Joe clasped his brother's hand with his brown one. Then the two embraced, squeezing tight and clapping each other on the back.

It had been far too long since he'd seen his foster brother. Sure, he was surrounded by brothers in the military, but there was nothing like being in the presence of the man he'd grown up with.

Charlie and Joe and the other four Matthews boys had been through a different kind of trenches together. They'd come up through the foster care system and survived. There should be a medal for fighting on those battlegrounds. But the six boys from Bright Horizons had been rewarded with something far greater; a father in the form of Haran Matthews.

"It's good to see you, man." Joe gave Charlie another squeeze before letting him go.

Charlie smelled like home. Like hay, homecoming, and horses. Joe had a sudden itch to be back on the ranch. To be back in open fields. To mount a horse and race through the valley. To hear his father's laugh and see the sparkle in the old man's eyes.

"Good to see you again, Rich," said Charlie.

"You, too," said Rich. "Just remember, we have shared custody of your brother now. I need him back by lunchtime."

Charlie snorted, but he didn't disagree. Though Joe and Rich had been tight during college, no one could compete with the bond the brothers shared.

"You ready to go?" Charlie asked Joe. "Savy's double-parked outside."

"Sav's here?"

"Yeah, she couldn't wait to see you."

"So, it's just the two of you?" Joe asked, hoping no one could hear the eagerness in his voice.

"Yeah, it's a hike out here. We kinda used the car ride as a date night. We don't get much with the kids at home."

Joe nodded, his mind not on his brother's words. Instead, he was trying to think of another way to ask where Foxy was. No one knew about his heart's long-ago decision that Foxy was the one for him. He'd kept it from his brothers and from Foxy herself.

Foxy had told him as a kid that she'd had a premonition about her one true love. As soon as she'd said those three words, *one true love*, Joe had known she was his. Even when Foxy insisted she wouldn't meet her mystery man until she was older.

"So, Tricksy's at the ranch with the kids?" asked Joe.

"No, Tricks is still on the road." Charlie hefted one of Joe's bags over his shoulder and began walking toward the exit doors to Ground Transportation.

It took Joe a moment to get his feet to move. There was still no mention of Foxy.

"Who's minding the kids?" Joe tried again.

"Dad is," said Charlie.

Finally, Joe just gave up and came out with it. "And Foxy?"

"Ummm," Charlie thought about it for a moment. The silence stretched on so long that Joe thought he might've forgotten the question. "I think she went to town to see Travis Ramos."

Joe's heart skipped a beat. Not the upbeat skip of a man in love. The thunk down into the stomach of a man who'd been gut-punched.

The love of his life was dating someone. She was older now. It was the future. Travis might be her dream man. He might not. The fact of the case was that Foxy hadn't seen Joe in that vision. Even if she saw him now, he still wouldn't be the man of her dreams. So what was he waiting for?

Before he stepped out of the airport, Joe turned to Rich and said, "I'll see you and your friend at lunch."

CHAPTER TWO

"*T*ravis, why won't you give me a reference?"

"You mean to tell me that as a psychic, you don't know?"

Foxy bit her tongue, trying to hold back the familiar retort. Why was that always the taunt everyone threw at her? *Didn't you know I was coming? Didn't you know the answers to the test you just epically failed? Didn't you know that guy, or girl, was a scumbag before you befriended them?*

No, she didn't know those things because she was not a psychic. Foxy hated the term psychic. It was such a catchall for anyone who had a heightened sense of awareness like her.

That heightened sense could come in many forms. Some people heard things in their minds. Kinda like Yoda and other Jedi masters using the Force to communicate or put suggestions in weaker minds. Though the sense of clairaudience was typically one-sided.

Others who were gifted might see images and scenes play out in their mind's eye. This clairvoyance might be in the form of metaphorical symbols. Sometimes they might see a flash of actual events from the past. Sometimes they might foresee a hazy possibility of the future.

Foxy wasn't afflicted with that ability either, and she was thankful for it. Her day-to-day life rivaled that of what could be seen on movie screens most days with an irresponsible mother who had dragged her daughters out on the road, into back-alley dives and smoke-filled bars where they saw all manner of things no adolescent should've witnessed.

Foxy was also thankful that she wasn't claircognizant. She didn't experience the feelings of others. Living in a house full of troubled youth both as a child and now as an adult, she would've never gotten to sleep buried under the weight of their feelings, much less her own. It was the thought of the children currently in her care that made her humble herself and try again with her former boss.

"I'm not psychic," she explained patiently. "What I am is clairsentient. It means the messages come through to me as a strong feeling. Like a gut reaction."

"Hmm," said Travis as he rang up the order of a departing lunch party. "And your gut didn't tell you that you were the worst waitress in the history of this restaurant?"

"Was not," was Foxy's professional retort.

Travis closed the cash register with a smack of his palm that made the machine ding. "You argued with people over what they chose to order off the menu."

"I didn't need my abilities to tell me that Mr. Jensen was one more steak away from a heart attack."

Mr. Jensen had barely fit into the booth. His breath had been short as he'd battled with the furniture over the effort. Once uncomfortably inside the booth, his belly had pushed so far up on the table that he could've balanced his glass of soda on it. He alternately reached for his cup of sparkling sugar and scratched at his jaw and chest, clear signs that a heart attack could be imminent. It hadn't been her gut. It had been her own eyes that had told Foxy that one more sip, or one more bite of rich food, could be his last.

Foxy had been wrong. It had been ten more steaks before Mr. Jensen landed himself in the hospital. And even after his bypass, she'd seen him sneaking into the fast-food joint in the next town.

"Then we developed those long waits because you started doing readings for dining customers," Travis was going on as he wiped down the plastic-covered menus, giving the grime more attention than he did her.

"I don't do readings because I'm not a psychic," Foxy corrected. "What I did was tell my neighbors who came into this fine establishment what my gut told me about them. It would be irresponsible of me not to."

Travis slapped the semi-clean menu down on the counter. "That wasn't your job. Your job was to take their orders and serve them with a smile. You weren't capable of that."

"I did smile at—"

"And now you want a job being a psychic for troubled youth?"

Foxy opened her mouth to tell him once again that she wasn't a psychic. It was a moot point. So, she shut her mouth and breathed in through her nose, trying to tap into the calm in her gut that told her that getting a letter of recommendation from Travis was a sure thing.

Clearly, she'd gotten this one wrong, too. That was the thing about being gifted with heightened senses. She was aware enough to get the message. But she didn't always interpret the meaning correctly.

Foxy often got the feeling that someone was about to call or come over. The phone might ring that moment or an hour later. They might show up on her doorstep later that day or next week. The feelings didn't come with a date-time stamp. But they always came true... eventually.

Now clearly wasn't the time when Travis would give her a glowing review. The problem was, she needed that letter of recommendation sooner rather than later if she was going to complete her application as an Elevated Care Foster Parent. She had kids counting on her, one in particular.

With that sense of urgency, Foxy turned on her heel and left the restaurant. Working here at Ramos's Deli and Cafe hadn't been her only job. She'd had other odd jobs in the town since she'd left the stage behind.

She and her two sisters had once toured the country as a singing trio, even after their mother had passed away from an overdose. But singing hadn't been Foxy's passion. People were. Especially younger people.

Like her older sister, Savy, Foxy had chosen to dedicate her life to helping troubled youth in the foster system. Kids with no responsible parents, or available guardians, or no family at all. But Foxy wanted to help on a higher level.

Too many of the kids in foster homes suffered from trauma and emotional shock. They often had long-lasting psychological effects that traditional foster parents couldn't manage. Having been there and done that, Foxy could help. Foxy wanted to help.

She'd completed the pre-service training. She'd passed the Fingerprint Criminal Record check, to many others' surprise. Now all she needed to complete the approval process was to gain two letters of reference. Surprisingly, this was proving the trickiest part.

She only had one letter so far. From Father Matthews. She needed one more. But she didn't bother trying to contact any of the old bar, club, or stage managers, thinking they wouldn't be the best judges of character.

The Danillos remembered her at the pizza parlor. But they wouldn't give her a recommendation since she'd only worked there for three weeks as a teenager. And she'd left without notice when her mom had snagged her and her sisters for a two-month gig on the road.

Being the youngest of the James sisters, Foxy hadn't stayed in high school long enough for the teachers to get a feel for her. Ms. Wright, her chorus teacher, remembered her. But what she remembered most was Foxy mentioning she had a feeling that Ms. Wright and Mr. Gerken, the football coach, would get together.

Foxy had been right. Sort of. They'd gotten married. Had a child. And then the football coach up and left the chorus teacher for the home economics teacher. It had been one of the biggest scandals in Honor Valley history.

Technically, Foxy had been right. Just not right enough to warrant a glowing recommendation from the first Mrs. Gerken. Foxy was running out of options.

Lifting her head to the wind, Foxy waited for a feeling to tell her which way to go. The wind picked up to her right, and she turned to put the air at her back. There had to be someone in this town who would vouch for her.

And then she saw it. A sign in the sky. Charlotte O'Dell, Family Law Practice. Ms. O'Dell had gotten Foxy out of a jam once. She only hoped the lawyer could do so again.

CHAPTER THREE

here was nothing like the smell of home. The Flying Cross Ranch smelled of fresh-cut grass, of turned earth laced with manure. Joe's nostrils flared as he took in the familiar scent. He opened his mouth so that he could gulp down lungfuls of the stuff. It was the smell of belonging, the scent of security, the knowledge that he was safe in this place.

In his younger years, his sense of smell had been his first defense. Clean smells were far and few between. Joe had spent the first part of his life sleeping on lumpy mattresses that had sometimes been used as toilets. He'd hid in corners that smelled of rotted food. He'd cowered in closets of unwashed clothes.

Joe knew he was made out of love. The letter from his dead mother told him so. He could only just barely remember her face. Her blonde curls and blue eyes with pink lips that stretched into a smile so bright that it threatened to overtake the single memory he had of her.

His mother, Janie, had told him that she loved him and that his father had too. The father that Joe had never met because he'd been lost to an IED in Afghanistan. Sergeant DeSean Curtis had never met his only son because Janie Horton's parents hadn't liked the look of the tall, dark man covered in tattoos.

And so when Janie returned home after DeSean's burial, they'd pushed their daughter to give up the little brown baby for adoption.

When she refused, they cut her off for three years… until she passed away in a factory accident. It was when Joe was deposited on his grandparents' doorstep that he first learned to hide. By the time he was tossed into foster care, he'd gotten good at the survival tactic.

Joe had stopped hiding when he'd come to the home of Haran and Tessa Matthews. Every room smelled of wide-open spaces and blooming flowers. The beds were soft and warm. The clothes were always washed and folded in the closets. The bathrooms spotless and odorless, even after one of his brothers finished their business inside. The Flying Cross Ranch was the sweetest smelling and safest place on the earth.

The sky over the ranch house was a little dimmer with the absence of his adoptive mother. Joe had taken Tessa Matthews's death as hard as he had his mother's. It was the love of his adoptive father that kept him strong.

Haran Matthews smiled down at him from the porch. The clouds parted at that second, sending two rays of sunshine down as the two men embraced. Joe was certain that it was his two heavenly mothers shining down their love.

Joe's adoptive father had hugged him as soon as he came in the door to the ranch house. When Father Matthews moved to let his son go, Joe squeezed tighter, needing to hold on just a few moments longer to inhale his scent. He'd nearly lost the man that had saved his life to an overworked heart. And so, Joe held on a little longer.

When he finally released his father was when he saw a ragtag group of kids looking suspiciously at him. The look was reminiscent of anytime strangers came to the ranch when he and his brothers were young. For months, likely even years, the Matthews boys feared someone coming to Flying Cross to take them from their adoptive parents.

"Children, I'd like you to meet my son," said Father Matthews. "Joe, this is Denny."

The tallest kid nodded his head upward, his shrewd eyes a challenge as he eyed Joe. That was the leader of this bunch.

"This little princess is LaTisha."

A brown-skinned girl with braids bit at the inside of her lip as she regarded Joe. Where Denny might be the leader, this one looked like the brains of the bunch.

"This one here is Miguel."

Miguel was the only one of the group that offered Joe a smile and a wave. The dark-haired kid looked Joe up and down, but not as though he was sizing up whether or not he could take him. Miguel regarded Joe as though he were trying to determine what gift to bring him for his birthday.

"I'm making enchiladas for dinner," said Miguel. "Some with chicken and others with only fish because Tisha has decided she's a vegetarian."

"Fish isn't a vegetable," said LaTisha, her eyes rolled skyward as though this wasn't the first time she'd stated that fact.

Father Matthews smiled in his good-natured way at the two before turning to the last kid in the bunch. "The last kid here is Ashton, who prefers to be called Ashtray."

Ashtray's blond hair was done in neat little cornrows. He wore a Wu Tang T-shirt and jeans that sagged low on his skinny body. "Yo, you spit any lyrics, bro?"

Joe bit back the retort that was on the tip of his tongue. This was just a kid. Still, this kid needed to learn some respect.

"You can call me Captain Joe, Ash… tray." Joe figured if he was going to ask the kid for some respect in how to address him, he'd have to show respect as well. "And I'm not a lyricist. I'm a lawyer."

A tendril of fear shot through the kids' eyes. They all took a step back and closer to Father Matthews. Even Denny, the fearless leader, looked piqued around the eyes.

"Relax," said Joe. "I'm not here to take any of you away. This is my home, too. I used to be a foster kid until Father Matthews adopted me."

"Ms. Savy and Mr. Charlie are going to adopt us," said Miguel.

"I know," said Joe. "I'm helping them with that paperwork."

That statement broke the tension in the crowd. But there was still a wary unease. Joe understood the sentiment. He was the new guy to them. It always took foster kids a while to trust adults.

"Why don't you go and get settled, son. I had Savy make up the guest room."

"Oh, um, I was going to stay in the guest house."

"Savy and Foxy are staying in the guest house."

"Oh? Well, I thought, since Savy and Charlie are getting married, that…"

"That what?"

Joe couldn't meet his father's gaze. If he dared, he knew the man would see right through his intentions. But what exactly were Joe's intentions toward Foxy?

"This is still a Christian household," his father was saying. "Savy and Charlie can sleep in the same room after they take their vows."

The children giggled but were quieted after a stern look from Father Matthews. When that stern look came back to Joe, the grown man squirmed in his shoes.

"Although you and Foxy are like brother and sister…" Father Matthews waited a couple beats before finishing his thoughts. "It would be improper for a man in your position to be bunking with a single woman."

For long moments after, Joe thought on that pause his father had taken. Did Father Matthews know about his childhood feelings for Foxy? Were they still just childhood feelings? Joe had already established that Foxy couldn't be the woman of his dreams, not if who she was was antithetical to him achieving his dreams.

In the kitchen, Joe opened the fridge to grab a cold drink. As the cold air sailed out of the icebox, so did the scent of strawberries. The sweet and tart scent sent Joe back into a time that had felt like a dream.

There had been strawberries on her breath. There always was. Either from the lip balm she applied or the fruit itself. It was her favorite.

Joe had never cared for the fruit. The seeds always got stuck in his teeth. He'd avoid them at the dining table until that day. That day, when Foxy James had looked up at him and pressed her berry-glossed lips against his.

He had always been a practical child, not prone to emotional outbursts. He hadn't cried when his mother died. He hadn't cried when his grandparents abandoned him. The one and only time Joe Matthews had cried was the day Foxy James had kissed him because the moment her sweet, berry lips met his, a single tear slipped down his cheek to turn the kiss bitter.

Foxy had taught Joe about soulmates. He'd thought that she was his. But she'd never said that he was hers. Logically, if she didn't see him that way, then she couldn't be his soulmate. Someone else must be.

Or maybe there were no such things as soulmates at all.

What Joe did know was that his sole purpose for being on this earth was to keep the scales of justice in balance. He could do a lot of good in this world with a bit more power in his hands. Becoming the District

Attorney would afford him some of that power. Dating a woman like Rich had suggested—what was her name again? Charlotte?—could give him a stronghold.

With that thought, Joe closed the refrigerator door, shutting out the scent of tart berries.

CHAPTER FOUR

oxy rolled the gloss onto her lips. The sweet taste of strawberries touched the tip of her tongue as she did so. The fruity taste instantly settled her, bringing her racing mind back to the simple pleasures of childhood.

The James sisters had grown up so poor that candy was an unattainable dream. Fruit from the fields was their only treat. When strawberries were in season during the summer months, Foxy would run through the fields and gorge, feeling like she was the richest kid on earth.

She had her hands out now as she stood at the door to Charlotte O'Dell's offices. Foxy pressed her top and bottom lip together, smoothing out the gloss. This was her last shot at not only making her dream come true but of helping children in need.

That's what Ms. O'Dell did. She helped kids in need. She wouldn't say no. She couldn't say no.

Throwing her shoulders back, lifting her chin, and stretching her mouth into a wide, friendly grin, Foxy entered the offices of Charlotte O'Dell, Family Law Practice. Sitting in the center of the white-walled reception room was Foxy's first obstacle.

"Do you have an appointment?" asked the secretary. Her dark hair was pulled back into a severe bun. The glasses sitting on the tip of her nose had lenses too thin to be prescriptive.

"No, but I am a former client of Ms. O'Dell," Foxy said as she skirted around the secretary's desk. "I just have a quick question to ask her."

The woman might be small, but she was quick. She shot out of her chair and was around the desk, blocking Foxy's way in an instant. "I'm sorry, but Ms. O'Dell is on her way to lunch."

"I just have a quick question about some paperwork."

Foxy feinted right, but unfortunately, the other woman predicted her move and threw out her spindly arms to block Foxy. Foxy heard the taunt in her head; *Didn't you see that one coming, little Miss Psychic?*

"I can schedule you for next week," the secretary said through clenched teeth.

Foxy put on her most winning smile and tried diplomacy again. "Really, what I have to say won't take more than—"

"Foxy James? Is that you?"

A pretty blonde poked her head out of the office door. Charlotte O'Dell was forever put together. She wore a deep purple business suit that belted just under her breastbone, accentuating her small waist. Her lips were a muted pink, but there wasn't a smell coming off her mouth like Foxy's berry gloss. That's because it was likely actual lipstick from a fancy department counter or retail cosmetics store and not gloss bought from the corner convenience store.

"What is it this time?" Charlotte asked as she slipped a scarf around her shoulders, which perfectly matched her pulled-together outfit. "Did you attempt to ride another man like a horse?"

The secretary dropped her arms and stepped back. She looked up at Foxy with interest now. Foxy took in a deep breath and let it out.

"It's not what you think," said Foxy.

Charlotte chuckled. Though she was a woman, no one would ever accuse the serious lawyer of giggling. Charlotte's voice was smokey, like Foxy's oldest sister Savy. "I represented Ms. James a year ago when she was charged with assault."

"It wasn't assault," Foxy explained. "It was self-defense."

Charlotte raised a perfectly plucked eyebrow.

"It was," insisted Foxy. "Just not for myself. For the horse."

The secretary turned from Foxy and looked at her boss for clarification. That rankled Foxy. It was her story, after all. She was the one with the firsthand account.

"Ms. James accused Auggie Fenton of animal abuse. Which is what any animal-loving citizen should do if they witness such a thing. Only Ms. James had never met Mr. Fenton."

The secretary turned to regard Foxy again. When Foxy opened her mouth to explain herself, the woman turned back to Charlotte for the facts of Foxy's story.

"The police went on to question Mr. Fenton. Only to learn that he didn't own any pets. When the police returned to question her, Ms. James said she'd had a feeling that Mr. Fenton was abusing animals. She's a psychic, you see."

Now the secretary scrunched up her nose as she peered at Foxy. Foxy peered back, certain now that those thin lenses held no prescription.

"I'm clairsentient," Foxy corrected the record. "It means I get feelings."

Foxy couldn't tell if the secretary was now looking at her with interest or scorn. Charlotte was grinning with amusement that was uncommon for the serious lawyer. Foxy supposed her case had been one for the books.

"Turns out she was right," Charlotte continued. "Mr. Fenton had horse manes in the trunk of his car. He'd been going to ranches and cutting off horse manes for weeks and selling them on the black market for hair weaves and extensions."

The secretary subconsciously touched her tightly wound bun. On second glance, her mane looked far too thick and lush to be all her own hair. She likely was a customer of store-bought tresses.

"It's an awful crime," said Foxy. "Horses use their tails to communicate, for warmth, and pest control. Imagine someone coming and hacking off your limb. It takes them a year to grow back."

"Mr. Fenton only got away with a misdemeanor," said Charlotte. "That still chafes."

Even though Charlotte O'Dell was a bit of a stiff, with little imagination, and often took things literally, Foxy had liked her lawyer. Charlotte was laser-focused when it came to the scales of justice. That trait reminded Foxy of her childhood best friend, Joe Matthews.

Even as a little boy, Joe had been a serious man. He'd trail behind Foxy as the voice of conscience on her right shoulder. Foxy had never been interested in breaking the law. She did have a habit of telling people about the feelings she got that involved them. That got her in a stitch or two. Joe was always there, bailing her out with his calm logic.

Joe was due back to the ranch soon. Foxy couldn't wait to see her old friend. She should introduce him to Charlotte. The two would be a perfect match. That is, if Charlotte would help her.

"What can I do for you, Ms. James?"

"I was hoping to get a letter of recommendation from you."

"Recommendation? For what?"

"I want to be an Elevated Care Foster Parent."

Charlotte tilted her head like a bird. The movement again reminded her of Joe Matthews. Joe would often gaze at Foxy in the same way, as if she were some creature that he didn't understand. A creature that might open its hand with a treat or turn a trick where she'd pounce on him and swallow him whole.

"All right," said Charlotte.

"All right?" asked Foxy.

"I'll do it."

"You will?"

"Give me until the end of the day. I have a lunch date in just—" Charlotte looked up and smiled. It was a smile of someone who saw a tall drink of water coming toward them on a hot desert day. "I think that's him arriving."

A sensation came over Foxy. One that told her something important was about to happen. Whoever this guy was that was coming for Charlotte, he was soulmate material. Foxy could feel it in her gut.

It was the warm sensation, like the brush of the ocean against the tip of her toes on a sandy beach. Like the snuggle under the covers after the sheets came out of the dryer. Like the security she felt anytime Father Matthews gave her a hug and a smile.

Foxy turned around, eager to witness the first awareness of true love unfolding in real life. She was met with a familiar face. A face from her childhood that had aged into the sharp angles and strong lines of a fully grown man. A fully grown man with a muscled chest that pushed against his collared shirt and filled out his long slacks.

When Joe Matthews's gaze found Foxy's, his head tilted to the side in the same birdlike motion of his youth. Treat or trick, it seemed to ask. Foxy didn't give him a moment to make up his mind. She launched herself into her friend's arms and let herself drown in the warm ocean feel of him, the just-dried sheets of him, the same secure hug that his father was famous for giving to those he loved and cherished.

Joe Matthews, her best friend from childhood, was home.

CHAPTER FIVE

"That's her."

Never had a truth rang so loudly in any man's ears. Those were the words that played in his ears over the last hour as Joe tried to convince himself that Foxy was not the one for him. That this childhood infatuation with her was long over. That there had to be someone else out there, a far more appropriate woman that he was meant to spend his life with.

The moment that he walked into the doors of Charlotte O'Dell's law offices, the first thing he saw was Foxy's dark, springy curls. The second thing he saw were her bright, expressive eyes. The last thing he saw was her brilliant sunshine of a smile.

"That's her."

The words were spoken out loud, but they hadn't come from Joe's mouth. They were from Rich, who walked into the offices beside Joe. So, he saw it too? He saw that Foxy was the only woman for him? Joe now had no reason to ever doubt or question his friend again.

And it looked like Foxy finally saw it too.

Her entire face lit up like a Christmas tree when she turned and saw him. The springy curls atop her head bounced as though they danced to a spirited jig as she clapped her hands together and bounced up and down in delight. With each step she took toward him, her grin spread wider, lighting him up from the outside in and then from the inside out.

Foxy spread her arms like a new bird taking its first flight. There was no fear of falling. No thought of failure. Because Joe was there to catch her as she flung herself into his wide-open arms.

Joe was forever catching her. Foxy had a habit of not looking before she leaped. Of speaking before she thought through her words. Of taking action before making a solid plan.

As kids, Joe had always trailed behind Foxy. He never told her not to go and do something crazy because then he wouldn't have a reason to catch her. And Joe was always waiting for any opportunity to catch her.

He caught her now. He wrapped his arms around her lush form. His fingers interlaced and locked the moment she was inside his embrace.

His nose went into her hair. The curls tickled him, bunching around him and welcoming him home.

He inhaled the sweet scent of strawberries, and his stomach grumbled, reminding him he hadn't eaten since he'd landed. In fact, he couldn't remember the last time his belly had been filled. Suddenly, Joe was starving. He had never wanted anything more in his life than he wanted the woman in his arms.

The woman of his dreams tilted her head up and looked at him. With her grin firmly in place, Foxy said his name. "Joe."

It was a sigh. It was a homecoming. It was the answer to a prayer.

Joe was transported back all those years ago to the time when he'd tasted her lips. It had been a dark moment, the darkest of his life. The day that she had been taken from him. Just as his mother had. Just as his father had.

Only it was different with Foxy. Because Foxy still walked this earth. But he couldn't walk beside her. He couldn't catch her if she stumbled. He wouldn't be there if she fell.

All that was over. Because she was here now, and he would never let her go again.

Joe had Foxy in his arms. And now she saw it. Everybody saw it. They belonged together.

A throat cleared behind him. Joe ignored the intrusion. He was far busier, calculating if he could kiss her now or if he should wait until later.

"I didn't realize how much I missed you until just now," said Foxy.

"I've missed you every day since the last time I saw you," Joe said, thrilled that he could finally speak his truth out loud. "Three thousand five hundred and sixty-seven days."

Foxy threw her head back and laughed. Joe still held her tightly. Had he not, she may have toppled backward. He would've never let that happen. In fact, he locked his arms tighter around her. How had the woman survived without him?

"Do you hear that, Ms. O'Dell?" Foxy said over her shoulder. "Joe is excellent at math. Whenever I had an algebra problem, I went to him."

O'Dell? Why was that name familiar? For the first time since he'd come into the building, Joe cast a glance at the other woman in the room. Tall, blonde, dressed in a power suit that was tailored to highlight her slim assets.

"He's smart," Foxy continued. "And handsome."

The woman, Ms. O'Dell, lifted an eyebrow and nodded. Again, a throat cleared behind Joe. All of his attention was on Foxy. Foxy made a move to step back, out of his embrace. Joe held tight, reluctant to let her go.

"I thought we weren't expecting you until later," said Foxy.

"What?" said Joe. "Don't tell me you didn't see me coming."

"As a matter of fact, I did see you. We were just talking about you." Again, Foxy motioned behind her to the blonde woman. "Wasn't I just telling you about him, Ms. O'Dell?"

"You were, indeed." Ms. O'Dell extended her hand. "Hello, Captain Matthews. It's nice to finally meet you."

Why did that name sound familiar? Joe didn't have time to remember. With his attention diverted to Ms. O'Dell, Foxy was pulling out of his hold. Joe supposed he should let her go. They would have time to embrace when they were alone. Besides, he was being rude to her friend.

Joe took the hand offered him by Foxy's friend. "Please, call me Joe. Any friend of Foxy's is a friend of mine."

"I was hoping you and Charlotte would become good friends," said Rich from behind him.

Joe had entirely forgotten the man was even there. He'd hardly noticed anyone else the moment he'd seen Foxy. Only just now, he realized there was a third woman in the room. She sat behind a desk, watching the small group with rapt attention.

"Joe," Rich spoke slowly, as though Joe were a slow learner, "this is Charlotte O'Dell. The one I was telling you about."

The one? What one? Foxy was the one.

If possible, Foxy's face lit up even brighter as she looked from Joe to

Charlotte. "Is Joe your lunch date?" Foxy asked her friend. "I knew it. Didn't I tell you you two should meet? And now you are."

Joe had barely glanced at Charlotte, but now he took a good hard look at her. As he did, his entire reason for coming into town came back to him. He was here to meet Charlotte O'Dell, a woman Rich thought would be perfect for him to date in an effort to win over the very conservative Board of Commissioners in charge of appointing the next District Attorney.

"I have such a good feeling about this." Foxy reached down and grabbed Joe's hand. Then she reached out and took Charlotte's hand. She raised them both to her chest as though she were blessing the two of them.

Joe's brain was still trying to catch up. Foxy hadn't been the one that Rich had brought him to meet. It was Charlotte. Not only did Rich think that Joe and Charlotte were a perfect match, apparently, so did Foxy.

"Don't let me interrupt fate." Foxy lowered both of Joe's and Charlotte's hands and joined them together. Once Foxy clasped their hands together, she stepped back and gave Joe a wink. "You can tell me all about your date when you get home tonight."

And with that, Foxy walked backward toward the exit. She didn't look where she was going. She didn't watch her step. Miraculously, she didn't trip, or stumble, or fall.

At least this time, Joe hadn't been left with a mess to clean up. Instead, he was left holding another woman's hand while the woman his heart beat for didn't cast a single glance backward.

CHAPTER SIX

There was a pep to Foxy's step as she left the law offices of Charlotte O'Dell, Family Law Practice. The sun was no higher in the sky, but the day felt brighter. That's because Foxy loved when she got to witness one of her feelings come to light. And Joe Matthews had always been a bright light.

When they were kids, he'd balked at the notion of a soul mate. He'd demanded that Foxy prove her theory of one true love with facts and figures. She could only offer him her feelings on the matter.

That chemical reaction that only she could experience inside her own body did not suffice for Joe. Yet, still, he remained her shadow while they were kids. Always at her back or by her side when her gut feelings got her into scrapes. And now, today, Joe had come face to face with the mate to his soul. He would finally know what she meant when she told him of those feelings of light and warmth and happiness.

A shadow crossed over Foxy from above. She knew it for what it was; jealousy. For years, Foxy had watched as a spectator looking from the inside out as she got the feeling that two people were meant to be together. She watched them meet. Watched the recognition dawn that they were in the presence of something big. Watch them fall in love and begin their happily ever after. Or sometimes, their happy for now.

All the while, she waited for her dream man. Where was he? He was running super late. That's where he was.

More than anything in the world, Foxy wanted a man that she could lean on when life got hard. She wanted arms to fold around her and keep her warm. She wanted a strong heartbeat to pound against her cheek while holding her close. She wanted the security that came with knowing that she'd found her person, the one who would stick by her through thick and thin and never let her down.

Joe had once filled that role when they were kids. Even though he thought most of her schemes and actions harebrained, he'd always watched over her and was there when things didn't go as planned. And if she remembered correctly, even as a scrawny kid, Joe Matthews had given the best hugs.

Maybe Foxy could sneak in a few more of those hugs from Joe while she waited impatiently for her soulmate to show up? Though that would have to depend on Charlotte. The family law legalese didn't seem like the jealous type. Though Charlotte's eyebrow had raised when Joe held Foxy a little too long.

Charlotte didn't have anything to worry about. She and Joe had been childhood friends. There wasn't anything between them except fond memories and a few heart-pounding moments that were typical in foster care.

While their older siblings Charlie and Savy had had an epic love affair, Joe and Foxy had never so much as held hands or shared a chaste kiss. And why would they? They were only friends.

Charlotte O'Dell was a lucky woman. The universe had matched her to a great guy. Foxy just hoped the powers that be would finally get around to plopping her soulmate on her doorstep.

Turning the key in the foster care van, the old bag of gears coughed and sputtered. With a second turn of the key, the engine turned over. She and her sister were supposed to take the vehicle in for a tune-up. They hadn't had the time with the move from the foster house to the ranch. Foxy hadn't had any premonitions of the van breaking down, so she decided to put it off another day.

The van carried her safely back to the Flying Cross Ranch. When she put it in park, it gave a satisfied shudder, as though it knew it would be idle for the rest of the day. The van was the only thing on this ranch that would be idle for the time being. Chores were in full swing on the land.

Savy, Miguel, and LaTisha were in the garden. From this distance,

Foxy couldn't tell if they were weeding, seeding, or tossing a salad. Whatever they were doing, the plant life was definitely winning.

Foxy turned on her heel, getting the feeling that that was not a battle she wanted to join. Instead, she headed toward the horse barn. Inside, she could hear her soon-to-be brother-in-law barking orders as was the Matthews boys' way.

Even before the lot joined the Armed Forces, they all spoke in commands that they expected others to immediately obey. Peeking inside the barn, Foxy saw the recipient of those commands was the most ornery foster kid of the bunch. True to form, Denny was as combative as ever.

"They're not listening to me," said Denny.

"You have to show them who's boss," said Charlie.

"I thought you were the boss."

Foxy failed to hide a giggle as she watched the two face off. Denny was as lanky as Joe had been when they were kids. But unlike Joe, who always had a thoughtful expression, like he was doing math in his head, Denny wore a perpetual scowl.

As always, Charlie Matthews was calm and in command. Foxy doubted it even occurred to him that someone would disobey a direct order from him. "You need to make sure the horse is aware of you."

"He can see me," said Denny. "He still won't lift his foot."

"Run your hand down his leg. Then squeeze the tendon."

"The what?"

"The place above his ankle—yes, that's it. Now he'll lift his own foot."

There was a spark of triumph in Denny's eyes as the horse did as he commanded. When the kid looked up, he was met with the same spark in Charlie's eyes. So of course, being ornery, Denny wiped the triumphant look from his face and replaced it with a scowl.

And of course, Charlie being certain that his orders would always be followed, the former pilot gave a self-satisfied nod at the kid and the horse. "Now, you can remove the shoe with the tools. Hey, Foxy. How'd it go with your old boss?"

"He said no."

Charlie wrinkled his nose, giving Foxy a clenched half-smile.

"But someone else said yes," Foxy said, stepping up to one of the stalls and petting the head of the horse that poked its nose over the gate.

"Oh?" Charlie's eyes went wide, and the half-smile rounded into an O of surprise.

"What? You didn't think I would get them?"

Charlie shrugged, his good-natured smile slipping back in place. "Well, you do leave an impression wherever you go."

Foxy decided to ignore the quip. She and Charlie poked at each other like brother and sister since they were foster care kids. In fact, all the Matthews boys treated her that way, except one. Joe never poked or prodded. He'd always stood by, making sure she didn't get into too big of a scrape or dusting her off if he hadn't gotten to her in time.

"You'll never guess who I ran into while I was getting the recommendation?"

"Just tell me," said Charlie, as he turned his attention back to Denny and the horse. "You know I hate guessing. I'm not psychic."

Foxy gritted her teeth at the P-word, knowing Charlie only said it to get a rise out of her. "I saw Joe."

"Joe came to find you?"

"No. Why would he come to find me? He was on a date."

"Joe was on a date? With another woman?"

"Another woman? Is he dating more than one? He just got back into town."

Charlie stared at her dumbly.

Foxy got the sense that she was missing something. Whatever it was that went over her head, the gut feeling she'd gotten when Joe had come into Charlotte's offices was much better gossip. "The woman Joe's out with now, I think she might be the one."

"You do? Your psychic powers tell you that?" Charlie's tone was doubtful, but all Foxy heard was the P-word. She wouldn't ignore it this time.

"I'm not psychic," she hissed through clenched teeth.

"Yeah, I'll say."

"I'm clairsentient. It means I get feelings that—"

"Mr. Charlie, I'm done. Can I go now?"

"Denny, you know better than to interrupt adults when they're talking," said Charlie.

Denny rubbed at his temple. The kid looked a little green behind the gills. Foxy reached for Denny's hand to tug him out of the stall. The moment her fingers touched his, she got a sharp pain in her gut.

"Denny? What's wrong? Are you not feeling well?"

Denny pursed his lips. He looked from Foxy to Charlie and then down at the ground. "It's nothing."

"It's not nothing," said Foxy, gripping his hand tighter. She knew that much in her gut. If it was nothing, her gut would be quiet. If it was something good, there'd be a tingling warmth. Instead, her stomach growled and grumbled like she was going to be sick.

"I'm not sick," Denny said finally." But I… you'll think I'm crazy."

"Everybody thinks I'm crazy because I get these feelings I can't always explain."

"I have a feeling, a bad feeling."

Foxy waited patiently for Denny to finish. The more seconds that ticked by, she grew certain that she knew what he was about to say.

"It's Daria. I have a bad feeling she's in trouble."

CHAPTER SEVEN

"You got your law degree at the University of Montana Western? I went to Montana State Northern. What a coincidence."

Joe blinked, but the motion didn't bring the woman sitting across from him into focus. In his mind's eye, he'd been replaying the reunion with Foxy over and over again. His arms tingling as they'd tightened around her. His fingers aching where they'd come in contact with her soft, warm flesh. He wanted to shove away the chicken dish, whose herbaceous aroma was muddling his memory of Foxy's sweet and fruity smell.

"My goal has always been to earn partner by the time I'm thirty. At my old firm, I got there just a couple of years early. Then I left and opened my own firm."

Joe blinked again, bringing Charlotte O'Dell into focus. It was the woman's ambition that finally wrangled some of his attention away from Foxy and to his lunch date. Joe had had a similar ambition to Charlotte when he'd first started law school. Though instead of making partner in a law firm, he'd risen to the highest rank a lawyer could in the military as a JAG. Now his sights were set on becoming a District Attorney. Maybe one day Attorney General.

"I had thought I wanted to become an A.G. one day," Charlotte was saying. "But I like my work too much."

"You practice family law?" asked Joe, at last pulling his own weight in the conversation. If Charlotte noticed the inequity, she didn't say.

"I do," Charlotte said after taking a sip of her sparkling water. "My family is amazing. My mom stayed home and did the traditional wife thing. Dad was the breadwinner, but he was home every night for dinner, at every after-school game or function. I remember looking up around the lunchroom at school one day and realizing not every kid had what I had, and wasn't that a shame."

If there was one thing that Joe could not abide, it was do-gooders offering pity or handouts. That wasn't Charlotte. He could see it in her crystal clear blue eyes. Charlotte's palm wasn't open. It was balled into a fist. Like she wanted to knock out the injustice she witnessed in the family courts.

"It never occurred to me that anyone would take advantage of a child," Charlotte said. "Not their parents. Or worse, their own government. Someone needs to be their champion."

A tendril of sunlight snuck into the window from behind the curtains. It made its way across the floor and up the table. That single ray landed on the side of Charlotte's wrist. When she moved her hand to lift a slice of strawberry from her fruit salad, the clouds shifted, and the light was gone.

"I'm a practical woman, Captain Matthews."

"Joe. I told you to call me Joe." Joe looked up into the sky. The sun was still there in muted yellow. If he waited a while longer, it would surely shift back and shine its light inside the restaurant again.

"Because I'm a friend of Foxy James?"

Joe shifted his gaze from the window to the woman. Charlotte's blue eyes pierced him like a prosecutor who sniffed a confession that was forthcoming.

"She's a character, that one," Charlotte continued in Joe's silence.

"That she is," Joe agreed, cutting into a slice of his chicken dish.

"So, the two of you..."

"The two of us?" Joe speared the slice of meat onto his fork. "No. We're... not."

"When she ran into your arms back in my office, and you held on so tightly for so long, I thought..."

Joe waited a beat before he spoke. When Charlotte held back what she thought of him and Foxy, he filled in the blank.

"We're childhood friends. I haven't seen her in years."

"About nine years? Three thousand, five hundred and sixty-seven days to be exact."

"I have a thing for numbers."

Charlotte grinned, but there was censure behind that smile. Her walls were up. Joe knew that with the right words, he could knock them down.

"There's nothing between me and Foxy."

It hurt his tongue to say it. But it was the truth. It was just an old childhood crush. Foxy didn't even think of him that way. Not then. Not now. He had to get over this.

Before him sat a woman who was perfect for him. And despite his poor behavior on this date, she still showed interest in him.

"I'm glad to hear that there's nothing between you and her." Charlotte moved another strawberry from her salad and speared a mandarin orange instead. "She doesn't seem your type."

"My type?"

"You seem like the kind of man that needs a serious woman on your arm."

"A serious woman like you?"

"Why not? Foxy seemed to think so. I think she was going to try to match us together before you walked in the door."

It should not hurt. But it did.

"She fancies herself a psychic."

"She's not psychic. She's clairsentient." Joe sat his knife and fork down. The sliced and diced piece of chicken untouched. "She gets feelings. But they're not always clear, and they're not always right. Sometimes she gets things wrong."

"Do you think she could be right about us?"

Charlotte sat her fork and knife down. All the fruit in the bowl gone except the strawberries. She fit the bill for the perfect political wife.

"I think the two of us could make a great partnership, Joe. We would be assets to each other's careers."

There it was. A clear, logical plan. Something quantitative that he could measure. It did not matter that she didn't make his heart skip beats when he looked at her. Not only would the woman be good for his career, she would be good for his health, too.

Joe paid for the meal after a cursory tug of war with Charlotte over the check. She might be a successful career woman, which Joe definitely found attractive, but she was also from a traditional household, which

Joe craved in a woman. Then they were outside the restaurant, gazing awkwardly at each other.

Joe leaned in. However, it was just as Charlotte reached out her hand, palm up, for a shake. Quickly, she withdrew her hand and tilted her head up. Unfortunately, it was as Joe thrust his hand out and just barely missed groping her chest.

They laughed. The sound burst from them in awkward gasps. Then there was silence. Finally, Joe leaned down and pressed a peck on Charlotte's cheek.

"You'll call me?" she said.

"I'll call you," he agreed.

Hopping in his car, Joe took off toward home. That kiss had sealed the deal for him. He'd closed off his past and decided he was taking his future in both of his hands.

Charlotte was the right choice. The logical choice. That was the only choice since Foxy didn't feel about him the way he felt about her.

With his future decided, Joe took a left turn to head toward Rich's place in town. It would be better if he stayed there the night instead of on the ranch where he'd be too near temptation. And so Joe cut a U-turn and drove toward the sun, which would lead him away from his homestead.

He had to blink a couple of times when he saw the rainbow-colored van on the side of the road. By the third blink, recognition dawned. It was the Bright Horizons Foster Care van. When he had ridden in that van as a child, it had been a dull yellow. The James sisters had since painted the old jalopy in bright shades to befit the home's name.

Beneath the hood of the van, he saw a shapely figure. Joe didn't remember telling his foot to press the brake. He didn't remember hopping out of the car and coming to her side.

"Thank the saints you saw me," said Foxy when he came up to her. "It just stopped working."

"Have you taken it in for regular maintenance?"

"I was going to, but my gut told me I'd be okay. And I am because here you are."

Joe opened his mouth to protest the warnings of a check engine light—which was on—and the grumblings of an upset stomach. He knew that with this woman, it would be a moot point. The words came up regardless.

"You have to keep a regular repair schedule if you want your car to remain dependable."

"Something important came up," Foxy said.

"More important than your safety? Or one of the kids' safety? What if one of the foster kids had been in the van with you?"

"That's what this is about. It's about one of the foster kids. My gut tells me that one of them is in trouble."

Joe pursed his lips. So much of his past mishaps started with this woman saying those words; *my gut told me.*

"I just want to check on her," she said. "She's at the state home."

"That's an hour's drive."

"Will you give me a ride?"

"You should call your sister and have her pick you up."

"There's no time. Visiting hours will be over soon and... Joe, I've got a bad feeling."

He should say no. He should call Savy, or his brother, to come and deal with this. He should take Foxy home himself. This situation could easily be handled with a phone call or on the next day.

Instead of doing any of that, Joe said, "Okay, hop in."

CHAPTER EIGHT

oxy gazed out the passenger side window as the sun slipped lower in the sky. The city skyline gave way to open fields as the miles clicked away. There was a warm glow outside of the car in the sinking sunlight. Inside the car, it felt as though storm clouds were moving in.

Joe sat in the driver's seat, silent and tense. It would have alarmed her if it was anyone else. But it was Joe. And this was his normal stasis.

He'd always been a quiet kid. Thoughtful. Only speaking when he was asked to provide an answer. Or speaking up when he saw an injustice taking place. Joe was not one to stand silent when someone was doing something wrong. Be it his brothers or the James sisters. He was the group's conscience. Even when he stood silently by them, everyone would always think twice about their actions under Joe's watchful gaze.

His gaze was on the road now. That strong jaw of his ticked, as though he wanted to say something but wouldn't. Why wouldn't he speak his peace to her? They were still friends, even after all these years.

"Bad date?" Foxy asked when she could take the silence no more.

"I'm sorry, what?" Joe squinted, but he didn't take his eyes off the road.

"With Charlotte? Did you have a bad date?"

He opened his mouth, then closed it. Foxy couldn't get a feel for what he had been about to say. She didn't need her gut to tell her what had happened earlier. Her feminine sensibilities told her that the date had not gone so well.

"Don't worry about it," Foxy soothed. "It doesn't always take the first time."

"What doesn't always take the first time?"

"True love," she said. "It doesn't always happen at first sight."

Joe's gaze left the empty road and turned to her. His lips parted. His eyes wide as he took her in.

There was surprise on his handsome face. Just as soon as Foxy named the emotion, his expression changed. Joe's lips pinched together. His fingers gripped the steering wheel. With the way he looked at her now, Foxy felt like she had just committed a grave injustice. But against whom?

"Love takes its own time to grow," she assured him. "Trust me. I've been waiting for my true love to show up for years. He's super late. But I'm trying to be patient."

"Right," Joe scoffed. "Your true love. Your mystery hero."

Foxy nodded, pleased that he remembered the vision she'd told him she'd had when she was young. "He's going to show up in my greatest time of need."

Joe rolled his eyes and turned back to face the road. The pinched expression remained in his eyes and his lips. He shook his head and muttered something under his breath. It sounded like he might've said *unbelievable.*

"What?" Foxy cocked her head, swiveling in her seat to face him. "I thought you believed in my gift."

"I've never believed in extrasensory perception," he said. At least he didn't insult her by calling her a psychic. "We have five senses that make up reality. The most prevalent one being sight and seeing what's right in front of your face."

"Light is energy. Energy that your eyes interpret as colors and depth to form an image. Feelings are also energy; electrochemical energy, which the mind makes interpretations of."

How did Foxy know that technical, scientific definition of her abilities? Because Joe had looked it up in a textbook at the library and explained it to her after some kids made fun of her. Of course, back then, when she'd tried to explain that to the juvenile delinquents in the face of their taunts, they'd only jeered at her even more.

"I seem to remember," Joe was saying, "that every time you got one of your feelings, I was the one that wound up coming face to face with reality."

"What are you talking about?" said Foxy.

"Like that time in elementary school, when you got the feeling that if you climbed to the top of the monkey bars and sang, it would push the gray clouds away."

"It did. Though just not exactly how I imagined it. Mrs. Reed had been sad, and when I sang, she was happy."

"Before you finished the song, you lost your balance and fell."

"And you caught me."

"That's my point. You got a feeling, and I faced the reality. Like that time you got a feeling that a spirit was in the closet at the foster home."

Foxy winced at that memory. There hadn't been a spirit there. Will Matthews had put a Chucky doll in there after they'd snuck into the theater one Halloween to watch the horror film.

"When I opened the door for you, and Chucky fell down from the heap, you knocked me down in your effort to get away, and I wound up with stitches."

"Yeah, but it was a really good scar. Will and Charlie were envious of you."

Foxy could see remnants of the outline just above Joe's temple. She reached her hand up to touch it. As her fingers brushed Joe's temple, his body tensed. Sensation flooded her finger when she connected with his warm skin. More memories of their time as children came tumbling back into her mind.

"You were always there for me. No matter how out there my visions were."

Joe didn't answer. He held his breath. He kept his eyes on the road.

Foxy remembered Joe hadn't liked being touched as a kid. It was a common occurrence with kids who had been abandoned by their birth parents. As far as she knew, she was the only person Joe had allowed this kind of contact. So, she took liberties.

Foxy brushed her thumb over the scar. Her palm tingled where it met the sharp angle of Joe's cheekbone. His jaw tightened and then relaxed in her hold. Just as she had when she was a child, Foxy felt a profound sense of gratitude that she could bring him comfort.

"I'm glad you're home. You're going to make a great District Attorney."

He shut his eyes. Only briefly. In that brief moment, Foxy felt the weight of the world lift from his shoulders.

Joe was a crusader for justice. It was one of the things she loved about her friend. He would need someone there to shoulder that weight.

"Charlotte is the perfect political girlfriend," said Foxy.

She supposed that someone would be Charlotte O'Dell. The lawyer would understand Joe's trials and tribulations far better than Foxy ever would. But Foxy would still be there for her friend to help him, not take everything so seriously.

Joe pulled away from her touch then. "What makes you say that about Charlotte?"

"You're both lawyers. Both crusaders for justice. You both will take on a case for the underdog. You two will probably change the world together."

Foxy folded her hand down into her lap. It still tingled with the reminder of Joe's warmth. She balled her fingers into a fist, trying to hold on to some of that warmth.

"Don't worry," she said. "I'll stay in the shadows, so no one sees your woo-woo psychic friend."

"You weren't meant for the shadows, Fox. You're too bright."

There was a spark in Joe's eyes as he turned back to her. His gazed roamed over her features. The embers in his hazel eyes were so bright they reminded Foxy of sparklers.

A match struck in her gut. So loud she swore she heard it in her ears. The flame inside her caught quick, so hot it burned its way up her chest and scorched the recesses of her heart. "You shouldn't be looking at me like that, dear."

"Why not?"

Had Joe's voice always been that deep? Like a sleeping bear roused in the dead of winter looking for his next meal?

"Why not?" he repeated, his hot gaze still on her.

It took Foxy's muddled brain another second to figure out the answer to Joe's question. From the corner of her eye, she saw the meaning of the gut-check.

"Joe, there's a deer."

Everything happened in a split second, but time appeared to slow to Foxy. She saw as the fire in Joe's eyes was snuffed out and replaced with fear. She saw the tips of his fingers turn first red with blood, then white when the blood drained as he put a death grip on the steering wheel. Joe's right forearm reached out and slammed into Foxy's chest, holding her back as he floored the brakes, and they both crashed forward into the dashboard of the car.

CHAPTER NINE

A light flashed before Joe's eyes. The light was bright, but it did not blind him. He saw everything clearly. In the moment before Joe Matthews thought he would die, all he saw was Foxy James.

Foxy singing at the top of her lungs from the playground monkey bars.

Foxy grabbing his hand and telling him to come with her on an adventure.

Foxy smiling up at him as she taught him how to dance the two-step before the middle school dance.

Foxy in tears when she'd learned that her mother had returned to take her and her sisters away. Foxy, the most spirited person he had ever met, looking up at him with an expression of helplessness. Foxy sighing softly as he pressed his lips so carefully, so gently to hers. Foxy closing her eyes and resting her head against his shoulder after sharing their first kiss.

She'd fallen asleep in his arms that night. In the morning, she was gone. Her mother had come to get her to take her and her sisters out on the road as her backup singers. He hadn't seen her again after that moment.

Foxy's eyes were closed right now. Her hand pressed to her forehead. Her beautiful features contorted into a grimace of pain.

Joe threw off his seatbelt to reach for her. He ignored the protest of the bruises forming on his arm as he did so. Somehow, Joe had survived not being near her for the last few years. What he could not bear was to be in a world where she didn't exist.

"Don't move," he insisted. "There could be internal damage."

"I'm fine," Foxy insisted. But the words were said through clenched teeth. "It's just a bump on the head."

"It could be a concussion." Joe took her head in his hands. Then he commanded, "Open your eyes for me."

Foxy did as he asked. For a moment, Joe could only stare dumbfounded. Firstly, because no James sister did what she was commanded to do. Secondly, because she looked up at him with tears in her eyes. Her expression was helpless, just as it had been all those years ago when he'd had his first taste of heaven.

Joe stared into Foxy's eyes. Foxy stared back at him. They were close enough to repeat that kiss. Joe could even taste the berry sweetness of her breath.

Foxy reached for him. Her fingers brushing his temple for the second time today. Just like he'd done earlier, Joe closed his eyes at her touch and let himself get lost in the dream. When her fingertips met his forehead, he felt something warm, wet, and sticky.

Joe opened his eyes to find that Foxy wasn't lost in a dream like he was. She was staring in horror at the blood on her hands. His blood.

"You're hurt," she said.

He was hurt. Hurt that she didn't remember what had happened between them. Hurt that she wouldn't even acknowledge the kiss that they'd shared. Hurt that she still searched for her true love, the man who was supposed to be there at the most difficult moment in her life when he had been the one there for her when her life had been turned upside down. Angry with himself that even after all of that, he could not walk away from her.

"Joe, you're bleeding."

"I'm fine."

"You threw your arm out to protect me."

"Of course, I did."

She reached for him again. Joe dodged her touch. He couldn't bear another friendly touch from the woman he craved. Not when she showed no signs of hunger for him.

Instead, he turned away from Foxy and climbed out of the car to inspect the damage. She'd called him dear. But that had been a misinterpretation.

A deer had run into the road a second before Foxy had warned him. Joe had swerved, but the motion drove them off the road and landed them in a ditch. The back wheels of the car were not touching pavement. Joe was able to get out, but the car was well and truly stuck.

"Stay here," Joe told Foxy as he pulled out his cell phone.

He held the device up to the darkening sky. Not a single bar of service joined him under the setting sun. There was no reception out here in the middle of nowhere.

The bars left him stranded, but Foxy was preparing to join him. The passenger side door creaked open as she tried to emerge. Joe was around the car before Foxy was all the way out.

"I told you to stay put," he admonished. "You might be injured."

"I'm fine. You're the one who's hurt."

Foxy wobbled as she stood. Joe pulled her to him. They stood there for a moment, chest to chest, gazes locked. Heat coerced up and down his forearms where he caged her in. Foxy's lips parted, and a gasp escaped. Her nostrils flared, but her gaze narrowed in clear confusion. She still didn't get it. Instead of pushing her away, Joe pulled her closer.

"If anything would've happened to you..." He couldn't finish the sentence. He couldn't voice the thought. Luckily, she did it for him.

"If anything would've happened to me, my sister would've killed you."

Joe grinned at that. Foxy mirrored his smile. Her hands rested on his chest, right where his heart beat out an erratic rhythm for her.

They were still standing so close. Almost like an embrace. Exactly like when she'd taught him to dance in preparation for the school function. His hands were at her hips. Her hands were pressed against his chest. They weren't swaying, but the world around them seemed to be.

"Déjà vu," she said.

"Are you remembering teaching me how to dance?"

Foxy nodded. "You were pitiful."

"Blame it on my teacher," he said.

There was a slight wind drifting past them as dusk began to settle. Slowly, they began to sway in time to the breeze.

"I've gotten better since then," Joe said as they swayed to the right.

"I'm sure you have," Foxy said as they swayed to the left.

"Fox..."

Foxy dipped her forehead and rested it against his chest. Joe's arms instantly closed around her.

"My head is so foggy," she said. "My emotions and feelings are all over the place. I can't think straight."

That's exactly how Joe felt every time he thought of her. Foxy was always telling others about her feelings. For once in his life, he needed to tell her how he felt.

They'd stopped swaying and were still now. The wind continued to whisper between them. The words Joe wanted to say were on the tip of his tongue. They were nearly out of his mouth when the sound of a loud motor and a honking horse broke the silence he'd been about to fill.

"You two okay?" called a gruff voice from the driver's side window.

Joe turned to see an old couple in a beat-up pickup truck pull to a stop beside them.

"You're not going to get a tow truck out here until morning," said the old man in the driver's seat. "You can come stay with us until then."

CHAPTER TEN

There were streamers in her memory. The theme of the dance all those years ago had been Enchanted Forest. Foxy knew she had danced all night long with each boy in her class. The funny thing was the only face she could remember swaying in time to the slow beat with her was Joe's.

The dance lessons had been awful. Joe had stepped on her foot with his left foot, then again with his right foot. She didn't remember a single second of the pain from her toes.

All Foxy could remember was how the two of them had laughed. How big Joe had smiled. How safe and secure she'd felt in his arms, even as her toes had been at the height of danger.

At the dance, there hadn't been any laughing or joking. He hadn't stepped on her toes a single time. Even while she'd made the rounds with other boys in the class, Joe hadn't danced with any other girl.

Again and again, Foxy had gravitated back to him with every slow song. Though she'd been abandoned as a child like Joe, she had never had any hang-ups about being touched. Still, no one had ever made her feel as grounded and steady as Joe Matthews.

Even in the midst of the car crash, Foxy had known that Joe would take care of her. As evidenced by the forearm he'd flung out to protect her. She knew he had to be bruised as well as bloodied. It wouldn't be the first time he'd put himself in harm's way for her.

Joe would never let anything bad happen to her. Even the times when he hadn't been able to protect her, thoughts of him and his steady smile had always reminded Foxy of the good in this world.

Joe wasn't smiling now. He wasn't even looking at her as they sat in the back of the pickup truck. As the older couple ambled down the long, deserted road, Foxy let Joe speak for them all the way until they reached their farmhouse. She let Joe take care of scheduling a tow truck in the morning. She let Joe call their family and tell them where they were and that they were fine.

"We only have the one room," said Mr. Drummond, the old farmer who had happened upon them on the side of the road.

Joe stopped walking. That would've been fine if they weren't on the stairs and Foxy wasn't walking behind him. She bumped right into his broad back, his broad back that was ripe with muscles. With all those muscles, Foxy would've expected him to be hard planes. Instead, she walked into the center of his back and fell into the same cushion that was at the front of his chest. Instead of instantly stepping back, Foxy reached her hand around to the front of Joe's waist. She told herself it was to steady herself, but when she met with even more muscles at his abs, her brain momentarily fried. Instead of letting go, she got it in her mind to count the number of abs she found.

Yep, it was a six-pack.

"One room is fine," Joe said as he unfurled her fingers and removed her hands from his waist. "We were raised together. Like brother and sister."

The words tasted like sandpaper as Foxy said them silently to herself. Joe continued up the stairs, leaving her standing there. She felt cold in her belly, the premonition that something was off. But she couldn't tell what.

Joe only had a bruise after he'd let Mrs. Drummond clean up the cut on his forehead. Neither of them were exhibiting any of the signs of a concussion. So what was wrong?

"You take the bed," said Joe once the door was closed behind them.

Those words felt wrong as well. The cold sensation in the pit of her belly increased. Foxy realized the last thing she wanted was to have any distance between herself and Joe. She wanted him to hold her close like when they were kids.

"Joe, we can share the bed. It wouldn't be the first time."

"We were kids back then. We're not kids anymore."

"What?" Foxy scoffed. "It's not like you're going to ravish me?"

Joe didn't laugh at the joke. Foxy wasn't laughing, either. That coldness in her belly was starting to spread. She knew what would make it go away, another one of Joe's warm, secure hugs.

"Tell me something…"

Foxy waited for Joe's question. It took him a moment to formulate it. His jaw working as though he wasn't sure if he wanted the words to get out. Which was odd. Didn't he know he could tell her anything?

"Why are you so sure about me and Charlotte?" was what he finally asked.

"Because of the feeling."

"What did you feel?"

Foxy searched for the words. It was always hard to convey the sensations she felt in her gut. "A rightness. An inevitability. It's the same thing I feel when I think about my true love. I felt that feeling when you and Charlotte were in the room together earlier."

"Maybe it was Charlotte and Richard?"

"No." Foxy shook her head, the warmth of certainty returning to her belly. "It was for you."

Joe was quiet for a long time. Then he sat down on the edge of the bed. Foxy came over and sat next to him.

"Did you ever think…" He stopped and cleared his throat. "Maybe it was for the two of us?"

Foxy smiled at that. "I've always felt a rightness with you. Whenever you would give me a hug, even as a kid, I've never felt more safe and secure."

"But not romantic?"

"Joe, you know I'm saving myself for my true love. There's never been anything romantic between me and any other guy."

"What about when we kissed?"

Foxy's mouth fell open. She was so surprised that she had to try a couple of times before she could get any words out. "We never kissed."

Now it was Joe's mouth that fell open. "You really don't remember, do you?"

"Remember what?"

"It doesn't matter." Joe huffed through his nose and rose from the bed.

"Where are you going?"

"You're psychic, can't you guess? Can't you feel it?" He turned and glared at her before going out the door. "I'm going to sleep on the couch downstairs."

Foxy wanted to reach out to him, to call him back. But she lost her voice. The coldness in her stomach came back and snatched all the warmth Joe's nearness had brought.

What had that been all about? What kiss? She'd never kissed anyone before, let alone her closest friend?

So why did the denial of that increase the chill in her gut?

CHAPTER ELEVEN

"An accident? Wait, where are you?"

Joe held the phone away from his ear. How was it that the rotary landline phone was loud and crisp and made Rich sound like he was shouting right beside him? It had taken three tries as the old dial up rang and rang before Rich even picked up his cell phone to answer the unknown and unlisted number.

"I'm on Route 29."

"What are you doing out there in the middle of nowhere?" asked Rich. He wasn't shouting this time, just speaking at his normal volume, but his voice still boomed in Joe's ear. Likely a side effect from bumping his head on the dash.

"I had some business to attend to." Joe looked up at the stairs where Foxy was resting her pretty head behind a closed door while he cleaned up the mess.

Here he was again. She got one of her visions or feelings, and he got the short end of the stick. Joe rubbed at his head. His fingertip bumped the band aid Mrs. Drummond had placed there. The blood flow had long stopped, but a bruise had formed under the bandage. Rich would have a literal cow when he saw it. It would certainly mess up the publicity photos he had planned for this weekend.

"What kind of business?" asked Rich.

"Family business," said Joe.

Because that was all he was to Foxy. Just a surrogate brother who was always there to catch her when she wasn't looking where she was going. Which was every single day. How had the woman survived without him all these years?

There hadn't been another man in her life. He knew that now, after she confessed that she was still waiting on her soul mate's arrival. And since Joe was not him, Foxy didn't even remember the kiss they'd shared all those years ago.

Whereas Joe had thought of Foxy every day. Nearly every second of every day. To the point where her name had been doodled on court dockets a time or two.

The imaginary Foxy had been his happy place. It was the live one who caused him pain. Especially now that he knew that she wasn't pretending the kiss never happened. She truly didn't remember it.

Joe remembered every second of it. Every scent. Every sigh. Every single one of her eyelashes as they'd brushed against his cheek.

There had been tears at the corners of her eyes as she'd hid from the adults when her mother arrived. Foxy had had a bad feeling for days, but she couldn't pinpoint where it came from. She wouldn't leave her room, fearing the monster was coming to the door and not hiding under the bed or in the closet. When she learned who the monster was, she'd called out for Joe. She'd sat huddled in his arms as the moments to her departure ticked down.

The sun rose and set, and he held her.

The moments ticked by, becoming hours, and he held her.

At one point, Foxy had looked up at Joe with those long lashes, the scent of strawberries on her breath, and her lips had brushed his.

So softly. Just for a heartbeat. Joe's entire world had changed in the space of that heartbeat.

When he opened his eyes, hers were closed. She tucked her head into the crook of his neck and went to sleep. Soon after, he followed her into dreamland. When he woke, she was gone.

"I'd hoped you were spending more time with Charlotte," Rich's voice boomed from the phone. "She said the date went well, and she thinks it can be a great partnership."

"Yeah, about Charlotte."

"She's great, isn't she? I told you she's perfect."

"She is. Perfect for me."

"I'll check with her people to see if she can make the photoshoot this weekend."

"No, don't do that."

"Why not?"

"Charlotte's not the one."

"You just said yourself, she's perfect."

"She is."

"Man, you're not making any sense."

"Matters of the heart rarely do." Joe rubbed at the bruise on his forehead. "Charlotte's a good woman. She deserves a good man."

"You're a good man. You're the best man I know."

"I can't love her. It would be wrong to pretend."

Rich let out a long sigh over the phone. He knew better than to argue with Joe when the decorated soldier and lawyer brought up right and wrong.

"I'm just going to be a bachelor candidate," said Joe. "On the bright side, the society pages will splash my eligibility all over the gossip pages. That'll keep me in the press."

"That could work." Joe couldn't see his friend, but he could all but hear Rich stroking his chin like a dastardly villain formulating his master plan. "You just need to stay out of the tabloids. Wait, look who I'm talking to. You are a veritable Boy Scout."

"Eagle Scout," Joe corrected. He was the only one of his brothers that had stuck through the Scouting program to earn his wings.

"All right, Eagle Man. We'll move the announcement of your candidacy to tomorrow night. Do you need me to send you a car to get you home?"

"No, it's fine. Don't go out of your way. I'm in a safe place, and they'll have my car ready in the morning."

After a few more instructions and a couple more tries to get Joe to reconsider a relationship with Charlotte, Rich let him go. Joe slipped the phone back onto its holder base. He looked up at the darkened staircase.

There hadn't been a peep from Foxy, which was not usual. If Joe was a veritable Eagle Scout, Foxy was a twittering parrot. Quiet was not her modus operandi.

He supposed she was sleeping.

But she did get bumped on the head.

She might have a concussion.

From his time in sports and his military training, Joe knew that protocol was to wake a concussed person every three to four hours.

Joe looked at his watch. It hadn't been an hour yet. She also might not be asleep just yet. He should make sure he would be starting the countdown from the right hour, lest he wake her just as she went to sleep in three hours.

Joe placed his foot on the first rung of the stair. It held his weight silently. It was the third step that creaked and announced his intentions.

Mrs. Drummond poked her head out of the kitchen, a washrag in her hand, a curious expression on her face.

"I'm just going to check on her," said Joe. "She might have a concussion. You're supposed to wake a concussed person every few hours."

Mrs. Drummond nodded. "You're a good brother."

Joe sighed at the characterization. He was tired of being cast as Foxy James's friend or surrogate brother. But if that's how he was going to stay in her life, then he'd swallow the bitter pill. Because his heart simply wasn't interested in trying to find sweetness in another woman.

He knocked quietly on the door. When there was no response, he pushed it open. Foxy lay on the bed. Joe came to the side of the bed and stared for a moment. One arm was flung over her head, the other lay off to the side. The white sheets bunched up around her, making her look like a fallen angel.

"Joe?" Foxy spoke without opening her eyes.

"I thought you were sleeping."

"I was, but I felt your energy." She opened her eyes and stared up at him. There were unshed tears in those beautiful eyes. "I don't understand why you're angry at me."

"I lost you back there."

It was an understatement. He'd almost lost her in that car accident. He had truly lost her when he realized she did not, and likely would never, feel the way about him that he felt about her.

"You would never lose me," Foxy said. "You're my safe place."

She reached out her hand to him. Joe took it. He took her hand, and he took those words, unable to keep himself from grasping at any straw she gave to him.

Joe climbed atop the mattress. He stretched out his body, laying on top of the sheets that the woman for whom his heartbeat lay under. Foxy curled his arm around her. She lay her head down in the crook of his elbow and went back to sleep.

It took only a few moments, but with the steady pace of her heartbeats and the even sighs of her breath, Joe allowed himself to be lulled to sleep. He did not wake himself or her in three hours. If they were both concussed, he'd rather stay wrapped up in this dreamworld than wake.

CHAPTER TWELVE

It was the best sleep Foxy had had in days, weeks, years. It was so soul reviving. It was spirit-lifting. It was so safe, secure, filling her with so much love and warmth that she didn't want to leave it.

It was also not like any other dream she'd ever had. She didn't see anything in the dream. Just a peaceful darkness. It was the feel of the dream that Foxy didn't want to part with.

It felt like a homecoming. It felt right. It felt inevitable.

It was like the times she dreamed about her true love. She hadn't had that dream in a long time. Having it now must mean he was near. It must mean that she was going to meet him soon. Maybe even today.

In her mind, Foxy's eyes flew open, eager to greet this momentous day. In reality, her eyelids lifted slowly, shirking away from the soft sunlight that peeked behind the curtains. With only one eye open, a toasty brown chest was revealed to her.

Foxy was lying in someone's arms.

As she moved from dream world to real life, the feelings didn't leave. Inside these arms, Foxy felt the same safety. She felt completely secure, as though these arms would never let her fall. It felt right having her body alongside this stranger's.

When she lifted her head, she wasn't surprised to see Joe gazing down at her. As one of her oldest and closest friends, Joe had always been a safe space for her. But he wasn't her dream man. He wasn't her soul mate. She would've known that years ago.

Foxy blinked the crust out of her eyes. There was no sleep crud in her eyes. She squinted, but there was no need. She saw things clearly.

Joe's handsome face stayed in focus. The feelings of security, safety, and warmth remained. Her heart insisted this was where it wanted to be. Her gut was a calm sea of tranquility.

What was going on with her?

It was then that Foxy glanced at Joe's mouth. Those lips were a soft pink pillow she wanted to rest her own lips against. The urge was so sudden, so palpable, that it took her by surprise. The surprise took her back years ago to a dream she once had. A dream where she kissed her true love good night and fell asleep in his arms.

Only that wasn't a dream. That had happened.

The last night she'd spent as a ward of the state at the Bright Horizon's foster home, Joe had slept in her bed. She'd been terrified at what life would bring her when her mother came to collect her and her sisters in the morning. As always, Joe was there.

He'd been there with her all day, as she'd stayed cooped up in her room. He'd been there with her all night, as she'd refused to leave her bed. Joe had simply sat beside her as silent tears fell. Then he'd held her as she fell asleep. But not before Foxy had tilted up her head and brushed her lips against his.

Holy stars, she had kissed Joe Matthews.

She hadn't meant to kiss him. She'd only meant to say thank you. Only her lips hadn't formed the words. The brush of his lips against hers had said all she'd needed to say, and then she'd fallen asleep. The same contented sleep she'd just experienced now. And when she woke from a night surrounded by his strength, she'd felt strong enough to face the new reality of her life.

How had she forgotten that? How had she forgotten him? How had she not remembered that the silent strength she'd carried around from that day had been from Joe?

"It's you?" she said.

Joe's eyes were open, wide open. His nostrils flared at her words. His heart skipped a beat. Foxy knew because her hand rested on his strong chest.

Foxy shifted in Joe's arms so that she could take all of him in. There was the strong chin that could argue a case if it would lead to justice being done. There were the bright hazel eyes that had watched over her, looking out for any sign of danger as she blindly dashed into the fray to deliver her own brand of justice that came from her gut. There were those two soft lips that always spoke up for her, even when he didn't agree with, or even understand, what she went on about.

"You're my true love?" Foxy couldn't stop the question mark from tagging along at the end of that sentence. Her gut was sure. Her heart was onboard. It was her head that was foggy. How had she not seen this so clearly?

For his part, Joe's features were screwed as he looked down at her. "Are you asking me or telling me?"

"How could I have not seen this?" Foxy sat up in the bed, the sheets falling away from her body to reveal that she'd fallen asleep in yesterday's clothing.

Joe sat up as well, resting his back against the headboard of the bed. "I've been asking myself the same thing for years."

"Years?" Foxy reared back and gaped at him. "You've known this for years, and you didn't tell me. How could you keep this from me?"

"Me? How could I...? Me?"

"Yes, you." She jabbed a finger in his chest. "We're supposed to be friends, and you didn't tell me you were my one true love."

"This is my fault?" Joe jabbed his own finger at his chest. "How is this my fault? Aren't you the one who's supposed to be psychic?"

Foxy threw her hands up in the air in exasperation. "I'm not psychic."

"I know, I know. You're clairsentient. You feel things." Joe motioned his hand over his heart."

"It's in the gut," Foxy corrected, but he wasn't paying attention.

"Except when someone has feelings for you. Then you block it out and forget that it ever happened."

"But you felt it." Foxy rose to her knees on the mattress so that she could tower over him. She only came up to his chin. "I can't believe you, Joe Matthews. We wasted all this time when we could've been..."

"When we could've been what?"

Joe came to his knees as well. Foxy had to tilt her head back to look up at him. She opened her mouth, but not a single protest came out. She barely kept herself from drooling with desire for him.

And so instead, Foxy flung herself at him. Like always, she leaped before she looked and nearly toppled off the bed. Like always, Joe caught her securely in his arms.

For the second time in their lives, Foxy's lips met his. That first kiss had been chaste in comparison. This kiss was a blazing inferno.

Sensations and emotions flooded Foxy. Warmth. Desire. Fire. Need. Satiation.

This was it.

He was it.

It was Joe.

Joe was the one.

She'd found her soulmate. She was wrapped up in his arms, experiencing pure bliss as Joe deepened their kiss. Not a single one of her visions, or gut feelings, or even her imagination, could possibly compare to being embraced and ravished by Joe Matthews.

Gone was the quiet boy with a calculating mind. Here and present was a grown man with a raging appetite, and it was for her. Foxy hungered right back for him. But her stomach felt settled. Everything in her felt right and whole and perfect.

A voice cleared from the doorway. That was what finally broke them apart. With Foxy still wrapped inside his arms, she and Joe looked up to see the farmer and his wife standing in the doorway.

"Brother and sister, huh?"

Joe and Foxy looked at one another. What she felt for this man was beyond sibling affection. Still, a cold shiver replaced the warmth that had overcome her in Joe's arms. Foxy pulled back when she got a bead on the sensation.

"Daria! We have to get to Daria."

CHAPTER THIRTEEN

*J*oe took the turn slowly. He mainly used his left hand to make the left-handed turn. His right hand was currently and irrevocably preoccupied, locked in gear with Foxy's left hand.

After thanking the bewildered farm couple whose gazes were fixed on Joe and Foxy's joined hands, the newly minted soulmates had made their way out of the house and to Joe's towed car in the drive. Joe had held onto Foxy's hand down the stairs, out the front door, and to the passenger seat. He reluctantly released her hand to climb into the driver's side, then he scooped her fingers back into his and reclaimed his woman. He wasn't looking forward to putting the car in park as they pulled up to the state foster home, but it had to be done.

Turning off the ignition, Joe bent his head and pressed a kiss to each of Foxy's knuckles. She grinned down at him, eyes shining brightly. Joe could've sworn he was looking into a supernova as her gaze focused solely on him. He never dreamed he could be this happy, feel this content. All that could make this moment better was another kiss from the woman he had loved for as long as he'd known what the word meant.

And then he realized he now had that right.

Joe leaned over the console. Foxy met him more than halfway. Their kiss was an actual supernova.

Gravity pushed in on him, causing Joe to fall deeper into Foxy's touch. He felt as though his world were expanding and collapsing at the same time. While stars and galaxies died and were reborn around him, Joe reached for the bright light that was Foxy. He kissed her until he was senseless, only coming up when the oxygen finally ran out.

"I can't believe it was you all along," she said after she gasped in not one but two lungfuls of air.

"I didn't need any extrasensory powers to tell me you are an amazing woman," he said once he caught his breath. "I knew the first moment I met you."

"The first moment you met me, you stuck your tongue out at me and made a face."

"I was seven," Joe protested. "I thought girls were gross. But you were the first person I warmed up to."

Foxy ran her fingers along his temple and down to his chin, tracing the contours of his face. With each touch, Joe felt like he was being reborn into a new man. A stronger version of himself.

"Now," Joe said after another quick peck, "let's go in and check on this kid."

"Her name's Daria. You'll love her. She wants to be a superhero when she grows up, right all the injustices of the world. Like someone else I know."

Joe had never had a vivid imagination as a kid. He'd just had an innate sense of when something was wrong. When he saw it, he had the urge to right it.

Looking up at the state foster home, he got that inkling that something was wrong. Walking in through the doors, he was hit with a pungent smell of unclean. Bright Horizons had been an old structure, but each care worker that had been in charge had kept it neat and tidy.

Walking down the halls, the children looked unclean. Not filthy. Just not cared for. At Bright Horizons, daily baths or showers were nonnegotiable. Many of these children looked as though they had gone a whole week without getting any parts of their bodies under a running faucet.

They flinched as Joe and Foxy came near them. None would hold their eye contact for longer than a second. In the distance, Joe could hear the muffled sounds of crying.

Foxy's fingers tightened their hold on his. Joe pulled her tightly to him. Foster care had been hard on both of them, but neither of them had suffered serious abuse. The signs were here that this place was darker than Bright Horizons.

Being brought up in the foster system after both of his parents died, and his maternal grandparents turned over their rights to him, had been a large part of the reason why Joe went into the law. He'd hated that, as a kid, he didn't have the power to speak up for himself. He had to rely on adults, and that wasn't something that came naturally to kids that had been abandoned. It wasn't until he had his law degree in his hand that Joe finally felt a real shift in power. Looking at these kids, he was reminded of the powerlessness he'd run from all those years ago.

As District Attorney, he would have the power to do something about this situation. As D.A., who would be the legal representative for the Department of Family Services. He could make a change that would improve these kids' lives.

Joe ached to tell the forlorn kids he passed this. He wanted them to lift their chins and know that change was on its way once he was in power. He would use his power to make their lives better.

A door at the end of the hall opened. A tall man who looked like he'd been a linebacker a lifetime ago walked out first. He was followed by a gray-haired woman who brought to mind a scarecrow with her black hair and perpetually narrowed gaze. Actually, on second glance, Joe realized the woman's hair was a pattern of black and a gray so pale it could almost pass as white.

"Thank you for coming, Commissioner Benson," said the scarecrow of a woman.

Benson? Why did Joe know that name? The man in question looked up, and recognition dawned in both men's eyes.

Rich had shown Joe a picture of this man at some point over the last week. This was Roger Benson. Benson sat on the Board of Commissioners, who would appoint the new D.A. to fill the vacant seat.

"Captain Matthews?"

Commissioner Benson looked Joe up and down twice. When the man's shrewd gaze came back to Joe's a second time, Joe was certain he saw disapproval in his gaze.

"I thought we weren't meeting until tomorrow." Commissioner Benson straightened his tie as he took a step closer to shake Joe's hand. "I see you're eager."

Joe let go of Foxy's hand and held out his to shake the commissioner's. "I didn't realize you were here, sir. It's a happy coincidence. I'm here on family business."

"Family?" Commissioner Benson looked at Foxy. "This is your sister?"

"No, Foxy is my…"

"I'm his soulmate." Foxy supplied when Joe's silence went on a beat too long.

Soulmate hadn't been the qualifier Joe had planned to use. Girlfriend seemed childish. Fiancée wasn't accurate as he hadn't asked. Soulmate was accurate but not necessarily the best description for the serious man who stood gaping at the two of them.

Commissioner Benson dropped Joe's hand. Foxy promptly picked it up and laced her fingers with his.

"Soulmate?" said Benson. "And you say your name is Foxy?"

Foxy nodded. "Foxy Morningstar James."

"Foxy works with another foster home," Joe interjected before she could add any more details. "She's working on her Elevated Care Certification as part of her job at the Bright Horizons Foster Home."

"Commendable," said Commissioner Benson, his disapproving features relaxing slightly.

"I'm also clairsentient," Foxy offered. "We're here because I felt that one of the kids in this home was in distress."

Commissioner Benson's gaze went back to Joe. For his part, Joe gave the man a weak smile, wondering if his dream job was right now slipping through his fingers. One thing Joe did not let go of was his soulmate's hand. He'd waited too long to win that particular reward. Whatever the future threw at him, or withheld from him, he would do it with this woman at his side.

CHAPTER FOURTEEN

"Ms. Foxy, you came to rescue me."

A skinny bundle of arms and legs and tangled hair flew against Foxy's middle. Even though Daria was slight, the little girl nearly knocked Foxy over with her embrace. Foxy squeezed the child back tightly, feeling worried that she mostly felt skin and bones.

When Daria had first come to Bright Horizons, she refused any kind of touch. It was common amongst foster kids. Those children had been abandoned by the first people who were meant to love them unconditionally. So it was no wonder that they had trouble accepting affection from strangers.

"This place is full of villains," Daria whispered in Foxy's ear.

Though Daria's idea of a whisper was loud enough for those at the back of a movie theater to hear her. They were standing in a common room with a few other foster kids. Most of them looked over at Foxy and Daria, sending Daria derisive looks.

Foxy knew those looks well. Before she and her sisters had come to stay at Bright Horizons, they'd been in a few unsavory places where kids and adults preyed on the vulnerable. But she'd been a James.

With one James, you used caution. With two, you ran. All three of them together had climbed to the top of the food chain of every foster home they'd been dropped in. And now, they ran what had once been one of the more notorious homes in the state.

Not only were they running Bright Horizons now, but they'd uprooted it and settled the establishment into new digs on a ranch. Daria was one of theirs. She was here at the State Home temporarily until they got her back. Part of the deal with them getting her back was Foxy earning her Elevated Care certification.

The State believed Daria was special needs due to a little misunderstanding. The little girl may have believed she was a superhero. There may have been a stack of medical records of bruises and sprains and broken limbs at the ER. And maybe a representative from the state witnessed the child leaping onto a horse because she believed it was magical and would help her flee being taken by the state.

Yeah, just a bunch of misunderstandings. Joe was helping file the paperwork for Savy and Charlie to adopt Daria's older brother Denny. Once that ink dried, and Foxy had her Elevated Care certification, there should be no reason that they couldn't get Daria back home with them where she belonged.

But first, Daria had to survive this State Home. Unlike the James girls, Daria was here all by herself. Neither did she have her brother looking after her. Worse than that, the little superhero was without her cape.

Without the cape covering her pale flesh, Foxy saw that there were a few more bruises on her arms and legs. They could've been from Daria's superhero antics. But Foxy somehow doubted it. The cold feeling increased in the pit of Foxy's stomach.

"Did someone hurt you, Daria?" Foxy held the little girl's bruised arms gingerly.

"Oh, this? I got this from spying on Ms. Monroe."

"You were spying on the head care provider here?"

Daria nodded. "Have you seen her? She looks like Cruella Deville, but without the polka dots."

Foxy couldn't deny the comparison. Ms. Monroe had a stern, shrewd look about her. And her black hair had uniform white streaks that couldn't have come from a dye job. That hairstyle looked like something from the supernatural.

"Ms. Benson looks like a villain. But also," Daria leaned in close to give Foxy another one of her stage whispers. "She's never tried to hug me like you and Ms. Savy. None of these kids have ever been hugged. I asked. They don't even do chores here."

That was a complaint after Savy's heart. But which one of Daria's statements would Savy love more? To know that Daria not only missed hugs, but she missed doing chores.

"That's how I knew there was something off about this place," Daria continued. Her voice was now low enough to be an actual whisper. "So I crawled through the air vents."

Foxy seized her thin shoulders. "You crawled through the air vents. Daria, that's dangerous."

"I was careful. No one saw me."

Foxy gentled her hold. Daria really required twenty-four-seven supervision. Not because she was a troubled youth. Because trouble attached to her like the smudges of dirt on her chin.

"This morning, Ms. Monroe and that creepy guy were in the office."

Creepy guy? She must mean Commissioner Benson. Foxy had gotten creep factor from him too, but she'd held her tongue. The man had something to do with Joe getting appointed as District Attorney. In fact, Joe was talking to him right now.

Foxy didn't know much about politics. She knew that a commissioner was some kind of politician. She supposed she'd have to deal with the likes of them if she was going to be a politician's wife.

Huh, look at that. Foxy James never thought she'd be anywhere near politics. But if that's what Joe wanted, then she would make compromises. She was serious when she said the world needed a good man like Joe. She'd just have to be the woman at his side protecting him from the evils of politics and power-hungry politicians. It would seem that that crusade might have to start with Commissioner Benson.

"They're making kids sick," said Daria.

"What do you mean?"

"They're making them mental on purpose."

"Daria, that is inappropriate language. People with mental disabilities need our compassion and understanding."

"But they're doing it on purpose, Ms. Foxy. I heard them say it. They're trying to make me mentally disabled too."

Tears welled in Daria's eyes. She didn't even try to fight them. They spilled down her cheeks, leaving tracks through the smudges of grime.

Foxy pulled the girl to her and held her tight. "I know this is hard, sweetheart. We're going to get you out of here soon. I promise."

"I want to go home now. I don't want to be mentally disabilitied."

Foxy took a deep breath. She stared at Daria. She knew this was an unfounded fear. But for some reason, the cold dread that had first brought her here wouldn't leave her belly. Not even now that she'd seen that Daria was somewhat healthy and mostly whole.

Something was still wrong.

CHAPTER FIFTEEN

"As you can see, we are all up to code here." Ms. Monroe's kitten heels clacked on the linoleum as she strode down the hall.

The sound reminded Joe of gunfire. However, instead of felling any of the bad guys on the opposite side, every kid in the vicinity of the sound jerked to attention while also flinching away and disappearing around a corner or into a nook or behind a door.

Joe peeked into the room that Ms. Monroe indicated. Inside, things were a little untidy. The floors were sticky and squeaky under his shoes. And there was still that ever-present smell of something unwashed.

It didn't cling to Ms. Monroe. She was dressed impeccably in a pristine blouse and a skirt that rivaled what Charlotte O'Dell had been wearing the other day. Her nails were polished to perfection. Her eye makeup expertly applied. It didn't make her look pretty. It made her look severe and intimidating.

The foster kids in the room shuffled about under her scrutiny. All conversation stopped the moment Ms. Monroe darkened the doorway. Every little body went as still as a cockroach, holding its position on a wall, hoping that as long as it didn't move, it wouldn't be noticed by the predator.

For his part, Commissioner Benson's gaze kept flitting back to his watch as though there was someplace else he'd rather be. He did not cross the threshold with Joe and Ms. Monroe. Neither did he lean on the doorjamb. His upturned nose wrinkled as though he smelled the unwashed scent as well and was doing everything in his power to make sure none of it touched his person.

Joe took in the room of silent kids. A few of them snuck glances back at him, but no one said a word. Foxy's voice sounded in Joe's head that something wasn't right with the place. He couldn't disagree with her. But neither could he find any evidence that something was out of place.

"When I was in foster care, it was never this quiet," said Joe.

"That's because they didn't have good drugs when you were a kid."

Joe blinked once, then twice. He looked over to Ms. Monroe, hoping to hear a jesting laugh or see a joking smile. The black and white-haired woman looked as serious as ever.

"A number of these children have major issues," Ms. Monroe went on to say. "Everything from panic attacks, PTSD, anxiety, and depression, along with physical disabilities."

A lot of children in the foster system had some form of PTSD. It could be a result of being born addicted by what their parents put into their own veins. Or it could be trauma that came postnatal. These kids weren't born with the same deck as others, which is why they so desperately needed advocates.

"I understand you came from the foster system yourself, Captain Matthews?"

Joe nodded. "My father was killed in Iraq not long after I was born. My mother's parents wanted her to give me up for adoption because I was biracial."

One of the kids looked up at this admission. The kid didn't look biracial, but it was hard to tell just by looking at anyone what their cultural make up was. Joe had always hated when someone asked him *what are you*. The kid wasn't looking at Joe's skin color trying to place his ethnicity. He stole a glance directly into Joe's eyes as though to ask *who* was he.

"It looks like you've made something of yourself," said Commissioner Benson, finally joining in on the conversation but not stepping over the threshold and into the room. "Law degree, JAG officer, and now a candidate for District Attorney. You're an example to these kids."

Joe nodded, his gaze still holding the kid, who was silently eyeing him. "I was fostered at a home and then adopted by wonderful people. Then I used the VA benefits from my father to pay for college."

"VA benefits?" said the kid, rising from his place on the worn sofa. "What's that?"

"Justin." Ms. Monroe's voice was like a whip cracking across the room. "We only speak if spoken to."

Justin pursed his lips. There was a quiver about his lower lip as though he desperately wanted to speak.

"It's fine," said Joe. "I'm happy to explain. VA benefits means Veteran Benefits. They're monies provided for any surviving member of a military person."

"My mom was a soldier," said Justin. "They say she fell and died."

This kid's mother was a fallen soldier. That meant she'd died in the line of combat, not that she'd necessarily fallen down.

"Do you think I'd have something like that? I want to go to college, too."

"Of course you do," said Joe, stepping forward. "I could—"

"Justin, Captain Matthews is busy," Ms. Monroe cut Joe off physically by stepping in front of him, as well as with her terse words. "This is something we can discuss later."

She turned with a perfect about-face that made Joe wonder if she was also a product of the military. Maybe the daughter of a drill sergeant, if she wasn't one herself.

Ms. Monroe marched Joe out the door, shutting it behind her. "I'm sorry about that," she said.

"No, I don't mind at all. I'd be happy to talk more to him or any other kid about military benefits and how to use them to pay for college or anything else."

"Like I said, most of these kids have disabilities that would preclude them from succeeding at college, let alone getting acceptance."

Joe wanted to protest that. A disability didn't preclude anyone from higher education. Soldiers who served their country came back daily with wounds gotten in the line of duty. Every day, they continued to give more, even in their wounded capacity. Before Joe could raise his voice, Commissioner Benson chimed in.

"What this place needs," said Commissioner Benson, "is more funding. It's expensive to take care of all these kids. It taxes the county and state budget."

"I agree," said Joe. "And if I become DA, foster care and funding will be one of my top priorities."

Commissioner Benson grinned at that. Something in the man's grin brought to mind a snake slithering up the path. "I think you would make a good DA. You'd certainly have my vote…"

Any thought of hissing left Joe's mind at those words. He'd done it. He'd won Commissioner Benson over. And it hadn't taken a fake engagement to do so. It had just taken Joe speaking from his heart about one of his passion projects; the care of foster kids.

"It's just that… soulmate of yours…I don't know if she's D.A. wife material."

Joe's shoulders caved at Commissioner Benson's words. But his heart refused to sink. It was too buoyed by Foxy's returned affection. It looked like he was back to square one because there was no way he would throw over his soulmate for his dream job.

"You're right," Joe admitted. "Foxy definitely isn't D.A. wife material. But she cares about these kids as much as I do. Likely more because she wants to work with the ones who are most troubled as an Elevated Care Provider. With her by my side, she'll help me in my crusade to ensure foster homes get the funding and staffing they need to take care of these kids."

Joe's heart pounded in his chest. He wasn't sure if it was for the loss of his dream job or if it was the adrenaline of standing up for his dream girl. As he looked at Commissioner Benson and Ms. Monroe, he witnessed a silent communication take place between the two of them.

Finally, Commissioner Benson turned back to Joe. He held out his hand. "I think I believe you. And I think you'll be the perfect man for the job."

CHAPTER SIXTEEN

Once the car door shut and they were enclosed in the car, Foxy and Joe reached for each other's hands. Foxy wasn't sure if Joe reached first or if she did. Foxy entwined the fingers of her left hand with Joe's right one. Joe pressed the palm of his left hand until it was flush with Foxy's right one.

They held onto each other tight. Both clearly needing the contact. Was it being in a less than savory foster home that had ignited the need? Was it the sparks of new love that still burned bright around them? Did it matter?

Foxy turned to Joe. He was already gazing down at her. His face was so familiar, so dear to her. Joe looked at her like she was a buried treasure he'd just unearthed. Had he always looked at her like that?

How had she missed these clear signs of adoration? How had she not realized that this was the man she was meant to spend the rest of her life with?

"It's pretty much a done deal," Joe said.

"Yes, I suppose it is."

Gone was the comforting security that always surrounded her in Joe's presence. In its place was a raging desire that Foxy wasn't entirely sure what to do with. She wanted to kiss him. She wanted to hold him close. She wanted him to feel just how fast he made her heart beat.

"We'll announce it next week," said Joe.

Announce it? He hadn't even asked her to marry him yet. They hadn't even gone on a single date.

Though did that matter? This was more than a done deal. It was the real deal. They were each other's soulmate.

No man had ever been as close to her as Joe. No man had her trust the way he did. No man had her heart.

"Rich will be thrilled," Joe said as he rubbed his thumb across her knuckles.

"Rich? Your campaign manager? I didn't get the sense he liked me very much."

"No." Joe barked a laugh. "He thought you'd be a liability to my campaign."

"A liability?"

"Now it doesn't matter because Commissioner Benson just gave me his blessing."

"Benson? The creepy old guy blessed our engagement?"

Joe blinked, and when he did, a little of the haze of desire cleared from his eyes. "Engagement?"

The clarity in Joe's gaze confused Foxy. "Joe, what done-deal-blessing are you talking about?"

"My appointment as District Attorney. Commissioner Benson was the last hold out. After meeting me today, he gave me his endorsement."

"Oh." Foxy let her fingers unfurl from his.

Joe did not let her go. Instead, he held tight and quirked an eyebrow. "Engagement?"

"It was a misunderstanding." Foxy tried again to pull her hand away.

Joe would not let her go. Joe took both of her hands, turning them until his palms were on the back of her hands. Then he pressed both of Foxy's palms to his chest, right where his heart beat.

"I understand it perfectly well," he said. "I am going to marry you."

Tears pricked Foxy's eyes. She closed her lids, but that didn't hold them at bay. "Even if I could be a liability to your career?"

Joe pressed his hands into Foxy's until her fingers jumped with every beat of his pounding heart. "This is yours. Has been since we were kids. It won't beat without you. The true liability, the only danger to my life, is not having you in it."

Foxy let out a long sigh, not realizing until then that she had been holding her breath. Joe caught the tear that slipped out of one eye. Before the next tear could fall, his lips were at her temple. He caught that tear and the others that fell. Then his mouth was on hers. Foxy should've tasted the salt of her tears. It was sweet warmth that filled her mouth as Joe ran his lips across hers.

When Joe pulled away, Foxy was floating. She hadn't known that such happiness was even possible. So why was her gut still tightening with dread?

Looking out the passenger side window, Foxy saw a small figure standing in the doorway of the state home. Daria's lip trembled as she looked at the two of them. Then a hand snaked out, and Ms. Monroe pulled the child inside and shut the door.

"I'm sorry we can't take her with us yet," said Joe. "You saw that she's okay."

Daria was physically okay. The adoption paperwork was moving forward. She would be back at the ranch soon.

All of those facts did not negate what Foxy felt. The cold twisting was still there. Though muted.

"She thinks they're trying to make her sick," said Foxy.

"She thinks someone is trying to poison her?"

"No. She thinks they're trying to make her crazy. She said she heard the Commissioner and Ms. Monroe talking about disabilities."

"Yeah, Ms. Monroe said many of the kids there have physical and mental disabilities."

"Daria said they were trying to give her one."

"She's what? Seven? I'm sure she misunderstood. In fact, they're working to bring in more funding for the kids to help them with their issues."

Foxy knew he was right. It was the logical explanation. No one could make a kid have a disability.

"Still," she said, "something felt off about that place."

"It's not a perfect place, but everything is run to the letter of the law. I think with more funding, they could make it more comfortable for the kids."

That sounded good. But the feeling still nagged at her.

"Fox, you can't always rely on your feelings. You yourself once said you have a fifty-fifty accuracy."

"Not about danger. Are you sure there wasn't anything weird about Commissioner Benson?"

"Foxy, you can't go around disparaging people based on the gas in your stomach."

Her stomach went numb at Joe's words. Her fingers clenched into fists at his chest.

"Don't do that. Don't pull away." Joe held her hands tight. He bowed his head and sighed before speaking again. "I'm sorry. That was wrong of me to say it like that. I believe you. I believe in you. But, sweetheart, we can't chase down every sensation you have, especially when lives are on the line. I can make a difference as D.A. I will make a difference, but I gotta get the job first."

Foxy knew Joe would make a difference. He always did the right thing. Joe would never rest when something was wrong. He'd come with her and investigated, and they'd found nothing wrong. This had to be one of those times when her gut was wrong.

Joe kissed her knuckles before he gave them back to her. Then he kissed her forehead before making sure she was buckled in tight. When he started the car, Foxy settled back in the seat and decidedly ignored the nagging in her belly.

CHAPTER SEVENTEEN

*J*oe settled his shoulders back into the driver's seat. He shifted his form, turning his body so that he could gaze down at Foxy. She wasn't asleep, as he'd suspected. She sat still in the passenger seat, eyes out the front window, staring at nothing. She was quiet like she'd been for the last twenty minutes on the ride home.

They were parked in the drive of the Flying Cross Ranch now. Their hands were still entwined. He knew they couldn't sit here all day, even though he wanted to. The last thing he wanted to do was let go of Foxy's hand.

It had taken too long to gain a hold of her hand, of her heart. The cold words he'd said to her before departing from the State Home still hung in the air between them.

If he let her go now, what if she wouldn't reach for him again after this? She held his fingers tightly now. Her fingers pressed into his, down to the webbing. Joe returned the caress, wanting desperately to remain a part of her.

"Foxy..."

Joe's words were lost when she turned to face him. His breath caught in his throat as those bright eyes lit upon him. The gold flecks that had always been ever-present in her hazel gaze were dim.

Had he done that? Had his words cut her so deeply that he'd dulled her shine. If having his career dream meant pulling a shadow over his dream woman, there would be no contest.

"Fox, I'm sorry."

"I know." Foxy curled her fingers over his. She brought Joe's hand to her lips and kissed the back of his flesh softly. "You have to get ready for this evening."

That had not been what Joe was about to say. It was true that he had to get ready for this evening. To get ready for the announcement that he was throwing his hat in the ring to become District Attorney.

But was the announcement even necessary when he now had a nod from every commissioner on the board? Joe didn't want to go to a party to talk to people. He wanted to stay in the car, in this little cocoon that he and Foxy had made.

"You were right," Foxy said. "Once you get this position of power, you'll be able to do more for those kids, for the whole community, than anyone else. You are the perfect man for this job, Joe. And I am so proud of you."

There was the spark back in her eyes. The golden flecks flashed at him, warming Joe from the outside in. He pulled her to him, tucking her face into his neck, pulling her chest flush against his until he felt her heartbeat sync with his.

"You'll be with me?" he asked.

"Are you sure you want me there?" she said. "Maybe we should keep our relationship quiet until after you secure the position."

Joe pulled back to look down into her face. There, he found what he feared. Foxy was serious.

"We're a packaged deal, Foxy. They can't have me without you."

Foxy traced Joe's bottom lip with her index finger. "Then I'll try to be quiet. Not talk about any of my gut feelings if I get any."

Joe opened his mouth to refute that. But he promptly pressed his lips together to hold back any sentiment. It would be better if she didn't say anything tonight. Just for tonight. Just to these people. They would figure out the rest as it came.

Lifting their joined hands, Joe pressed his lips to Foxy's knuckles. He kissed each one in turn. When she pulled away to get out of the car, he let her go.

Joe watched Foxy walk away from him. He sat, tracing her every step until she was behind the door of the guest house. Finally, he climbed out of the car.

"So, that finally happened."

Joe looked over to see his father leaning against the front porch. Haran Matthews held a glass of pale brown liquid in one hand. Condensation ran down the sides of his fingers as he sipped his tea in the afternoon sun.

"You knew?" said Joe.

"Everyone knew," said Father Matthews. "Except, of course, Foxy."

The two Matthews men looked to the guest house. From this distance, Joe saw Foxy's shadow move across the curtained window. He hated this short distance between them and wanted to go to her. To bring her back into his embrace. To kiss her lush mouth. Or simply to hold her hand again.

"The two of you are not sleeping there together before vows are said."

"Yes, sir." Joe sighed. Then he let out a chuckle. "I did it, dad. District Attorney is mine."

Father Matthews tilted his head and regarded his son. He sat his empty tea glass on the railing and opened his arms. Joe felt like a schoolboy as he went into his father's embrace.

"I'm proud of you, my boy. You worked hard, and all of your dreams are coming true." Father Matthews pulled back to regard his son. "So, why don't you look happy?"

"I am," said Joe. "It's just... I met this kid at the state home. He could've been me if I didn't have you. Lost his parents to the war in Iraq. He wants to go to school but doesn't have the means."

"If his parents were in the service, then he should qualify for the GI Bill?"

"He didn't even know about it. I want to get a program going to make sure the kids in foster care know about their benefits."

"He should have survivor's benefits now to help him along."

"I don't think he knew about them either."

"The staff at the home would know," said Father Matthews. "Though your mother and I had to fight to get yours."

"You had to fight Bright Horizons to get my benefits?"

"No, your maternal grandparents. They tried to keep what your birth mother left you for themselves. They were pocketing your benefits from both your father and your mother while you were in foster care."

"You never told me that."

"You were a kid. As your guardian, I did what was necessary to take care of you and make sure you had the best shot at life."

Joe gripped his father's shoulder. If it weren't for this man, he had no idea what his life would've turned into. "I wish there were more like you, Dad."

"There are," said his father. "Those James girls are going to save the world, one foster child at a time."

Joe followed his father's gaze to the east side of the ranch. Savy was in the garden with the four foster kids currently in her care. She threw her head back and laughed at something one of the kids said. The children, even the sour-looking one named Denny, all laughed and grinned. Those kids were the lucky ones. They couldn't find anyone better to care for them, to fight for their futures than Savy and Foxy James.

"Before I forget," Father Matthews pulled an envelope from inside the door to the big house. "This came for Foxy while you were away."

The envelope read that it was from the law offices of Charlotte O'Dell. "What is this?"

"I believe it's a letter of recommendation from the family law practitioner that helped Foxy a couple of years ago. It was Ms. O'Dell's father that helped us when we fought your grandparents for your benefits. It's my understanding that Ms. O'Dell is still fighting for foster kids and getting their benefits from the state."

"From the state?"

Joe thought back to his lunch date the other day with Charlotte. She had said something about getting benefits from the government. Joe hadn't thought much of it, until now. A light wind blew, prickling the hair at the nape of Joe's neck. A roiling began in his belly. It grumbled like he was hungry. But food was the last thing on Joe's mind. A cold feeling settled in his gut, a feeling that he couldn't ignore.

CHAPTER EIGHTEEN

The shower didn't do Foxy the good she needed. It washed away the dirt and grime of the last two days, but it didn't make the gnawing feeling in her stomach go away.

Something was off.

Foxy took a deep breath and let it out slowly. Then another and another. Slowly, the cold, twisting feeling began to recede. What took its place was the warm, soothing love she felt for Joe.

That love had always been there. Foxy just hadn't taken the time to examine it. She'd always been so preoccupied with what was going on in other people's lives that she had nearly missed out on the love of her life.

That way of thinking, that way of feeling, was done. From now on, Foxy was going to keep her nose—and her belly—out of other people's business and focus on her own life. She was going to be the wife of the District Attorney. Those would be big shoes to fill. Likely high heels, which were not her favorite.

She'd had to wear them when she'd performed with her mother and her sisters. Foxy preferred flats and sneakers so that she was grounded. The stems had taken her body too high from the earth and its natural vibrations.

She'd wear heels for Joe. He was her soulmate. She would be everything he needed her to be. And that was not a woman who walked in flats and was led around by her bellyaching.

Foxy turned her head toward the door. But at the last minute, she closed her mouth and looked the other way. The door opened, and Savy came in.

"What?" said Savy. "You didn't hear me coming?"

"Hey, sis."

"The van is back, and it's had a tune-up. Thanks for that."

"That's great." Though it hadn't been Foxy. It had likely been Joe that had made that call. Like when they were kids, he was watching out for her and anticipating her needs.

"So, you and Joe spent the night together." Savy plopped down on the sofa and waggled her eyes up at her sister. "How did that go?"

A slow smile spread across Foxy's face at the thought of waking up in Joe's arms. And then there was that first kiss. Well, actually, the second kiss. Soon, she would be waking up like that every morning for the rest of her life.

"No way," said Savy. "He finally made his move?"

"What do you mean, he *finally* made his move? Did you know about the kiss?"

"He kissed you last night?"

"Not that kiss. The one from ten years ago?"

"Ten years ago? Do you mean when you were fourteen? I'll kill him."

"You will not. You and Charlie were getting up to the same thing at that age."

"The two of you are not staying in this guest house together without vows being exchanged."

Foxy rolled her eyes. Then she flew into her sister's arms. "It's him, Sav. He's the one. He's the man I've been dreaming about all these years. Only it wasn't a dream. It was a memory. I forgot all about it. What kind of psychic does that make me?"

"You're not a psychic."

"No, it's even worse." Foxy wrung her hands as she paced the length of the room. "All my life, I've had all these feelings. And now I've come to realize that I don't even know what they mean half the time. How could I have missed him when he was standing right in front of me for so long? He even kissed me, and I didn't see it."

"You have him now." Savy stood and stopped her sister, bringing her into a hug. "And he has you. That's what matters."

"Yeah." Foxy sniffled into her big sister's shoulder. "Yeah, I do, and I'm gonna focus with my eyes instead of my stomach."

"What?" asked Savy, pulling away.

Instead of answering her sister, Foxy turned to the door a second before the knock sounded. It had to be him. It had to be Joe.

Maybe he'd come for another kiss. Maybe he'd come just to be near her. It didn't matter why he'd come. Foxy simply wanted to be in his presence. But when she opened the door, it wasn't Joe.

"Is she okay?" asked Denny.

"Yes, Denny. Daria is fine. Impatient, up to her old superhero tricks and spying, but she's not hurting."

"You said you got a feeling," said Denny. The anxiety in the boy's voice was palpable.

Foxy bit her lip. She hated that her gut had caused this kid to worry. "I did. But she's okay. She'll be home with us soon. I'm sure of it."

"Because you got another feeling?" Denny's tone was biting, accusatory.

"That's enough, Denny," said Savy. "Go finish your chores."

Denny scowled at them both as he took off down the steps of the guest house. The fluttering in Foxy's belly turned back to angry bees. She took a deep breath. And then another. The sensation wouldn't stop this time.

She thought of Joe. Pulling up an image of his strong, certain face. But the vision was hazy.

"Denny's right," said Foxy. "I have to help Daria. And the only way I can do that is to get the right credentials."

"I thought you said you got the two letters," said Savy.

"I had. But I kinda stole the man of the woman who agreed to write the second recommendation letter. When she finds out, I doubt she'll have anything favorable to say about me."

"Where are you going?"

"Into town to get another letter of recommendation."

Foxy grabbed the keys to the van and left the guest house. The drive into town was a blur. Her mind was far too focused on settling the nagging in her gut. But the more she hushed it, the louder it grew in her mind.

Pulling into the parking lot of Ramos's Deli and Cafe, Foxy put the van in park and hopped out. The roiling in her stomach was feeling more like a belly ache than any clairsentient feeling she'd ever gotten before. This was the only way she knew to solve the problem with Daria.

She was going to march into the restaurant and get Travis to write her a letter of recommendation. The parking lot was near to full. It hadn't been that way a couple of years ago before she worked here. Foot traffic had increased at Ramos's when she worked there and gave out unsolicited advice and predictions. Customers may have come for the spectacle of the psychic waitress, but they stayed for the food. Travis owed some of his success to her, and she wasn't leaving without that letter.

Foxy marched up to the door of the restaurant. But something nagged her, causing her to pause. A light wind blew over her shoulders, causing the hair at the nape of her neck to prickle. She glanced over to the left and what she saw stopped her heart.

Joe stood at the door of Charlotte O'Dell's law offices. Charlotte stood in the doorway, a huge flirtatious smile on her face. She leaned in and kissed Joe on the cheek. He did not pull away. He followed her into the office as she beckoned him inside.

The whole scene left Foxy feeling cold and numb. She had not seen that one coming.

CHAPTER NINETEEN

"Thank you for seeing me, Ms. O'Dell."

"Ms. O'Dell? I think if we're seeing each other, Captain Matthews, then it should be on a first-name basis." Charlotte pressed her palm to Joe's chest and came in to kiss him on his cheek. When he flinched at her touch, her smile sank, and she stepped back. "Unless we're no longer seeing each other."

Joe took a deep inhale. He let the breath out with an apology. "I'm sorry, Charlotte."

Charlotte beckoned him into the building. Joe followed, girding his loins for what was to come. He hated breakups, which is why he had avoided dating for much of his adult life. No matter how perfect the woman was for him, she could never be Foxy.

"Tell me what I did wrong?" said Charlotte once they were in her office with the door shut. "Is it my high-powered job? Is it the six-inch heels? I'm always taller than the men I date, but my high arches can't stand flats. You still have a good inch on me with my stilettos on."

"Charlotte." Joe held up his hand to stop her diatribe. "It's none of those things. You're great. You're perfect."

"Logically, I can't be perfect if you're dumping me."

"It's not you. It's me."

Charlotte balked at that.

"Actually, it's someone else."

"You're not making any sense, Captain Matthews."

"I was already in love with another woman before I even met you."

"And let me guess, she realized what she was missing when you started dating me?"

"No, she didn't even remember that there was anything between us. She actually encouraged me to date you. Until she had a vision of our first kiss as kids and then realized that I was her soulmate and—"

"This has to be the most nonsensical conversation I've ever had in my life," said Charlotte.

She looked at Joe as though he were crazy. Because the words coming out of his mouth were crazy. Had he have been talking to Foxy, the words would've made complete sense. That thought made Joe grin.

"No, I take that back," said Charlotte. "I've had crazier conversations with your friend, Foxy."

The despair of being dumped dissipated from Charlotte's face and was replaced by suspicion. Joe quickly changed the subject before the lawyer's deductive reason focused too pointedly on Foxy.

"Never mind," said Joe. "That's not why I'm here."

"So, you're breaking up with me and also here to ask for something else?"

"It's work-related. You practice family law. You help foster kids. Can I ask what the nature of your work is with the kids?"

"You know I can't break client-attorney privilege." Charlotte crossed her arms over her chest. It was a move Joe pulled many a time. She was in full counselor mode now.

"I'm not asking you to reveal anything that isn't public record. I'm just not sure what I'm looking for. I was at the state foster home earlier and something one of the kids said just won't leave me alone."

Charlotte uncrossed her arms and leaned a little forward. "What did they say?"

"Well, it's what they didn't know. He was a soldier's kid. But he didn't know he had access to the GI bill being the survivor of military personnel. And when I tried to give him more information, the care-taker steered me out of the room."

"I see." Charlotte leaned back in her seat, but she didn't cross her arms over her chest to ward him off. She tapped her index finger on her lower lip and regarded him.

"You see?" said Joe. "You see what?"

Charlotte continued to tap her lower lip as she regarded him. Just a moment ago, she had looked up at him with the trust that came with believing they were going to be life partners. Now she looked at him as though he was an adversary.

"Charlotte, I want to help these kids. If there's anything you know that could help me help them, please..."

"You'll want to look into The Marshall Project."

"What will that case tell me?"

"It's not a case. It's a nationwide investigation."

"An investigation of what?"

"I think you suspect what it is."

Joe pursed his lips. He tapped his index finger on the wooden arm of the chair he sat in. He did not want to voice what was formulating in his mind about what was happening back at that state home. When Charlotte voiced it for him, it was no better.

"You know there are bad foster parents who pocket kids' benefits."

Joe nodded. His own maternal grandparents had done that to him. "But this kid doesn't have any other family, as far as I know."

Charlotte remained mute again, waiting for him to voice what he didn't want to acknowledge.

"It's the state, isn't it?" Joe didn't need Charlotte to confirm. It all added up. Especially when he remembered Ms. Monroe hushing him about the GI Bill and survivor benefits. It was still a hard pill to swallow that a state agency would be taking money from children. "That can't be right."

"It's not illegal," said Charlotte. "It's unethical. It's downright dirty, but they're not breaking the letter of the law. They're saying it's being used to fund their care. I've even found evidence that they're looking through these kids' school and health records to see if they can be labeled as mentally disabled, so that they'll collect more money."

Mental disabilities. That's what Foxy said Daria had told her. Foxy had been right. Her clairsentience had uncovered a huge conspiracy.

"The Marshall Project has found at least thirty-six states where state foster care agencies are using this practice of taking kids' benefits to pay for their foster care, that includes survivor benefits, veterans' benefits, and Social Security benefits. They're raking in millions every year."

"But foster homes are funded through taxpayer dollars and federal and state grants," Joe said, his mind giving a last grasp of denial.

"They say they use the funds to pay for the children's daily expenses like shelter and food, rather than just giving them cash. My law firm is a part of a class-action lawsuit regarding this matter."

"Class-action? Who are the defendants?"

"The county and the state. This was one of the ways they were trying to get more funding for children's services. By making the kids pay for this public service."

Commissioner Benson's snakelike smile popped into Joe's head. The man had mentioned that they needed more funding. Is this how he meant to get it?

"Since you're in line to be the next District Attorney of this county, you'll be representing the state for this matter."

CHAPTER TWENTY

oxy squeezed her hands in her lap. Her fingertips felt cold. She pressed them together, rubbed them on her knee, and finally rested them on the console between the driver and passenger seat. Joe did not reach for her hand to cover it with his warmth.

"Is everything okay?" Foxy asked.

"Hmm?" Joe's gaze was out the window. His hands were at ten and two, ever the responsible driver. "Yes, of course."

"You just seem distracted."

"It's a big night. This will be a big announcement. It's going to change our lives."

He'd said *our* lives and not *my* life. That was something. At least he was still including her in his life. Or was the *our* referring to Charlotte O'Dell.

Foxy should just come out and ask him about it. Ask him what he was doing at the woman's office today. Her stomach was in absolute knots over it. She couldn't form the words.

Joe parked the car and came around to her side to hand her out. The moment his fingers touched hers, Foxy got a jolt of warmth that coursed all through her body. The nagging feeling that had been pressing her all day fled, and all she felt was the love she'd always had for the person standing beside her. Though now it was so warm, so bright, that it burned for the man kissing her fingertips.

She'd been a fool to think anything was wrong. Clearly, Joe still loved her if he was kissing her fingertips like this. It just went to show that her gut didn't know everything.

"I'm going to have to leave you," said Joe when they entered the venue.

"What?" Foxy gripped his hand tighter. "No."

"Just for a little while. Rich will take care of you."

Foxy wanted to protest that she didn't want Rich. She didn't want anyone but Joe. But Joe was already walking off. His strides were long, sure, and purposeful. His direction would take him right onto the path of Charlotte O'Dell.

The woman looked stunning in a white dress that did wonders for her complexion. She took one step toward Joe. Her legs impossibly long in six-inch heels. Meanwhile, Foxy wobbled in her one-inch kitten heels.

"So, you're the psychic he's going to throw his career over for?"

Foxy turned to see that Rich had come up behind her. She'd barely glanced at him the first time they'd met, but she remembered him. The man had a movie star's good looks, along with a grin that might've given a shark pause.

"I'm not..." She couldn't finish that sentence. The doubt in her abilities had grown so much over the past couple of days that Foxy wasn't sure what she was any longer.

On the one hand, she knew with a certainty that she and Joe were meant to be together. On the other hand, she knew that being with him would bring challenges to his dream life. Why was her happily ever after turning into a nightmare?

"I know," Rich was saying. "You're not a psychic. You're a clair... something or other. Someone who feels things deeply. I won't hide the fact that I feel that Joe choosing you will make things difficult for him to advance in politics. If he'd stuck with Charlotte, like I said, he would have a clear path to State District Attorney in a matter of years. Maybe even a shot at President one day."

Foxy's gaze ping-ponged around the room until she found Joe. Charlotte was still beside him. They weren't arm in arm, but she was clearly introducing him to important people. Something Foxy couldn't do, not unless he wanted the best table at Ramos's Deli and Cafe. Or to get good seats at a few of the state's dive bars.

"Right now, he's only the county D.A.," Rich was saying. "So, I don't think there's much harm you can do here in your own backyard."

The dark, twisty sensation knotted inside Foxy's gut. Despite the wrenching, she had a feeling Rich was wrong about that. The sensation warmed to a near burning when someone cleared their throat behind them.

"Commissioner Benson, good to see you," said Rich, sticking out his hand for a greeting.

The commissioner ignored Rich's hand. His gaze was on Foxy. The way the older man looked at her made her feel dirty inside and out.

"I hear you're getting certified in elevated care for foster kids, Ms. James," he said.

"That's correct."

"You came to visit a little girl at the state home earlier today."

"Daria. Her name's Daria."

"Can I take it that your interest in her is because she has a history of mental health illness?"

"No, Daria's a healthy adolescent."

"Who believes she's a superhero."

"So do some adults and any Marvel or Star Wars fan."

"I'm a DC guy and a Trekkie myself," said Rich. The man's sharklike grin faded with a single glance from Commissioner Benson, whose glassy eyes brought to mind those of a killer whale.

"Ms. James," said the commissioner, turning his attention back to her. "You do understand that when children are properly diagnosed, they get the additional care they need."

"I understand that," said Foxy. "Daria should not be in state foster care. She should be with her family, who love her."

"She has no family."

"I'm her family."

"Oh, it makes sense now." Commissioner Benson flashed her those sharp white teeth. "You think you're psychic. The kid thinks she can fly. Clearly, you both have mental health issues."

Foxy opened her mouth to take this man to task. Then she promptly shut it. In hindsight, she'd like to say that her discretion came from thinking about Joe's future. That would be a lie. Instead, what gave her pause were the addled words of a child.

"You're trying to make her mental." The wrenching in Foxy's gut ceased, and an eerie calm settled. A calm that felt right. "She said you were trying to make her mental."

"Thank you for stopping by Commissioner Benson but—"

Rich didn't get a chance to excuse the commissioner because Foxy went on.

"You're trying to diagnose Daria with a mental illness." The flash of acid roiled in Foxy's belly. It left behind the taste of metal, like the copper of a penny, in her mouth. "Money? You're doing this because of money?"

Once again, Rich tried to come between the two, perhaps to smooth the waters. But these waters were shark-invested, and Foxy had caught big game on the hook.

"If you want your fiancé to prosper," said Commissioner Benson. "If you want your certification rubber-stamped, then you'll play along."

Foxy shook her head, a warm glow of certainty radiating from her entire being. "Whatever you're doing, Joe would never play along with this."

"Excuse me." Joe's voice was amplified throughout the room. He stood on stage at a microphone stand. Standing by his side was Charlotte O'Dell. "I dreamed of this day since I was a child."

A hush fell over the room as they all waited for Joe Matthews to accept the honor that had been bestowed upon him. Foxy had the urge to run to the stage and yank him away from the dangerous pool he was about to wade into. Something in her gut told her she didn't have to.

"Ever since I was put in the system as a foster kid," Joe continued, "I knew that I wanted to help those who felt powerless. The best way to do that was through the law. Or so I thought. I've always prized logic over feelings, facts over emotion. This time I'm choosing feelings and emotion."

Joe's gaze found Foxy in the crowd before he continued. And when he did, Foxy knew with certainty that everything between them for now and in the future would be just fine. She didn't feel it in her gut. She knew it in her heart.

CHAPTER TWENTY-ONE

oe's toe bumped against the riser at the podium. The jolt sent a screech of feedback through the microphone. Inside his body, he felt his gut, his heart, his head shake with turbulence. He had a moment of doubt where he wondered if he was truly prepared for this new turn his life was taking.

Searching the crowd, he found a beacon when he saw Foxy. He caught sight of her where he'd left her, standing with Rich. She wasn't smiling. She looked very concerned. Her gaze followed Commissioner Benson as he walked off.

Joe wanted to leap down off the stage and go to her. To go to Benson and deck the commissioner for what he might have said to upset Foxy. But Joe knew he didn't need to. He could see it in her narrowed gaze. Foxy had already made the man out to be the villain without any need for the awful facts that Joe had collected. Because Foxy trusted her gut, she saw things clearly. Where he needed facts and figures.

When her gaze found his, she didn't smile. She still looked concerned. Did she doubt him? Did she think he would take this job after learning the facts? Well, if she did, Joe was about to make his stance on the matter crystal clear.

He turned his attention back to the microphone, took a deep breath, and took that hard left turn that would change his life's trajectory forever.

"I dreamed of this day since I was a child," he began. A hush fell over the room as they all waited for him to accept the honor that had been bestowed upon him. "Ever since I was put in the system as a foster kid, I knew that I wanted to help those who felt powerless. The best way to do that was through the law. Or so I thought. I've always prized logic over feelings, facts over emotion. This time I'm choosing feelings and emotion."

A restless rustle went through the crowd as they tried to gauge where this speech was going. The only person's opinion Joe cared about was Foxy's. When he found her again, a beatific smile crossed her face. A smile that said *I know you. I'm with you. I love you.*

Joe nearly forgot what he was about to say in the prepared speech. All he wanted was to kiss that smile on Foxy's face. Not yet, but soon. After he took the first step on the long path of the work he chose to do.

"I will not be accepting the appointment as county District Attorney. I will be going into private practice." Joe motioned Charlotte to his side. "With the help of Charlotte O'Dell as my partner, we'll be launching a lawsuit to stop the taking of foster children's survivor benefits, veteran's benefits, and Social Security benefits by the county and state."

A gasp went up through the crowd. Joe ignored what his ears heard and only focused on what his eyes saw. His Foxy didn't look surprised at all. Of course she didn't. Because she knew.

"Just as my family and my friends, and the love of my life stood by me, I hope you all will support me in this crusade to do the right thing for the most vulnerable amongst us; the children who have no parents to turn to."

There were a few seconds of stunned silence. Followed by raucous applause. Joe clasped Charlotte's hand in his and thrust their arms into the air.

The crowd swarmed the stage. Joe moved through quickly as possible, his eyes on Foxy as she stood still, waiting for him. There were many claps on his back. Many hands reaching out to shake his.

When Joe reached Foxy, he reached for her hands. They were warm and familiar. He brought them to his lips and kissed each of her fingers before finally placing his lips upon hers.

"Why didn't you tell me?" she said.

"It honestly didn't occur to me that you didn't already know," he said. "You told me you felt something was wrong."

"You listened to me."

"But I didn't believe. I won't make that mistake again."

Foxy wrapped her arms around his neck. "I had a feeling it would all work out between us."

Joe pulled her in closer until there wasn't a breath of space between them. "Well, this was the only logical conclusion to our story."

He bent his head to her and captured her lips. Their kiss ignited a fire inside him. The blaze burned so brightly Joe had a moment's fear that everyone in the vicinity might be burned by how much he loved this woman. That fear quickly died as the embers grew. The love he and Foxy shared was now and would continue to be a force for good.

EPILOGUE

The chime let off a high-pitched shrill, breaking up the sounds of the music coming from the stage. A few listeners turned to glare at Will Matthews. He shrugged unapologetically. It wasn't as if his ringing phone during the performance had made things any worse.

The drummer was a beat behind the keyboardist. The guitarist's E-string was out of tune. The vocalist had mixed up the words of the popular song that they were butchering.

Will was sure his ringing phone couldn't possibly make the cacophony of sounds any worse. Still, he put silenced the device. Though he knew that wouldn't stop the person on the other end of the phone from reaching out to him.

He was right.

Barely a second later and the phone was vibrating on the dining table. The light from the face of the phone flashed an alert in case the bumping and jumping around of the device weren't enough. Again, the guests at the table next to him sent him a glare.

Instead of a shrug, Will sent the man a glare right back. It was clear the man was a lightweight because after only three seconds into the stare-off, the other man dropped his gaze. As if the man stood a chance against a Matthews. Including this one.

Will had stood tall, with his chest puffed up while he disappointed the man who meant the most to him in this world. When Will had broken the news to his adoptive father that had broken the old man's heart, Will hadn't blinked. Haran Matthews had taught him better than that. But Will's mind had been made up that day, and though he knew his father would never be as proud of him as he was of his other son's, Will had down what was best for himself.

He had no excuse why he was now in a dive bar listening to the butchering of old songs made into something unrecognizable by today's rebel youth. The last act had taken an old Beatles song and made it sound like frogs croaking to their death. The current act was thankfully finishing up a poor man's rendition of an Ella Fitzgerald song that made Will certain he was dreaming a little nightmare.

As that band cleared off, Will's phone took another opportunity to vibrate and flash once more. He knew this would continue until he answered. Now that Joe was out of the military, his brother would dog him until Will answered.

"Shouldn't you be in court or something?" was Will's greeting to his older brother.

"No, because I'll be headed to church instead."

"Not surprising being the kid of a preacher."

"She said yes."

Will paused to stare down at his phone. On the face of the receiver was his brother's name and number. He placed the device back to his ear.

"You finally told Foxy how you feel?"

"I did."

"And now you're getting married?"

"We are."

"Bro that's the best news I've heard in a long time."

Will was truly happy for Joe. He was the most serious brother of the Matthews clan, but he'd been head over heels in love with Foxy James for as long as Will could remember. Their brother Charlie had been in love with Savy James for just as long. What was it about those James sisters that stole a Matthews boy's attention?

"Sav and Fox want a double wedding," Joe was saying. "We'll need you home."

"Yeah… yeah."

Will wasn't sure if his brother could hear the lack of enthusiasm in his voice. He'd made his visits back to the Flying Cross Ranch fewer and far between after he'd disappointed their father with his choices in life. The pang in his heart was still a real thing. Though when he saw the next act walk out onto the stage, his heartbeats picked up a few beats.

"There's so much to do, and we're going to need you," Joe was saying.

"Yeah... right."

The sultry songstress wrapped a slender hand around the microphone. Every man in the room leaned forward as her vibrant red lips came close mic. Will included. But he'd always leaned forward whenever she parted those lips in song, or just to say hello.

"You never know," said Joe. "By the time you get here, there might be three weddings. I wouldn't be surprised if Topher finds Tricksy and proposes."

That brought Will out of his stupor. He blinked once, twice. But his vision was still filled with the songbird on stage. She opened her mouth and the sweetest sounds began to fill the room.

"Hey, is that Tricksy I hear-"

"Joe, I gotta go. I'll talk to you soon."

Will hit disconnect before his brother could ask any more questions, or hear any more incriminating evidence. Namely the fact that Will was seated at the back of a dive bar, in the shadows, listening to his brother's ex as she crooned a somebody-done-somebody-wrong love song. Because if his father, or his brothers, knew of his latest life-altering decision, it would definitely be a long time before they saw hide or hair of him again.

———

You may think you've guessed Will's secret.
But his secret crush on his brother's ex is just the beginning.
Find out the rest in *His Vow to Adore*,
Book Three in the Flying Cross Ranch Romances!

VOW TO ADORE

A FLYING CROSS RANCH ROMANCE 3

CHAPTER ONE

The chime let off a high-pitched shrill, breaking up the sounds of the music coming from the stage. A few listeners turned to glare at Will Matthews. He shrank down in his seat a bit, hating the momentary spotlight on him.

In fact, Will detested any added attention on him. Luckily, he was the third eldest in a family of six brothers -right smack-dab in the middle of the family, making it easy for him to hide. With two older and three younger loud, rambunctious, opinionated and sometimes quick-tempered boys, Will had no problems hanging out at the back of the line. Or better yet, off to the sides while his siblings shouted their imminent approach, drew attention to their presence, and were often asked to leave as a result of all of it.

Will did not like to be a bother or cause a ruckus. People would've called him quiet, except he was always flanked by at least one of his noisy brothers, who would quickly shoo away any notion of quiet. Though he sat at the table alone, it was one of his brothers calling him on his cell.

Truth be told, his ringing phone during the current stage performance was not the true ruckus being caused. It was the sad excuse for music that was bothersome. The drummer was a beat behind the keyboardist. The guitarist's E-string was out of tune. The vocalist had mixed up the words of the popular song that the whole band was butchering.

Will was sure his ringing phone couldn't possibly make the cacophony of sounds any worse. Still, he silenced the device. Though he knew that wouldn't stop the person on the other end of the phone from reaching out to him again.

He was right.

Barely a second later and the phone vibrated once more on the small, round and quite unsturdy dining table. The light from the face of the phone flashed an alert in case the bumping and jumping around of the device wasn't notification enough. Again, the guests at the wobbly table next to him sent him a glare.

Will could've glared right back. Or he could've straightened his shoulders and puffed out his chest. He had a good fifty pounds on his glaring adversaries -combined. But confrontation was not his way. Something his family of active duty Air Force and vets had often used against him. Being the sole Matthews boy who was a pacifist, Will took it all in stride. Except the one time Will had stood his ground without backing down.

On that day, Will had stood tall, with his chest puffed up while he disappointed the man who meant the most to him in this world. When Will had broken the news to his adoptive father that had broken the old man's heart, Will hadn't blinked. Haran Matthews had taught him better than that. But Will's mind had been made up that day, and though he knew his father would never be as proud of him as he was of his other sons, Will had done what was best for himself.

And now he was going to have to do it again. But he could do it later rather than sooner. Which was the excuse he gave as to why he was now in a dive bar, listening to the butchering of old songs made into something unrecognizable by today's rebel youth. The last act had taken an old Beatles song and made it sound like frogs croaking to their death. The current act was thankfully finishing up a poor man's rendition of an Ella Fitzgerald song that made Will certain he was dreaming a little nightmare.

As that band cleared off, Will's phone took another opportunity to vibrate and flash once more. He knew this would continue until he answered. Now that Joe was out of the military, his brother would dog him until Will answered.

"Shouldn't you be in court or something?" was Will's greeting to his older brother.

"No, because I'll be headed to church instead."

"Not surprising being the kid of a preacher."

"She said *yes*."

Will paused to stare down at his phone. On the face of the receiver was his brother's name and number. Instead of the picture of his brown-skinned brother, there was the image of a woman with honey-golden skin. Her wide eyes were looking dreamily off into space. Foxy James was the woman of Joe's dreams, but Joe had never told the woman that all these years. It looked like that had just changed.

"You finally told Foxy how you feel?"

"I did."

"And now you're going to the church because... you're getting married?"

"We are."

"Bro!" Will fist pumped the air, his excitement too great to be contained. "That's the best news I've heard in a long time."

Will was truly happy for Joe. He was the most serious brother of the Matthews clan, but he'd been head over heels in love with Foxy James for as long as Will could remember. Their brother Charlie had been in love with Savy James for just as long. What was it about those James sisters that stole a Matthews boy's attention, and soon after, their hearts?

"Sav and Fox want a double wedding," Joe was saying. "We'll need you home."

"Yeah... yeah."

Will wasn't sure if his brother could hear the lack of enthusiasm in his voice. He'd made his visits back to the Flying Cross Ranch fewer and far between after he'd disappointed their father with his choices in life. The pang in his heart was still a real thing. Though when he saw the next act walk out onto the stage, his heart picked up a few beats.

"Will you be able to take time off from the airline?"

"Yeah... sure." Will was going to be able to take all the time he needed off from the airline, seeing as that was no longer his career path.

"There's so much to do, and we're going to need you," Joe was saying.

"Yeah... right."

The sultry songstress wrapped a slender hand around the microphone. Every man in the room leaned forward as her vibrant red lips came close to the mic. Will included. But he'd always leaned forward whenever she parted those lips in song, or just to say hello.

"You never know," said Joe, "by the time you get here, there might be three weddings. I wouldn't be surprised if Topher finds Tricksy and proposes."

That brought Will out of his stupor. He blinked once, twice. But his vision was still filled with the songbird on stage. She opened her mouth and the sweetest sounds began to fill the room.

"Hey, what's that playing in the background?"

"Oh, it's just the radio."

"It sounds like Tricksy singing. Where are you?"

"Joe, I gotta go. I'll talk to you soon."

Will hit disconnect before his brother could ask any more questions, or hear any more incriminating evidence. Namely, the fact that Will was seated at the back of a dive bar, in the shadows, listening to his brother's ex as she crooned a somebody-done-somebody-wrong love song.

Will knew the actors in this particular song. It was his brother Topher who had done Tricksy wrong. But the truth was, it wasn't Topher at all who had been the culprit. It had been Will. And Will could never let Tricksy find that out.

He could never seem to stay away from the woman for too long, either. And so he slunk down once more in the back and listened to the songbird that he would never catch because she was in love with his brother.

CHAPTER TWO

he butterflies had set up shop in her belly. They were old friends of Tricksy's. They came fluttering about every time she found herself at the back of a stage. She would've worried if they hadn't come with her.

They tickled her belly. They danced in her heart. They got choked up in her throat because they wanted to get out and get into the world. Much like the songs Tricksy wanted to sing. That's where the words to all her songs lived; in her belly, in her heart, all rising up to her chest wanting to burst out.

Tricksy took a deep breath, willing the winged creatures and her words to hold on just one more second. It was almost time for them to fly out of her and flit about the room, dazzling the audience with their color and beauty.

Tricksy shut her eyes and reached out her hands. Unfortunately, her palms came away empty. There was no Foxy at her right to grab hold of her hand. There was no Savy at her left to grab hold of the other.

She was alone. A solo act. Which was what she had thought she wanted.

Her older sister Savy had always been a spotlight hog with her alto voice. Savy often made it hard for Tricksy to harmonize her soprano voice with hers. After the last fight they had backstage, Savy had walked out the backstage door and never come back. Foxy had followed.

But that was fine. Tricksy was just fine. She had found harmony in her own voice. She didn't have to sing an octave lower. Now, on her own, she could hit those high notes.

Her cue came from the MC.

Tricksy took a deep breath, letting the butterflies and the words know they were about to take the spotlight. It was show time.

She stepped onto the stage. The first thing she noticed were the lights. It was hard not to. The stage lights were always blinding. It was hard for the performers to see the crowds. That's why once she stepped onto the stage, the butterflies fled. The insects were searching for flowers and nectar. Tricksy was a creature that sought the applause.

It greeted her the moment she stepped onto the stage. Not as loud as she would've liked. But this was a new crowd. She had to win them over if she wanted a more permanent spot here at Ronny's Dive.

Yes, Ronny had called his bar a dive. And it fit the definition. The food was fried to within an inch of its life so that customers couldn't tell that it was at the end of its shelf life. The bar top was sticky, and so were the floors. Likely because they were both cleaned with the exact same rag.

She'd sung in worse places when her mother was alive and shepherding her and her sisters' careers. Those dives had been in places where preteens should never have set foot in. Ronny's was a few steps up from that.

Tricksy navigated the sound cables in her heels and made her way to the microphone. Once there, she wrapped her fingers around the cold metal and came up close to the bulbous grid of the mic.

The music started. She opened her mouth, and the world fell away.

Tricksy found the note. She hopped on and rode the strings to the high pitch where she belonged.

It's you, my dear, whom I adore.

The song was a slow melody, perfect for her voice. She got in her trills and rolls -something she could never do when Savy's deep voice brought the performance down.

Divine worship for my devoted mon amore.

As she sang, Tricksy felt weightless. The higher her voice went as she sang a song about giving her heart away to her first and only love. It should break her heart to sing about Topher Matthews every time she got on stage. But her heart joyed in the song because it got to sing. Even if it was singing about the man who had spouted poetic words to her one day only to say the same thing to Judy Cartwright a few weeks later under the bleachers.

Tricksy poured all her angst and heartbreak into break up songs about Topher. If the songs ever made the radio, they would give Taylor Swift a run for her money.

Out in the audience, the women in the crowd appeared to feel the same way. They got up, throwing their hands in the air as Tricksy's voice rose higher. They swayed their bodies in time to the beat as she belted the notes out.

Clearly, these girls all had a Topher in their past. A gruff boy with a handsome smile. The kind she was sure just needed her tender loving care to pull him out of his bad boy ways.

Yeah, right. Last she'd heard of Topher, he was breaking hearts on other continents. His Instagram account showed that he'd left behind a trail in Afghanistan. There were tweets about his escapades in Germany. For a time, his name had been a trending hashtag on TikTok.

Not that she was stalking him or anything.

All girls reported the same lines he'd used on her. Telling them that she was a dear whom he adored. That his adoration was one of devotion for his life. But a few days later, he would inevitably show his true colors. Topher Matthews wasn't the passionate poet he pretended to be. He was a womanizing rake.

Tricksy hit the highest note of the song. She belted it out, using every last bit of the breath in her lungs. When she was through, she was met with raucous applause.

She took a bow. Not because of the gratitude for her audience. She bowed because she had nothing left in her. Her body simply collapsed in half.

A few deep breaths and she could stand again. She was herself again. The butterflies returned from their flight and settled back in her belly. Her words, now that they'd gotten out of her heart, out of her chest, went back inside her to relax until she called on them again.

That song always took it out of her. When she rose, the lights weren't so bright. She opened her eyes and saw a single face. The face of the owner. Ronny didn't look pleased.

His gaze narrowed at her. They'd talked about this. The customers weren't here for a sad, somebody done somebody wrong song. Most of the time, only the women would get up and dance.

A look out in the crowd told Tricksy that it was only women up on their feet. The men hung back, fidgeting and looking uncomfortable. Many looked at their watches, at their phones, and at the door.

Bars like this weren't about the art of the performers. The people came to shake off their blues, not be reminded of them. Customers came to dance. If they danced, they'd get thirsty. If they got thirsty, they'd get hungry. It was about the money, not the art Ronny had told her time and again. Which meant that Tricksy had to change her tune.

She raced to hop on the new beat the band played. The song was a Top Forties hit that could be heard all day on the radio. It was a song about shaking one's backside while wearing a trendy outfit. It was about finding company for just that night with no strings attached. They lyrics flew by fast, faster than the beat of butterfly wings. But Tricksy rode it out.

By the chorus, the men were out of their seats. People threw up their hands. They began to shimmy their bodies to the music. No one was listening to her voice anymore, just moving along to the beat. Which is why they were here.

It appeared everyone, men and women included, wanted what this song had to offer. Fashionably, free fun for just one night. This music had nothing to do with the vocalist. Anyone could sing the song. In fact, everyone was singing along. Her voice was drowned out as the crowd sang along.

Tricksy's high voice got lower and lower.

A man shimmied his large body up to the edge of the stage. He put his hand out as though asking her to dance. Tricksy demurred and moved to the other side of the stage. He followed, hand still out, insistent.

Tricksy backed up, but the man took a step onto the stage. His steps halted as he went tumbling back. There was another man behind the first, and Tricksy raised her fist again, ready to meet her next assailant.

Only to pause. She knew a Matthews when she saw him. Though this wasn't the Matthews she expected.

"Will?"

CHAPTER THREE

ill knew something was wrong when the music changed. He hadn't particularly enjoyed the lyrics to the song about his brother. Mainly because the words to the poem Topher had recited to win Tricksy over had been first butchered by Topher, then later butchered to unrecognizability in the song.

The dear that I adore
Devoted to mon amour.

Those were the original words. They'd been in church that morning all those years ago, which is the only reason Will could fathom Topher had tacked on the notion of worship and divinity. It had completely wrangled the rhyme of Will's verse. But as he hadn't been the one to deliver the words, he really couldn't be the one to complain.

Though Will did complain a week later when his brother further butchered his poem about Tricksy when Topher used it to steal a kiss from Judy Cartwright beneath the bleachers where everyone could see. Then everyone hastened to run and tell Tricksy, who had been inconsolable.

Will knew, because he'd been the shoulder she'd cried on. He'd wanted to tell her not to cry over his brother. He'd wanted to tell her that the words she'd thought belonged only to her, and not to Judy Cartwright, and later Bess Goodman, and then a little later beyond that Delia Thomas, had been written expressly for her. By him.

But Will knew telling Tricksy the whole truth would bring her nothing but even more pain. As a conflict avoider, Will wasn't willing to take that step. But also as the man in love with Tricksy, he couldn't bear the thought of causing her a single second of upset.

For the past few years, Will had found Tricksy in the dive bars she'd performed in and sat in the back and listened to her voice. The places had gotten seedier and seedier as the years had gone by. But her voice always rang true. Except for right now.

This song wasn't her. She wasn't a pop singer. Nothing Tricksy James did was in line with the synthesizing and syncopated beats of a Top Forties song because she was far too unique to even be considered on that list.

He'd watched her face as she sang. All of the joy had seeped out of Tricksy's eyes as she'd bopped to the beat. The notes fell flat to his ears. But the people around him continued to dance and sing along, further muting her voice.

Will stood to leave. In all his years of checking in on Tricksy, she had never once caught him lurking in the background. Now, with this upbeat tune that belied her voice, he didn't want her to catch him baring witness to the scene.

This wasn't the life she'd told him she wanted all those years ago. She was settling, something she told him she'd never do. Something he himself had never done.

Except when it came to her.

Will had settled for her friendship when he'd wanted her soul. He'd settled for her kindness when he'd wanted her passion. And now he was turning his back on her when she was clearly in distress.

He turned back and was instantly enthralled by her face as she sang. She might not enjoy the words she was singing, but she loved singing. The sight made Will eager to do something he said he'd never do again. He wanted to give Tricksy his words to sing.

Tricksy's gumption had inspired Will to stick to his own guns. He was the only Matthews boy who hadn't gone into the service. But he still had his wings.

Flying commercial airplanes had given him a sense of belonging in his family of Air Force pilots. Like all his brothers, Will loved soaring high. The possibility of shooting an enemy down had never sat well with him. Instead, he spent his time getting people safely where they needed to go for work, for pleasure, for family.

His downtime between flights allowed him to pursue his hobby of poetry. The poems had piled up over the years. Until he'd had enough to publish in a book. His debut would be releasing soon and Will would be hanging up his wings for a new career.

The weight of his decision forced him back down in his chair. If he'd had the courage to reach for a dream he never considered making come true, perhaps now was the time to reach for the woman that had always been there when he'd closed his eyes.

Will sat in the darkness of the club and listened to the only woman he'd ever loved sing a song about having a one-night stand. He had just about had enough when a guy approached the stage and began to get handsy.

Will looked over to the security. The buff guy who had manned the door was now eying a girl in a miniskirt who looked far too young to be in here. He was not paying the artist on stage any mind. Nor the fan that was too attentive.

The bartender was filling drinks. A man off to the side in a suit, who looked like he might own the dismal dive, was all smiles at the performance on and off the stage. He looked like he was in no hurry to come to the songstress's aid. In fact, he looked like he approved of the show.

That was enough for Will. He couldn't leave Tricksy in distress. Will rose from his table.

He made his way through the writhing bodies on the dance floor. More than one woman tried to sway him into a dance. Will sidestepped them all until he reached his target.

He tapped the guy on his shoulder. The man didn't even turn to glance at Will. His hands were still trying to grab at Tricksy who fought him off while still maintaining her pitch.

Will felt anger boil up in him. It was short lived as all anger was with him. In the foster care system, he'd always managed to stay invisible. In a house full of alpha males, he was never bothered to take a back seat. He knew from the short time he spent with his parents in North Korea that if one person fought, the entire family would be hurt. His father had fought back and his mother had been killed for his efforts.

Words were the best weapons in situations like these. Will's fist unfurled and came to hang loosely by his side. Yet somehow, the burly man went tumbling back.

Will stepped aside to let the man fall to the ground. He looked up to find Tricksy's fist extended. Just as everyone knew not to cross a

Matthews boy, or a Silver sister, high up there was the warning to never, ever, cross a James girl.

The bar descended into chaos as the music stopped and the man flailed on the filthy floor. Tricksy's eyes landed on him.

"Will?"

She reached for him. Will caught her up, lifting her down off the stage and into his arms. She stared up at him in wonder. For a brief moment, Will experienced a moment of nirvana. He had everything in his life that he'd ever coveted right here in his arms.

"Is Topher here?" she asked.

And then it all came crashing down at the mention of his brother's name.

CHAPTER FOUR

ricksy's voice felt hollow. Her chest felt empty and her soul weary. It was mostly from the song that had been shoved down her throat. But that didn't account for her sore hand. The skin at her knuckles smarted where she'd connected with the handsy man wanting a private dance.

It should've been evident to him that she wasn't *that* kind of performer. For one, she had on all her clothes. For two, she could hit the high notes without a synthesizer. But all Mr. Handsy heard was another person's lyrics which, to his brain, suggested that he could shoot his shot.

Well, if you shoot your shot at a country girl, raised by a drug addicted mother, who'd grown up in foster care, you would get exactly what you deserved. And that was lying flat on your backside with your meaty hand clutching at your bloody nose.

Somewhere in the midst of the indignation and the ache in her hand, Tricksy felt like she was floating. She felt secure. Safe. Protected. Cared for.

There was a delightful smell of spice that made her feel rejuvenated. Spice and something musty, like old books. Its mix of scents reminded her of home. The only home that had been a constant in her life. The Bright Horizons Foster Care.

But that couldn't be right. Bright Horizons smelled of harsh chemicals that didn't quite mask the unclean smell of bedwetters and unwashed bodies. Though there had been a few books on a shelf in the common room. One person had always been sitting on the floor beneath those shelves with his nose in a book.

That's what she was smelling. That corner and the boy at the bookshelf. She'd had a few hugs from that boy when she was feeling down. He always seemed to be there when she was sad and needed a shoulder.

Tricksy was wrapped up in someone's arms now. But this was a man's arms. Not a boy's. Still, there was no mistaking the scent of him. No mistaking the feel of Will Matthews.

A memory of leaning into Will hit her mind. Topher had forgotten about a date they'd planned. He'd kept her waiting for a half hour, but Will had been there. He'd sat next to her and allowed her to lean on him. At some point, he'd wrapped an arm around her and they sat just like that.

Will had always given the best hugs. He was gentle, but strong. The kind of man a girl could trust.

In reality, Will Matthews was a unicorn. He wasn't the kind of man that songs were written about. Because no one would ever believe he was real.

But he was. And he was holding onto Tricksy, giving her his magical strength and quiet comfort.

In that comfort, there was one thing Tricksy knew. Wherever Will was, Topher was not far behind. The two of them had been inseparable in their youth. Though Tricksy had always suspected that it was Will who attached himself to Topher's hip. Because where Topher always managed to find trouble that he would solve with his fists, Will's calm head would always prevail by talking the offended party down until a peace treaty was reached... or long enough for his other brothers to join the fray.

"Is Topher here?"

Will's hold loosened on her. But not before it tightened for a brief second. Or maybe that was Tricksy's imagination?

"No," Will said, releasing his hold on her. "It's just me."

There was a hint of resignation in his voice. But that had always been there. Will was the quietest of the Matthews boys. Always keeping to the shadows. It was no wonder he'd latched onto Topher, who was loud and talkative.

Tricksy had always liked sitting next to Will at the foster care dinner table. She never had to say anything to him. She never had to make her voice louder than his, like she had to do with her sisters. It had been so long since she'd had a moment of quiet.

"You broke my nose!"

The shout didn't come from the floor because the handsy private dancer was stumbling to his feet. He reached for Tricksy. Before she could put up her dukes to deliver another deserving blow, she was tucked out of the way and behind Will's back.

Mr. Handsy threw a punch. That punch would've landed right at Will's right eye. But in his quiet and careful way, Will simply stepped aside. The punch flew through air and the momentum sent Mr. Handsy crashing down into a table full of guests and drinks.

Glass splattered to the floor. The table gave out under his weight and split in two. Girls screamed as their dresses were doused with cheap alcohol. Guys leaped out of the way as their pristine, expensive sneakers were threatened by the brown liquid and fruity concoctions.

"That's it, James. You're outta here!"

Tricksy whirled around to face Ronny. She opened her mouth to protest, to fight. But all the fight had gone out of her. Mainly because her throat was still sore from belting out the hit song. The truth was, Tricksy wanted to get out of there.

She reached out to the left, but Foxy wasn't there to take her hand. She reached out to the right, but Savy was nowhere to be found. She took a step back and a strong arm came around her.

Will's forearm pulled her into his strong chest. He shifted his weight and pulled her into his side. Tricksy's body sagged into his, letting him take all her weight as he gave her his strength.

She was done being strong. She was done lifting her chin up and pretending everything was okay. She was done doing it on her own.

This had been her last shot at a break. She was low on funds. She wasn't going to get paid for tonight. Ronny would surely deduct this destruction of his property from her cut, and she was likely to owe more since she was being paid so low.

She had no idea what to do. But right now it didn't matter, because she wasn't the one holding herself up. It was Will. And once again, like when she had had her spirit broken, he let her lean on him.

CHAPTER FIVE

ill kept a hand around Tricksy's waist as they made their way to the back of the club to get her things. He slung her travel bag over his shoulder, noticing how light the bag was. He said nothing to her about it. As a frequent flyer himself, he'd learned the art of packing only the essentials. But he would admit, his carryon was twice as heavy as Tricksy's pink rolling duffle bag.

Instead of commenting on it, he carried the excess baggage on his back, and he reached for her with his free hand. Tricksy came willingly. She seemed too dazed and exhausted to protest. She hadn't said another word after being fired from the dive bar. Will hadn't seen her this silent since the day Topher broke up with her.

Just as she had that fateful day, Tricksy rested her head against Will's chest. Her steps matched his as they crossed the threshold out the back door. The moon was high in the sky. The night filled with the sound of revelry that came from Friday night fun seekers. When they came to a stop at a streetlight in the parking lot, Tricksy shut her eyes to the yellow spotlight.

That's when he knew all wasn't well. For any James sister to turn away from a spotlight meant that something was wrong. "Tricks?"

Tricksy let out a long, low sigh. The sound was weary and off key. It came from somewhere deep in her belly. When she was done, her shoulders slumped as though she'd emptied her body of every last bit of breath she'd carried for a while.

"Tricks, you okay?"

She didn't lift her head. She didn't open her eyes. She took in another deep breath, and let it out long and low like the first one. She looked defeated.

"Hey, don't let that jerk get you down. You're too good for this place. I'm sure you have other gigs lined up."

She snorted at that. "No one else wants me."

The reply was on the tip of his tongue."

"All the clubs want a pop singer in a mini-skirt. That's not me."

No, it wasn't her. Tricksy was a fan of the 1940s era pin-up girl. Many of her dresses now and when she was younger had a cinched waist with a flaring skirt. The striped dress she wore tonight brought the eye down to her long legs. Even though they were covered from her waist down to her calves, it still let the mind wonder.

Her hair was always in curls pinned atop her head. The swoops and lulls of her lustrous hair would make a man dizzy if he followed the curves around her head. Her lipstick was always a vibrant red that gave a man ideas that weren't always gentlemanly.

Not Will. He had been raised a gentleman. He averted his gaze from Tricksy's mouth and looked her in the eye. Her gaze was watery, but not a single tear had spilled. That left her dark eye liner giving her catlike eyes an even more exaggerated flare. It was her lips that still slanted downward into a frown.

The sight only served to make his heart squeeze. He could never stand to see this woman sad. Which is why he fed his brother the lines that he knew would make Tricksy's romantic heart smile.

Will had often come to her rescue when they were younger. Oftentimes when his brother forgot about a date he'd made with her. Having a girlfriend hadn't ranked high on Topher's everyday to do list.

Tricksy was the first thing Will thought of each morning that he woke up. She was his last thought every night. Even now, he thought about her at least every ten minutes throughout the day. Her happiness and contentment meant more to Will than his own. So, when he realized that Tricksy only had eyes for his brother, Will decided that she would have him.

"Let me take you home," he said to her now. "Where do you live?"

That rattled her. She stepped away from him. She looked up at him, but not directly into his eyes. She looked at his ears.

Will had quietly studied Tricksy all of his younger years. He knew that that look, that slight avoidance of meeting his eyes, meant she was about to skirt the truth.

"I'm between places right now," she said.

"Where are you headed next?"

"I don't have a gig lined up. But I should be getting a call soon." She focused on his other ear.

From that, Will knew she was both homeless and without any prospects. He racked his brain trying to figure out away to give her money without it seeming like charity. With them both being foster kids, he knew how much she loathed the idea of a hand out.

"Wait, Will?" She met his eyes then. One of her catlike eyes lifted, as though she was taking him in for the first time tonight. "What are you doing here?"

Will's gaze slipped to Tricksy's right ear. "I was on a layover. I was looking through the local paper's entertainment section for something to do, and saw your name on a billboard and decided to come see an old friend."

That was mostly true. He was on a layover, but only because he specifically looked up where she was performing and got on that particular flight rotation.

"Where are you flying off to next?"

Will glanced at her other ear. "Home."

"You're headed back to Flying Cross?"

"My presence has been requested. I'm sure yours has been, too."

"Why?" Tricksy's hand landed on his chest in a jerky motion. "What's happened? I thought your dad was okay."

Haran Matthews had suffered a heart attack a couple months ago. The old man had overworked himself out on the ranch by himself. But now he had a full house of orphans and foster kids to help shoulder the work, thanks to Joe and Savy moving the Bright Horizons Foster Care Home into the Matthews' old bunkhouse.

"Dad's okay."

The relief on her face was instant. Tricksy's hand fell away from his chest. Will had to stop himself from catching her wrist and holding her hand there.

"I'm headed back for the wedding," Will continued.

"Which of the Silver sisters is getting married this time?"

"They're all married."

"No kidding?"

"It's your sisters' wedding."

Tricksy blinked. "Charlie and Savy are finally gonna do it, huh?"

"I said sisters, plural. Charlie and Savy and Joe and Foxy."

Again, Tricksy blinked.

"They didn't tell you?"

Tricksy looked down. With that look, it appeared that no one had. The next words out of Will's mouth shocked them both.

"Come home with me."

CHAPTER SIX

*T*ricksy watched Will's lips move as he formed the words. There were tons of words coming from his lips. Words like *married, sisters, home.*

Instead of focusing on the words he was saying, she chose to focus on Will's mouth. Will had nice lips. Not the thin lips he'd had as a child. Or at least she thought they were thin? Had she noticed?

No, she definitely hadn't. Because if she had, she would've seen how plump Will's lips were. The top one was perfectly symmetrical on both sides as it formed the top part of a heart.

No, not a heart. A bow string. Because Will was a Matthews. Those boys were all warriors to their core. Fighters ready to step into battle.

Except Will. Will had never been the first to run into a fight. But he had done a lot of talking. Talking with that mouth. And those lips.

She would've noticed that bottom lip. It was as plush as a pillow. Not a motel room pillow that she was used to sleeping in for these past few years. No, it would've been a five-star hotel pillow that stayed plump and firm even after someone flounced back onto it.

Will's bottom lip looked sturdy enough for a woman to fling herself at him. He'd catch her with that bottom lip. Trap her in the bow of his top lip. And hold her securely.

Tricksy shook her head. Firstly, because what the heck was she doing waxing poetic about Will Matthews's lips? But secondly, and most importantly, she did not wax poetic. She wrote angsty songs of heartbreak and loss at the hands of Mr. Wrong. Not flowery ballads of kissing Mr. Good Guy.

And Will Matthews was definitely Mr. Good Guy. He was *the* good guy. Mr. Good Guy with some seriously kissable lips. She would be willing to bet a lot of women appreciated the way those lips would move across theirs.

But no. Will wasn't a player. He likely had a steady girlfriend even now. One he would never consider cheating on. One who was likely missing having his kissable lips pressed against hers.

Topher was an excellent kisser. Tricksy had thoroughly enjoyed the way his lips had moved across hers. But she couldn't remember what his lips looked like. She was having trouble even grasping exactly what they felt like. Even though she sang about how his lips had done her wrong in her songs.

Had Topher's lips been thin or heart-shaped like Will's? Had they been wide like Will's or just a small slash in his face? Tricksy couldn't remember. How could she not remember her one true love's lips?

"Tricks? Do you want to come home with me?"

There were so many emotions roiling around in Tricksy's head and in her heart. Home? Did she want to go home? She hadn't been home in over a year. And the last time she was there, she'd fought with her sister Savy.

And now Savy was getting married. That wasn't a surprise. Savy and Charlie Matthews had been engaged since they were twelve. What was a surprise was Foxy's engagement. And to Joe Matthews, of all people?

Whereas Savy and Tricksy had been engaged in a silent war, Foxy had been in contact with Tricksy. Foxy had failed to mention she was even dating Joe, much less marrying the guy.

Foxy had declared herself Switzerland in the cold war between her two older sisters. But Tricksy supposed now her younger sister had chosen sides, and once again Tricksy been left to go it alone.

Will reached a hand to her forearm. His strong fingers wrapped around her flesh and squeezed. With just that singular touch, Tricksy felt instant relief.

It had always been like this with Will. He'd always brought her comfort. Topher didn't like dealing with her emotions, and Tricksy James was an emotional woman.

Her ex always tapped his foot when she tried to have a heart to heart with him. He'd constantly tried to change the subject when she wanted to discuss her feelings.

But Will? Will would always listen intently to her every emotion, be it happiness or sorrow.

"You don't have to go," Will was saying.

He pulled her in for another hug. Tricksy didn't protest the affection. She felt like a well that had been empty for years. Will was filling her to the brim with just his presence.

"I'll fly you wherever you want to go," he said.

Tricksy didn't want to go anywhere. She wanted to stay wrapped up in Will's embrace. A funny thought settled in her scrambled brain. That thought was that Will Matthews, with his spicy-musty-book scent and his huggalicious arms, was as good as being at home.

"I want to go home," she said.

Will squeezed tighter. Tricksy did the same. They stood like that for long moments.

Tricksy pulled back to look at him. She had to blink a couple of times. In her memories, Will still had baby fat around his cheeks. That was gone and what was left was chiseled features. A strong jaw. Two compassionate eyes. And those kissable lips.

She gave herself another shake. At this rate, she should worry about getting brain damage with all the shaking going on. In her mind, the image of Will blipped between him as a kid and him as a man. When she looked back up at him, only the man remained.

Tricksy stepped out of his embrace.

Will shoved his hands into his pockets. The movement brought attention to his chest. There had been no definition there when he was a kid or a teen. He'd been scrawny and malnourished. She remembered the day he'd arrived at the foster home. Soon after, he and his grandfather had escaped with their lives from North Korea. Will had lost his parents to the regime. A few weeks in America, and he'd lost his grandfather, too.

He'd been nothing but skin and bones back then. He hadn't known much English. But when a book had been placed in his hands, he'd gobbled up the language and soon spoke it better than all the other kids who'd been born in the country.

That skinny kid with little to say was a thing of the past. Will Matthews was all defined muscles and sure words now. A solid chest poked against the front of his shirt, stringing the buttons. A six pack poked at the bottom of his shirt just above his buckle. And those lips kept saying the most comforting things to her.

"Topher will probably be coming home soon for the weddings."

And now her ex was added into the mix. Well, at the worst-case scenario, she needed to write some new songs. And the artist who suffered was the one who made the most beautiful art.

CHAPTER SEVEN

Their suitcases lay side by side. Neither were large. Both would easily pass the new carryon regulations airplanes gave for luggage stored in the overhead compartments.

Most of Tricksy's life had been as a performer on the road. Will knew she was fond of both clothes and shoes. It awed him, at the same time as it worried him, that her life had been reduced down to the size of a carryon.

For Will, this was a necessity of his job as a commercial airline pilot. His former job as a commercial airline pilot. He'd have to get used to saying that.

He waited for the twinge of loss to come at having to hang up his wings. His pulse was steady at the thought. His heart jumped at the sharp, unexpected turn his life was now taking. Especially in light of the passenger he handed into the seat beside him.

Will slid his suitcase over a nudge, giving Tricksy's prime real estate in the trunk of his car. He took a moment to stare down at the two vessels laying side by side. Her pink case and his utilitarian black case. They did not look like they belonged together, but they fit snuggly one beside the other.

Before he'd pulled onto the main road, Tricksy's eyes had closed. She'd been out like a light before they'd turned onto the highway. Will had been hoping to talk to her, to catch up, to simply listen to the sound of her voice.

He made sure to hide the CD recording she'd made of her demo years ago. Even though the disc was years old and well traveled, it had not a single scratch on the surface. Despite being played on a daily basis.

As Will drove into the darkness of night, he couldn't help but notice the bags under Tricksy's eyes. She hadn't been sleeping well. The only time he'd seen any life in her eyes had been when she was up on the stage singing about her heartbreak over his brother.

It troubled him that she still carried the burden of that pain all these years later. He'd once read in a *Cosmo* article that the time it took to get over a breakup was the duration of the relationship plus half. By that calculation, Tricksy should've been over Topher years ago. The entirety of the affair had barely lasted a couple of months.

Despite all of her assurances that she was fine, Will knew that she still suffered. The joy and satisfaction at seeing her last night and hearing her sing dissipated under the burden of her sadness. It was a weight he could not bear. He knew what he had to do.

At the next exit, Will pulled over at a rest stop. The gravel under the wheels was loud to his ears as the car came to a slow stop. The gentle hum of tractor trailer engines made his ear drums ache when he pulled the keys from the ignition.

A glance at Tricksy showed she still slept fitfully. That was a good thing. He didn't want her to witness what he was about to do.

Stepping out of the car, Will put a good bit of distance between himself and his car. Though he didn't go so far that Tricksy was out of his line of sight. He pulled out his cellphone and tapped his favorites contacts. His father held spot number one. Will tapped on number two.

He had to hit redial a couple of times to escape the voice message. Finally, on the third try, Topher picked up.

"Do you have any idea what time it is over here?" came his brother's gruff reply.

Topher Matthews was not a morning person. He wasn't a night person either. The man could catnap all day if left to his own devices. Which served him as a soldier; the ability to grab rest whenever there was downtime, and be wide awake during every other hour of the day.

"I need you to come home," said Will.

"I already told Charlie that I'll try and get time off for the wedding. But I can't guarantee it."

Topher's voice was gruff with sleep. But it sounded like he was pulling the phone away from his face with those last words. Which could mean that he thought the conversation was over and he was about to hang up.

"Toph," Will called into the line. When he realized he'd raised his voice, he raised his head. But Tricksy hadn't stirred in the passenger seat. "It's not for Charlie and Sav."

"Yeah, I know. Joe and Foxy are getting married, too." Topher's voice was louder, letting Will know that he hadn't put the phone down. Unfortunately, it was now even more disgruntled.

"Not for them either. For Tricksy."

There was a pause. Followed by a grumble in the shape of a sigh. "Tricksy's getting married?"

There was a pang in Will's heart at that notion of Tricksy getting married. Will knew Tricksy could never be his, not when her heart belonged to his brother. But he had never thought through the idea of her being completely off limits once some other man put a ring on her finger.

"No," said Will. "She's not getting married. She's coming home."

Another unintelligible grumble sounded from the receiver. There was a ruffle of sheets. At least Will now had his brother's full attention.

"I think it would do her good to see you," said Will.

"Why? She hates my guts."

"She doesn't hate you." Will pressed his lips together before uttering his next words. "I think she's still in love with you."

There was silence on the other end of the line. Will thought Topher might've hung up. Or fallen back asleep.

"We both know that's not possible," came Topher's reply. "I'm not the man she thinks I am."

"But you could be."

"No, I couldn't be. Because it's you."

Now it was Will's turn to let out a low sigh. Though his sigh sounded less like a bear prematurely woken from hibernation, and more like a bear trying to catch a salmon swimming upstream.

"Why don't you just tell her the truth, bro. Tell her that it was you that wrote those poems. It was you who told me what to say. It's you that she fell in love with. I was just your stand in."

"Toph-"

"I'm not gonna be your Serious de Burke anymore."

"Cyrano de Bergerac. And you would've been Christian, the man Roxanne was in love with."

"Whatever. I'm not doing it. I don't want to be in a relationship. I'm not cut out for them."

"That's not true."

The silence on the other end of the line was pointed. Will could swear he saw Topher's brow raise on the cellphone's face.

"You're a great guy," Will said.

"Yeah, I know. And so do a lot of women. I'd like to keep it that way. Go put your big nose in somebody else's love life. Preferably your own."

"Did you just call me big nose?"

"Are you gonna keep pretending to be a man unworthy of love?"

"Wow, Toph, that was kind of poetic."

"It's what you get when you pull me out of a good dream. I'm hanging up on you and going back to sleep. Go tell Roxanne how you feel, Big Nose."

And with that, Topher hung up the phone.

For long moments, all Will could do was stare down at the device. His sole obstacle for telling Tricksy his true feelings had been removed. He could march up to the car, wake her from her dreams, and tell her that his heart was hers.

CHAPTER EIGHT

ricksy had slept in many a car over the course of her career. She'd fought her sisters over seats in their mom's beat up Chevy when they were kids traveling on the road. The fight was always over the right back passenger seat because the left back passenger seat had a spring loose in the side of the seat.

She'd rock, paper, scissored who would get night driving duty when she and her sisters were a singing trio. She'd hurried onto discount buses, aiming for a seat just a few rows behind the middle where she wouldn't hear the door opening and closing of the main door with each stop, and she would be far enough away from the bathroom and wouldn't get a whiff of something unpleasant as she tried to slumber.

Car sleeping had always been a chore. But this ride was the smoothest she'd ever been on. When the sun tickled her cheek from the passenger side window, she came to wakefulness slowly, eagerly, without a crick in her neck or a protest in her spine. She felt absolutely rejuvenated, like she'd slept on a thousand count sheets in a five-star hotel.

Even better, this hotel had room service. The smell of eggs and bacon greeted her nose, along with the aroma of a strong brewed cup of coffee. Tricksy wondered if she'd died and gone to heaven at some point on the highway.

"Good morning."

A comfortable cushion, a delectable breakfast, and the gentlest wake up call any girl could ask for? Yes, this was heaven. Will Matthews smiled at her from the driver's seat. His gaze on her was observant and kind. Never leering or calculating. The woman who caught Will's heart would never have hers broken. No, she'd always have a strong and comfortable set of arms to hold her, kind words whispered in her ear, and an attentive man to see to her every need.

Lucky girl.

"We're home."

Tricksy looked out the car window as Will set the food on her lap. Sure enough, she saw the small town of Honor Valley. The town's main street was bustling with a crowd of at least ten people walking on either side of the road. The tallest building was only three stories high, nothing like the skyscrapers of the major cities she'd toured in. Pedestrians waited at the crosswalk while trucks came to a full stop to let them cross without need of a flashing sign.

There was the pizza parlor where she and her sisters would sing for change on the street.

There was the ice cream shop their mom had taken them to and left them one time when she went to score and forgot her maternal duties.

There was the one-screen movie theater where she and Topher had their first date.

"You okay, Tricks?"

"Yeah." Before Will could ask her anymore questions, Tricksy took a sip of coffee and then gave the most pleasurable sigh in her life. "It's perfect."

It was an honest answer. The coffee was perfect. A strong, light brown roast with one cream and four sugars.

"A little bit of coffee with your sugar," said Will. "I remember."

He did indeed. And since he'd put at least half a cup of sugar in the beverage, Tricksy wouldn't have to be embarrassed about how much she put in.

"We got in a little late and I figured they'd be finished with breakfast at the ranch and out doing chores. I didn't want you to starve while you waited for lunch."

"Thanks, Will. That was thoughtful."

But that was Will. Always thoughtful. Always attentive.

Whereas she'd been a bad friend. Every time Topher had disappointed her, Will had been there. Yet she hadn't once thought to reach out to him after their breakup all those years ago.

Well, that was ending now. She needed a friend like Will in her life. She needed to be a friend.

She just wasn't sure how to go about it? Every man who'd come into her life always wanted something from her. Usually something she wasn't willing to give. Will had never asked her for anything. What could she possibly give him?

"Tricks… there's something I've been meaning to tell you."

"Yeah?" she asked when the silence stretched. But her attention was diverted to a billboard across the street on the door of the local bar. There was an announcement for the bar's regular talent night. "I can't believe they still have that."

On those nights, the twenty-one and over bar allowed families and young children onto the stools to sample the town's talents. Fond memories hit Tricksy of her and her sisters singing in the show. She and her sisters always got the most applause when they sang together. Tricksy had even done a few solo acts on that stage. It was where she'd debuted the breakup ballad about Topher.

At first she'd been met with stunned silence. Likely because everyone in the audience knew who the song was about. But on the last note, the crowd -of mostly women- were on their feet.

Tricksy had insisted on including the song in their act. Savy had scoffed. They sang upbeat, happy songs. Lots of show tunes that catered to her alto voice. But Tricksy had gotten a taste of what it felt like to have applause for her own creation, and she wanted more of the accolades.

It was around that time that she and her sisters had performed together less and less. It had also been the time when she'd been going through her breakup with Topher and she didn't want to sing any happy songs.

"You're thinking about him, aren't you?"

Tricksy turned back to Will. She knew she didn't have to clarify who. Not with Will. He'd been there through all of it.

But the truth was, Tricksy hadn't been thinking about Topher. Not really. That breakup was always somewhere near the front of her mind. Today that particular dissolution wasn't what caused the pang in her heart.

"I think I've been on my own too long," she said.

"You do?"

"I think it's time I do something about that."

"Really?"

"Yeah." Tricksy turned from the bar and the old memories. She faced Will. There was a light in his eyes and a smile full of expectation on his face. Seemed he was happy with her decision as well. "I'm gonna work on my relationship with my sisters."

"Oh?" Will blinked and his smile wobbled.

Tricksy cringed. She'd done it again. She'd leaned in on Will's shoulder and went on and on about her problems, when he'd wanted to talk to her about something.

"I'm sorry, Will. What was it you wanted to tell me?"

"That we should get a move on if we want to make it to the ranch before sundown."

CHAPTER NINE

He hadn't blown it. Will had to stop thinking that. He just had to find the perfect way to tell her his feelings. Along with the fact that he'd coached Topher all those years ago.

The moment sitting parked on Main Street had not been that moment. Not with all the memories of her past and his coming out of the shadows and into the sunlight at every street corner.

His words could wait. They could wait because right now, Tricksy was singing. She'd finished her breakfast and coffee and was now singing along to the radio.

She'd turned on an old, jazzy station on the car's radio. Tricksy's voice drowned out the accomplished singer who had sold out stadium seating. They were now her background singer as she took center stage in the passenger seat of his car. He only wished he could record this impromptu performance right now and play it back for the rest of his days.

Tricksy bopped in her seat, shimmying her shoulders. Her voice was light and airy as though she had no care in the world. Like the past that had weighed on her shoulders only moments ago had flitted away like a kaleidoscope of butterflies.

He drove in the slow lane and took the long route home. Tricksy didn't seem to mind. He doubted she even noticed. All too soon, the sight of the Flying Cross Ranch came into view.

The place looked the same, but different in the noonday sun. The porch needed a fresh coat of paint. There were a few pieces of wood missing from the fence in the north pasture. Though the bunkhouse looked as though it had gotten some care since his time there.

Will knew that that's where the new batch of foster kids was staying. The five kids living there were a mixed bunch. In race and ethnicity like he and his brothers, but also in gender. That had been a sore spot when Charlie and Joe had tried to get their adoptive parents to also adopt the James girls.

Will never knew why his parents wouldn't budge on the matter. But they never turned the girls away when they came by.

Now, two James girls would live on the ranch, becoming Matthews themselves. And the third was coming to stay for a time. If Will had his way, Tricksy would have a permanent place on the ranch -a place at his side.

Looking up at the big house, Will expected to see his father and brothers out in the pastures, but there was no one in sight. He knew they had to be here because he saw his father's old truck in the drive. Perhaps they were all in the house for a late lunch?

Rounding the car, Will handed Tricksy out. She wrapped her fingers around his, pressing their palms together. The jolt went all the way through his body on down to his toes. He kept hold of her fingers as she stepped into the rich soil in her heels. As they climbed the porch steps, he didn't neglect the fact that their fingers were still entwined.

Tricksy squeezed his hand as though he were a lifeline. She was likely nervous to see her sisters again. Will would take that. He would be her strength now. He would lend it to her indefinitely.

He opened the door and was met with even more silence. It was odd. The house had always been filled with noise. And now that there were new foster kids here, it should be even louder than when he and his brothers were boys.

No sooner had Will had the thought, then a chorus of shouts rang out from every corner of the house.

"Surprise!"

Will clutched Tricksy to his chest. They both looked around wildly at the people who materialized from the stairs, the hall, and the kitchen. There were only a few faces that Will recognized; namely his father's old wizened face and his brother, Joe.

There were a handful of kids that eyed them skeptically. The kids were indeed made up of all shapes, sizes, and colors. There was a brown-skinned girl with long braids hanging over her shoulders. Her gaze was the most skeptical as she eyed Will and Tricksy. The other three kids were boys. The tallest fairly glared at the two of them. While the dark-haired one and the blond haired one looked on in awe. Not at Will, at Tricksy, who he still held firmly and securely in his arms.

"OMG, I knew it!"

That came from Foxy.

"I saw this," she said as she materialized from behind a closet door. She pointed a finger at Will and Tricksy. "Didn't I tell you I saw this, Joe?"

"Will, what are you two doing here?" asked Joe. "We weren't expecting you for days. We weren't expecting you at all, Tricks."

In his arms, Tricksy bristled. If they weren't expecting them, then who had they shouted surprise for?

"I was expecting you," said Foxy, grabbing her sister's hands. But Tricksy didn't let go of Will. "I saw you two together in one of my visions a few days ago. Actually, it was years ago, but you -in real life- were so convinced that you were in love with Topher. But, you know what, to tell you the truth, I was convinced my true love was someone else when it was Joe all along. So, this makes total sense, doesn't it?"

Tricksy looked at Will. Will looked at Joe. They all looked at Foxy.

Will had forgotten how trying it could be to follow Foxy when she spoke. Especially when she spoke about her psychic abilities. Even more especially when Foxy only got her predictions right about half the time. Will that hoped this was one of those times she was half right.

"Now we all three can get married," Foxy was saying. "Can you picture it? All three Jameses on a stage again. Well, an altar. It'll be epic."

Tricksy let go of Will's hand then. She clasped onto her sister's hands at those words. Will wanted to clasp onto Foxy's hands at that sentiment. Because he could picture it; he could picture himself at the altar with Tricksy.

Will looked at his father. The old man watched the scene play out with his trademark look of quiet contemplation. Will ached to know his father's true thoughts about this matter.

"Wait?" said Foxy. "Am I getting ahead of myself? Has Will even popped the question yet?"

Tricksy opened her mouth, but no words came out. Will wanted to fill the silence.

"You do know he's always been in love with you, right?" Foxy continued.

Tricksy turned to Will with wide eyes. Will's first instinct was to deny it. But it was the truth.

"Oh, no. It looks like he hasn't. So you won't be getting married with us. Such a shame," Foxy sighed. "I was all ready for the James sisters to be a trio again."

Behind them, the door opened again. Savy and Charlie entered with a little girl between them. Everyone scrambled to shout surprise again, but the effect was disjointed. The little girl didn't seem to care. She bolted into the house and jumped into Father Matthews' arms.

"Tricksy?" said Savy. "What are you doing here? And Will, is that you?"

"Yes," said Tricksy, coming to stand by Will's side and taking his hand. "We're here together. We're… together."

CHAPTER TEN

The show must go on. That was the saying in show business. It was a saying Fanny James often slurred after she'd fallen off the stage, or was bowing down to the porcelain gods when the drugs were running rampant in her system.

Though none of her daughters had much respect for their mother, they did have respect for that rule. And so, despite the unexpected guests showing up, despite the botched surprise, as well as the surprising new relationship that was unveiled, the show had to go on.

But this wasn't Tricksy and Will's show. It was the little girl, Daria's, show.

Tricksy hadn't met Daria the last time she'd come home, when Savy and Foxy were still living in the Bright Horizons Foster Home. She hadn't met any of this new batch of kids who all must have arrived sometime within the last year.

Daria, who was the youngest of the new foster kids, had been taken away from Savy some time ago. After a legal battle with the state home, and the finalization of adoption paperwork of Daria's older brother, the kid was finally able to return to her forever home.

A twinge knotted in Tricksy's belly. Someplace deeper than where the butterflies lay in rest. She'd never had a home to call her own. Her early life had been far too unstable for that.

Like her sisters, Tricksy had dreamed of coming to live at the Flying

Cross Ranch, marrying one of the Matthews, and never leaving. That dream was coming true for Savy and Foxy. It was even coming true for all these new foster kids.

Once again, Tricksy would be the odd one out. Left to fly solo after her brief gig here. And because this wasn't the Tricksy show, she had to step aside and let the light shine on the little girl.

As everyone showered love and praise on Daria, Savy kept sneaking furtive glances at Tricksy and Will. Tricksy did not let go of Will's hand. Not for a single second. She was sure if she did that, Savy would see through the whole thing.

Tricksy didn't understand her need to impress her sister. To show Savy that she was her equal. And, in a lot of instances, to one up her.

No, wait. Tricksy did know why. It was because of that brow of Savy's. She raised it like it was the kind of armor that could pierce into the person it was aimed at. And it was always aimed at Tricksy.

Tricksy felt her knees knocking under her sister's stare. Her upper lip quivered under the weight of the lie she'd told. Her bottom lip was about to spill all. But something at her back stopped her.

Will slipped his hand from her death grip and slid it around her waist. His large, warm hand rested just off the center at the small of her back. It felt like an anchor. She was halfway into his embrace. All she needed to do was turn slightly, and she'd find herself fully in his embrace.

Tricksy turned, and she felt herself lock into place at the center of Will Matthews's chest. She looked up. Will smiled down at her.

He hadn't balked at her lie. He hadn't even twitched a brow. He truly was the most decent man she knew, and she was using him. Again.

Only a couple of hours ago, she'd pledged to be a better friend to him. To not use his shoulder as a tissue. Yet here she was again, physically leaning on him when her feelings were hurt.

As cake was being passed around, Tricksy gave Will a tug. He came willingly, though his gaze lingered for a quick second on the iced cake. They headed out onto the porch, out of earshot of everyone in the house.

The kids' glee at having cake in the afternoon could still be heard. So could the horses chomping down on their hay. The chickens Father Matthews kept treated the noonday sun like it was the early morning sun and the roosters crowed.

"I'm so sorry, Will. I don't know what came over me."

Will said nothing. He just lifted his head to the sky. The rays warmed his sun kissed face. The angles were sharp as the sun cast shadows under his eyes and beneath his chin.

"It's just that Foxy was talking about being together in the wedding, being a group again, and something in my head just snapped."

"You miss your sisters."

"I doh…" That lie wouldn't roll so easily off her tongue. "I'll tell them the truth."

Will said nothing. Only turned that piercing gaze on her. The rays of the sun softened as he looked down at her, chasing the shadows away.

"It won't be the first time Foxy got a prediction wrong," Tricksy said.

"She didn't get it wrong."

Now it was Tricksy who went quiet. The sun slipped from Will and shone its rays on her. She felt heat at her back, between her shoulder blades. She felt warmth between her brows.

"I have feelings for your, Tricks."

"Feelings?" She felt sweat in her palms, followed by an instant cooling.

"Beyond friendly ones. Far past sibling feelings." Will lifted his hand to just above his head. "They're right up against the border of love."

Part of Tricksy's brain itched for a pen and paper to write down the poetic words. It was her heart that was racing too fast to allow her to move.

Was she making this up? Was she hearing things? Topher had said lovely words to her before, and he'd never lived up to a single one.

Her fool heart should take a chill pill. But this was Will it was racing for. Will, who was kind and compassionate and had those kissable lips that she had just started to notice.

"You love me?" Tricksy asked.

Will inhaled slowly, deeply.

Tricksy felt the breath leave her body as she waited for his response. What did she want it to be? Did she want Will to love her? Did she love Will?

Of course, she didn't love Will. She loved Topher. Didn't she?

"Listen," he said finally. "You've already told them that we're together. So why don't we try it out?"

"Try out being together?"

"Well, marriage might be a little too soon." Will shrugged, his good-natured grin firmly in place.

That good-natured grin that featured his pillow soft lips. If they tried out being together, Tricksy could get the chance to kiss those lips. But what happened after the kiss?

After a few kisses and Topher had called it quits. He'd gone on to kiss other girls and Tricksy hadn't been kissed again. Instead, she'd written angry lyrics about a broken heart.

"I'd like to take your out for a romantic dinner, or a picnic in the woods, or a horseback ride on the trails. Just the two of us. We can talk and spend time alone and see if you might develop feelings for me that are stronger than friendly or sibling-ly."

Will's hand reached up to brush her temple. The sweat that had started to pool there cooled. Her shoulders relaxed as she leaned into his touch. She was meant to be answering his question, but all she could do was watch his lips. She wanted him to say more beautiful words to her.

She had been tricked by a man's beautiful words before. But this was Will. Will had always been decent and kind. If Will kissed her, he wouldn't call it quits soon after to go off kissing other girls. Because Will Matthews was the exact opposite of his brother.

Tricksy tilted her head up. Will's nostrils flared as he gazed down at her lips. She would answer him. She would give her answer just as soon as she tasted his lips to know for sure.

Will leaned down. Tricksy went up on her tiptoes. And then-

"Excuse us."

They sprang apart as Charlie and Joe darkened the porch door.

CHAPTER ELEVEN

*S*iblings were the worse. Will hadn't known that in his early days, having been born an only child. When he'd been brought to America and later placed into the foster care system, he'd had an adjustment to the noise of all the other kids. There was often a lot of silence and discipline in North Korea. There had never been a moment of quiet at the Bright Horizons Foster Home. Even less so in the Matthews's house.

His five brothers joyed in playing pranks while others were sleeping. But they never managed to wake Will from his silent nightmares. Not the ever present feeling of hunger pains that felt all too real in his dreams. Not the teeth clenching need to be silent less the government think your traitorous.

Will's parents had been traitors. They had both wanted to defect. When his father had had the chance, his mother had shoved Will into his arms. As the two males had gotten across the border, they learned his mother had been killed for their efforts.

Along with his parents and siblings. That was the way of the country. If one person rebelled, anyone connected with that person was killed.

So Will had learned it was best to stay silent, even when the nightmares came. Even when the dreams were good ones. Will's boyhood dreams had always been about Tricksy James. The girl with the big voice who wasn't afraid to use it.

Will wasn't even sleeping right now. He had Tricksy in his arms. He had everything in his life he'd ever wanted. He was about to have his first taste of his dream. So, of course, his brothers had to show up and ruin it all.

"Excuse me," Tricksy said before stepping down the porch and heading towards the horses.

It took everything in Will to let her go. He'd finally done it. He'd told her how he felt, and she hadn't laughed at him. She hadn't looked at him with pity.

Her nostrils had flared. A spark of curiosity had lit in those dark eyes of hers. Her gaze had landed on his mouth, as though she'd wanted to kiss him. He'd nearly kissed Tricksy James until his two nightmares of brothers ruined it.

Will wanted to turn to his brothers and curse them out using the foulest language he knew; and he knew a lot, having been raised in a state home and later around hardened soldiers. But he knew anger served no purpose other than to hurt the ones he loved. Besides, he couldn't take his gaze off Tricksy.

He'd finally told her how he felt. She hadn't run screaming. She hadn't shot him down. She'd seemed surprised... and interested. He knew he could've won her over if only he'd stolen that kiss.

"So, we're stealing our brother's girlfriends now, are we?"

Will rounded on Charlie, his fists clenched. "Tricksy and Topher were together for a few weeks years ago. Practically a decade."

Charlie's mouth fell slack. Will knew why. It was a rare occurrence indeed to hear Will raise his voice, or his fist.

Though his fists weren't raised. Just clenched. Still, it was more anger than anyone had seen from him in all his years at Flying Cross combined.

"Still," said Joe. "It's bro-code. You're breaking bro-code. Thou shalt not date his brother's ex."

"Fine." Will unclenched his fists and opened his palms towards his brother. "Show me the law book where that's written."

Joe and Charlie shared a look. The slack left Charlie's face and was replaced by a look of sheer mischief. Joe's brows lowered, like a gavel hammering out a final decree of judgement.

Will didn't have time for his brother's shenanigans. He turned back to the fields. But Tricksy was nowhere to be seen.

For a second, he panicked. Had she slipped through his fingers just when he'd gotten ahold of her?

Then he saw the door to the guest house swaying a bit. That's where the girls always stayed when they came to visit when they were younger, and that time after their mother had passed. That was likely where Savy and Foxy were staying until Charlie and Joe put rings on their fingers and said their vows before their father and God -in that order. So that was likely where Tricksy must have gone.

"Besides, Topher was never in love with her," said Will. "He was only into the notion that she had a crush on him."

Both before and after Tricksy, Topher had never had a serious girl-friend. Topher had never had a girlfriend, period. There were tons of girls. Some of them friends. But the only one who had ever gotten that combined label, even if for a brief period, had been Tricksy.

"Are you sure that's all it was for Tricksy?" asked Charlie. "It looked to me like she was in love."

That called Will up short. Tricksy had believed she was important to Topher. The relationship had meant more to her than it ever had to Topher.

"That was my fault." Will had told Tricksy his feelings, but he hadn't told her the whole truth. Now was a good time to practice. "I told Topher what to say to her."

He'd expected surprise on his brothers' faces. Or at least censure. The two men shared a look that was a mix of disappointment and understanding.

"It was what I was feeling," Will went on. "I just wanted her to be happy."

"You Cyrano de Bergerac'd her?" said Joe. "Bro, that's even worse."

And now, Will couldn't make any eye contact with either of them. His gains of only moments ago felt cheapened. "What was I supposed to do? She only ever looked at me like I was her buddy."

Charlie came over and clapped him on the back. His large hand gave Will a brotherly squeeze. "But you guys got that out in the open now, right?"

Will winced.

Charlie loosened his grip on Will's shoulder and dropped his hand.

Joe's brows came down again, the judgement even heavier this time.

"You don't want to start off a relationship with a lie," said Charlie, sounding very much like their father.

Again, Will couldn't hide his wince.

Joe raised his finger as though he was in court making an objection. "You are in a real relationship with her? Or was that just to show her sisters up? I know Tricksy and Sav have a weird competition thing going on."

"I told her how I felt," said Will. "Now I just have to hope I can convince her to feel the same way."

"How are you going to do that?"

"Same way I helped Topher win her heart. I'm going to romance her with my words. Only this time, it's going to come straight from me."

CHAPTER TWELVE

*T*ricksy had stayed in the Flying Cross Ranch guest house a few times in her life. Namely, right after her mother had passed away from a drug overdose. Mrs. Matthews had taken the girls in after they'd heard the news and for a few days after the funeral.

It had been a handful of days filled with warm food, clean sheets, and caring hugs whenever the girls wanted. Most of the time, they didn't have to ask. Even all six of the Matthews boys were kind and careful with them. Charlie never let go of Savy's hand. Joe had dogged Foxy's steps. Topher hadn't hung close to Tricksy, but that had never been his way.

He'd given her a few niceties like *sorry for your loss*, but not how are you holding up. Then he'd disappeared into the bunkhouse, a place the girls weren't allowed. She hadn't seen much of him after that, but she had seen Will.

Will had asked after her feelings. Will had asked what she needed. Will had sat quietly by her, offering his shoulder. All the while, Tricksy's eyes had never strayed from the bunkhouse, hoping for a sighting of Topher.

Tricksy could see the bunkhouse from the guesthouse's window. It had been painted a different color since her time here. She saw the two little girls, LaTisha and Daria, coming out of the doorway of the now coed space. The girls grinned at each other and broke into a run.

Looking for all the world like two wild and carefree children who were exactly where they belonged.

The Jameses had all had hopes of an adoption when they were that age, but their mother would never let them go completely. She'd always kept herself just well enough to look like she was trying for rehabilitation. As soon as the authorities' backs were turned, she'd put a needle in her arm. By the time she'd passed on, Savy was a legal adult and Tricksy wasn't too far behind. The door on their opportunity to become a Matthews had closed.

Then they'd lost Mrs. Matthews. Tessa Matthews's death had been a far bigger blow than their own mother's had. Because, despite not being able to take the girls on as her own, Mrs. Matthews had shown up for them time and again because she actually cared about the girls. When Tricksy wondered if someone might be proud of her accomplishments, it was always Mrs. Matthews's face in her mind.

"So, you and Will?"

Tricksy didn't turn at the sound of her sister's voice. She kept her gaze on LaTisha and Daria as they ran towards the end of the drive. In the distance, a school bus ambled its way down the road. The silence in the guesthouse was so loud that Tricksy heard the giggles of the girls outside clearly. Finally, she turned and faced the silent inquisitor.

Savy stood with her arms crossed over her chest. She was decked out in a pair of jeans that fit her curvy form to a T. Tricksy's lower lip twitched to hold shut. She desperately wanted to ask to borrow the denim, knowing that if they fit Savy, then they'd fit like a glove on her.

Tricksy remained quiet.

So did Savy.

It was a power play. One Tricksy knew she'd lose. As a singer, Tricksy couldn't abide silence for too long.

"Will's a good guy," she said, breaking the stalemate.

"I know," said Savy.

"You know?" Tricksy crossed her arms over her chest, affecting the same stance as her sister. "Let me guess, since you know Will's a good guy, you're wondering what he's doing with the likes of me."

Savy's hands moved to her hips. "I didn't say that."

"You didn't have to." Tricksy mirrored the movement. Then, when she saw that she was in the exact same pose as her big sister, she clasped her hands behind her back. "You always judge me."

"I have never judged you." Savy raised a finger as though it was a point of order. "Except when you're off key."

Tricksy's hands shot from behind her back and punched downward to the floor. For good measure, since her hands didn't make a sound, she stomped her foot. "I have never sung off key a day in my life. Except that time when you decided to change the key of that Whitney Houston song."

"Don't blame me cause you don't have the range." Savy waved her hand in the air as though she were brushing notes off an imaginary musical scale.

The sound of disbelief that escaped Tricksy's throat hit the range in question. "I don't have the range? You don't-"

"Guys!"

The two sisters turned to see their baby sister in the door of the guesthouse. Clouds moved into sight in the blue sky behind Foxy, threatening a storm on what had been shaping up to be a perfect sunny day.

"If your voices get any louder, you'll scare the horses," said Foxy.

Savy affected a look of innocence. It was a look Tricksy had seen many a time in their youth. It was a look that told Tricksy that Savy knew that she was in the wrong, but she would deny it if an authority figure asked.

Foxy wasn't exactly an authority figure, but she was often the buffer between her two big-voiced siblings. It was often Foxy, the psychic in the family, who was the voice of reason during Savy and Tricksy's arguments. Instead of launching into a lecture, Foxy opened her arms to Tricksy.

"You're home!"

Tricksy allowed herself to be swallowed up by her baby sister's embrace. It felt good. Foxy smelled the same. She felt the same. But different.

Tricksy knew why. "You're getting married," she squealed.

"I'm getting married," Foxy squealed back. "And so are you."

The squeal died on Tricksy's lips. Her heart thudded with excitement at the thought of getting married. It was something she had always wanted; a man to sweep her off her feet after going down on one knee. She'd dreamed that man was Topher when she was younger. But now her dream man wasn't a brooding blond. The man of her dreams was slowly morphing into a dark-haired man with a heart-shaped smile.

"I knew it," Foxy was saying. "I saw it happening in one of my visions. Will was sitting in the dark, watching you in the light. Each vision, he got closer and closer."

That dream sounded creepy and not at all like Will. But Tricksy had learned it was better to smile and nod when Foxy relayed one of her visions.

"Will moved in sooner than I had expected. You two are ahead of schedule. But that's great. Now we can all get married at the same time."

"Foxy, that's a bit premature," said Savy.

"What are you saying?" Tricksy turned a glare on her oldest sister. "That I'm not good enough to be a part of your wedding?"

"I didn't say that." Savy held up both her hands. "I just figured you weren't at the same stage as the two of us."

Tricksy grit her teeth at the word *stage*. No, she wasn't on the same stage as her sisters. They'd gotten off the stage. Tricksy was the last woman standing, the last woman singing.

"How long have you and Will been dating, anyway?"

"Not long," Tricksy begrudgingly admitted. "But we've been friends forever. And he told me he's had feelings for me for a long time. I'm just catching up now."

It was the truth. It was all the truth. Her heart was racing even now. But the question was, could it catch up to Will's?

CHAPTER THIRTEEN

ill grabbed fresh fruit from the fridge. He knew that Tricksy had a thing for apples. Her favorite movie as a kid was *Snow White and the Seven Dwarves*. She had fixated on the apple that the old hag had given Snow White. True, it had poisoned the princess and put her into a sleep, but that sleep had given her her prince. Therefore Tricksy found it romantic.

Will tested two apples, making sure they were firm, which meant they would be sweeter. He placed those into the picnic basket. Satisfied with his wares, he closed the fridge and turned around.

A sound coming from the closet pulled him up short. The sound was too large to be a rodent, and not a single rodent had ever dared come into Tessa Matthews's house. The boys were sure her ghost came in the night to dust away the cobwebs and tidy up the corners.

A second sound came from the closet. It was a definite squeak. But not a vocal squeak that would come from a tiny throat. More like the squeak of a pair of sneakers against the floor.

Since it was a Monday morning and all the kids were off to school, Will could hazard a guess what, or rather who, the culprit was. He pulled open the closet door and his suspicions were confirmed.

"Nothin' here to see. So why don't you just let me be?"

Will winced at the kid's bad rhyme. He'd been treated to it all last night during dinner whenever Ashton, who would only answer to the nickname Ashtray, spoke.

As a quiet kid who preferred books to people, the closet had been one of Will's favorite hiding places as a kid. There were a number of times he'd been in there and had forgotten to make it to the school bus. Since there was no book in his hands, Will was fairly certain Ashtray had missed the school bus on purpose.

"Did you find what you were looking for in there? A dust pan? Broom?"

Ashtray looked around the small place as though he was just now realizing it was a broom closet filled with cleaning supplies.

"I assume since you decided to stay home from school, and that you're in the broom closet, you're going to help my father and Charlie with the day's chores?"

The gulp down the kid's narrow throat and into his small chest was audible. "Uh, yeah, yo. I'm about to clean up, bro. That's why I'm behind this doh."

Will had read and heard some truly bad poetry in his days, but this kid? Oh, this kid's verses were brutal. Ashtray stepped out of the closet and into the light. That's when Will saw another sign of brutality.

Beneath Ashtray's shirt collar, between his neck and his shoulder, was the unmistakable outline of a handprint. It looked as though someone had grabbed him there, very roughly. The handprint was smaller than Will's, but slightly bigger than Ashtray's hands.

"You having some trouble at school, Ash?"

The kid pursed his lips. Whether in preparation for another ill-constructed rhyme, or a stalling tactic to determine what lie he could tell, Will wasn't sure. He knew he wouldn't get the truth from this kid who had known him for less than a day. If Will wanted to be trusted, he'd have to give some of his own first.

"It was hard for me when I first came to this country. I didn't speak the language, and I looked different from everyone else."

Ash swiped a blond braid from his startlingly blue eyes.

"I got picked on a lot."

Ash's eyes lit up at that. "But you hit them with that kung fu. Made them do what they do."

"I'm Korean, not Chinese."

Confusion darkened the kid's gaze. He clearly didn't know much about the differences in culture. Especially not when he was affecting an urban accent. An accent that vacillated from the sunny West coast, and other times to inner cities of the East. The kid meshed up the slang from Snoop Dog to Puff Daddy, which made his speech pattern all the more messy.

"Things got better for me when I learned English, and I began to use my words. You see, no one could understand me at first. Once I could speak to them, using my own words, we saw that we had a lot in common."

The we in question were his brothers. Topher and the twins, Mateo and Aldo, had been Will's first bullies when he came to live at Bright Horizons. They pushed and shoved and stole his food. They played pranks and made him miserable.

Once he learned English, he was able to tell them to stop. No, Topher didn't listen to his plea at first. Instead, he'd laughed at Will's garbled accent. But that was only at first.

The more words Will learned, the more words he used. The more words he hurled at Topher, the more Topher began to listen. Until the two saw that they had a lot in common. Pretty soon, Topher didn't stop talking to Will. Then, if anyone else dared push, shove, or steal from Will, it was Topher who stepped up to Will's side.

"You clearly have a lot to say, Ash. But I think it might be hard for other kids to understand your rhymes when they're still learning proper English themselves. Maybe if you spoke more plainly, you'd have a little better understanding?"

The kid pursed his lips again. He scratched at his side, where his pants hung low on his skinny frame. "You not gonna rat me out to Ms. Savy?"

There was no rhyming in that sentence, so Will felt he'd been heard. "I think if you get on with those chores, she might not be so mad."

Savy loved chores. If the kid got a few done before she found him, he wouldn't come away with too big a punishment for missing a day of school. Maybe?

But when Ash grabbed the mop and headed out the backdoor, Will wasn't so sure it was going to work out for him. He couldn't deal with that drama anymore. He had a more pressing arrangement to get to. When he turned around, he came face to face with his father.

"Hey, Dad."

"Son," his father nodded at him, an easy smile on his face.

It was rare to find Haran Matthews frowning. Even with a house full of rambunctious, mostly feral boys. That smile was a loaded weapon. If it even began to turn downward, the Matthews boys would hop into formation to complete whatever chore or correct whatever wrong that had displeased their father.

"I helped with chores this morning already," said Will. "I was just headed out for lunch."

"With Tricksy."

Will Matthews wasn't one to blush, but he felt his cheeks heat. "I love her, Dad. Always have. I finally got the courage to tell her so."

"I know you were in love with her. Never understood why you stepped aside for your brother." Haran Matthews looked him up and down. "Though, no, maybe I do understand."

Will waited for Father Matthews to explain his meaning. When the silence stretched on for a couple of seconds, he knew it wasn't coming. His father was not a fan of spoon feeding his boys the answers to questions. In grade school, he frowned at calculators, preferring to have the boys do long division and algebra on scrap paper. Said it built character.

So whatever Father Matthews thought Will had to learn about making way for Topher to sweep the woman he loved off her feet, he would have to wait until Will completed every step of the problem. But that was fine. Because Will wasn't going to make the same mistake in coming to a solution to this.

"I got some mail for you," said Father Matthews.

He handed Will an envelope. Will cringed when he saw the From address. It was from the FAA, the Federal Aviation Administration.

This was not how he wanted to tell his father about his decision to stop flying. Will's decision to start in the commercial flight business instead of joining the Air Force, or even the reserves, had been a slap in his father's face. Though the old man had never said so. But Will still knew.

"Congratulations, son," said Father Matthews.

Will blinked a few times. Had he heard his father correctly? Was the old man being sarcastic? That wasn't his way.

Father Matthews handed his son another package. This one was opened. "I'm sorry that I opened it. I couldn't figure out who it was addressed to with only the initials and I thought the contents would give me a clue."

Inside the opened envelope was the proof of a book. A book of poetry. The author was J. Matthews.

"How'd you figure this was by me?" he asked his father.

"Aside from knowing my son's true name," Father Matthews grinned, "which other of my sons has a gift for the written word?"

Will's Korean name was Ji-Hoon. When he'd come to America, the case worker had trouble saying it and began calling him William.

Father Matthews didn't ask Will why he hadn't published the book in his family name. But he didn't have to. Will had found the courage to tell the woman he loved about his feelings, but he still wasn't ready to tell his family about his other passion.

"I'm proud of you." Haran Matthews opened his arms. Will came obligingly. But he wasn't certain he'd heard his father right.

"You said you're proud? Not mad?"

"What would I have to be mad about?"

"I quit flying to become a poet."

"Ah," Father Matthews nodded. "So you're telling me you finally stopped doing what you thought I wanted you to do and you're doing what's in your heart?"

"Um… well, yes."

"Words have always been your greatest strength, son. I'm happy you're taking the credit for them instead of hiding them away in notebooks or giving them to your brother to use for his purposes."

There was a twinkle in his father's eyes as he said the words. Will felt like that was a part of the lesson he was supposed to learn. Well, after years of long division with no calculator, he'd finally come to the solution. He'd told Tricksy how he felt and now he was headed out to spend the afternoon with the answer to all his heart's desires.

CHAPTER FOURTEEN

The sun played peekaboo with the clouds. The clouds were white, fluffy affairs, so Tricksy doubted it would rain. Despite the turbulent morning, the day was far too perfect for a storm.

She'd had a good breakfast with her sisters. Foxy had gabbed during most of it, trying to fill Tricksy in on a year's worth of town gossip. Savy had kept casting Tricksy sidelong glances, but she hadn't said too much. The two of them had come to a truce of sorts. Though Tricksy was certain she was doing far more to keep the peace than her older sister.

There were only two clean forks in the guest house. Instead of insisting that the actual guest in the house get the utensil, Tricksy ate her eggs with a spoon. Savy and Foxy were headed out to do chores, whereas Tricksy had a date. But Tricksy waited patiently for twenty minutes while Savy did her hair, which would easily come down under the noonday sun and the chores she had planned.

When Tricksy emerged from the bathroom and headed for the path behind the house instead of the barn, Savy had sucked her teeth. It was evident her older sister wanted Tricksy to participate in the chores. But she was going on a date and she was wearing a sundress.

Yet did Tricksy put up an argument? Nope. She smiled sweetly and turned on her heel to take Will's arm. Luckily, her back was to Savy as her smirk spread across her face.

Tricksy felt like a princess as she walked arm and arm with Will. He led her into the forest, near a small pond that was bordered by the Flying Cross Ranch and the Silver Star Ranch. The spot was idyllic, romantic, like something out of a Disney movie. She expected bluebirds to land on a branch and serenade them.

Unfortunately, that didn't happen. The lack of cartoon avians didn't detract from the magic of the day. She and Will had had many a meal together when they were younger. But the air was different this time.

Tricksy stepped off the path and her heel instantly stuck into the rich earth. Will gave her a tug, and she came into his arms. Their lips were just a few inches away from each other. It was the perfect moment for a kiss.

They both pulled back.

Will took her hand again. He lead her on a sturdy part of the path, pointing out places to avoid stepping in her impractical shoes. She knew the shoes were impractical. But she'd wanted to make herself pretty for Will.

After Will laid out a blanket, he held out his hand to help her into a seated position. No man had ever done that before and Tricksy was charmed. When Will joined her on the blanket, they gazed at each other shyly. Their smiles were wide, but neither of them spoke. Tricksy tugged at the bottom of her lower lip. Will tugged his upper lip into his mouth. When he caught her staring, she turned away.

A giggle escaped her lips and Will looked over at her.

"Is this insane?" she asked.

"What?"

"Us?"

He blinked.

"Not insane like crazy, or bad. Just insane, like unexpected? Not that I was expecting it? I just... Why am I all of a sudden tongue tied around you? We've always been good at talking to each other."

"Maybe because now you know how much I want to kiss you?"

The breath left her in a whoosh. Will had never spoken to her like this in all their years of knowing each other. He'd never looked at her like he was now. There was heat in his gaze, but he held himself back.

Suddenly, Tricksy wanted to kiss his lips more than anything in the world. It wasn't her belly that was grumbling. It was something in her throat, a dark desire that wanted to be addressed.

"But you didn't," she said. "Just then, when I fell into your arms. You... didn't."

"No. I didn't."

"That kind of makes me question just how much you want to do it, then."

She was goading him, and she knew it. She wasn't determined not to be the kind of girl who chased men. She wanted to be chased. She wanted him to make the first move.

"I will," he said.

"When?"

"When I've earned it."

Tricksy wanted to argue more, but she decided to hush. Will had declared his feelings, but he wasn't pushing her. He was chasing her, but allowing her to be just beyond his reach. In truth, it was a bit thrilling.

Will reached over to open the basket. Out of its belly, he pulled sliced apples and buttery croissants.

"My favorite," she said.

Will nodded. He arranged the treats for her on a plate. He picked up the neatly arranged dish and presented it to her. When Tricksy's hand met Will's, a spark of electricity zapped her fingers. She knew he felt it too, by the flare of his nostrils.

A bird cawed in the tree above, further adding to the Disney-like feeling of the scene. In the midst of the song, the bird promptly did its business. The little gift landed at the center of her plate.

Tricksy glared up at the bird for ruining her perfect moment.

Will chuckled and put the plate aside. He pulled a single slice of apple from the basket and held it out for her. Instead of taking it in her hand, Tricksy leaned forward, parting her lips.

Will stared for a moment, his features dumbfounded. Then he got himself together and raised the morsel to her mouth.

Tricksy crunched down on the apple. It wasn't the sexiest sound. Nor was it the most elegant food to eat when trying to flirt with the guy you're dating. But the fruit was sweet and the guy who gave it to her was just as sweet.

Will fed her another apple slice. Followed by a torn piece of croissant. Each bite was better than the last. Likely because they had been carefully selected and were now being presented to her by a man who truly cared for her.

"Thank you for this, Will," she said.

"It's my pleasure." He smiled, his gaze on her lips as she swallowed down the last bite.

Tricksy wasn't going to play coy anymore. She wasn't going to wait for Will to think he deserved her. She reached for him and pulled him down to her lips for a searing kiss.

Fireworks went off behind her eyes. Her heart pumped out an erratic series of beats. It had been so long that the organ had been broken that it didn't realize it was skipping beats.

When they pulled apart, Will looked at her. His dark gaze appeared just as dazed as she felt. "We probably shouldn't get married."

"What?"

"Next week, with our brothers and sisters."

Now it was Tricksy who blinked. She wanted to cup her hand to her mouth and breathe into her palm. Perhaps she'd bitten into a bad apple and the smell was on her breath?

"I don't want to rush this," Will was saying. "There's so much we need to learn about each other. And I want to do this right. I want you to see that I'm the man for you. And there are things I haven't told you."

"What things?"

He hesitated. He opened his mouth, and that's when the sky decided to pour out its heart.

Will clutched her to him as the rain poured down. He stood with her in his arms and used the picnic blanket to shelter her. It didn't matter that she was getting soaked through. It didn't matter what he wanted to tell her that he hadn't. Tricksy knew that this man would never hurt her and that let her know that she was safe with him and they'd weather any storm.

CHAPTER FIFTEEN

Will held his hand out flat. The apple contained in his palm was snagged quickly by the mare. Duff had been his favorite when he arrived on the ranch. The stallion had always been the gentlest of horses, never showing any signs of temper. He was getting on in years now. So Will snuck him a second apple.

His good deed done for the day, he turned. Only to find that the gate was open. A new to him stallion was out and about. The young buck grazed in the open pastures. Having a horse outside of the pen with no one attending him could be a danger. It would be best if the horse was back in the pen with the gate closed firmly behind him.

Will approached the horse with slow steps. The horse raised his head and eyed Will warily. Will took in his options to get the horse back in the pen.

He knew he had to watch the pressure he put the horse under as he systematically cut off options for escape. He could run the horse until the beast tired itself out. But he only wanted the animal to move as much as necessary, and only in the direction he wanted. Anything that would hurt the horse was out of bounds. His father wouldn't abide any kind of animal cruelty.

Will kept his demeanor calm. He didn't want to give off any negative vibes or do anything that would cause the horse to aggress. He grabbed a coiled lariat, not a lunge whip. His father had taught him to use the lariat as an extension of his arm to get the horse to follow his commands.

Horses were extremely intelligent creatures, but also empathetic. Will focused his gaze on the horse's hip. He made a kissing sound with his lips. Then he motioned with his hand. The horse took a step forward. Will relaxed his stance even more, letting the lariat hang loosely. It appeared the two understood one another.

Will made another sound and another hand motion. The horse took a few more tentative steps. Will nodded his head, speaking soothingly to the animal. Within a minute, the horse was back inside the gate. Will hadn't had to raise his voice or the lariat.

He did wonder at who would've left a gate open on the ranch. It couldn't have been one of his brothers. They'd had it drilled in the head that you always close a gate behind you on a ranch or an animal would get out. Or get in, which could be even worse.

It had to be one of the foster kids. But they were all at school today. Except Will saw a pair of sneakers peeking out of one of the stalls in the barn.

Once again, Will approached the animal with caution. He placed the lariat on a hook on the wall. At the stall, he leaned over slowly and looked down.

"Ashton?"

"No," said the kid. "It's Ashtray."

"Right. My mistake. Do you mind if I call you Ash? Ashtray is a place where you discard something you no longer want. I don't think that represents you."

The kid stared at the ground. With the toe of his shoes, he kicked up some of the dirt. Then, when a few specks got on his shoes, he balanced on one foot to rub the dirt off onto his low hanging jeans.

"Did you miss the school bus again, Ash?"

He looked up now. His eyes were red, as though he'd been crying. Will averted his gaze and stared at the wall. The last thing a little boy wanted an adult male to know was that he'd been crying.

"I'm taking the day off. I need a self-care day."

"Self care day?"

"Yeah, Ms. Foxy takes them all the time."

"Ms. Foxy is a grown woman." Though that was debatable sometimes with the antics her visions had her get up to. "You haven't earned that right yet."

"Please. I can't deal with him today. I'll go back tomorrow."

Will opened the door to the stall slowly. He made his movements small, just like he'd done with the horse. He came inside and crouched down next to Ash until they were at eye level. "Somebody giving you trouble?"

"I'm handling it."

Will nodded, remaining mute. In his experience, if he waited patiently, the other person would always fill the silence.

"I tried being myself. But he doesn't like who I am, so he grabbed me by the neck and shoved me and ruined my pants. I had to hide it from Ms. Savy because she would go down to the school and call his teachers and his parents and probably the mayor, too. Then I would never have any street cred."

That sounded like Savy.

"I can't tell Mr. Charlie because he'll tell Ms. Savy. And I've been avoiding Ms. Foxy because I don't want her to see what's been going on with her psychic powers, because she'll tell Ms. Savy."

Ash ended his diatribe in a rush, with his small chest caving in. He must have been holding that in for so long that letting out had emptied him out. He leaned his head against Will's shoulder, a few of his braids unraveling as he did so.

"What do you think I should do, Mr. Will?"

"Me?"

The kid nodded.

"I think that every bully needs a victim. They need someone else to bully so that someone won't bully them."

"So, you think I should find the bully's bully and talk to them?"

"No, I think you should stay out of his path. Don't give him a chance to make you a victim."

"So, in other words, run and hide."

"That's not what-"

"So, I can stay home today and have a self care day?"

Will sighed. He'd been had, again. If he kept this up, Savy would have his hide. "All right. But you're helping me with chores. And you have to make sure you close doors behind you from now on."

"Deal," he said, headed out the stall door, leaving it flapping open behind him as he raced out into the fields.

CHAPTER SIXTEEN

Tricksy twisted her hair up into two pin curls. Looping the curls around the curling iron, she tamed her thick, dark hair into what looked like a series of waves that a surfer would love to ride. A few of the tendrils she left to hang down her long neck, hoping to draw attention there during the evening's festivities.

The thought of Will's gaze on her neck brought a flush to her cheeks. The thought of his lips brushing the bottom tendril of her hair spread that blush all across her neck.

A third tendril escaped the pinned up curls atop her head, likely eager to join the party at the bottom. Tricksy reached for her hairspray, only to realize she'd left it in the other bathroom back at the guest house.

She'd been trying to get into the guest house bathroom for two hours. With her two sisters also trying to get ready, she'd had to resort to coming into the big house to do her hair. If she tried to trek back across the yard to the guesthouse, more curls would likely riot and join the party around her neck. The only thing to do was to attack them with more pins to keep them in their place.

By the time Tricksy had stopped the rebellion in its tracks, and she was developing a migraine, there was a knock on the door.

"It's occupied."

The person on the other side rattled the locked doorknob. Tricksy turned, exasperated. She was certain it was Savy.

She pulled the door open and was immediately pressed back inside the room. A tall form loomed over her. Strong, muscled arms came around her. Lips in the shape of a heart captured her mouth.

Tricksy surrendered to the intruder without a sound. No, that wasn't true. A moan of pure delight escaped her lips when they parted as Will deepened the kiss.

Will's kiss was so gentle that it forced Tricksy to cling to him violently. Her back was pressed up against the door. The pins in her hair poked into her scalp. But Tricksy wouldn't stop Will's kiss to pull them out. Not for all the hairspray in the world. Not when the softest lips imaginable crashed down upon hers again and again like a tidal wave. She was going to drown, and it was going to be such a good death.

"You're gonna get us in trouble," Tricksy said when she could catch her breath. "Isn't this against your father's rules?"

"Worth it," Will grinned.

He brushed his index finger against the baby hairs on her forehead. He traced his finger down her ear tip. He took one of the tendrils she'd allowed to hang at her neck between his thumb and index finger. The loop of hair curled around Will's finger like a cat tucking in for a belly rub.

"You look beautiful," he said.

"I haven't even put on my makeup."

Will shrugged and pressed a kiss to her temple. It was the most intimate moment of her life, feeling this man with such strength in him handle her so gently. Tricksy felt his nostrils flare and ruffle the hairs atop her head. She felt his inhale and was certain parts of her soul left her body to settle inside this man.

This man was Will, her childhood friend. The shoulder she cried on whenever anything didn't go as she planned. That shoulder beckoned her now. Tricksy rested her head against his shoulder and found the safe space that had always been available to her. Now that place felt more like a warmth hearth that offered comfort, but also sparked with embers that waited to ignite something more.

Tricksy turned her head, tucking her forehead beneath his chin, she rested her hands against his heart. She felt it thumping against her fingertips. Will turned and pressed another gentle kiss to her temple.

Tricksy felt a shudder flit across her shoulders and run down her spine until it reached her toes.

She was so full of feelings, so full of emotions, that she didn't quite know what to do with herself. She itched for a pen and paper to write it all down in verse. But she didn't have a clue where to begin.

With her other songs, Tricksy would begin in a lower key. Recounting all the ways, the guy, namely Topher, had done her wrong. Then her voice would rise to its sopranic glory in the chorus as she let her anger and rage have at it.

Standing in the tender embrace of Will Matthews, Tricksy didn't want to start low. Not when she was so high. Could she start a song in a high C? She wasn't sure? She'd never written a song of about happiness.

Because that's what this feeling was. Happy. Secure. Love.

Will had said he loved her. No man had ever said that to her. And Will never lied, so she knew it was true.

The question was not could she write a song about him. The question was, could she love him?

Tricksy looked up at Will. Will gazed down at her. He didn't make any demands. He asked nothing of her but a chance. A chance to let him love her.

"Thank you," she said.

"For what?" he toyed with the tendril of hairs at her nape.

Tricksy shook her head, too embarrassed to confess what she was feeling. Anytime she'd told her true feelings in the past, she'd gotten hurt. But this was Will. Will would never hurt her.

"Thank you for being you," she said. "You're beautiful."

He let go of her hair and turned away with a sheepish grin.

"You are." Tricksy captured his strong chin in her palm and turned him back to face her. "I always thought the girl who won your heart would be the luckiest girl in the world. I never imagined it might be me. I wish you had told me sooner how you felt."

Something shifted in his eyes. "I would have." He took a deep breath, and let the air out away from her and towards the door. "But you were in love with my brother."

"I'm not sure that was love. A crush, maybe. It certainly felt like a crush." For years, the image of Topher was always at the forefront of her mind. Now, standing in the loose embrace of his brother, Tricksy was having trouble picturing the details of the man. "Topher said so many romantic things. But he never behaved the way he spoke. It's like he was two different people."

"Yeah," Will sighed again. His features were contorted in pain when he came back to face her. "About that…"

His lips parted. Then quivered as though he was about to form words. Only to jerk apart again at a knock at the bathroom door.

The door opened to reveal Father Matthews standing on the other side. His usually cheery face displayed a displeased frown.

Will and Tricksy broke apart instantly, retreating to the far corners of the small enclosure as if the two grown adults had been caught with their hands in the cookie jar.

CHAPTER SEVENTEEN

Will was living his dream. Thankfully, he was awake while all the goodness of his childhood hopes and yearnings were happening to him. To say that reality was better than his imagination was the understatement of the decade.

He walked down the street of his adopted hometown with his fingers entwined with the girl who had inhabited all of his childhood, pubescent, and adult fantasies. He was certain everyone was looking at them. That everyone envied him. And why wouldn't they?

Tricksy was a picture in her flaring dress and heels. Her hair done up like a pinup girl from the mid-century, though a few extra tendrils had escaped from the updo after their bathroom tryst.

The thought of their time together behind closed doors made Will grip her hand tighter. In his back pocket was the copy of his book of poetry. The plan was to show her the book, let her read his words, and then launch into the truth about what happened when they were kids. But later.

Right now Tricksy's head rested against his shoulder as they walked hand in hand. Her head on his shoulder had been a frequent occurrence in their youth. Normally, there were tears flowing down her eyes. But tonight, they gleamed bright with happiness.

He'd done that. He'd put that sparkle there. And he planned to do everything in his power to keep it there.

Tricksy deserved to be happy. She deserved to write songs that were heartfelt, not heartbroken. Will wanted to be the inspiration for those ballads.

He ached to hear his name on her lips on a high note. He wanted to hear their love story in a chorus sung over and over again as happy couples danced around a room. He never wanted to hear Tricksy James sing another sad song, not while she was on his arm. And Will had plans to keep this woman at his side for the rest of their lives.

"You don't know how much I needed a night out," said Savy. She walked ahead of Will and Tricksy on Charlie's arm, while Joe and Foxy brought up the rear. "Being a mother is hard work. I thought my parenting days were over after raising these two."

Savy chucked her finger over her shoulder in the direction of her younger sisters. Foxy and Joe weren't listening to a thing Savy said. They were in their own little bubble, too busy gazing at each other.

Will turned to gaze at Tricksy, but Tricks was glaring at her older sister. Her lips, which were coated in a deep red gloss, were pinched together as though she was trying to hold words in. It quickly became apparent that she was going to lose that battle.

"You didn't have to raise us that far. I'm only two years younger than you."

"Yeah, but you wet the bed until you were six."

Tricksy's hand was a death grip on Will's. The tension in her body radiated out to him. Then her face morphed from indignation to the kind mischievous grin he remembered seeing on the Old Hag when she offered Snow White that poisoned apple.

"Oh, you're still mad because I had an accident on Mr. Blankie. Charlie, did you know Savy slept with a special blanket until she was twelve?"

Savy's steps faltered, her features scrunched and her nose wrinkled as though she'd just taken a bite out of a bad apple.

Charlie's arm around her waist propelled his fiancée forward. He cast a meaningful glance at Will. The meaning that rung loud and clear in that glance was *I got mine under control. You keep a handle on yours.*

The command in his brother's gaze rankled, but Will knew Charlie was right. They had to keep the temperature amongst the female siblings cool if they all wanted to have a good time tonight. Luckily, Will was excellent at defusing tense situations.

"Is that Castro's Creamery over there?" Will asked. "I haven't had Old Man Castro's ice cream in years."

"Maybe we should go there," said Charlie, jumping on the distraction band wagon.

"What do you say, Joe?"

"Hmm? What?" Joe struggled and lost the battle to tear his gaze away from Foxy.

"But it's karaoke night at the bar," said Savy. "I'm in the mood to sing. What about you ladies?"

Now it was Will that cast Charlie a glance. Though Will's glance was one of uncertainty? Could more sibling squabbling break out if the girls were singing on stage? He wasn't sure? What he did know was that he wanted to hear Tricksy sing.

"What do you think, Tricks? You wanna share your gift with the undeserving people of this town?"

Tricksy smiled up at him and Will felt like he'd hung the moon. All the tension eased from her face. That's what let him know he'd made the right decision. He squeezed her closer as he steered her into the bar.

Once inside the bar, both Savy and Tricksy made a beeline for the sign-up sheet. At least when they came back to the table, they weren't pushing and shoving.

"When are you headed back on the road, Tricks?" asked Charlie.

"Um... I'm not sure."

"You gonna be traveling with our brother here? Is that legal? Can you fly with your significant other on board commercial flights?"

"I think you're thinking about the medical profession," said Joe. "Doctors can't operate on loved ones."

"I'm retired."

All eyes went to Will's. It was Tricksy's surprised gaze that he focused on.

"You didn't tell me that," she said.

"I wanted to tell my dad first."

The surprise melted away and was replaced with acceptance. Just like that, she gave a nod and appeared to move on. Will hoped his next admission to her went just as smoothly.

"So what are you going to do now?" asked Savy. "How will you support my sister when the two of you are married?"

"That's none of your business, Sav," said Tricksy.

"I think it is. You're my little sister."

"I'm a grown woman, and you're not in charge of my livelihood."

"Someone should be."

Tricksy sat forward, her fingertips holding onto the edge of the tabletop. "What's that supposed to mean?"

"Ronny's Dive bar? Not really an upstanding place."

The blood drained from Tricksy's fingertips as they gripped the table. Before she could get a word out, the announcer called Savy to the stage for her song. Savy rose quickly, smiling and waving to the crowd of townsfolk who knew her and her voice.

Will put an arm around Tricksy, trying to urge her body to relax after that tense exchange.

"You not singing tonight, Foxy?" said Charlie.

"Oh no," said Foxy. "There's a storm brewing."

It was a cloudless night outside. Still, something about Foxy's forecast sounded all too right. On the stage, Savy whipped the crowd into a frenzy with her deep-throated rendition of an Adele song. The applause that followed her performance was thunderous.

"Coming next to the stage is another town favorite. Let's give it up for Ms. Tricksy James."

Tricksy gave Will's hand a squeeze before leaving the table. Will couldn't take his eyes off her as she took the stage. So often he'd hidden in the backs of bars to watch her sing. Now he sat front in center. Not only that, her eyes were on him as she sang the Donny Hathaway classic *A Song for You* that had been made popular again in a higher key by Christina Aguilera.

Tricksy's rendition of the love ballad was pitch perfect. Especially the parts of falling in love with a friend in a place with no space or time. With each word belted out, her gaze never left Will's.

His heart thudded so loudly in his chest that he didn't realize that it was the audience applauding at the conclusion of the song. Even Savy joined in in praising her sister. The look on her teary-eyed face was surprisingly close to pride.

When Tricksy let go of the mic, the MC put up his hands to halt her motion.

"Not so fast," he said with a huge grin. "This is not on the schedule, but I know the crowd here would love to hear the song that made you a local celebrity."

The prickles started at Will's back. The song that had made Tricksy James a local celebrity was the song about her breakup with his brother.

Not exactly the thing the new guy wanted to hear when he was trying to win the lady's heart.

The crowd, made up of mostly women, started a slow clap, demanding the song. Tricksy cast Will a glance. In that glance, he could tell she was hesitant to acquiesce to the crowd's demands. Was it because of him? Or was it because she no longer wanted to sing that song?

Will hoped it was the latter. He also hoped it was the former. He wanted Tricksy to be over Topher and take into account his feelings. Unfortunately, what either of them wanted would be a moot point as the track began to play.

Trapped on the stage, Tricksy had no choice but to start singing the lyrics of the song about how his brother broke her heart. But it sounded different as each word left her lips. Usually Tricksy sang this particular song with a pang in her voice.

There was no pang. There was hardly any emotion. She rushed a few of the lyrics, as though she was just trying to get to the end. Near the middle of the song, which called for higher notes, she faltered.

Savy was out of her seat and at the mic beside her sister. She looped an arm around Tricksy's waist and sang into the side of the mic. In her alto voice, Savy managed to hit the note that Tricksy hadn't been able to reach.

The rest of the song they sang at a lower key, somewhere between Tricksy's high soprano and Savy's lower register. The two finished the song in perfect harmony and to the most applause of the night. Before the applause died down, as Savy was taking a bow with her arm still wrapped around Tricksy's waist, Tricksy ducked out of the embrace and ran off the stage.

CHAPTER EIGHTEEN

She had to get off that stage. She had to get out of there. She had to get away from the audience. She had to get away from her sister.

For months, years even, Tricksy had wished her sisters were standing on the stage at her sides. But that performance of Savy's reminded her of what it had been like. Savy had always taken the spotlight. She had always arranged the music to fit her alto voice when Tricksy wanted to go high and riff and trill.

Tonight, when the spotlight had been on her, Savy had brought Tricksy back down to a place she didn't want to be. Singing about her ex, in a key that wasn't for her, in front of the man she had an actual connection with.

Tricksy hadn't even wanted to sing that song. Her heart hadn't been in it. Not when her heart was now entirely focused on Will.

Will was a man who would never do those things to her that she sang about in the song. Will would never say one thing and then do another. Will would never leave her stranded. Will would never break her heart because Will would never lie to her.

Tricksy had not been in love with Topher, she saw that clearly now. It had been a crush. A silly girlhood crush, and she didn't want to sing about him anymore. She wanted to sing about Will. And she wanted to sing about him in her key.

She jumped when a hand landed on her shoulder. Whirling around, she saw Will. She saw the concern on his face. She saw his hand reaching for her. She saw that comfortable-looking space that was his shoulder and she dove for it.

Will's arms came around her. His lips brushed her temple. He said no words, just made reassuring sounds in her ear as he held her tight.

And that's when she knew. Tricksy knew everything would be alright, because she was with Will. Her heart had chosen Will. The choice was so simple, as if it had always been him.

She had spent half her life pining over Topher, but she'd fallen in love with Will in the space of a heartbeat. And it was the safest place she'd ever found herself.

"What was that all about, Tricksy?" called Savy.

Tricksy did not want a fight. She did not want to face what was on the other side of Will's shoulder. She wanted to stay hidden inside the comfort of Will's chest.

But this fight was long overdue. And so she turned away from Will's chest. She lifted her head from Will's shoulder. She took a step back from Will. She felt the reluctance with which he let her go.

"You always do that," Tricksy said as she came face to face with her sister.

"Always do what?" said Savy. "Come to your rescue?"

"Did I ask you to come to my rescue?"

"No, you didn't because you were choking on that song."

"I didn't choke. I didn't want to sing it. I've completely outgrown it. I've grown past it. I'm in a new relationship now. A good, healthy relationship with someone who cares about me and doesn't try to steal the spotlight from me."

"I think that last part was about the two of you, and not Will." Foxy said as she leaned over and spoke those words to Savy.

"Thanks, sis, but I didn't need a psychic to tell me that," said Savy.

"Hey," Foxy held up her hands as she stood between her two sisters, "I'm not a part of this fight. And I'm not a psychic. I'm clair-"

"And that's another thing," said Tricksy, her finger pointing at Foxy. "You never choose sides."

"Why would I choose a side?" said Foxy. "You're my sisters. We stand together."

"We never stood together," said Tricksy. "We stood behind her because we were her background singers."

Savy rolled her gaze skyward. "Here we go."

"And she's doing what she's always done now, which is to try and put me in my place."

"How can I be trying to put you in your place when you're the one who left," said Savy.

"You're the one who didn't stay," said Tricksy.

"How about this," said Foxy. "Here's the perfect time for you two to meet in the middle with me. Come on." Foxy opened her arms and made a hand motion, urging her sisters closer.

"Stay out of it, Foxy," both Savy and Tricksy shouted at their sister.

Foxy threw up her hands, lolling her head back and seeking answers from the same sky as Savy. The sky was still void of clouds, but the storm was picking up here on the ground.

"You say you wanted to mother me," Tricksy was saying, "but you left me to go and take care of people who weren't your flesh and blood. You left me alone to deal with the world."

"You wanted to stay on the road," said Savy. "I couldn't stop you from going."

"Yeah, you could've."

"How?"

"You could've told me you wanted me to stay home."

The two sisters stared at each other. Both of their chests heaving as though they'd been running hard and fast and came to an abrupt halt. Their postures both stiff and flinching at the same time.

Tricksy had thought she'd felt relief at having finally had it out with her sister. Instead, a weight settled on her chest. The butterflies that always danced in her belly before and after a performance were silent and huddled in a corner of her gut, uncertain of what the calm in the center of this storm would bring.

"What do we do now?" asked Foxy.

Savy let out a forceful breath, her shoulders heaving downward. "I want to go and have ice cream."

Tricksy let out a weary sigh, her arms coming around her middle. "I want to go home."

Savy turned left and headed with Charlie to the ice cream shop.

Tricksy turned right and headed back to the car with Will.

A glance over her shoulders showed Tricksy that Foxy had stayed where she was in the middle of the sidewalk, head swinging from right to left as she watched her sisters retreat to opposite sides.

CHAPTER NINETEEN

The moon was high over the barn. The ranch was quiet in the cool night. The sky was still cloudless, but Will had just weathered a storm for the ages.

For the second time this week, Will slowed the car to a stop on the ranch. The gravel under the tires was as quiet as the interior of the car. The lights were out in the main house, as well as the guest house and the bunkhouse. Even the bugs halted in their creeping, uncertain if it was safe to make any move.

Will had known things weren't perfect between the James sisters. When were things ever perfect in a family of differing views and temperaments? But he'd never known how wide the rift between Savy and Tricksy actually was.

A few miles back, the anger had dissipated off of Tricksy's face. All that remained on her beautiful features was hurt and sorrow. Will reached out to her. He couldn't help himself, not now when he had finally earned himself the right to touch her.

He placed his thumb at the center of her brow. With gentle pressure, he tried to smooth the worry lines that creased her forehead. What he got for his efforts was a long and weary sigh as Tricksy dipped her head so that the weight of it was cradled in Will's palm.

They stayed like that for long moments. Will brushed his thumb and forefinger idly across her forehead and temples.

"You should talk to her," said Will.

"I don't want to talk to her. She's a bully."

"Well, you know the thing about bullies?"

"They have big mouths and big heads and go by the name Savy James."

Will chuckled. Wrapping his fingers around the base of Tricksy's neck, he gave a tug. Will met Tricksy's lips with a slight brush of his.

"The thing about bullies is that they can only be if they have a victim."

Tricksy jerked her head out of Will's hold. "Are you saying I'm a victim?"

"No. No, that's not what I'm saying." Will reached for her hands. When he got hold of her, his hold was gentle, but absolute. There was no way he was letting her go now that he had her. "I'm saying you need to use your words."

"I tried that tonight. Didn't you catch the performance on the stage? She stole my spotlight. Like always."

"Not with that first song," said Will. "In that performance, you were brilliant."

Tricksy squeezed his hands, leaning across the middle console. "I didn't want to sing the second song."

"I know." Will squeezed back.

When Tricksy had sung that song back in the dive bar last week, her voice had been resonant. But tonight, it had been resigned and reedy. Her performance confirmed for him more than words ever could that she was finally over his brother.

It was his cue that she was ready to move forward. Which meant that it was the perfect time to come clean about his involvement in her past. The book in his back pocket was burning a hole in his jeans, eager to finally come into the spotlight.

"Tricksy… there's something I've been meaning to tell you. It's about our past."

"I don't want to revisit the past, Will. I want to talk about a future. Our future. Because I realized tonight that I want a future with you."

It was Tricksy that cupped Will's cheek in her hand. She brushed her lips against his. Softly, carefully. Will held still, letting her sample him. Tricksy was worthy of savoring every taste, every morsel.

"I realize that I deserve to be happy," she said, her mouth still pressed against his.

"You do." Will wobbled at her lower lip.

"I was worried about being happy and how it might affect my singing. Isn't that crazy?"

"Insane." Will moved his attentions to Tricksy's top lip.

"But tonight when I was on that stage, and looking at you, I hit notes I didn't even know I could."

Will pulled away, but only far enough that a breath could get between them. He stared into Tricksy's gaze and his heart banged against his chest in double time rhythm.

"It is insane," Tricksy said. "It's insane that I should feel this way about you so quick. But somehow I think this feeling has always been here inside of me. Even after all these years, I feel like we've never been apart. I feel like you've always been there, in my life, somewhere up high, watching over me."

Will opened his mouth to tell her that he had, that he'd always made a point to seek her out wherever she was performing. Though he doubted that would sound as romantic in his head as it would out loud. Besides, he still had to get to the part about him putting words in Topher's mouth.

"Tricks, I know you don't want to talk about the past." Will looked down at their joined hands. One day, he wanted to put a ring on her finger. "But there's something I need to get off my chest in order for us to move forward."

"Topher?"

"Yes, about Topher."

"Topher?"

Something in her tone made him look up. She wasn't looking at him. She was looking out the driver's side window. Her expression was one of wary incredulity.

A dark figure stood outside the car door. A dark figure with a square jaw and blond locks that had grown longer than Air Force regulation.

"Topher?" Will said.

Topher bent down. He tapped at the window and then made a motion for Will to roll it down.

"Hey, bro. Hey, Tricks."

"Topher?" both Will and Tricksy repeated.

"Sorry to interrupt the make-out session, but the front door is locked and I don't have my keys."

"Topher?" Tricksy said again, her voice losing its surprise and growing angry. "What are you doing here?"

"I live here. And I hear there's going to be two weddings. By the looks of you two, I'm guessing that's increased to three."

"You think Will and I are going to get married?" said Tricksy.

"That's what it looks like to me," said Topher. He turned his gaze from Tricksy to Will. "Looks like you told her everything, and it's fine."

"Everything?" asked Tricksy. "What everything?"

"You know; how he's the one that fed me those lines about adoring me amour back when we were kids-"

"It was the dear that I adore," said Will with a huff at his words being butchered even more. "Devoted to mon amour."

"Yup, that. What he said. The words that made you fall for me. Now you see that it was him you were really in love with and not me. I told you I wasn't the guy you thought I was. Now, you believe me."

CHAPTER TWENTY

"Will? What's he talking about?"

It was surprisingly easy to tear her gaze away from Topher. Tricksy had once believed his face to be so interesting. But today it looked tired. There were lines and dark circles under Topher's eyes. The indents of mischief that had always stretched at the corners of his eyes looked like they'd been carrying something heavy. The angles at the edges of his mouth weighed down as though he'd been frowning a lot recently.

In another life, Tricksy would've gone to Topher. She would've urged him to unburden himself in hopes it would draw them closer together. Right now, she didn't care a wit about what was bothering him.

Her gaze went to Will. Will didn't look much better than his brother did. The smooth planes of his forehead now creased with a burden that looked as heavy as Topher's. Will's soft lips that had kissed her silly a moment ago were pursed, as though he were holding back words. He hadn't been able to take his eyes off her all night, but now his attention was fixed on Will.

"Will?" she tried again. "Will, what's he talking about?"

The moment the words left her mouth, her own lips pursed. Will turned to her, and the look in his eyes made her heart thud. She had no clue what Topher meant about telling her everything. The way worry settling into the grooves of Will's brow told her it might be best if she were left in the dark.

But that wasn't the relationship she had with Will. They didn't have secrets. There were no lies between them.

"Tricks." Will reached for her, but she shrugged from his touch.

Her rejection shocked him as much as her. It was Will's touch she craved more than anything. Definitely more than Topher's. But she also wanted to be in Will's embrace more than she wanted her sister's hug.

Tricksy knew that whatever Will had to say, she didn't want to hear it. She knew it would unravel the beautifully woven fairytale she'd thread around their love story. The threads were all about to come apart. Then she'd be left standing alone, just like with her sisters.

And all because of Topher.

She glared at him as he stood outside the driver's side door. Tricksy reached for the passenger door handle, jerking the car door open and slamming it with all her might. She rounded on Topher, her index finger pointing at him accusingly.

"Why can't you just let me be happy?" she shouted at him.

"Me?" Topher pointed his thumb at his chest.

There had been a time that Tricksy had reveled in being wrapped up in his arms. Topher hadn't offered her many hugs. He wasn't the touchy feely type. Not unless there was making out involved. His hugs had never been about making her feel better. They had always been about him, about his wants, about his needs.

Tricksy took a step back from him. She didn't want to give anything away. She barely had anything left for herself. She just wanted someone to hold her, to comfort her.

Will climbed out of the driver's seat, his arms outstretched to her. More than anything, Tricksy wanted to go into his arms. She knew that everything she was missing could be found there.

"It's not his fault," said Will. "It's mine."

Those words called Tricksy up short. Will was meant to be on her side. So why was he standing in support of Topher?

Oh, right? Because there was something she hadn't been told? Something that would prove Topher wasn't the man she thought he was. Tricksy didn't need anyone to tell her that… anymore.

She'd figured it out on her own. Sure, it had taken years. But she'd learned her lesson.

"It was me," said Will.

That was something Tricksy now knew for sure. It was Will. It was Will she wanted to be with. It was Will that she was truly falling in love with.

"When we were kids and Topher was wooing you. It was me."

"I don't know what that even means?"

Will came to her, taking her hands in his. "I told him what to say to get him to go out with you. I feed him the lines."

Tricksy looked down at the hands that were always sure. She looked at the shoulder that had never let her down. She looked in to the eyes of the man she trusted above all others. "You... what?"

"Because it was what I felt for you." Will's hold tightened on her hands, as though he was frightened she'd try to get away. "I gave him all my feelings for you because you wanted romance in a package that was him."

Tricksy's head was hurting. Probably because it had begun playing a tennis match between the brothers. She looked at Will, then at Topher. Then back to Will, and once more at Topher.

It had always been Topher who had said one thing and did another. Now she saw that it was Will that did nothing while telling Topher what to say. Which was worse?

Finally, her gaze settled on Will. "You lied to me."

"I... yes. Yes, I did."

Will let go of her hands. He hung his head. All the fight gone out of him.

Tricksy turned on her heel to storm away. The sound of her stems impacting the ground was the loudest thing in the night. What she did not hear, what surprised her most, was that she didn't hear Will coming behind her.

CHAPTER TWENTY-ONE

"What are you doing here, Topher?" Will didn't take his eyes off of Tricksy as she walked away from him. Every fiber of his being told him to run after her, to whirl her around and make her understand. He hadn't done what he'd done to hurt her. He had just wanted to make her happy.

"Why does everyone keep asking me that?" Topher moved into Will's line of vision, but Will looked right through the man. "I do live here, you know. Technically, at least. It's my permanent address."

Will glanced at his brother. That one glance caused concern where Will didn't want to care. He tried not to see the bags under Topher's eyes. He tried to ignore the wariness in the frown lines. He tried to shrug off the tension he saw in his brother's shoulders.

The sound of the door to the guesthouse slamming shut broke the spell Tricksy had over Will and his full attention snapped to Topher.

"You're in trouble?" said Will.

Topher bit at his lower lip before opening his mouth to respond. Whatever came out of his mouth, Will knew to disregard. That lip bite was his tell. He was about to lie.

"I'm good, as always." Topher gave a shrug and looked towards the house.

That was his other tell. Whenever he lied, he always looked around to see if their father was nearby. Topher might mislead his brothers, but he would never lie to Father Matthews. It was late enough for their father to be in bed.

With the coast clear, Topher turned back to Will. "It's not me who's in trouble. I thought you told her?"

"I was about to," said Will. His nostrils flared at the words. When he inhaled, he caught the distinct smell of a woman's perfume on his brother's shirt. Here Will was about to lose the only woman he ever loved, and Topher had already picked up, and likely discarded, the next woman waiting in line for his attentions.

"I was about to tell her," Will said, casting a glance at the guest house, wishing Tricksy could hear him. "I had to make sure she was over you. And she is. She's over you."

Topher made a dismissive sound. "No woman is ever over me."

Will whirled back to his brother. His fists were clenched in anger. His exhale was loud and harsh as it passed his lips. The air was forceful enough to make Topher wince.

"This is not my fault," said Topher.

"Nothing is ever your fault, because you never take responsibility. Only credit."

In the distance, Will heard the sound of tires on gravel. Car doors opened and shut. He made out the soft murmurs of his brothers and their fiancées coming towards them.

"It's not like I want her." Topher waved a dismissive hand towards the guest house. "She was fun for a while. But you can go and have her."

"Go and have her?" Will took another deep breath. This one came out just as harsh as the rest of them. He was having trouble using his words because his teeth were grinding against each other so hard. "She's not a piece of candy we're sharing."

"No?" Topher flashed his wicked grin. "It seems like you were having a treat when I walked up on you making out just now."

Will rolled his eyes at his brother. His fists clenched harder. Topher could be callous. It was why Will had felt the need to feed him lines for Tricksy. He'd wanted her to have the romance and poetry she deserved. Now he saw exactly why she'd written that angsty breakup song. Topher did have a habit of mishandling things so that they broke, and the pieces never fit together quite right again.

"Sorry if I didn't realize how serious you were," Topher was saying. "I thought you'd just fulfill your boyish fantasies with a kiss or something and move on. Tricks is a handful."

There were no more words left in his throat. It closed up. As did his fists. But it was his fists that had something to say.

Will's fist lashed out before he could stop it. Topher went down to one knee, his hand covering his nose. Red oozed from between his fingers.

"Boys!"

Up on the porch, Father Matthews stood peering down at them. It was rare that the old man raised his voice in anger at his sons. The strain on his father's face had Will's hands instantly unclenched. The last thing he wanted to do was cause his father any stress or harm.

Will looked down at his father's side to see Ash. The kid's eyes were wide as he took in the scene. It was then that Will knew he'd caused more harm than he meant, and to more people than he wanted to hurt.

Charlie and Joe dashed between their brothers. Joe crouched down to Topher, one hand keeping him down, the other checking out the bleeder. Charlie made himself a roadblock in front of Will.

It was unnecessary. With that punch, all the anger had exploded out of Will. There was nothing left inside of him.

"Walk it off," Charlie said to Will.

Will did just that. He turned on his heel and headed into the woods. He walked until the red of his anger had dimmed and the darkness of night claimed him whole.

CHAPTER TWENTY-TWO

Tricksy flopped herself down on the sofa in the guest house. She stared at nothing in the silence. The silence grew so loud she couldn't bear it.

There wasn't a television set in the place. The Matthews had never been fans of that style of entertainment. They'd always insisted there was too much to do outside on a working ranch than to sit on one's backside and watch others do their business.

Tricksy switched on the old-fashioned radio on the counter. Every station played a love song. An old somebody-done-somebody-else-wrong love song. A new somebody-done-somebody-else-wrong love song. And even one I-love-me-some-him love song. After hearing that last one, she didn't change the station. She switched the device off and flopped back down on the couch, resuming staring at nothing in the silence. That's how her sister found her.

"I suppose this is somehow my fault, too," said Savy.

Savy stood in the door of the guest house. The moon cast her sister in an otherworldly glow. Tricksy looked up at her sister... and promptly burst into tears.

"Tricks, honey?"

The door slammed shut. The moon's light faded. Arms came around her and squeezed her tight.

"Baby girl, what's wrong?"

Tricksy hugged Savy back so tightly, so fiercely, that Savy tumbled down onto the couch beside her. Without wasting any time, Tricksy crawled into her sister's arms, practically climbing into Savy's lap. Savy didn't utter a sound of protest. She wrapped her arms around her sister like she was a baby and began to rock.

By the time Tricksy realized she had cried her eyes out, she opened her eyes to see that she was surrounded by Savy on one side and Foxy on the other. Savy had one arm wrapped around Tricksy, while the other held her hand. Foxy gripped Tricksy's other hand tightly in hers. It had been so long since her sisters had both stood by her side. A few more tears trickled down her cheeks before she could get herself together and come to sit on the sofa cushions between them.

"It's Topher, isn't it?" said Savy. "I saw him outside. Is that why Will gave him that shiner?"

"Shiner?" asked Tricksy.

"What did he say to you?" asked Foxy. "Did he try to win you back?"

Tricksy wanted to laugh at that. But she was still too tear-logged. Her humor had no purchase from which to launch even a small giggle.

Instead of laughing, she asked, "Will broke Topher's nose?"

"That he did," said Savy. "And all I have to say is *finally.*"

"Will's not a fighter," Tricksy insisted.

Tricksy had known Will Matthews for more than half her life. Nothing rattled the man. Not to anger, and not to passion.

Well, she'd have to strike the passion part. He'd shown her more passion in the last couple of days than any song she'd ever sung.

"He wouldn't have broken Topher's nose unless he made a pass at you," said Foxy.

"Did Topher make a pass at you?" asked Savy. "If he did, I'll bust his lip to match his crooked nose."

"Topher didn't make a pass at me," said Tricksy. "He implied Will was keeping something from me."

"What could Will possibly have to keep from you?" asked Savy.

Tricksy hated to admit it. More to herself than to her sisters. "It was Will that wrote those poems for me all those years ago, not Topher."

"So, Topher lied and said they were his?" said Savy. "The jerk."

Tricksy shook her head. "I think Will put him up to it."

"Why would Will do that?" said Savy.

"Because..." Tricksy sniffled at the realization. "Because Will knew I wanted Topher, and he wanted me to be happy, even if it wasn't with him."

"I'm not following you, sweetie." Savy shook her head, but she didn't let go of Tricksy's hand.

"I am," said Foxy, as she squeezed Tricksy's other hand. "Will has always been in love with you. But you've always had a crush on Topher. Will didn't think he could compete and so he tried to give you what he thought you wanted. That's his way."

"I mean," Savy began, "it does make sense that Will would've written those words than it does Topher."

It did make sense. But it didn't make it right.

"But he shouldn't have Cyrano de Bergerac'd you," said Savy. "That was wrong. They were both wrong. I'm gonna go give them both matching bloody noses."

Tricksy yanked her older sister back down onto the couch. Savy came with a begrudging grin. She wrapped her arms around Tricksy and bussed a kiss to her temple.

"Fine," said Savy. "You fight your own battles. We'll be standing by for backup if you need us."

That particular fight with the men in her love life would have to wait. Tricksy was far too preoccupied, and too happy, with being in the spotlight of her sisters' attentions.

CHAPTER TWENTY-THREE

ill's fist smarted where the skin tore after the impact with his brother's face. Topher had a hard head, so no wonder Will was in pain. But he wasn't the only one in pain.

From his place in the woods, he could see glimpses of his family. Charlie made angry gestures at Topher. Joe stood between them, making calming movements. Their father stood over his sons watching the boys with what Will knew was dismay.

A handful of words. One action and everyone he cared about had gotten hurt. This was why he didn't fight back. It did no good.

Tricksy felt betrayed. Topher was bleeding. And Will had no one to blame but himself.

He'd finally had the opportunity to use his own words himself and he had stalled. From his back pocket, he fished out the proof copy of the book of poetry he'd authored. In the dark, he couldn't see a single phrase. What good were his words now?

"Wow, what a punch! I thought you said you didn't know any martial arts."

Will sighed. He didn't need the moon's light to let him know that Ash had followed him into the woods.

"You gotta teach me how to hit like that. If I get in one good shot, those bullies will never mess with me again."

"That's not a bully, Ash. That's my brother."

Topher was the brother that had bullied Will the worst when he'd first come to the foster home. Topher was also the brother that had protected Will fiercely after they were finally able to communicate with each other. Tonight, Will had hurt his brother for simply speaking the truth.

A harsh truth. An inconvenient truth, but a truth no less. Tricksy was a handful. But she was a handful that Will wanted to hold on to for the rest of his life.

Will had had boyish fantasies about her for most of his life. But he was a grown man now. Not a child. He was purposeful with his words as well as his deeds. What was between him and Tricksy was real, and he wasn't giving up on it. It was worth fighting for.

"You gonna go finish him off?" Ash's gaze was down, focused on Will's hand.

Looking down at his hands, Will saw that he was flexing his fists. "No, Ash. Violence is never the answer."

"Yeah, but you look like you're ready to fight."

"I am ready to fight." Will marched back towards the house. Behind him he heard Ash mutter "Cool" and fall into step with him.

As Will neared the house, his father was the first to see him. Father Matthews's gaze narrowed on Will. But something in Will's expression told his father that there was no cause for alarm. He gave a nod that was as much of a blessing.

Will's heart filled with gratitude at the motion. His father knew that he wasn't a violent man. Even if his two eldest brothers moved in front of Topher as though they were his bodyguards. Will very nearly lost the battle with rolling his eyes.

"I walked it off," Will said, holding out his hand to Topher.

Topher looked down at Will's hand, then back at Will. He shouldered his way between Charlie and Joe to come to stand before Will. Topher took Will's hand -Will's injured hand- with his own and squeezed; hard.

Will winced.

Topher smirked.

"I love her," Will said.

"I know," said Topher.

Now it was Will who squeezed his brother's hand, hard enough for Topher to wince. "You disrespect her again, and we'll be right back here."

"Fair enough." Topher didn't quite hide the wince of pain at Will's grip. "That's some right hook you got there for a pacifist."

"She's worth fighting for," said Will.

"Then you better go to her." Topher released Will's hand and gave him a pat on the back. Though the pat was much more like a slap.

In his typical fashion, Will let that slide. Topher was an Alpha dog. Will had no issues running near the back of the pack. He had nothing to prove. Not when he was very close to having everything he could ever want in this life.

Will turned to find Ash studying the scene from the side of the porch. There was equal disappointment, as there was curiosity, on the kid's face. Will knew if this kid was to make it in this world, he would need the balance of those scales tipped a bit.

"You saw what just happened there?" said Will.

"Yeah," said Ash.

"You saw that the fighting didn't solve anything?"

"I don't know, Mr. Will? I think the big guy won't mess with you again."

"If I hadn't calmed down and come back and talked it over, it would've hurt my whole family. Fighting with fists never solves anything."

"Unless the other guy hits you first," said Topher.

"Excuse me." Will faced his brother. "Do we need to repeat the lesson we just learned again?"

"Nope," Topher grinned as the blood trickled down his nose. He peered down at Ash. "Use your words first. Fists second, but only if the other guy raises his first. Then you hit him hard enough so that he stays down."

Topher ducked into the house behind their father before Will could give any kind of response, verbal or physical.

"It's good to be home," Topher said as the screen door closed behind him.

Father Matthews let out a long sigh. Joe gave a shrug as if to say *What do you expect from a Matthews.*

Charlie came up and clapped Ash on the back. "I'll take over the after school special lesson from here. Will, you need to go sort things out with Tricksy."

Will did have to do that. But how? It was words that had gotten him into trouble. How could he use his words to get him out of it?

CHAPTER TWENTY-FOUR

ricksy was certain she'd woken the rooster up with all her moving about. But even long after the bird had made his cries, she still hadn't seen Will all morning.

Had he left? That was his way. Will Matthews avoided confrontations at all costs. Though one look at Topher's black eye and swollen nose told her differently.

"Ouch," she said, as Topher came out of the barn.

His eye was a light shade of blue mixed with a hint of purple. There was redness all around his nose. But instead of making him look a fright, it made him look like a rogue.

Of course it did. He was Topher.

"You should see the other guy," he said.

Tricksy's back went straight and tension radiated out to her fingertips, pulling them into fists. "You hit Will!"

"I didn't touch him." Topher put up his hands to ward off another impending attack. He jerked a thumb at his swollen face. "He did this for you."

"For me?" All the tension left Tricksy's body on a sigh. It was crazy that the thought of her sweet-tempered Will would do this kind of damage for her. Then she had to wonder... "Why? What did you do to make him act out?"

Topher shrugged, then winced at the movement. "I may have made an inappropriate comment."

"About me?"

"Look, I'm sorry, Tricks. For the comment, but also for how it went down between us all those years ago."

Tricksy gave her head a wobble. Was the mighty Christopher Matthews actually apologizing? Tricksy realized how much she'd needed to hear those words.

But what she wanted more was to talk to Will. To hear his words.

"He's in love with you, you know."

So everyone kept saying to her, including Will. "Then why didn't he just tell me that himself? Why did he give you his words?"

"Because you didn't feel the same way about him, and he wanted you to have what you wanted. So, he told me what to say to make you happy."

The anger and hurt that had grown inside Tricksy's gut last night evaporated in one instance. It was true that Will had mislead her. But the reason that he mislead her is what gutted her.

"I don't think he thought he deserved you. At least not back then. He knew you had a thing for me. Because, of course, what woman wouldn't -Ouch!"

Tricksy punched Topher in the shoulder. He was lucky it had been in the fleshy part of his arm and not in his face. She was sorely tempted, but despite the twinkle of mischief in his eyes, she saw something there she'd never seen before; sorrow.

What else did Topher Matthews have to be sorry about? No sooner had she spied it than he shuttered his gaze and turned away from her.

"Where is he?" she asked.

Topher pointed to the barn. "Helping Joe and Charlie with their vows."

Tricksy moved past Topher, finally leaving what she thought they had behind her, and headed into the barn. Inside, Will had his back to the door. He leaned against a wall with his brothers facing him. Joe and Charlie had their heads buried in a small book.

"These are good, bro," Charlie was saying. "Can I use this one for my vows to Savy?"

"Oh, that line would be good for Foxy," said Joe.

"No." Will snatched the book from them. "I wrote these for Tricksy.

I'm not letting anyone have those words from my heart about her again. I have, in fact, learned my lesson."

"Yeah?" said Charlie. His gaze had lifted and was fixed on Tricksy. "So, which of these poems are you going to use when you make your vows to her?"

"I've gotta win her back first," said Will.

"Just pretend," said Joe. His gaze also had found Tricksy standing in the doorway. "If you were down on one knee right now, what would you say to her?"

"There are too many words I want to say to her," said Will. "That's why I wrote them all down in this book of poetry. It's everything I couldn't say to her myself."

"You wrote me a book of poetry?"

Will whipped around to see her. His eyes went wide at the sight of her, as though she was the sun and he was soaking it all in on a cold day.

Tricksy walked closer to him. Joe and Charlie made their way past her and out of the barn. Once Tricksy was standing before Will, the two of them simply stood still and silent, gazing at one another as though seeing them anew.

"Tricks… I was going to come find you. To tell you everything. I had planned to tell you everything soon. I've been a coward about love."

"Tell that to Topher's nose."

Will let out a harsh laugh and then promptly winced. "You know that's not me. But I will fight for you. I'm going to fight to win you back. I'm going to sweep you so far off your feet you'll-"

Tricksy snatched the book from his hand. She gave him her back as she turned the pages. Inside the book was verse upon verse of the most tear-jerking and heartfelt rhymes she'd ever read.

"You say you'll do anything to win me back?"

"Yes," Will said. "Name it."

Tricksy held up the book of poems. "I want these. I want to use your words. I want to sing them."

Will's smile was slow, but as it spread, it lit up his face. "They're yours. Every last one of them."

"I'm going to give you credit this time," she said.

"All I'll ask is that you take my name."

Will wrapped his arms around her. Tricksy came into his embrace. She bypassed the inclination to rest her head on his shoulder. Instead, she went right for what she truly wanted. Her hand rested at his heart as she aimed for his lips.

Will met her kiss with the kind of passion that songs and poems were written about. In fact, once the kissing was done, the poet and songstress got down to just that. They composed a bevy of rhymes that were sure to make all who listened get up on their feet and sway to the rhythm of love.

EPILOGUE

opher scratched at his chest. The raised bumps he found there irritated him more than the fading bruise below his eye did. He'd had his nose broken many a time in his life. At times because he opened his mouth. At other times because his gaze had strayed to a woman who wasn't as free as her flirtatious gaze let on. But mostly he'd gotten his nose broken in the heat of battle.

Topher had been a fighter all his life. Even before joining the armed forces. He loved as hard as he fought.

Though love was a strong word. The raised skin over his heart agreed with him. He peered in the mirror at the angry scar. Thinking about how it got there had his heart skipping a beat.

"You all right there, son?"

Topher snatched the edges of his shirt together, fastening the buttons with quick fingers as he met his father's gaze. He hadn't meant to leave the bedroom door open. He'd only come in to grab a change of shirt after the day's chores.

Things were busier than usual on the ranch after the weddings. Both Charlie and Savy and Joe and Foxy were away on their honeymoons. By the time the two couples came back, there would be three prefabricated homes on the ranch. Three because Will had wasted no time in proposing to Tricksy, and that wedding would be happening at the end of the month. Joe and his dad were still hearing it from the Silver sisters that they weren't building the homes themselves as their father, the dearly departed General Silver, had had them do when they were just girls.

But the adults on the Flying Cross Ranch didn't have time to build new homes, along with fostering five kids, and managing a working ranch. Topher was home on borrowed time. He only had a few months left before he signed a new enlistment contract. He just had to take care of a few things before he went back into the Air Force.

"Dad..." he began and stopped. Topher had never been good at asking for help. He preferred to do everything on his own. Being a burden was what had gotten him thrown into foster care at a young age. He'd vowed never to be too much of a handful to his adoptive parents, not after everything they'd done for him. But this request wasn't for him. Not exactly.

"Dad," he began again.

"What is it, son?" Father Matthews came into the room, shutting the door behind him. It was as though his father knew he needed privacy to make this request.

"I know we're a bit crowded here on the ranch, but I was wondering if we could make space for one more?"

His father's face was a mask of patience as he regarded his son. Haran Matthews had to know instinctively that there was more to this story than Topher was letting on.

"Since the guest house will be empty, I wanted to let a buddy of mine use it while they recover from their injuries."

The scar on Topher's chest itched again, but he stopped himself from scratching at it. Still, his father's eyes went to that very spot, as though it called to him.

"A Wounded Warrior?" asked Father Matthews.

"Yes, Airman Toni Solis."

"Of course, son. Any friend of yours, and any fellow airman, is welcome here." His father gave a nod and headed for the door. "Just let me know when he'll arrive."

Topher gulped, trying to hold down the half truth he'd just let slip by. The whole truth was that Airman Antonia Solis wasn't a man. Even more of the truth was that it was Topher's fault that she had been injured in the first place. At least now he had the chance to make it up to her by bringing her here to the ranch to get better.

———

Are you the kind of reader that loves it when a bad boy falls hard for the right girl? Then you don't want to miss the epic downfall of Topher Matthews in
"His Vow to Trust"
Book Four in the Flying Cross Ranch Romances!

VOW TO TRUST

CHAPTER ONE

he *plop plop plop* sound of the stone skipping across the surface of the water wasn't calming. It was the number of skips that was satisfying to Toni Solis.

Six skips brushing light kisses on the water's rim. Six plops that left behind a concentric circle of ripples before a final splash. Always the same pattern each time. That's what satisfied her.

With the stone sinking into the pool of water after its performance, Toni went back to her lists. A number of columns decorated the single page in straight lines. A lineup of duty made its way down the page on the right. On the lefthand side of the page was a series of penciled-in dots, a few single strokes, and only a couple of Xs to mark where a task was completed.

Communications systems got a second stroke to form an X. So did weapons systems. Only a single stroke was placed next to the itemized list that included medevac and maintenance recovery. There was much to be done before all the necessary steps for mission readiness were completed.

Bending down to pick up another stone, Toni sent the rock out onto the water like a bullet. *Plop plop plop plop plop plop~splash.*

Toni inhaled then exhaled along with the expanding circles in the water. She flipped the sheet of her notepad and went over the list again.

"Senior Airman Solis?"

Toni turned at the sound of her rank and name. It was still new to her; that attachment of *senior* to her status. Each time she heard it her heart skipped in thudding plops inside her chest.

"They're ready for you, ma'am."

Toni nodded and folded the pages of notes in half like a hotdog, then in half the other way like a hamburger. Making sure the edges were straight, she tucked the pages into her pocket and turned to leave. But not before picking up one more stone and casting it off into the water.

Plop plop plop plop plop~splash.

Her shoulders jerked as the stone sank into the water on the fifth plop. Her eyes scanned the ground, searching for another rock. She wasn't a superstitious woman, not by any stretch. What she was was methodical, regimented, orderly. She knew that running through tactics again and again, thinking through every eventuality, making a list and checking it twice, that was what saved lives on the battlefield.

"Senior Airman?"

With a purse of her lips, Toni abandoned the water and headed back to the base. It was a short walk from the pond to the military post in the village on the east coast of the African continent. The area was relatively safe, but Toni kept sending glances over her shoulder back to where the stone had prematurely sunk.

On the other side of the water was the small Somalian village where she and her team had been deployed for months now. On the bank, she saw people that looked like her. Women with skin the same color as the fertile earth. But where she wore muted fatigues, they wore vibrant skirts. Where her hair was in two lopsided braids that crowned the sides of her head, their hair was woven in tiny, intricate braids that zigged and zagged in precise patterns.

Toni had had one of the village women do her hair once. Only once. They had gushed over her texturized hair, calling her a White woman even though they could have been long-lost cousins. But anyone who wasn't from the country, or even the continent of Africa, was often called white by those born to the land. And that included African Americans. Regardless of whether their ancestral line was mixed with European or not. It was a prejudice Toni had not expected.

Though the country of Somalia was poor, they had all the basic resources necessary, including fertile land, livestock, and fish. But many kept looking west. Toni had had many marriage proposals, a few even forceful despite the uniform on her back and the weapon slung over her shoulder.

Airman Solis wasn't interested in marriage. Her career in the military would be her only beau for the foreseeable future. Her children would be the medals she intended to collect as she rose through the ranks. Men were a distraction that was not included on her list.

Inside TOC, her team was assembled. The Tactical Operations Center was the hub of the specially trained military personnel on the base. It hummed with a different energy, a seriousness of the dangerous and daring missions the men and women inside these walls were prepared to take. Checking the digital clock on the wall, Toni saw that they had time to run over the mission details one more time before departure.

"We're ready to go." It wasn't a question that Senior Master Sergeant Sinkins posed. He stood with his hands behind his back in an at-ease stance. Though the man was never at ease, he was always at the ready.

"Sir," Toni began, "we have time to run through the details one more—"

"No time for another prep."

Her heart skipped a beat at that voice. Just one skip and then a splash because she knew she could never manage to stay afloat in the presence of a man like him. Which was why she always tried to keep a body of water between them. Which was why she didn't turn to look at him as she spoke.

"A rush through prep is a rush to failure," said Toni.

"We have the element of surprise," said Captain Topher Matthews in that deep, arrogant baritone of his. "Missions never go exactly as planned. You have to account for the unexpected."

"Not when I plan them," said Toni. "You either learn by mindless repetition or blunt force trauma."

She'd avoided looking at him for almost a whole minute. She could have lasted longer. Instead, he disrupted her plan and came around to stand directly in front of her.

Toni bit her lip to hold in her gasp. No man should be this beautiful. And worse, he knew how good looking he was. Even worse than the worse, he knew the effect his looks had on women.

His golden locks were just a touch too long. His blue eyes were clearer than the skies he loved to fly in. His grin was a flash of white teeth that warned he was a wolf in pilot's clothing.

"You know how to make God laugh?" Matthews snatched the folded notepaper from her hands and held it up. "You make a plan. And that's coming from a preacher's kid."

Matthews liked to throw that in their faces from time to time. As though he was holier than thou, even though he was the biggest womanizer on the base. And the most irresponsible. He hated prep and often went off script while on a mission. But because he always got the task done, he rarely to never was dressed down over his actions.

"Time is of the essence on this mission," said Sinkins, his at-ease stance at full attention now. "Solis, gather your team and head out."

"Yes, sir."

That was the end of the argument. The command was given, and she'd have to obey. It was her favorite thing about being in the military: the orderliness of it. The rank and file of it. Everyone knew where they belonged and what they had to do. If ever there was a question, it was clearly spelled out, or rather barked out, by the person above you.

It was also the thing she hated about the military; the orderliness of it. It meant that a corner cutter like Matthews could pull rank and override her, even if she knew she had the right of it.

She ignored the grin Matthews shot her way, refusing to catch his eye. He just wanted to rub it in that he'd gotten one over on her. He could be childish like that.

Fifteen minutes later, Toni and her unit were in a copter with Matthews at the command. As the aircraft lifted off, she spied the small pond that bordered the base of the village. The waters were still under the cover of night. Nothing skimmed the surface. Not a ripple in sight.

Toni turned her attention back to the mission at hand. This should work. She'd drilled her team enough. She'd thought of every eventuality. They were ready.

Her stomach dropped as the bird went up higher. It was the irony of the decade that she was an airman that got woozy with each takeoff. Especially the way Matthews flew -the show-off.

The aircraft jerked. It wasn't the jerk of acceleration. It was the jerk of an impact.

Lifting her head, she sought Matthews. He had one hand on the yoke, tugging with all his might at the control wheel. But it was to no avail. They were dipping down in dizzying circles.

Matthews sent a glance over his shoulder. His gaze connected with hers. Toni had always avoided looking directly into his eyes, afraid she'd fall like so many women before her. But now, when she looked at those blue eyes, they were the only thing that she could hold on to.

Toni felt like a stone skipping across the skies. One plop. Two plops. She lost count of how many plops there were as they skidded through the air. The sound of the splash on the ground was deafening to her ears.

And then everything went black.

CHAPTER TWO

opher scratched at his chest. The raised bumps he found there irritated him more than the fading bruise below his eye did. He'd had his nose broken many a time in his life. At times because he opened his mouth. At other times because his gaze had strayed to a woman who wasn't as free as her flirtatious gaze let on. But mostly he'd gotten his nose broken in the heat of battle.

The last battle he'd fought had been two months ago. Though the wounds on his body were all but faded, something inside him hadn't healed quite right.

Every time he closed his eyes, he saw it. The bright light of the blast. The inkiness of the dark sky. The flashing lights of his console. The spark in Toni Solis's eyes that had gone out when he'd lost control of the craft.

For some reason, seeing her fear had kicked him into high gear. He'd managed to land the craft, but not without extensive damage to the copter and those inside. The one who had been injured the worst had been Solis.

Topher had been a fighter all his life. Even before joining the armed forces. He loved as hard as he fought.

Though love was a strong word. The raised skin over his heart agreed with him. Thinking about how it had gotten there had his heart skipping a beat.

The streaks across the sky that had looked like lightning but weren't. The ground coming at him fast. Then black. Then red.

Topher peered in the mirror at the angry scar he'd gotten as he'd climbed over burning metal to get to her. To make sure the fire that was always in her eyes was still there. But her eyes had been closed. Her body was limp and broken.

"You all right there, son?"

Topher snatched the edges of his shirt together, fastening the buttons with quick fingers as he met his father's gaze. He hadn't meant to leave the bedroom door open. He'd only come in to grab a change of shirt after the day's chores on the ranch.

Things were busier than usual on the Flying Cross ranch after the weddings. Both his brother Charlie and his long-time girlfriend Savy and his brother Joe and his first love Foxy had said their vows. Now Charlie and Savy were headed away for their honeymoon. By the time the couple came back, there would be three prefabricated homes on the ranch.

Three because his brother Will had wasted no time in proposing to Tricksy, the girl who had been Topher's first love. Though there was that word again—*love*. It hadn't been love between Topher and Tricksy. At least not on his part.

There had only been one woman he could ever profess to loving. He'd fallen hard for his adoptive mother at the tender age of nine. Tessa Matthews had been everything to the mistrusting foster child that Topher had been. He'd lived for her smiles, happily did the dishes for a hug, and even remembered to always flush the toilet for her winks.

He'd only ever felt emotions like that for her. He couldn't imagine feeling them for any other woman. He didn't care to. Especially not when the hurt of losing his adopted mom still weighed down his heart.

So, no, Topher hadn't loved Tricksy in the way that she wanted to be loved. The way that Will loved her back when they were kids and now that they were grown adults. But he would be here for their wedding at the end of the month. He'd stay a few days to make sure the homes got delivered. But after that, he needed to decompress, and to do that, he would go camping alone in the wilderness for a few weeks until his next deployment.

But first, he had a mission to complete. "Dad..." he began and stopped.

Topher had never been good at asking for help. He preferred to do everything on his own. Being a burden was what had gotten him thrown into foster care at a young age. He remembered his biological father shouting at his mother that he couldn't afford her and *the kid.* He never called Topher by his name. Even when he went out the door that final time, he'd told his mother he wasn't going to be responsible for her and her kid any longer. A year later, and his mother left and didn't come back.

They were both alive and well. He'd looked them up while in high school. Topher had vowed never to be too much of a handful to his adoptive parents, not after everything they'd done for him. The request he was about to make wasn't for him. Not exactly.

"Dad," he began again.

"What is it, son?" Father Matthews came into the bedroom, shutting the door behind him. It was as though his father knew he needed privacy to make this request.

"I know we're a bit crowded here on the ranch, but I was wondering if we could make space for one more?"

His father's face was a mask of patience as he regarded his son. Haran Matthews had to know instinctively that there was more to this story than Topher was letting on. Because Topher never asked for anything that he couldn't get for himself.

"Since the guest house will be empty," Topher continued, "I wanted to let a buddy of mine use it while they recover from their injuries."

The scar on Topher's chest itched again, but he stopped himself from scratching at it. *Buddy* was the wrong word. He and his intended guest had never done a buddy thing the entire time they'd known each other. Other than to come out alive after their last mission together. The others on the mission had come out as well. All a bit broken and bruised, but none as banged-up as Solis.

Everyone else had been able to get to their feet and get clear of the crash. She was the only one who'd had to be carried. As he'd picked her up and into his arms, the folded paper with her readiness plan on it had slipped out of her pocket. Before he could grab it, the fire had claimed one edge and consumed the document whole.

"A Wounded Warrior?" asked Father Matthews.

"Yes, Airman Toni Solis."

"Of course, son. Any friend of yours, and any fellow airman, is welcome here." His father gave a nod and headed for the door. "Just let me know when he'll arrive."

Topher gulped, trying to hold down the half-truth he'd just let slip by. The whole truth was that Airman Antonia Solis wasn't a man. Even more of the truth was that it was Topher's fault that she had been injured in the first place.

She'd had a plan. Maybe if he'd followed that plan, maybe if he'd listened, then…

No. That wasn't the way they were trained to think. Things could go wrong in missions, and they had that time. But they'd lived to fight another day.

Topher would do just that. He would go back to the battlefield and fight once more for his country. Just as soon as he got Solis settled.

At least now he had the chance to make it up to her by bringing her here to the ranch to get better.

CHAPTER THREE

*P*lop *plop plop*—splash.

Plop plop plop plop—splash.

Toni rubbed the surface of the next rock in her palm. She waited for the waters to settle. The surface of the pond was clear and blue, just like the waters had been back in Somalia. That was unusual for a lot of bodies of waters in the States where things were often polluted from overcrowding and dumping.

If she stared hard, she might see the rock sink to the bottom of the pond. But the blue got darker the deeper she looked. The dark blue reminded her of the sky swirling around her.

Toni shut her eyes. She found no solace behind her eyelids. She stayed awake, eyes wide open, most nights with all the lights on to avoid walking in a nightmare of shadows.

Raising her arm, she let the rock fly. The perpetual twinge in the muscle of her forearm called the throw up short. Her fingers released the stone before her wrist could get the proper flick on it.

Plop plop—splash.

The stone sank instantly, barely causing a ripple. It hadn't skipped far enough to make any real impact. But the impact remained in her forearm and alerted her shoulder that there was something for it to complain about. The wound that had been plaguing her since she'd hit the ground during the crash came to life with all the agitation of tossing the rocks.

She raised her arms out in front of her in a Y shape, like an eagle spreading its wings. Crossing her arms one over the other, she pressed her forearms together in the yoga pose known as The Eagle. She repeated the motion, opening and closing her arms like the proud bird about to take flight.

The relief from the pain was instant. But that's where the relief ended. So long as the injury remained completely unhealed, Toni would not be taking flight any time soon. She was still grounded by the United States military.

It was a temporary setback. She had a plan. Of course she did. So long as she went over every step, she would be ready again. Soon.

There were still rocks on the ground. She reached for one. As she bent down, her left knee wobbled, unprepared to take on more of a load.

Toni managed to grab the rock and not tip over before bringing herself back upright. As she stood to attention, the ache returned. The doctors said it would always be there. No matter how much rehabilitation she did.

Doctors didn't understand her determination.

Rubbing her thumb over the face of the stone, Toni lifted her hand and tossed again. The rock sailed a few feet away from her, gliding over the surface of the calm water before landing with a splutter just off the bank of the pond.

Toni cursed under her breath and knelt down again. Her knee hadn't given out on her. Sometimes the weight of everything she'd been through, everything she'd yet to face, came crashing down on her injured shoulders.

"Senior Airman Solis?"

Toni bristled at the call of her name. During her time at the hospital, she'd been *ma'am* and *soldier*, or even *Ms. Solis* a few times. She missed hearing the rank she'd worked so hard for. She turned to the sound of the voice and was confronted with a metal leg. Looking up, she found Dylan Banks waiting patiently at the end of the pier.

"It's time," said the vet and founder of the Purple Heart Ranch.

Toni carefully put her feet under her. She came to standing with only a wobble. That was the easy part. The first step was a doozy.

"You've done very well during your time here, Toni."

Toni had been skeptical about coming to the rehabilitation ranch. Planting seeds and weeding flowers for dexterity? Caring for animals to help combat PTSD? Turns out there was something to it all. But it was riding horses that had improved the functionality of her injured leg the most.

"Too bad I can't stay and continue my healing," she said.

"You know the rules," said Dylan.

"I'm pretty sure the rules are against the law."

The Purple Heart Ranch was a rehabilitation haven for veterans and Wounded Warriors from all legs of the Armed Services. But a local zoning law indicated that only families could stay and live on the ranch. That meant that any soldier who came to stay had three months' worth of healing provided at no cost to them. If they wanted to stay longer, the cost would be a marriage license. Meaning they'd have to get hitched. It was a restriction Toni was not willing to abide by.

"No one here's complaining." Dylan had a grin on his face as he looked out at the ranch he'd helped build.

Toni followed the trajectory of his line of sight. In the distance, she saw his pretty wife, Maggie, and their toddler trailing behind her. Maggie threw her head back and laughed as the child tried to keep up with a ragtag pack of dogs. As the woman leaned back with her hands on her low back, her pregnant belly was pronounced in her sundress.

Toni snuck another glance at Dylan. The pride and love were so bright in his eyes that Toni had to divert her gaze. She had one memory of her mother's smile. She had none of her father.

Smiling moms and dads were plentiful here on the Purple Heart Ranch. Toni had met a number of the couples, and they all looked happy. Happy with each other. Happy with their offspring. It was unfamiliar territory for Toni, and she wouldn't be too sad about leaving the anomalous terrain. Soon, she would be heading back into the military to reclaim the career that made her proud.

She would miss this place, though. She'd grown up in the city. Not the inner city. Just a nice suburb adjacent to a big city.

She'd been raised by a single dad after her mom passed away when Toni was just eight years old. Her dad had never remarried. He'd never even dated again, as far as Toni could tell. He was married to his career and had little time or attention to give to another woman… and that included his own daughter.

At the end of the drive, Toni saw a golden-haired man who was getting a lot of attention. A small group of women surrounded him. They all grinned up at him with little cartoon hearts in their eyes.

Toni rolled her eyes at the display. When she brought her gaze back around to the scene, Topher Matthews's eyes weren't on any of his admirers. Those baby blues were locked on her.

Matthews had walked away from the crash that had put her career on hold. He'd walked away with only a scratch on his chest, where her body was banged up and bruised. But she'd been told that he'd walked away from the crash carrying her in his arms. If he hadn't done that, she would be dead.

And now he was coming to rescue her again.

Her time at the Purple Heart Ranch was up. She could've gone to her father's home, but he had moved into a one-bedroom apartment recently which was a hundred miles away from the nearest VA hospital. She needed to be near a clinic to continue her rehab so that she could get cleared to go back into active duty. Which left Matthews as her only option.

Not that she'd asked him for his help. He'd offered. She'd opened her mouth to refuse, but nothing came out. She'd meant to ask for details, for facts and figures, at least a direction so she'd know where she'd be going. For the first time in her life, she was stepping forward without a plan in place.

Hopefully, this was the way to get God to stop laughing at her.

CHAPTER FOUR

She looked thinner than before. Or maybe that's because Topher had never seen Toni Solis out of her fatigues.

He had to blink and turn away at that thought. He'd never had one like it before, seeing Solis out of uniform. He'd never thought of her like that, like a woman.

Of course, he knew she was a woman. He'd simply always thought of her as a soldier. One of the best. If a little too regimented and analytical for his liking.

Solis was as straight-laced as they came. Except for her hair. For a woman who liked to line up everything nicely, the parts in her hair were almost always askew and crooked.

That included today. The two braids woven around her head like a crown were uneven, one higher on her head than the other. The other was lower but thicker, as though she was off balance.

He liked it. Liked seeing Little Miss Perfect, Little Ms. Orderly in some form of disarray. That wasn't the only thing he was noticing about her.

She wore a T-shirt and jeans that hugged her curves. Curves that had always been hidden beneath the baggy uniform. Curves that were now on display as he looked his fill.

Beside him, he heard the distant notes of feminine chatter and giggles. He'd completely forgotten about the girls that had been flirting with him while he waited for Solis. He left them standing and met Solis at the back of his truck.

She avoided his gaze. Looking down. Looking up. Looking everywhere but at him.

"You ready?" he asked.

All he got was a bob of her head. The nodding gesture was canted a little to the left, the side where the braid was thicker. His gaze caught and held on the tight curls that had escaped the weaving.

He caught her looking at him then. Her gaze narrowed, and she frowned. She ducked her head, but not before running a self-conscious hand over her hair.

Topher had parked in front of the small cabin she'd been staying in. On the porch were bags. Solis was headed for them, but he beat her.

"I can do it myself," she said, brushing past him.

But her brushing past him was a couple of limping steps. Topher halted in indecision. He knew Solis was one of the best, but he'd seen her go down. He'd tasked himself with picking her back up. Seeing the bright light go out of those eyes, holding her limp body in his arms as he raced to get her to safety, had shaken him.

Topher wanted nothing more than to see the female soldier back in her top form. But that limp told him that she wasn't there yet. The wince when she hefted the bags up and onto her shoulder screamed that she needed help.

Topher looked at Dylan, who pursed his lips. Dylan gave a slight shake of his head, but his eyes remained watchful of Solis's every move, as though he was prepared to jump in if the load became too much for her. Topher followed that cue.

Like all Matthews men, Topher loved a strong woman. His adoptive mother had been tough as nails. Tessa Matthews had had to be to wrangle six high energy boys. But Tessa had been strong enough to let a man do things for her. Solis was a violently independent woman, one who Topher had witnessed bite a man's head off if he dared offer to carry her gear for her. So opening the car door was likely the wrong step, too.

Balling his hands into fists and putting them behind his back, Topher watched her struggle with the bags as she dumped them into the bed of the truck. It went against everything he'd been taught by his father to let a woman struggle. But Solis was a military woman, and Topher knew how important it was for women warriors to be seen as equal.

He stepped around the car to the passenger side door. He knew he'd catch it by opening it for her, but he would take this heat.

She didn't look up at him as he held the door open for her. Once she was safely inside, he shut her in, feeling panic rise in him. They'd be in the truck for over an hour as they headed back to the Flying Cross Ranch. What would they talk about?

Hopefully not that last mission that had left her wounded and her military career in shambles. He was set to head back in less than a month, where she couldn't be on her own yet. Which was why he was picking her up.

Topher turned and thanked Dylan. The man sent him off with a *good luck.*

When he climbed into the car, Solis was sitting rigid in the passenger seat like the soldier she was. Her gaze was trained out the window. Her lips pursed.

In her hand was a stone. She rubbed at the smooth surface, reminding him of a gambler rubbing at dice. He knew she had a habit of skipping stones. He wanted to tell her that there was a creek on the ranch. He wanted to tell her that he'd skipped stones there as a kid. But all those were personal matters, and he never discussed details like that with women. It gave them the wrong idea.

The women who'd been flirting with him watched with pouts as he pulled away from the curb. Clearly, they had the wrong idea about him and Solis. They weren't a couple. They weren't even friends. But he felt responsible for her, which was why he was taking her home to heal.

The Purple Heart Ranch had done as much for her as the place could. But on the Flying Cross Ranch, with the strength and guidance of his father, Solis would be as good as new in no time. If that ranch could turn around six wild foster boys, it could easily heal one wounded woman.

He'd drop her off. Make sure she was settled with his dad looking over her. Then he'd be on his way, his debt to her repaid. With that plan in place, Topher settled back into the long drive.

"You're a cowboy?" said Solis, breaking the silence. "Why doesn't that surprise me?"

"I wasn't born on a ranch. I grew up in the inner city."

Solis looked at him as though he was lying. She had the most judgmental eyes. But at least the spark was back in them. Her eyes were the color of coffee, his favorite beverage. Coffee never judged. It gave energy and comfort and strength. All of a sudden, Topher found himself very thirsty.

"I'm the product of an affair," Topher found himself saying. "My mother tried to use me to get my father to leave his wife. He stayed for a while, but then he went back to his family. She left shortly after he did."

"She just left you with other family members?"

"No, she left me completely alone in the apartment. I stayed until the landlord came looking for rent. By then, I'd eaten all the food and was starving."

"How old were you?"

"Five."

Topher had no idea why he told her this. He was never this chatty with women. He would always get them talking as he found a way to steer them back to their room or his. He wasn't steering Solis anywhere. She was coming home with him to live on the ranch. So it didn't count.

"What about you? Your mother was in the Army?"

"She was."

Topher waited for her to add more. Women always filled silences with chatter. Not Solis. "She retired?"

"She died. Not combat related."

"So your dad raised you?"

Solis shrugged. "I pretty much raised myself. My dad was a workaholic. I was a latchkey kid since first grade."

"That explains it."

Her head whipped to him. "Explains what?"

"Your independence."

"You say that like it's a bad thing."

"People need people."

"Look, you don't have to worry about me. I mean, I appreciate you letting me crash at your place. But I won't overstay my welcome. It should just be a few weeks more of rehab at the VA. Then I'm applying for reinstatement."

Topher pursed his lips. Her injuries were severe. He knew that for certain. He'd held her broken body in his arms. She was one of the best strategists he'd ever worked with. But he wasn't so sure about that timeline.

It wasn't going to be his problem. He'd drop her off. Get her settled in the guest house. Then he'd be off soon.

CHAPTER FIVE

$\mathscr{I}$t was blessedly quiet on the drive. But Toni was still tense. It wasn't that she didn't trust Matthews behind the wheel. The man had flown an aircraft in a war zone with heavy enemy fire that had taken them down, and still he'd managed to get them on the ground with their lives.

They were on a country road, not in contested airspace. Their only adversaries were the deer dotting the lines of the forest. The occasional herd of cows busied themselves in the rolling pastures. In the distance, wild horses ran fast and free, their manes streaking behind them.

Toni turned in her seat to watch as the horses ran past. Her eyes were big, her mouth slightly open. In her hand, she'd taken the stone out of her pocket and was rubbing at the smooth surface of the rock. Her heavy limbs felt weightless as she watched the beasts run. Her heartbeat picked up as they disappeared over the horizon.

She caught Matthews's gaze on her, and her heart thumped. She turned back around in her seat and faced forward. The weight resettled in her limbs.

Matthews didn't say anything, and she was grateful. The honk of a truck idling down the road caught his attention. With a closed fist, he pounded the center of the steering wheel, giving off a short, friendly beep.

She eyed those hands. Her mind flashed back to how he'd held on to the yoke in the aircraft back in Somalia. When the next truck zoomed past them at the speed limit, Toni's entire body tensed.

She pinched the skin at her throat when Matthews got too close to the edge of the shoulder. She tugged at the edge of her braid each time he took his hand off the steering wheel to reach for his bottled water. She nearly had a heart attack when he reached for the stereo dial.

"You can choose," he said.

"Beg pardon?"

"The tunes," he said, resettling his hand on the steering wheel. "You can choose what we listen to."

Toni let loose a slow exhale. She had to unfurl her fingers from the seatbelt before she could reach for the radio dial. So much of her life had been out of her control for the last three months. From the time she'd lost in a coma while on a base hospital for nearly two weeks. To the time at the Purple Heart Ranch where she wasn't sure if she would walk unassisted again.

She was so used to being in control that her brain was having trouble functioning. Reaching for the dial, she turned the knob too far in one direction when she knew that tuning into any one station was done in small turns. When a familiar tune hit her ears, Toni stopped the twisting of the dial. She settled back against the headrest and let out another sigh.

A baritone voice that she didn't remember from the song hit her ears with the melody. Toni opened her eyes and glanced over at Matthews. Sure enough, his lips were moving, and it was his voice singing the lyrics.

"You know Mahalia Jackson?" she asked.

"Of course I do." When the look of shock didn't leave her face, he continued, "I told you, I'm a preacher's kid."

It was still hard for her to believe that Topher Matthews was even a child of God, much less that he could actually go into a church without being smitten down. The man had broken so many hearts, many at the same time.

Mahalia Jackson crooned on about helping somebody as she traveled along. The gospel singer's voice had always felt like a warm blanket to Toni's ears. She reached to turn the volume up. At the same time, Matthews was reaching for the knob. Their fingers brushed.

Toni couldn't hide her gasp. A zing from her index finger spread through her palms. From there, warmth spread through her entire body, making her shiver with the impact of it.

"You cold?" he asked, completely unaffected. His long fingers moved from the volume and reached instead for the AC dial.

There was no need to. Toni's entire body felt like it was on fire. She tugged at her braids again, wishing that her hair was long enough to hide her face.

She shifted in the seat. It was difficult for her to sit for long periods of time. Her leg was already cramping, her knee threatening a tantrum if she kept it cooped up much longer. But she needed to get out of this car and away from close proximity to Matthews as quickly as possible. That meant staying put as they drove to their destination. So she didn't complain.

When Topher turned the wheel and pulled off at the next exit, she opened her mouth to protest, but her foot was too busy tapping at the floorboards. Her body was far too eager for a reprieve to let any words escape.

"Hope you don't mind," he said as he parked the car. "Just need to stretch my legs a bit."

Toni eyed the man as he got out of the truck. She eyed his long, lithe body that moved with ease and power. She watched as his powerful legs carried him to the front of the car without a wobble or a misstep.

Matthews raised his arms over his head and stretched his big body. A sliver of golden tan skin was exposed as he did so. Toni couldn't take her eyes off the spot. She wasn't the only one.

A few other women scattered around the rest stop were enjoying the show. Some covertly sneaking gazes as they looked past the men or children talking to them. A few overtly as they flipped their long hair over their shoulders and tugged at pouty lips.

Matthews grinned at them as he brought his arms down. Emboldened, or invited, a couple of the women came over, boobs first. Toni swore that each of those girls had somehow lowered her T-shirt the moment she stepped up beside Matthews.

Toni curled her lip as she reached for the handle and shoved the passenger door open. Matthews glanced at her as he continued to speak to the women. The women didn't look over at her, not even eying Toni as competition.

She wasn't competition. She certainly didn't want to be in the running for that man's heart. Or any man's heart. She was on a mission.

She would crash at the Matthews ranch, go to the VA to continue her rehab, and then get reinstated. That was the plan. Those were the check boxes on her list. That was all that mattered.

She stepped out of the vehicle, but her leg wasn't ready. When her heel impacted the ground, she stumbled. The top half of her body pitched forward. She held out her hands to brace herself, but her palms never hit the dirt.

Strong arms came around her. Those arms caught her forearms and lifted her upright. Toni looked up to find Matthews's face close to hers.

Her hand was against his chest. On the warm flesh just inside his button-up shirt. There were more than a few buttons undone, which allowed her index finger to rest on raised skin.

She knew he had come away with a scratch. Was that it? Right over his heart?

Matthews set her away from him. Then he reached up to his shirt and yanked the buttons through their holes, closing up his shirt and hiding his wound.

"Let me know when you're ready," he said in his gruff voice. Then he walked away from her.

CHAPTER SIX

opher kept an eye on Solis's leg. Her left leg was closer to him, though he knew it was the right one that had sustained the injury. Both looked shapely encased in the denim of her jeans. Long and lean with a dainty foot encased in dark running shoes. He wanted to remove the shoes and replace them with boots. He'd bet a pair of cowboy boots would make her impossibly long legs even longer and accentuate the curves of her hips.

Realizing he was checking out her shapely thighs and making plans for her curves, Topher averted his gaze.

He didn't know what to do with this woman. Any evidence he showed of trying to care for her needs was met with haughty suspicion. If he feigned ignorance, he was dealt a twisted curl of her lip.

What was he supposed to do?

All he knew to do was to get her to the ranch. His father would know what to do. His father could fix anything. Haran Matthews could heal any wound, whether it be physical or emotional. Solis clearly had both.

He'd seen her try to hide every wince of pain as the truck bumped over dips in the road. It was why he'd kept to the speed limit on their drive, even though it was evident she was having trouble on the long ride. Her mouth had remained mute, but each tightening of her lips, every narrowing of her eyes, he'd caught.

Topher knew how to dress a physical wound. He had military training for it. He also had five brothers who'd roughhoused as kids and young adults and needed to hide the evidence of any wound from their parents.

There was nothing he could do for her leg or shoulder. She wouldn't even let him lift her luggage. And he sure as all the hay in the world didn't know what to do with an emotional wound. Which is what girls seemed to get most of the time.

Most times, to heal something on the inside required words. He was known as a smooth talker, but those coffee dark eyes of hers had met any of his words today with a bitter glare that left a foul taste on his tongue.

Solis wasn't one to be charmed. And if a man couldn't charm a woman, then what was he supposed to do with her?

Didn't matter. He didn't need to answer that question. His father would handle it.

Though there was a slight problem with that plan. Topher hadn't told his father that Toni Solis was a woman.

It wasn't a lie.

He'd just neglected to correct his dad when he'd made the assumption that the gender neutral name belonged to a woman and not a man.

Topher knew Father Matthews would take her in. He was like that. The man had taken in six wild boys. Though he and his wife had opted not to take in the three James girls who had also been in foster care with his foster brothers.

Topher had always assumed that was because Savy and Charlie had declared they were in love with each other before they'd reached double digits in age. He later learned it was because the girls' parents refused to relinquish their parental rights, even though the drug addicts kept coming close to having their rights terminated with each passing year that they didn't straighten up. By the time the drugs did the James adults in, Savy was legal and took on the care of her two younger sisters herself.

And now, with the old foster home being demolished and moved to the bunkhouse of the Flying Cross Ranch, Haran Matthews had taken in the adult James women and their five foster kids. At least he was bringing his dad a grown woman to fix.

His father would use his booming preacher voice, give Solis the words of wisdom she needed to hear, and the soldier would be back on her feet in no time. Topher's debt to her would be repaid with the only currency he had—his father's love. Because lord knows Topher didn't have any love to give himself.

At last, he pulled into the lane that lead to the Flying Cross Ranch. His heart sighed at the sight of his home. His brothers and their neighbors, the Silver sisters, had made great progress on the new additions. Three of his brothers had decided to come back home and live with their wives.

The prefab homes were settled on new foundations. One was painted red brick, another white, and the third was a riot of colors. That one belonged to the clairsentient Foxy and his straight-laced brother Joe, who'd just given up a chance at being appointed DA in favor of working with state foster kids.

With his brothers and their wives and wife-to-be getting settled in the new houses, that left the guest house available for Toni. Topher pulled up to the main house first. There he saw his father sitting on the porch in his old rocking chair.

"There's my boy," Father Matthews said as he came to standing.

Topher wasn't a boy. But any time this man used that term, a sheepish grin spread over his face. Father Matthews opened his arms, and Topher came into them.

"Hey, Dad."

"I thought you were off to pick up your friend Toni."

"I'm Toni." Solis waved from the side of the truck. She'd hung back, looking uncomfortable at the display of emotions between father and son.

Father Matthews looked at Solis, who bit her lip. Then at Topher, who fixed his gaze on the old barn. It looked like the roof needed some work. The old man shook his head and then offered Solis a bright smile.

"Welcome to the Flying Cross Ranch," said Father Matthews.

"Thank you for having me, sir. I promise I won't be a bother, and I'll be out of your hair as soon as possible."

Father Matthews looked Solis up and down. Topher wasn't sure if she saw it, but his father had taken her number right then and there.

"You stay as long as you need," said Father Matthews.

That had gone easier than Topher had imagined.

"Of course you'll stay in the guest house, while my son stays in the main house," Father Matthews continued. "Forgive me, but I am—how do you kids say it? Old school."

"Oh, no." Solis held up her hand. "No, no, no." She flicked her fingers between herself and Topher. "There's nothing going on between Matthews and me."

As though to make certain it was definitively clear, she made a slicing motion with her hands as though severing the very idea of the two of them in a relationship.

"She needs a place to stay that's close to the VA hospital," said Topher. "And she's been doing well with equine therapy, so I thought you could give her some lessons."

"Horses?" said Solis. "You didn't say you had horses."

There was an almost smile on her face. Topher got lost a minute in that wide-eyed gaze of hers. He suddenly remembered just how thirsty he was for a hot, large drink of coffee.

"I'd be happy to give you lessons," said Father Matthews. "We can start when I get back."

"When you get back?" Topher jerked to attention, like hot coffee had spilled on his chest.

"I'm away for the long weekend. Charlie and Savy insisted I come on their honeymoon cruise with them."

"You're going on your son's honeymoon cruise?" asked Solis.

"I'm not going to say no to a cruise. And I like my son and his wife."

Solis pursed her lips, as though she tasted something foul or unfamiliar. But she didn't say anything.

Father Matthews turned to Topher. "You can see to her riding lessons during that time."

"Me?"

"You're an excellent rider and teacher. Why not you?"

Because he'd planned to drop her and go on a solo camping trip before his next deployment. But it looked like he was stuck with her.

No good deed goes unpunished, right?

CHAPTER SEVEN

Stairways were her nemesis, with steps being the villain's minions. Toni had learned that there was a difference between steps and stairs. Stairs was the plural of stairway. A stairway was a structure made up of individual risers, or steps, that moved a person upwards.

It was an important distinction for someone who had mobility issues. If she had to climb stairs, meaning multiple stairways, then it was something she wanted to be prepared for. However, if there were just a few steps to climb, her mind and her body wouldn't hold too much tension as she faced the arduous task. But at the end of the day, whether it be stairs or steps, the whole point was to carry the person upwards.

There were only a few steps up and into the guest house. Toni placed her uninjured leg on the first riser. Bending that knee, she lifted her injured left leg onto the next step. Slowly, she straightened that left knee, wincing not from pain but from the *snap, crackle, and popping* sounds her knee made -and was likely to make for the rest of her life.

She only let the full weight of her body rest on her left leg for a split second before calling on the right leg to lift her up onto the last step. Letting out a sigh, she looked over her shoulder at the hill she'd just climbed. There had been a time in her life where she had scaled mountains at a fast clip without taking any rest stops or breathing too heavily.

Those days were in the past. But she still had a bright future ahead of her. She just needed to stick to the plan. A cloud moved over her head, but it was only there for a second.

Once she was inside the guest house, she shut the door behind her, leaving Matthews on the other side. She'd felt his stare on her back as she climbed the steps. Luckily, he hadn't come over to help her. But a glance out the door's window told her that he might be questioning that decision. His handsome face was pinched.

Had he expected her to let him in? Was this offer a place to stay just some ploy to try to romance her? Toni let out a laugh at that notion.

A glance in the mirror hanging on the wall just inside the door told her that that was a joke. She was not Matthews's type. Though she knew he dabbled with female soldiers from time to time, he preferred civilians. As a lot of committed bachelor soldiers did. They could get in and out with little to no excuses aside from the major one: *Sorry, babe, but I'm being deployed. Duty to country.*

Sometimes that was true. Often it was a lie. A lie women who hung out at bars around the base bought because they just wanted to land a soldier. Just another reason Toni happily neglected her love life.

She loved the career she'd chosen, and she was anxious to get back to it.

As though it heard her heart's desire, her leg throbbed. She'd been inside Matthews' truck for far too long. The stopover had helped, but she needed to stretch it out.

Looking around the guest house, she saw that there was an embroidered rug she could use for stretching in front of the wooden coffee table. The place was done up cozy. It was clear that it had a woman's touch. But there were masculine accents, as though a woman had lived here and thought a man was coming to stay.

Clearly Matthews's father had been expecting a male buddy of his son's to arrive. Toni had seen as much in those bright hazel eyes when they'd landed on her. He'd been surprised, but not angry.

She'd felt the urge to apologize to him for the inconvenience. To promise that she wouldn't be a bother, wouldn't even make a sound. She'd clean up behind herself, so he'd have no cause to be annoyed at her presence.

But Mr. Matthews, or rather Father Matthews, as he'd told Toni to call him, was headed out. That was something Toni was used to. Her father was forever married to his job and never around. But his presence always hung huge in his house. Even in her closet of a bedroom that he'd turned into a home office the day after she'd enlisted.

A knock at the door had Toni turning around. Had Matthews changed his mind? Was he coming inside to press his suit? She was probably the only woman around for miles.

Toni quickly disabused herself of that notion. Not because of the ridiculousness of Topher Matthews being attracted to a woman like her. Because there were three beauties crowding the doorway.

The women had tanned skin, as though they were of mixed heritage. Their springy, dark hair was at all lengths. The tallest had a halo of soft curls around her head. The shortest one had her hair cut into a bob that bounced around her heart-shaped face, while the one in the middle had her hair pulled back into a tight bun, but a couple of tendrils wrapped around the base of her neck.

When Toni opened the door, she realized she'd miscounted. Coming up to mid-height of the women was a young girl. This fourth member of the group was clearly of African descent with her coca-colored skin. Her hair was done in neat cornrows, making the girl look like a little princess. Toni took a moment to envy the hairstyle, especially the evenly parted rows of braids that were all ruler straight. Toni ran a self-conscious hand over the messy part in her hair.

"Hi, you must be Toni," said the tallest woman. She had a deep baritone of a voice. "I'm Savy, and these are my sisters Foxy and Tricksy."

The names took Toni back. Were these women performers? Or were their parents just on something when they named their kids?

"And this here is LaTisha."

The young girl eyed Toni with the open curiosity of a child. Her gaze went above Toni's eyes to her hairline. LaTisha frowned, but she didn't say anything.

"We just wanted to welcome you," Savy continued. "And make sure you have everything you need before we head out."

Savy pushed her way past Toni as she spoke. The other two women and little girl walked single file behind their leader into the house. They weren't slight women. But Toni was a highly trained soldier. Yet, with her injury, even little LaTisha might get the best of her.

"I'm headed on my honeymoon with Charlie, that's Topher's brother, and his dad."

That bit of information hadn't registered when Toni had heard it the first time outside with Matthews and his dad. Now that it was confirmed, she had to give a shake of her head. Not only was the dad not mad for the unexpected visitor plopped down on his property, but he was going on his kid's honeymoon? What a weird family.

"Foxy is going to be running around with her husband Joe while he does some legal work for state foster kids."

Foxy, the one with the short bob, gave a wave and an apologetic grin.

"But Tricksy will be here to watch over the foster kids."

Tricksy was the only one that, along with LaTisha, hadn't offered Toni a friendly smile. Where LaTisha eyed Toni with child-like curiosity, Tricksy eyed Toni with wary suspicion.

Danger bells should have been ringing in Toni's head. This woman clearly looked at her as an adversary. But for what? It was the first time Toni had met the woman. What did she have against her?

Something else registered louder in Toni's mind. "Foster kids?"

"Didn't Topher tell you?" said Tricksy. "There are five fosters living here."

Toni's gaze landed again on LaTisha. The kid held Toni's stare. Her parents had given her up? Yet she looked so clean and tidy with her pressed clothes and straight cornrows.

"Did he tell you he was a foster kid himself?" asked Tricksy, suspicion oozing from her tone. Her lower lip curled in cynicism. Or was that jealousy?

Toni's gaze dipped to the woman's hands. It was instinct for her to look for a weapon when faced with an adversary. What Toni found on Tricksy's left hand confused her more. There was a sparkling engagement ring on her fourth finger.

"There's nothing between Matthews and me." Toni made an emphatic gesture with her hands, slicing the air. "I needed a place to stay near the VA hospital. He feels guilty for crashing. So here I am."

The three women winced. Toni felt only a slight pang of guilt for speaking about the crash in such a callous manner. But she knew what she'd signed up for, and she wanted to get back to it. Even with the danger she knew it presented. With all its faults, the military had been the only place that had accepted her without conditions.

"We're just glad you're all safe," said Savy, breaking the tense silence.

"Just don't get back on the horse too soon," said Foxy.

Toni wasn't going to listen to that bit of advice. Horseback riding was the one thing that had sent her recovery off the charts. Matthews had promised her a ride, and she was going to take him up on it.

"I can see you're not going to listen to me," Foxy was saying. "When your heart gets thrown, know it's okay to let Topher catch it."

Toni wanted to balk. Matthews hadn't caught her the first time. He was the one who'd made her fall. She definitely had no intentions of falling for him in the emotional sense. But she fixed her face and showed her manners. Luckily, Savy quickly ushered all the women out of the house with an apologetic smile cast Toni's way.

Such a weird family. They didn't have to worry about Toni overstaying her welcome. As soon as she got better, she'd be out of here on her next deployment.

CHAPTER EIGHT

opher walked the property line. In the distance, he could see the white-capped mountains. A mix of sky-blue and forest-green clashed all around him as nature made its mark on the vista.

Outside of this land, he always felt the need to rush and go as fast as possible, push himself as far as possible. But when here on the Flying Cross Ranch, he felt as though everything around him stood still. And so could he.

He also saw that the ranch needed repairs. The roof of the big house showed wear and tear since they'd last replaced it ten years ago, before they'd all been at home together. When he and his brothers all lived here, everything was in tiptop shape. But they'd all been gone for so long. Because they were all around the same age, there had been a mass exodus. That move had left their father high and dry, the recent victim of a heart attack because he worked himself so hard to maintain his home, their home.

Topher's hand curled into a fist. His father had given him so much. He would not be the man he'd become without him. He probably wouldn't be here on this earth without Haran Matthews.

Luckily, three of his brothers were back home for good. Charlie, Joe, and Will could help keep the place in good form. Topher wasn't ready to settle down. He didn't think he'd ever be. He didn't see why he ever would need to be. But while he was here, he would get as much work done as possible.

This was his home base. It would always be. Whenever he needed to stop, whenever he needed a moment to breathe, whenever he needed to retreat from the world, he'd come back here for a spell before zooming off again.

Three days was a fair price to pay to hold still while his father got a well-deserved vacation. He could do work on the farm and get Solis off to a good start for her rehab.

"Is that a pig up there in the sky?"

"No, I think it's hell freezing over."

Topher rolled his eyes at the sounds of his brothers' voices. He knew what was coming. So he steeled himself for the punches they would swing.

"It must be," said Charlie, "because I never thought I'd see the day that Christopher Matthews brought a girl home."

Topher ducked his brother's jab. Then threw one of his own. It was two against one as Joe snuck up behind him. Those were not fair odds... for his two brothers.

Joe went for a body check. Topher side-stepped the man and got in a shot at Charlie's side. That left his two opponents tending to their wounds while Topher did a Mohammed Ali style dance away from them.

Except Topher hadn't seen Will come up behind him. Will wrapped an arm around Topher's neck and took him down. The brothers rolled on the ground, both trying to gain the upper hand.

At one point, they switched sides. Joe, always angling to get the scales of justice to balance, dove onto Will. Charlie, loyal to the end, took that opportunity to reengage Topher.

It was utter chaos. But that was the Matthews boys.

"I can't wait to meet the woman who's finally tamed The Topher Matthews," said Will as he brushed dirt from his pants. Unfortunately, that grass stain would live on those pants from now on.

"It's not like that," said Topher, swiping at his bottom lip and coming away with blood. He wiped the fluid on his pants and came to standing, unperturbed.

"You told Dad she was a man."

Topher shrugged. "Sometimes I forget Solis is a woman."

Though he hadn't when he'd seen her this morning on the Purple

Heart Ranch. Not in those jeans that hugged curves he'd never known were there. Not when she'd leaned her head against the passenger-side window as the sun's rays had kissed her brown skin.

"Yeah, right," said Charlie. "I caught a glimpse of her on the way here. She's definitely all woman."

"Shut it, or I'll tell Savy," said Topher, throwing out another jab, which Charlie ducked.

"Tell my wife whatever you want. She knows she has me wrapped around her little finger."

"And she knows you like it," said Joe.

Charlie grinned wide in confirmation.

"Solis needs help," said Topher, ignoring his brother's antics. "Dad always says to help each other."

In a chorus that their musical wives would've appreciated, all three of his brothers snorted.

"I'm sure you were going to help her," said a feminine voice. "That's why you were about to drop her and run."

Topher tried not to groan, but he couldn't hide his wince. For years, anytime he came face to face with Tricksy James, he steeled himself for the blow that would inevitably land square on his nose.

Like all the James girls, Tricksy knew how to fight dirty. But she didn't come to Topher. She went into Will's arms. Still, that didn't mean she wasn't coming for him.

Tricksy had fancied herself in love with Topher for more than half her life. She'd even written a song about it that had become a popular breakup anthem on the local charts. Though he hadn't heard her singing it lately. Topher supposed he had Will to thank for that.

Will Matthews had been in love with Tricksy for longer than Tricksy had thought herself in love with Topher. It had taken a little white lie for the two of them to finally see the truth that had been right in front of them all along.

What the two of them had was real, Topher knew that beyond a shadow of a doubt. He could spot love. Enough to know that he wanted little to nothing to do with it.

He'd seen how his birth had contributed to the loss of his biological father, who had been and still remained married. He'd seen how the loss of his adoptive mother had affected his dad. He'd felt the loss himself. Still felt it. Topher didn't want anyone to have that kind of power over him.

"I wasn't trying to drop her and run," he said. But looking around at his brothers' faces, he saw he had no support. Because everyone knew that had been his ultimate plan. "Dad's good at this stuff. So is Savy. Solis is in better hands with them."

"Any woman is in better hands so long as they're not yours." And with that, Tricksy gave Will a passionate kiss, a wink, and walked off.

Will looked stupidly at her as she walked away. Then he turned to glance at Topher. "You know you're going to have to fix that."

Topher sighed. Another reason he'd planned to drop off Solis and get out of here. Everyone kept insisting that he and Tricksy have a talk. Topher hated having talks, especially when they were about feelings. It was why he didn't do relationships.

He wasn't even in a relationship with Tricksy, but to make his family happy, he'd have to sit down and have a talk about their feelings. Or rather, she would. Because he didn't have any feelings on the matter. He didn't think she should have any feelings left for him now that she was with Will.

But to make everyone around him happy, he'd do it. He'd just let her yell at him until she tired herself out. Then his dad and Savy would be back. And he could go off on a solo camping trip. Then he would leave for his deployment. And that would be that.

CHAPTER NINE

*T*oni woke to silence as the sun's rays crept into the bedroom. The bright light trod a muted path across the sheets on the bed. Nothing stirred, not even the dust motes in the air. The hushed stillness reminded her of her childhood.

It was always quiet in her father's house. Either he came home late after she'd already made herself a microwave dinner and went to bed. Or he was gone early in the morning before she got herself up and dressed, toasted a Pop Tart, and made her way to school.

Most days, they talked through notes left for each other on the kitchen counter. His notes were always short, quickly scrawled, and barely legible. There wasn't much Toni had to communicate with him about. He'd given her permission to forge his signature on permission slips as soon as she'd learned cursive writing. If he'd ever signed something of importance himself, the school administration would definitely have thought his autograph was the forgery.

In the military, it was never quiet. Definitely not on the base. There was always motion or action. Or snoring. Or farting. Or low conversations over electronic devices to loved ones in different time zones.

Toni had loved every minute of it. Loved the shards of light that always seemed to shine at every minute of the day and night. Loved the frequency of the sounds—no matter how vulgar. She had never been alone on base. And there was always someone looking out for her.

Here, on the Flying Cross Ranch, all Toni could hear was the sound of the wind rustling leaves. Even the chickens were relatively quiet. She rolled out in the comfortable bed and prepared for the day. It was early in the morning, just after dawn, but she saw she wasn't the only one up.

Five kids moved about the ranch. There was a mix of boys and girls. They were of differing heights, which told her they were a range of ages. They were also of differing races, by the looks of the hues of the skin tones ranging from the brown-skinned LaTisha to a little girl who was just a touch too pale for someone clearly used to working outdoors.

The children moved about the farm carrying pales, moving bales of hay, and tossing out feed to the penned-in animals. What Toni didn't see were any adults around them. Were the Matthewses running a child labor farm here?

No. She doubted that. Not when all the kids wore grins on their faces as they went about their chores.

"Thought you'd sleep in."

Toni's heart slammed against her chest at the sound of Matthews's voice. It wasn't easy to sneak up on her. Especially not for this man whose location she made sure to always know when they were in a room together.

"Training," she said, turning to face him.

Looking directly at his face was a mistake. He'd let his blond mane of hair grow wild since he'd been off base. And by wild, she meant there was a good two inches of locks radiating around his face. She felt over-heated gazing up at him.

Matthews nodded as though he didn't need her to expound on that one-word answer that she'd given. They'd had the same training. His more extensive than hers because he'd been in the Air Force longer and had risen higher.

"You want breakfast first? Or do you want to get started?" Matthews asked.

"Started?"

"With your rehab."

"I don't have a VA appointment until Monday."

"I know," he said, stepping closer.

Instinct warned her to step back. Everyone knew what happened to those who flew too close to the sun. Instead, she held still, letting his warmth seep into her aching limbs.

"I was going to take you out for a ride. Equine therapy worked on your leg."

Toni perked up at that, an unguarded smile starting at the corner of her mouth. She'd loved riding on the horses at the Purple Heart Ranch. Sitting atop the majestic beasts had restored some of the power she'd lost after the crash.

"Yes, please."

Matthews's grin was like a heatwave. It singed the hair on her forearms yet still managed to leave behind goosebumps. It was the heart-stopping grin she saw him give to other women.

Toni crossed her arms over her shoulders. "I mean, yes, that would be agreeable. If it's not too much trouble."

"No trouble at all. I want you well."

Of course he did. Because he wanted her out of here and out of his hair. Well, he'd get that soon, sooner if she could help it.

He held out his hand in a gesture for her to precede him. She took a deep breath and braced herself for the descent down the three steps. Down was always harder than up.

Though she took that deep breath, there was nothing to actually brace herself with. No handrail to lean on. All that was there was Matthews's strong bicep, which she refused to reach for.

She stepped down onto the first step with her good leg. That meant her injured knee only need carry her full weight once for the second step. Toni transferred the weight quickly, but she couldn't hold back the grunt of pain.

She glanced over at Matthews, but he was looking away from her, his face turned off into the distance. But Toni caught sight of the tension in his jaw. When she looked down, she saw both his hands clenched into fists.

His body relaxed once they were on level ground. He kept his pace slow as they headed to the barn. Toni tried to go double pace. Partly to show him she didn't need coddling. Mostly because she was eager to get to the horses.

"This is Mahalia," he said as he brought out a beautiful black mare. "She's been with us since I was a boy."

Toni couldn't imagine Matthews as a boy. She couldn't see this majestic beast as a pony. Like all females, the horse nuzzled at Matthews's hand.

"Let me just grab you a saddle and—"

"I can do it."

Matthews bit his lip as Toni pushed past him to the array of saddles lined up in the corner. The saddle she chose was slightly different from what they had on the Purple Heart Ranch, but the mechanics were the same.

Matthews brought out another horse and had him saddled up while Toni was still fussing with the straps. A few seconds later, it looked like her time was up with the saddle. He took the straps from her hands and made quick work of the saddle. With that in place, he turned, his hands reaching for her. A zing went up and down Toni's spine as Matthews put a hand on either side of her waist. With a gasp, she smacked his hands from her body.

"What do you think you're doing?" she demanded.

"I'm helping you on the horse."

"I can get up myself."

"That's enough, Airman."

The rigidity and command in his voice made her snap to attention. Matthews always had a jovial look on his face. Even when things were serious. His expression was all flat lines as he regarded her now.

"You need help." His tone brooked no argument. "Whether you want to admit it or not, you need a helping hand. I have help to offer you. We're on the same mission."

"Fine."

"Fine."

They both stood with their arms crossed over their chest. Matthews moved first. He unfolded his arms and placed his hands on her waist again.

As she went up, Toni unfolded her arms. Her hands came to rest on his shoulders. She felt the play of muscles there as he lifted her up. Her breath caught as she looked down at him. She saw his pupils dilate and his nostrils flare. Was that heat she saw in his eyes? She'd never know because once she was settled down on the back of the horse, he turned from her.

Sitting astride the horse, Toni realized she didn't care. She'd lost so much of her power since that crash. She'd nearly lost her faculties when Matthews had lifted her off the ground. Now that she was on the horse, she felt she had her power back.

CHAPTER TEN

opher knew this trail like the back of his hand.

He frowned at that saying as the words rolled through his head. He had never spent much time looking at the back of his hand. He doubted he'd be able to pick it out of a lineup of photographs. But if he saw the roots poking out of the ground on this trail, if he saw the wind of the path and the types of rocks that were off to the sides, if he saw the way the wildflowers grew, he would know he was on his favorite path.

He'd been walking it, running on it, riding on it for more than half his life. But he'd never brought a girl on it. Not even Tricksy during their ill-fated relationship—if you could call a few group dates to the ice cream shop and a couple of unfinessed kisses a relationship.

Tricksy had called that a relationship. Up until a couple weeks ago, she had called him the love of her life. In the same breath, she'd also called him her worst mistake.

That debacle, like his biological mother's heartbreak and his adoptive mom's death, taught Topher that love was not in his cards. Mostly because it was a game he had no interest in playing. Which was why he preferred to get in, have a little fun, then get out before feelings could develop.

Luckily, he didn't have to worry about feelings with Solis. He didn't think the woman had any. Not with how she grimaced and bared the physical pain she was clearly in. He saw that, like he'd had to scoop her injured body up and into his arms to save her life after the crash, he'd have to drag her bodily to get her to ask for the help it was clear she needed but for some reason was too stubborn to ask for.

He glanced over his shoulder at Solis. She wasn't even looking at him. She rarely did. Which meant he didn't have to worry about the idea of a relationship between the two of them entering her head.

All she wanted was to get well so that she could return to the service. It was what he wanted too. Not just for himself, but for her, too.

Solis eyed the trail with a small smile. He'd never seen the woman smile before. It made her look like… well, like a woman. Almost pretty.

The two thick braids that wound around the crown of her head were crooked. They were always crooked, if he remembered correctly. She was often wearing a helmet, so he hadn't paid much attention.

The haphazard part down the middle of her head, which was out of alignment, made her appear more accessible. Like she was someone who could make a mistake and not worry too much about it. Much like the trail that stretched out before them, twisting and winding on a circuitous path. Topher wondered about running his fingers across that track in her hair.

He gave himself a shake. What was a thought like that doing in his head? This was Solis. She wasn't a woman. She was an airman. And he wouldn't be staying long enough to run his fingers anywhere on her body. His only interest in her body was getting it back in shape so she could move on with her life.

Her gaze caught his, and she frowned. That was another thing about her. Whenever women caught Topher looking, they never frowned. They smiled demurely, doing that hair flick thing or leaning forward with their chest on display—all those things to keep men's gazes lingering and offering an invitation. Solis's glare was a loud and clear door slammed shut.

"Your form is good," he said, trying to cover from his wayward eyes. "On the horse, I mean. I mean—riding the horse."

Topher pursed his lips. He'd never been tongue-tied around a woman before. Why was this one making him nervous?

"Thank you," she said, her shoulders straightening at the compliment.

Something sparked in Topher's chest. He liked what that compliment elicited from her. He wanted to see it again.

"You could loosen up on the reins a bit."

Her shoulders went rigid, but not like before. There was a stiffness to them now. The smile had dissolved from her face.

"I know the procedure to ride a horse. I aced the checklist they had at the Purple Heart Ranch."

"Is everything a checklist to you?"

"I like to be prepared. We can't all fly by the seat of our pants."

"I don't use my pants to fly."

"That's not what I heard."

She said it under her breath, but Topher heard it clearly. She likely meant it as an insult, but the joke was funny, and he laughed. She glared at him. Instead of a chin lift or a light in her eyes, she bristled. Of course she did. She was Solis.

"Who exactly did you hear it from?" he asked, curious to know which woman had kissed and told about him to her. He'd always thought her clipboard and pens were her only friends. He never saw her gossiping with the other female soldiers.

"Like you'd even remember their names," she said.

Wow, she was tough as nails. But she had the right of it. Topher didn't mind having a love-them-and-leave-them reputation. It made things easier when it was time for him to go.

"I'm surprised your family even remembers my name," she went on.

"I've never brought a woman home."

"Of course you haven't. No commitment on your part. Though Tricksy seems to have stuck around."

"Me and Tricks…" Topher sighed. "We're complicated. She followed me home because her sister Savy was dating my brother Charlie."

"And you plucked her off."

"There was no plucking. It was never real. Just—what do they call it? Puppy love."

"I wouldn't know. I'm a cat person."

Again, he laughed at the insult that he chose to interpret as a joke. Turning to face her, he caught her crack a smile. But it was there and gone so fast. Topher wracked his brain to determine how to get it back, how to make it linger. What came out of his mouth was a truth he rarely spoke of.

"I'm not the bad guy here. I don't believe in love. Not love like that.

Not love between two people that are essentially strangers. Now the love between a parent and a child, that's different."

"You loved your biological parents?"

"No, they were both selfish people." Thinking about it now, Topher realized he might have a bit of their selfishness in him with how he interacted with the fairer sex. "My adoptive parents, they chose me. Even when I didn't deserve it, they still chose me. I can't imagine doing that with some random woman."

They rode in silence for a few yards. Topher wanted to fill the silence, but with what? He didn't know. He felt raw after having exposed that piece of himself. Would she turn around and use it to hurt him? She was a trained soldier.

"I'm no expert," Solis finally said at another turn in the path, "but I believe that's what dating is for."

Another non-joke. But this time, he didn't laugh. "That's not what dating is for."

"Pig."

Topher made a snorting sound that mimicked the animal he was accused of imitating. Solis laughed at him. A genuine laugh that time.

It had been a long time since he'd enjoyed his time with a woman without fear of her falling into imaginary love with him. Solis had zero interest in him. She'd made that clear. It allowed him to let his guard down even more.

"You don't have to worry about me falling for you," she said. "Again."

"Again?"

"I fell out of a plane because of you."

"I caught you."

There was a charged moment. He watched her throat work as she swallowed. Her eyes were huge in that round face of hers. Her chin tilted up so that all he saw was the crown of her braids and not the crooked part.

His smile was nervous, not the confident one he always wore around women, around anyone. He wanted to open his mouth to make an excuse, to joke the sentiment of those words away. But the words were out there. He couldn't take them back. And so he looked away.

"Any way," he went on, "I'm going to help you get back on your feet. I owe it to you."

"You don't owe me anything, Matthews. But... thank you."

He hadn't expected to hear those words. "You're welcome. Don't worry, you won't have to deal with me for long. I'll be deploying again soon."

The silence was deafening. He looked over, and the look on Solis's face was thunderous. Without any warning, she took off at a gallop.

CHAPTER ELEVEN

*T*oni leaned into the horse as it took off. The wind whipping against her face stung, but the air dried any tears before they could form. The bouncing of the horse made her leg throb as she fought to keep her seat, but better endure that pain in her knee than the ache scratching at her chest. She should stop before she fell, but it was already too late. And so she held on tight and urged the horse faster.

How had she fallen for it?

She was such a fool.

Her backside protested the rough ride. But Toni wasn't sure if it was that pain or the pain of the fall that had her running faster, farther.

She ducked her head to avoid a tree branch. She heard her name being called in the distance. Matthews was chasing after her. But why?

Toni urged the horse faster. She'd never gone this fast before. The trainers at the Purple Heart Ranch had only ever let her go as fast as a trot. This was a full-on gallop, and she was close to losing control. But the power she felt, the freedom she felt atop the horse at this speed was too good to pull on the reins.

As long as she was moving forward, no one would leave her behind. As long as she was running, she wouldn't hear anyone's words to stop her in her tracks. Or worse, their silence wouldn't make her shiver with its cold completeness.

Except it wasn't silent out here on the trail.

Toni heard the sound of hooves pounding the ground behind her. She knew there were wild horses roaming free in this part of Montana. Was one joining her run?

A quick glance over her shoulders disabused her of that notion. It was Matthews. And he was gaining.

But why was he following her? He'd just said he was leaving. Leaving here. Leaving her.

Before those words had left his lips, Toni had felt high on the horse. She'd let that man lift her up on this pedestal, the pedestal of a horse at that. She'd learned he'd never brought a girl home. It felt like he'd never shared this special place with another woman, either. For a moment, Toni had felt special.

His talk of not believing in love didn't bother her. She didn't believe in it either. Her own father had made the choice to neglect her each day of her life since her mother's death. So no, she didn't expect Matthews's love. But she had warmed to the notion of being special to him.

Until he told her he'd be leaving her behind. Going back to work. Just like her father did every day of her life. Because she was a burden.

The tears stung her eyes now. The drops were falling too fast for the wind to catch them. She couldn't lift a hand to swipe them away. She couldn't let Matthews catch her. She couldn't let him see her like this. She couldn't.

"Toni!"

Matthews had never called her by her first name. She was surprised he even knew it. Her grip slipped on the reins, and she wobbled in the saddle.

Looking ahead, Toni saw a small log lying on the path. The mare would have to jump to clear it. Toni hadn't practiced jumping back at the Purple Heart Ranch. She had no clue of what to do. She was going to lose her seat and be thrown from the horse.

Gripping the reins, Toni pulled on them, trying to slow the horse down. But she couldn't sit up straight to tug hard enough. It felt as if when she tried to right her body, she would lose her grip and fall.

"Toni!"

She dared a glance to her left and saw Matthews riding right beside her. He reached out his hand to her. But Toni was too frightened to grab for it.

"Give me your hand, soldier."

The command in his voice was absolute. She had to follow the order. But her fingers wouldn't loosen their death grip on the reins.

Cold seeped into her body under the warm glow of the midday sun. Her fingers were icicles as they curled around the leather. Her lips trembled and her teeth chattered as she ducked her head against the wind slamming into her face.

And then there was heat.

Matthews's warm hand was on hers. The reins were being taken from her. Mercifully, the horse began to slow until she came to a dead stop.

Toni could feel the animal's pounding heart against her thighs. It made her knee throb. Her hunched position made her shoulder ache.

And then she was weightless.

An arm came around her waist. She was airborne, being lifted off the horse. She didn't fight it. But she did try to hide her face.

She was deposited with a deep, male grunt against a warm chest. An arm like a tight band came around her. The world slowed, but she felt another pounding all around her.

It was her heart. It pounded in her ear. Against her cheek.

No, that wasn't just her heart. It was Matthews's heart, too. He held on to her, breathing hard, squeezing tight.

It had been a long time since Toni had been held. She couldn't remember the last time. But she was sure it had been inside her mother's arms.

Her mother's arms had been strong. Her heartbeat a song Toni would remember always. Inside that embrace, Toni had felt safe, like she wasn't alone in the world.

She closed her eyes inside the safety of this hold. Her lips parted as she took in long, deep breaths that made her heart settle. The weight left her shoulders. The ache left her leg.

It was good. So good. Too good.

And then it was over.

Topher yanked her from him, far enough so that he could peer down at her with a stormy glare in his eyes.

"What were you thinking? Were you even thinking?"

Toni opened her mouth. All that came out was a choked cry. Followed by a deluge of tears.

CHAPTER TWELVE

opher slammed the hammer against the nail. It sank in in just two whacks. That was a bit disappointing. He wanted to pound something harder and for much longer. He grabbed another nail and repeated the process.

This time, it took him four whacks. On the first try, his fingers shook, and he dropped the nail. On the second try, he just barely missed his thumb, and the nail went in crooked.

This had been happening for two days now. For two days, a tremble would turn up in his hands. For two days, his hands would ball into fists out of nowhere.

No, not out of nowhere. Anytime he caught a glimpse of Toni Solis peeking out of the window of the guest house. Anytime he caught sight of Mahalia grazing in her pen.

Topher didn't blame the old girl for what had happened out on the trail. He blamed Solis. He just didn't know why she'd done it.

She'd clammed up after he'd pulled her from the runaway horse and held her tight. At first, he hadn't been able to speak, hadn't been able to get a single word past the pounding of his heart. When her tears fell, he hadn't wanted to say anything else.

Topher was a trained soldier. He'd been battle tested first by the crazed warriors that had grown up with him on the ranch and then by the best military personnel on the face of the earth. But his Achilles' heel? A woman's tears.

He'd never expected a display like that from the stoic Solis. And he wanted to know why she'd done it. Why had she taken off like that? Was it something he'd said? He couldn't imagine what. And she wouldn't tell him. She wouldn't even talk to him.

When he'd knocked on the guest house door the day after, she hadn't answered. Not being one to push, he'd left her alone to lick her wounds and got to work.

The work to be done on the roof was grueling for one man. Joe was in the city every day, trying to save the world through the muddy water of local politics. Will had his hands full with the five foster kids that were learning the ropes on the ranch. And the roof was just the beginning of the repairs that needed to be done. Not to mention the ongoing upkeep of running the ranch.

The Silver sisters from the neighboring ranch had been by to lend a hand when they could. Those six women knew their way around the land since they'd grown up thinking of the Flying Cross ranch as an extended backyard. They'd been the ones helping out Father Matthews while his sons were away flying around the world.

But Topher couldn't expect the Silver girls to stop their lives to keep tending to the Matthewses' lands. Especially with their husbands glaring at him as their pregnant wives picked up construction tools and corralled wily animals.

Topher needed more hands on the ranch. There were another two pairs of hands that could be helping at the moment. So he picked up the phone and dialed.

While the phone rang, Topher looked toward the guest house. He could see shadows moving behind the curtain of the front window. No doubt Solis was inside working on her PT. He knew the woman had a list and was sticking to it religiously. He had a sudden ache to bust down the door and snatch the clipboard from her, just to have her glare at him with those hazel eyes.

"Brooooo." The truncated word was drawled out in a deep, masculine voice that sounded as though it hadn't been used yet this morning.

"Bro," Topher answered.

"You know what time it is here?"

Maybe it was still night where Mateo and Aldo were. There was a lilting quality to the words, letting Topher know he was talking to Aldo.

Mateo had worked hard to eliminate as much of his Spanish accent as possible, where Aldo had embraced his Mexican heritage full bore.

Topher ignored Aldo's question. "We need you home."

There was a rustling of sheets. "Is it Dad?"

"Yes."

Topher heard his brother swear. Then he heard an identical voice swear. There were muffled sounds, and then a new voice came on the phone.

"Is it another heart attack?" asked Mateo.

"What? No. Dad's fine. He needs our help on the ranch. Things are in disrepair here. Charlie's on his honeymoon. Joe is slammed with his state foster care case. And Will is always making stupid eyes at Tricksy. Pretty sure he'll be wanting to go on a honeymoon soon."

"Is this about Tricksy?" Aldo drawled. "I thought you were over her."

"I was never under her."

There were boyish chuckles on the other end of the line. In their laughter, no one could tell the twins apart. Though Topher would always be able to guess who told the joke. Aldo was the trickster of their bunch.

"You two grow up," said Topher. "I'm being serious here. Dad needs help here."

"We'll be home soon. Meanwhile, he has you. Didn't you always say you could do the work of three men?"

"I can. But this isn't my only job right now."

The door to the guest house opened, and Solis came out. She tilted her head to the sun and pushed her hips forward, which also pushed her chest forward. Topher was far enough away that he couldn't see anything fun, but just the sight of her curves as she stood their unaware made his heart skip a beat.

He gave himself a shake. He should not be looking at that woman like that. He shouldn't even be looking at her like she was a woman. She was Solis.

"We heard about your little project from Charlie," said Mateo.

Topher pinched the bridge between his brows. "Does that man not know what to do on a honeymoon?"

"Sounds like you might be thinking of one yourself," said Aldo, his voice filled with mirth.

"What? No! It's not like that. I'm just helping her out until she gets back on her feet."

"By bringing her home and tending her wounds personally?" Aldo snickered.

"I owe her. It's my fault."

"You know better than to play that game, bro." Mateo's voice turned serious, leaving no room for joking. "We all know what we sign up for in this life."

All Topher could think about was watching Solis fall. Seeing the fear in her eyes. Then reaching for her, just like he'd done when she was on that galloping horse.

She'd closed her eyes then as Mahalia ran off with her. Closed them and seemed to accept her fate.

Well, screw that. Screw it then and screw it now. He wouldn't let her give up back on the battlefield. He wasn't letting her give up now.

He'd give her the rest of the day to sulk and lick her wounds, and then he was going to get back to tending to them himself. He'd have that soldier in ship shape before he deployed, and then they could all get back to the life they'd signed up for.

CHAPTER THIRTEEN

*T*oni stayed in bed as the sun rose. She didn't rise from the bed until the star was at its pinnacle in the sky. She puttered around the guest house all day, making sure to stay out of the sun's rays, sticking instead to the shadows, lest she be spotted. Now that the sun was starting to set and darkness was slowly creeping in, she finally poked her head outside the door.

The activity on the ranch had died down. There had only been one knock on her door. Foxy had stopped by to check on her and bring her a plate of food and herbal tea. A wary Tricksy had stood sentry in the background, her wavy hair pulled taut in a high ponytail that made her look like a disapproving warden and not a welcoming matron.

"I felt that you were hungry," Foxy had said.

"Felt?" Toni asked, taking the plate of food. As a kid who'd grown up on microwaveable foods and graduated to the mess hall of various army bases, she wasn't picky.

"I'm clairsentient," Foxy clarified.

Toni didn't point out that it was late in the day and it was a good bet that she would be hungry since she hadn't shown up for any of the appointed mealtimes. The guest house had a small fridge and a two-burner stove. But she was grateful for the home-cooked meal.

"And don't worry about Butch, the bus driver," Foxy continued. "His honk is worse than his bite."

With a smile and a wave, the woman bounced down the steps. Toni frowned at Foxy's retreating form.

Tricksy wrinkled her nose at her sister as she passed by. When Tricksy lifted her head, her and Toni's gazes connected. It would have been a shared moment, except Tricksy schooled her features and turned on her heel, effectively shutting Toni out.

Toni was used to that from other women. She hadn't had many girl-friends growing up. She hadn't had that many boyfriends either. And definitely not a real boyfriend. The school counselor had diagnosed Toni with attachment issues. That was before she left for a better job a couple of weeks later in private care. Though the counselor was gone, the diagnosis lingered. Toni didn't see the point in attaching to anyone when nobody was permanent in her life.

That's how she found herself later in the evening—sitting alone on the guest house porch without anyone else coming to check on her. She'd made it clear she didn't want or need company, and it looked like the Matthewses would respect that. Topher Matthews was clearly all too happy to keep his distance after she'd shed her tears, and that suited her just fine.

She reached for the end of one of her braids and began to uncoil it. Taking a fat-toothed comb, she ran the teeth through her hair, starting at the end. Toni had learned the hard way that any hair maintenance had to start at the end unless she wanted the mother of all headaches. That was a lesson she'd had to learn since she didn't have a mother to tend her hair, and her father didn't always remember to make her an appointment at the hair salon.

Toni's arms quickly began to tire as she went through the task of unraveling the second braid and pulling the comb through her tight curls. That ride had taxed her muscles, much more than it ever had on the Purple Heart Ranch. She'd never ridden that fast before. She had almost died before.

Twice now.

Twice she'd been trapped in a conveyance that she'd had no control over.

Twice she'd almost lost her life.

Twice Topher Matthews had been there to rescue her.

That craziness ended now. She didn't need rescuing. She was the rescuer.

It was time to get her rehabilitation back on track. She had her first doctor's visit at the VA clinic in just two days. She wouldn't ask any of the Matthewses for help getting there. She could Uber.

Though she barely had any cell phone service out here on the ranch. And when she tapped the ride share app, it was still searching for a driver twenty minutes later.

With three bars of service, she was able to pull up the local transit authority website. She saw the bus schedules listed. But she'd have to walk a mile up the road to catch the first of three buses that would take her to the clinic.

There; problem solved. A mile would tax her, but it would be worth it not to have to sit next to Matthews, who clearly didn't want to be around her. Or sit sandwiched between a chatty Foxy, who spouted nonsense and a scowling Tricksy, who clearly still had a thing for Matthews.

Toni put her phone to the side. Her arms had had a good rest from being raised over her head to fuss with her hair. Now that all of her tresses were unwoven and combed through, it was time to part the sections and rebraid. This was her least favorite part of hair care.

"That's not straight."

Toni looked up to find LaTisha staring at her from the porch.

"Here, let me." The little girl stomped up the steps in red cowboy boots and held out her hand for the comb.

Toni hesitated. This was a child. Could she even part straight? But she couldn't do worse than her own weary hands. Toni handed over the comb.

She felt the little girl's hands in her hair. Then the blunt tooth of the comb as it tracked across her scalp. It brought to mind sitting on the ground between her mother's legs as she did her hair as a girl.

The sound of her mother's laughter rang loud and clear in Toni's ears. Her temple warmed where she remembered her mother pressing a kiss there. Toni gave a shake and let the memory fall away.

"Are you going to marry Mr. Topher?"

That made Toni shake anew. "No. We're not even dating. I don't date."

"You're a career woman? Like Ms. Tricksy? She's a singer. She's really good, too. When she's not singing about Mr. Topher. She's marrying Mr. Will, you know. Are you going to marry one of the other brothers?"

"I'm not marrying anybody."

"Oh."

Toni wasn't sure if that *oh* was condemnation, accusation, or repudiation. But that single word made her shrink into herself.

"I want to get married," LaTisha continued as she worked the comb to the middle of Toni's scalp. "And be a mom, and have a husband that's also a dad. Sometimes dads aren't husbands, and husbands aren't dads. I think it would be best if I married a boy who wanted to be both."

"That's smart."

"Yeah, I know. I'm at the top of my class."

Toni couldn't hide her smile at that. "You don't want a career?"

LaTisha made a tsking sound with her teeth. "Being a mom is a career. It's Ms. Savy and Ms. Foxy's job to take care of us kids. But I don't want to foster. I want my own kids. Not all fosters are good kids. Ms. Savy says that's not always their fault. But I think sometimes it is. You can choose to behave."

LaTisha handed the comb to Toni. Before Toni could raise her hands to gather hair to start braiding, LaTisha's small fingers were weaving at the front of her head.

Toni sat back. Her shoulder blades rested against LaTisha's small body. She found that she was enjoying the feel of someone's hands in her hair so much that she didn't stop the little girl. If it looked bad, she'd just redo it later.

"Do you have a mom and dad?" LaTisha asked.

"Everyone has a mom and dad."

"Nope. Everyone has parents. Not all parents are moms and dads."

Wow, this kid was wise beyond her years. Toni didn't want to answer her. She felt that if she spoke about her mom while in this vulnerable position of having her hair braided, the tears from yesterday would return. But the words escaped her lips none the less.

"My mom died when I was a little girl."

"Was she a good mom?" asked LaTisha.

Toni nodded.

"Mine wasn't. She wasn't a mom. She was just my parent. But now I have two moms, so it worked out for me."

Toni looked up to see Foxy. She gave a wave. Toni waved back, as though to say it was okay for LaTisha to be here. Foxy gave her a smile and turned back to the house.

"Mr. Topher's a good guy," LaTisha said as she switched to start the other braid. "He plays games with us, even the girls. I think he'll be more than a parent. I think he'll make a good dad."

Toni would have disagreed. Matthews was leaving. She knew from experience that a good dad didn't leave their kids to their own defenses all the time.

CHAPTER FOURTEEN

opher slammed the truck's gate closed after making sure the supplies were secure. Packed in the back was lumber for fencing, shingles for roofing, and some specialized feed for a few of the chickens who were looking a little too lean.

He'd run out of space after tossing in the feed, but he still had more supplies to get to. He'd just have to take another trip. Or ask Joe to grab it on his way home from the law offices he shared with Charlotte O'Dell.

The problem with that idea was that Joe drove a luxury car. His brother might not get upset if the interior got a little dirty. There was still enough farm boy in him. But that high end car wouldn't fit a quarter of the supplies Topher still needed brought back to the ranch.

He'd just have to make another trip. He couldn't do it later today, and he couldn't come back tomorrow. Tomorrow he had Solis's appointment at the VA clinic.

A small voice in his head whispered that he could have one of the girls drive Solis instead. Topher flapped his hand at his ear, like he would an annoying gnat. Solis was as much his responsibility as was the upkeep of the ranch. He could manage both while he was here.

There was still so much work to do on the ranch. Repairs that had been part of his and his brothers' chores growing up had been neglected. How had his father maintained all this time? How had they not noticed the ranch slowly falling into disrepair?

The same way they hadn't noticed their father getting older.

Haran Matthews had always been a giant to him. Topher still looked up to the man like he held the world on his shoulders. He just hadn't realized his father's shoulders were slumping from the weight he carried. For as long as he was here, he'd lessen that weight while not adding more onto his father's back.

Which meant he'd get Solis back on her feet. But maybe not on a horse for a while. He could work out a loaner vehicle for her and show her around town and the way to the VA. Which meant he would have to finally go and see her at the guest house.

Climbing into the truck, Topher shoved the key into the ignition. The engine sputtered before turning over. Just another thing to add to his long list of chores. The twins had better get here soon to lift their own weight on the ranch, because Topher was starting to feel the ache in his own back.

Rounding Main Street, the engine sputtered again when Topher's foot slammed on the brake. Sitting at the bus stop was a sight he hadn't expected to see: Toni Solis.

She was hunched over, rubbing at her knee. It was her left knee, the injured one. He knew that because his arms had been covered in her blood when he'd scooped her up after the crash.

She pumped the leg in and out. A wince stayed on her face as she made the movements. Clearly, she was in pain.

Had she walked here? No, that wasn't possible. It was five miles from the ranch into town. But it was one mile from the ranch to the nearest bus stop. And there she sat, where the bus would have dropped her off.

Switching his foot from the brake to the gas, Topher pulled up to her at the bus stop. He slammed the truck into park and stared at her out the window. She looked up and started when she saw him.

"What are you doing?" he shouted.

"What does it look like?" she answered in that haughty tone of hers.

There was a sheen of sweat on her forehead. A trickle ran down her temple, making the tight curls at her nape cling to her neck. Topher felt an irrational sense of jealousy staring at those curls.

He lifted his gaze slightly to the crown of her head. Her hair was freshly braided. The rows in nice straight lines. The woven poufs made it look like an actual crown was sitting atop her head. Her nose in the air completed the regal look.

"How'd you get here?" he demanded.

Solis pursed her lips like an indignant child.

"Did Foxy or Tricksy give you a ride?"

She looked down the street at the bus ambling toward them. That answered the question for him. She had taken the bus. Which meant she'd walked to the stop.

Why? Why would she put herself, her body, through such an arduous task? Why hadn't she asked him for help? He would've taken her wherever she wanted to go.

"Where are you going?" The moment the words were out of his mouth, he held his breath, uncertain whether or not he wanted the answer.

"I'm doing a practice run for my appointment at the VA," she said. "I wanted to do the route before I had to actually go."

Topher's mouth gaped, but nothing came out for a full thirty seconds. Another second longer and he would've caught a fly. He chucked his thumb at his chest. "I'm taking you to the appointment."

"This time," she agreed with a nod. "But what about next week or next month? I need to make sure I can do it myself."

"When I'm gone, someone from my family will help you."

"I can't rely on your family."

"Of course you can." His family members were the most reliable people in the world. It's why he'd brought her here to them. He was getting nowhere with this conversation. Topher slammed the driver's side door open and hopped out.

"You can't park there. It's the bus lane. You'll get a fine."

"I'm responsible for you," he said.

"No you're not. You feel guilty. That'll wear off, and then I'll be right here, on my own."

"It's not guilt," he said, stepping up to her.

"Then what?" she came to standing, but she wobbled.

It was instinct. He reached for her. First to steady her. But once she was steady, he didn't let her go.

"I need to know you're safe," he said.

Solis's throat worked, but she couldn't get any words out. Good. He didn't want to hear any more lip from her.

Thinking about her lips, Topher couldn't help but dip his gaze to them. There were plump and lush. The type of lips that begged to be gently kissed and then bitten.

"We survived something traumatic," he said quietly. "That might not make us family, but it connects us."

She stared up at him with big eyes. He saw it again, the vulnerability he'd seen when he'd reached for her in the crash. The same look when he'd pulled her to him when the horse had taken off.

Couldn't she see that it was safe here? Safe with him.

"I need to know you're safe," he repeated. "Flying Cross is the safest place I know. My family will keep you safe if I'm not here. I want you to stay here, with them."

"For how long?"

He almost said forever. The word fluttered around inside his chest, banging at his lungs to get out. Instead, he said, "Stay until you feel independent enough to go."

He gazed down at her. The vulnerability was still there. Perhaps if he pulled her closer, it would—

HONK! The bus had pulled in behind his truck. In the driver's seat was Butch, the bus driver. The man had been running these routes since Topher was a kid. He loved to honk that horn, but he was unlikely to get out of the seat and do anything about it.

Topher corralled Solis to the passenger side of the truck while Butch leaned on his horn. Topher waited until Solis was safely inside and securely held by her seatbelt. Then he rounded to the driver's side. He caught sight of Butcher's glare in the rearview mirror as the man finally let up off the horn.

CHAPTER FIFTEEN

Toni watched the flames as they rose into the night air. The sparks hissed as they twirled up into the dark sky, circling each other and fizzling out. It was as though the flames in the hearth couldn't contain themselves. They crackled and popped, sounding for all the world like the smack of kisses.

Not that Toni knew what kisses sounded like firsthand. She'd never been kissed herself. She had never been much interested in the act. At first glance, love looked like a warm and cozy thing, but she'd seen far too much heartache. The angry and despondent tears had always looked to her like they burned the rejected.

And so she kept her distance from the bonfire and stood on the outskirts of the gathering. The people partaking of the fire's warmth were all couples. They stood with hands entwined, heads close together, bodies angled toward one another.

They were all from the neighboring Silver Star Ranch. A gaggle of six sisters and their husbands. Over a dozen people had introduced themselves to her. Toni was surprised she could remember all of the women's names. But then again, each Silver sister had a name related to the military.

The eldest, Scout, with her severe expression that softened each time her husband nuzzled into her neck. Sailor with a high ponytail and round belly who danced in her husband's one-armed embrace, even though there was no music playing. The prim and proper Mareen looked slightly out of place with her designer jeans and boots as she leaned against a green-eyed giant that reminded Toni of the Incredible Hulk. The giant's hands were gentle as they rested on the small bump at his wife's belly. There was even youthful Brigadere on the arm of a man who looked twice her age, but Brig carried herself in a way that seemed older than her years. And finally, the twins, Artillery and Gunnery, talked over one another and completed the other's sentences as their husbands watched them in mute fascination.

Each woman looked at Toni with friendly curiosity when Matthews led her to the spot. Someone had tossed a log into the pit, and the flames had sparked. Matthews had turned and angled his body so that she was shielded from the worst of the heat. Once the flames had settled, those friendly gazes had turned into open inquiry.

Toni had been peppered with questions about how long she'd known Matthews and how well. It had felt like an interrogation, done with pretty smiles and assessing gazes. The Silver sisters were the daughters of a general, but not a single one of them had joined the service. If they had, they would have managed world peace in under a week through sheer force of will.

Though she had no secrets to spill, Toni felt that she was close to cracking within the first five minutes. She managed to slip away when the two James sisters arrived, diverting attention away from her. Before she made her escape, her gaze locked with Matthews's.

It had been doing that since they'd arrived at the impromptu bonfire. It had been doing that on the drive back from town. It had been doing that over the dinner table as the foster children had all talked over one another, laughing and poking fun at one another while the adults refereed or joined in the ribbing.

Matthews's gazes were quick assessments. Rhetorical questions he clearly wasn't expecting verbal answers to. His blue eyes seemed to ask her the same thing each time.

Are you okay?

He never gave her leave to answer. His gaze would simply meet hers. Then he would do a quick scan of her person. Toni wasn't sure what his metric was to gauge her well-being, but she appeared to pass each time.

It was only his gaze that he rested upon her, and briefly. He didn't come within arm's reach of her again. He didn't reach for her again. He didn't glance at her mouth as though her lips were twin flames that he wanted to warm himself near.

In fact, a few times when she got close to him, his body jerked back from her. As though she might burn him. Clearly, he was regretting whatever it was that had passed between them earlier. If it had been anything at all.

Which it hadn't. He just felt responsible for her. He might deny his guilty feelings about the crash, but she knew that was all this was. He would be gone soon, and soon after his departure, she planned to make hers.

She was no one's charity case. She could take care of herself. She'd never liked being coddled.

Well, she hadn't thought she'd like it. She'd never actually been coddled. Though it was nice having his gaze search her out every now and again.

She felt his eyes on her as she stole between the trees. The hiss and crackle of the fire mingled with the babbling of the brook just beyond the bonfire. Her body was tired from the long walk she'd taken this morning, but she wasn't limping. The land was flat, with no stairs to climb or logs to step over. Picking up a stone, Toni rubbed the smooth surface and then let it rip.

Plop plop plop plop—splash!

Not so bad. She was almost back to her stone-skipping record. Looking down at the ground, she searched for another stone that would help prove that she was on the mend and returning to her former glory. She spied two candidates and bent down to retrieve them.

"He watches you."

Still in her crouch, Toni glanced over her shoulder to find Tricksy watching her. Toni didn't need to ask who *he* was. She also didn't feel like she owed this woman a response, especially not after the six-way Silver interrogation she'd just made it through. But she technically was a guest here where Tricksy lived.

"Matthews feels responsible for what happened to me," Toni offered up. "That's all."

"So you're saying it's guilt he's feeling and not love?" Tricksy's hands were clasped behind her back as she took slow steps toward Toni, looking for all the world like a lawyer who was making the case against a clearly guilty defendant. "Because trust me, that man doesn't believe in love."

Neither did Toni, but she didn't tell this woman that. However, there was something else she wanted to know. "Why do you care? I thought you were with his brother."

Tricksy unclasped her hands from behind her back and brought them up to her heart. "I am. I'm with Will."

Toni came to standing, the rocks in the palm of her hand. Not as weapons to use against the other woman. Even though Tricksy clearly regarded her as a foe.

"I love him," Tricksy was saying. "Will, I mean. I really love him. Not like some little girl crush or puppy love. The real thing, you know?"

Toni did not know. So she said nothing.

"Topher isn't capable of the real thing. So I'm just warning you; don't fall for him."

"Are you sure you haven't gotten up from that fall you had for him?"

Tricksy's pretty features soured. The light in her eyes when she had been talking about Will died a quick death as she glared at Toni. The rocks in her palm made a clicking sound as Toni rubbed them together.

"Look," Toni said, "I'm just here to get better and then I'm out. Topher's headed back into the service, anyway. There's nothing between us but duty."

Tricksy made a noncommittal sound. Toni thought the woman would argue more. Instead, she turned on her heel. But she didn't get far.

Standing in the path was Matthews. Like he had been doing all day, his gaze found Toni and did its assessment. Once he appeared to satisfy himself that Toni was in good health, he turned an ice blue glare on Tricksy.

CHAPTER SIXTEEN

The bonfire took place at a spot halfway between the Flying Cross Ranch and the Silver Star Ranch. It was neutral territory, so to speak. A place that both families claimed as their own. Though truly the only reason for fencing between the two ranches was for the animals and not the wild children who roamed free.

Topher knew both ranches like the back of his hand, which he had been studying of late. He knew how many paces it would take to go from the bonfire pit to the little creek. He knew what trees sprang from each side of the path and where their roots unfurled from the ground. He knew the path was well trodden with little to no tripping hazards. He knew the water was shallow, with no danger of drowning.

All these things he knew so well, but he itched to follow Solis to the clearing. The hairs at the nape of his neck prickled with the need to ensure that she was safe and well. There was a tickle at the corner of his eye where he needed to see for himself that she hadn't tripped over a new vine that may have sprung up since his last visit to this well-known spot.

His feet were moving before he finished making any demand of his body. But his progress was slowed as he fielded questions from the Silver sisters. Scout made kissing noises behind his back, something he would've had a witty comeback for just a couple of days ago, but now he let the childish action go as he picked up his steps.

Solis had been withdrawn for most of the party. He'd thought she might be fatigued if not overwhelmed by the nagging nosiness of those silver hellcats. He was sure the only reason their husbands put up with the girls was due to their time in boot camp.

Breaking free of the landmines his neighbors tried and failed to toss his way, Topher hurried down the path. Then slowed his steps. He didn't want to appear overeager. He was simply doing his duty, handling his responsibility.

The irritation that was scratching at his chest at having Solis out of his sight for more than a minute was due to his concern for her and her well-being. Nothing more.

She'd looked weary as she'd progressively made her way to the edges of the gathering. He'd been about to suggest she call it a night when she'd walked off. When he saw the direction of her steps, he relaxed a bit. He knew she liked water, had an affinity for it. He'd caught her on base skipping stones a few times. He'd watched silently, smug in the knowledge that he could best her in number of skips.

She was likely headed there to skip stones. Now would be a great time to challenge her. And just to make sure she was doing okay. Because she was his responsibility. And because of the panic he'd felt seeing her sitting at that bus stop this morning.

It had been the same panic he'd felt when he'd caught her gaze as he'd lost control of the aircraft. It had been the same panic he'd felt when she'd gone galloping ahead of him.

Topher knew the woman always had a plan. But he liked it best when he was the one in the cockpit when her plans were set in motion. He wanted to be the one in the driver's seat as her strategies were played out. He wanted to be in the lead when the orderly procedures she'd prescribed were initiated.

When he came into the clearing, he saw that someone else had beaten him to the helm. Tricksy paced before Solis, throwing kinks into an operation that had nothing to do with her.

"I thought we got past this, Tricks," Topher said.

Tricksy stiffened and looked up at him. For a moment, she looked like a kid caught with her hand in the cookie jar. He'd seen that look on her face before. He'd been the one next to her when she'd tried to steal the cookies, after all. She'd gotten in trouble, but he'd escaped.

Another woman who had gotten a scrape in her dealings with him. But Tricksy was all right now. She was head over heels in love with his brother, who should've been her first love in the first place. Not Topher.

"Oh, I am so over you, Christopher Matthews." Tricksy spat his full name like it was a bad taste in her mouth. "I've found real love with Will."

"Yeah, I know." Topher shrugged. "And I'm happy for you. I'm happy for you both. So what gives?" Topher made a motion between her and Solis, who stood at attention with her hands behind her back, like the good soldier she was.

"I'm just trying to mitigate any damage you might do to anyone else." Tricksy jutted her chin up at him.

That chin was as sharp as a sword, but the blow she'd tried to deal him was dull. He knew he'd hurt his old friend. Tricksy was the first, and the last woman whom he'd both befriended and dated. After the nightmare that was their breakup, Topher had sworn never to go down that road again.

Over the years, he'd missed Tricksy's friendship. He hadn't heard her laugh or seen her smile in years. Whenever she looked at him, it was with pain or anger in her eyes.

Topher's gaze found Solis. She didn't pretend to not listen. Her right palm was in motion, making clicking noises as she rubbed two stones together. She was trying to smooth the rough edges of the rocks before she flung them into the water. Unlike the stones in her hands, Topher's rough edges would never be smoothed away.

"You break every girl's heart you come in contact with," Tricksy was saying.

"We're not dating," both Topher and Solis said at the same time.

"Oh, please," said Tricksy. "I've seen the way you look at him."

Had she looked at him in some way? He only ever saw judgment and disappointment in Solis's gaze when he saw his reflection there. In answer, there was a crunching sound as Solis ground the rocks in her hands. Her eyes went wide, and her nose wrinkled.

"And I've seen the way you look at her." Tricksy pointed an accusing finger at Topher.

Now Topher's features reformed to incredulity. The only reason he looked at Solis was to assess her health and well-being. Sure, he'd started noticing other things about her. Like how her body curved in all the right ways outside of fatigues. With her hair parted straight, he noticed how it crowned her head. With her head up and not looking down at documents, he saw how her lips were heart-shaped and not a thin, judgmental line.

"You leave hurt behind," said Tricksy. "And the thing is, I don't think you mean to do it. You just can't help yourself."

And with that last missive hurled his way, Tricksy stormed back up the path. Topher stood stunned into stillness in the wake of her destruction.

No, he didn't mean to do it. But how was it his fault that women expected more from him than he was willing to give? He never lied. And when he was bluntly honest, it always made things even worse.

"Do you need to be alone?" asked Solis.

Her voice was a siren in the darkness. Topher stepped closer to it.

"There's no such thing as alone here," he said. The silence stretched between them, and he knew she would've let it linger. But he felt the need to fill it. "She's wrong."

"You do have the hots for me?"

The comment was so unexpected, it caught him entirely off guard. With his center of gravity knocked off its axis, he threw back his head and laughed. When the world felt steady again, he turned to look at her. In the moonlight, she looked more than pretty. Before she could catch him staring, Topher bent to pick up a few stones.

CHAPTER SEVENTEEN

*H*is hands were large. His fingers slim and agile. They didn't look soft or gentle. They did look capable, and they proved that they were as the stone skimmed across the surface of the water five times before making a splash and sinking into the dark waters.

Toni lifted an eyebrow. He had impressive skill. She would've said so, but she was enjoying the silence between them. Plus, if she kept quiet, she didn't have to admit that she thought he was good. The man's head was already big enough.

Except that it wasn't. His head was perfectly normal-sized, capped with those blond tufts of hair that moved with him as he put his whole body into his tosses.

Those blue eyes shone with a light that said he knew how good he was. He knew how attractive he was. He knew that she thought so. He inclined his head as though to tell her to simply give up trying to hide her attraction to him and admit it.

"Do you give up?" he asked.

"What?"

"It's your turn." He made a motion with those slim, agile fingers.

Toni swallowed. Her heart made a series of fast thumps inside her chest like it was skipping across the water. When she tore her gaze from his hand to look up into those blue eyes, she heard a decided thud and was surprised to see that she was still standing.

Matthews was talking about the game they had slipped into. He was talking about her turn at tossing a rock. Nothing else.

Intellectually, she knew that. Logically, she knew that. Sensibly, she knew that. There was no reason for her heart to have all these theatrics. No reason for her head to see something that wasn't there.

With a deep breath, Toni stepped up to the water's edge. She rubbed the two rocks she held in her palm against one another. The grating sound like nails on a chalkboard calmed her senses, or at least distracted them enough away from the silly thoughts she'd been engaging in a moment ago.

With a flick of her wrist, she sent one stone flying. *Plop plop plop plop...plop—splash!*

"Yes!" she shouted, throwing fists in the air. It was five plops, just one shy of her highest score of six. But she hadn't managed this many in months. Just more proof that she was truly on the mend, almost back to her old self.

Next to her, Matthews let out a low laugh. It was the second time he'd laughed at her antics this night. The first being after the joke she'd made about him having the hots for her.

It had been an absurd thing to say, but she'd hated the silence left behind when Tricksy had stormed off. Though Toni had the distinct feeling that Matthews hadn't been laughing at her when he'd thrown back his head and chuckled. He wasn't laughing at her now, either. He seemed relaxed and delighted… by her.

As the last of his laughter subsided, a grin remained on his face. He gazed down at her, his features further softening. Those blue eyes of his were hooded, but she saw something in them. She just wasn't sure what.

Interest?

Curiosity?

Toni knew she should move away from him. She had heard what Tricksy had said about him breaking hearts. She'd seen it with her own eyes back on the base. But she had never thought for a second that he was interested in her. He had never even looked at her. Not really.

He was looking at her now, his gaze taking in her features. What was he seeing?

Was it because she was the only woman out here to seduce? He usually was grinning or smirking at women when he was seducing them. She'd seen it because she'd watched him.

Toni's breath caught when his fingertips made impact on her temple. She'd been right about his fingers not being gentle. There were calluses on the pads of his thumb and index finger. Still, it was the softest touch she'd ever experienced.

It was the only tender touch she'd ever experienced like this, besides her fading memories of her mother. Definitely, no man had ever touched her like this.

She knew she should turn away. She knew she should pull back. Topher Matthews was a heartbreaker, and she was a wounded warrior.

Toni tilted her head back to receive the kiss he was about to steal from her. Because she was a trained soldier, and she would prefer to be at the ready to meet this mission. His lips did not crash down on hers. Instead, his fingers tangled in her hair.

"You've come undone," he said.

Toni blinked.

"Your hair. It's come undone."

Reaching up, Toni felt the free strands of her hair had come loose from its braid. She jerked away from Matthews. Giving him her back, she tried to work her fingers through the strands.

"I'm sorry," he said. "I know better than to touch a woman's hair without permission. I was just... I mean..."

He hadn't been trying to steal a kiss. He hadn't been preparing for a carnal attack. She wasn't beautiful to him. She wasn't desirable. She probably looked like a wild thing with her hair out.

"You're not parting it straight," he said. "Here, let me help."

He reached for her again. But she didn't want him to see her like this. However, the moment his fingers slid into her hair, it short-circuited her resolve.

Matthews's fingers weren't only in her hair, they were moving about the strands. Toni felt the edge of his nail as he parted the hair down to her scalp.

She thought that was it. But he didn't stop at the part. He towered over her, moving to her side and tilting her head for easier access. And then he began to weave her hair back into submission.

For long moments, Toni stood silent. Partly in shock that a young, White man was braiding a Black woman's hair. Mostly in a stunned sort of paralysis at how good his movements around the crown of her head felt.

"How do you know how to braid hair?" she asked.

"My mom. My adoptive mom. I saw her doing it to her hair one day, and I was curious. So she taught me."

His adoptive father was African American. There was a good chance Father Matthews' wife had been Black as well. Toni was certain the woman was Black when she reached up and felt the secure braid on the side of her head.

"There," he said. "Beautiful."

"You think I'm beautiful?" As soon as the words were out of her mouth, she wanted to take them back.

Matthews shrugged. "Of course you are. You're one of the few women who is and doesn't act like she knows it. I've always liked that about you."

Well, the joke was on him because she didn't know she was beautiful. She was fairly certain that she wasn't. But she wasn't going to argue with him. She wasn't even sure what to say now that he'd put her back together atop her head while everything inside was in an upwhirl.

"I'm not going to hurt you, Toni."

Right. Because he wasn't interested in dating her. So why did she have a sudden tinge of pain?

CHAPTER EIGHTEEN

opher pulled the truck door open for Toni as she came down the steps. Her gait was fine this morning, the limp not as pronounced. Her braids were straight, which made his nose wrinkle a bit. He liked it when she was a bit crooked. He wondered if that was still the same braid he'd woven into her hair last night out by the water.

His fingers clenched to a fist to try to dispel the itch that descended on the palm of his hand. He'd enjoyed the feel of her thick hair in his hands as he'd weaved the strands together. Solis had always appeared formidable to him, but her hair had followed his every command without a strand coming loose in protest.

Topher wished she'd come undone again. He wished he'd left behind a straggler that would give him the excuse to undo the braid, all so he could weave the loose strand back in line. But she was completely put together today.

She glanced up at him then. A shy expression shone in those coffee-colored eyes. Then she glanced away.

He resisted the urge to hand her into the truck. Well, he tried to. Without conscious thought, his hand raised to assist her. And wonder of wonders, she took it. The moment her fingertips met his palm, there was a zing of electricity between them.

He heard her gasp. His fingers closed around hers before she could pull away. But the spark was there and gone by then. And she was seated in the passenger seat. Leaving him no reason to hold on to her.

Topher shut Toni inside. The click of the latch was loud in his ears. He about faced and began to walk around the truck to the driver's side. Instead of heading around the front end of the car, he decided to take the long way around the back. His steps slowed as he got to the driver's side as realization dawned.

Solis was going to be fine. She was going to completely recover from her injuries. And then she was going to leave. The meeting at the VA clinic would likely confirm it today.

How long would they give her? Likely another month? Maybe two? Definitely not longer than the six months he would be deployed. She'd be gone before he got back.

Then she'd likely be on a mission of her own. There was no guarantee they'd serve together again. No guarantee they'd have more time together in the future.

Topher scratched at his heart. With his other hand, he leaned against the driver's side door before opening it. He ran his hand over the back of his head, tugging at the overlong locks of his hair.

This was a good thing. This was the goal they'd both hoped to achieve. She was getting better, and he would be leaving. His debt to her would be repaid.

This was a good thing. These were all good things. Yet the itch at his chest persisted.

Across the way, Topher caught a glimpse of Tricksy. She was giving him that evil eye that she'd given to him ever since they were kids and she claimed he'd broken her heart. The itch at his chest ceased, and he gave his former friend his back. Climbing in the truck, Topher put the vehicle in gear and pulled away from the ranch, leaving Tricksy in the rearview mirror.

The drive to the hospital was a quiet one. He appreciated that about Solis. She didn't care for idle chitchat. It was always about the mission for her.

On the radio, Mahalia Jackson crooned as they drove. Solis held a clipboard in her hand. On it, he saw a number of check marks next to her neat script. But he couldn't make out the script and keep his eyes on the road at the same time. Besides, he didn't need to know what gains Solis had made in her healing to return to active duty. He knew the woman was going to ace any exam the doctors gave her.

Taking one hand off the wheel, Topher scratched again at the itch at his chest. Foxy must have replaced the detergent in the laundry room with some environmental brand that he was having an allergic reaction to.

He parked in the visitor's lot as close to the entrance as he could get. Solis reached for the passenger side door handle. Topher's gaze landed on her hand. She must have felt the heat of his glare, because when their gazes connected, she put her hand back in her lap and looked forward. Topher couldn't hide the smile that lit his lips as he got out of the truck and went around to her side.

He offered his hand after opening the door. She took it, just lightly resting her fingertips on his palm. Topher's fingers curled around hers reflexively. She didn't pull away. Instead, she stepped down gingerly.

He glanced at a wheelchair and raised a brow. She snatched her hand from his and punched him in the shoulder with it. He was still laughing as they made their way into the clinic.

He was also still rubbing at his shoulder. Despite the woman being small and carrying around a shoulder injury, she had a good right hook. She was going to be fine.

Topher stood by quietly as she filled out the paperwork. His gaze rested on the braid in her hair. Even though she could throw a punch, she still struggled with her hair. If they were stationed together again, would she let him part it for her? Would she let him braid it?

A single strand had come loose from the end of the braid. It curled around the base of her neck. He should tell her. Or maybe he should fix it for her.

"You don't have to stay," she said.

Topher crossed his arms over his chest. He pressed his fists into his sides under his armpits as he did so. A glance in a mirror might have him resembling a toddler on the verge of a tantrum.

He wasn't going anywhere until he knew the timeline of when she was leaving. Finally, they were called back. Topher rose to go with her, but the nurse raised his hand.

"Sorry," said the male nurse in a shirt with colorful umbrellas. "Family only."

Solis's face went blank. Her coffee-colored gaze turned to a bitter shade as she looked everywhere but at Topher.

"I am her family," said Topher.

"Oh, my mistake." The nurse grinned. "Fiancés are welcome."

Topher saw Solis swallow hard, but she said nothing. So neither did he, and the nurse lead them both back.

The doctor was a middle-aged male that looked like he had once been a drill sergeant. His biceps were fairly bursting out of his white coat. His shoulders were back, his feet braced apart as he got down to the questions.

"Any new injuries?" he asked.

"No," answered Toni.

"Yes," said Topher.

They both turned to him.

"She was nearly thrown from a horse. Before that, she was riding pretty hard. I haven't seen her in any pain, but she often hides it well."

The doctor nodded, jotting down some notes.

Toni's mouth hung open as she looked at him incredulously.

Topher wasn't sorry for it. He wanted the doctor to have all the facts to make the best decision possible about Solis's future.

"Any prescriptions or non-prescription medications?"

"No," said Toni.

"My sister-in-law has been giving her echinacea tea and willow bark tinctures the last two days."

"Matthews!"

Topher shrugged, keeping his attention on the doctor and his note-taking. The man didn't bother to hide his grin, likely thinking they were, in fact, a soon to be married couple squabbling. At another time, Topher would've shuddered at the notion. Instead, he crossed his arms tighter over his chest and waited for the next question.

"I'm sure a cup of tea doesn't matter," Solis was saying.

"It's good to inform your healthcare provider about herbal reme-dies," said the doctor as he continued to scribble notes. "Their healing effects are widely known in the scientific community and have been known to impact some medications."

"I just want to know what I need to do to get back out there."

The doctor lifted his head then. "Back out there?"

"Back to active duty. Just give me the list of things I need to do and..." Toni's voice trailed off as she saw the doctor's expression.

"I'm sorry, Airman Solis. Your injuries are career ending. There is no going back on active duty."

CHAPTER NINETEEN

Everything hurt. The passenger seat had suddenly sprung coils that dug into Toni's back and sides. There was no longer enough leg room, and her knees ached from being in a tight crouch. The leather of the seat was hot to the touch. The windowpane was freezing cold. She needed to get out of here.

"Pull over."

"We'll be home in a minute," said Matthews, moving one hand over the other as he made a turn onto the Main Street of the small town.

Home? Toni didn't have a home. The one place she had felt like she had belonged had just denied her from ever returning.

She couldn't go back. They didn't want her back. So where was she going to go?

Her breaths came quick and shallow. Though she panted while turned toward the window, there was no chance for the air from her lungs to fog up the glass. No sooner did one puff present itself than the next breath of air wiped the vapors away.

"I need to get out," she said.

Matthews sent her a glance. His blue eyes shone clear in the passenger side window. She'd seen that worried look only one time before: the time just before he'd lost control of the aircraft and they'd crashed.

He hadn't been in control of that situation. Neither had she. She hadn't planned for that disaster, and she had no plan for the new blow dealt her. The military no longer wanted her.

Toni was this close to yanking open the door and leaping out when Matthews slowed and came to a stop. Toni looked up to note it was at the same bus stop from the other day. Luckily for him, the bus was nowhere in sight.

What did this mean that he'd brought her here? Did he want her to get on the bus now? Was her time up with him and his family now that there was no hope for her reinstatement?

"Are you going to be sick?" Matthews's hands reached for her but came short of touching her.

Toni's hand went to the door handle. She didn't wait for him to come around and hand her out like some dainty lady. She wasn't a dainty lady. She was a soldier.

No matter whether they wanted her or not. She was a soldier.

She yanked open the door and spilled out. Her foot hit the ground wrong, causing her knees to buckle. She bent over, but she didn't collapse onto the ground.

Strong arms came around her, lifting her back up. Toni was pulled into a warm chest. Arms came around to hold her steady. Hands pressed the back of her head against a thudding heartbeat.

Toni wanted to push against him. She wanted to fight him. But it felt too good. It felt too necessary when her world was falling apart around her.

And so she let Matthews hold her.

From the corner of her eye, she saw people glancing at them. She didn't care. Her lifelong dream had just been snatched away from her. When Matthews let her go, she would be facing a world of darkness.

"I'm going to have to go home," she said. Toni felt his nod as his cheek moved along her temple.

"I'll take you home."

"Not your home," she said, shaking her head against his chest. But she only managed two shakes before resting her head back at the center of his chest where his heartbeat was the strongest. "Not back to the ranch. I have to go to my father's home."

Matthews's hold tightened on her. His heartbeat kicked up a notch. He blew out a breath that sailed down the center of her head where he'd parted her hair into a straight line the other night.

"That is, if he's even there," Toni went on in the silence. "He's very dedicated to his career and often spends nights at his office."

Matthews said nothing. He only held on to her. When Toni shifted to break his hold, she felt the reluctance with which he let her go.

"Stay," he finally managed to say, though the word sounded choked. Like it had been forced out of him.

"I can't impose on your family indefinitely."

"You are my—" he cleared his throat. "I want you to stay."

"Why?"

"It's my fault."

Toni didn't need him to clarify what he was at fault for. "It's not your fault, and you know it. We all knew what we signed up for."

"I should've gone over your mission readiness list one more time. I should've..." Matthews sighed, resting his forehead against hers.

They were still standing apart. He didn't put his arms around her again. He just stood there, resting his blond locks against her dark braids.

Even though he wasn't touching her, Toni could taste his breath. She could feel his heat. He opened his eyes and stared into hers. His gaze landed on her mouth.

Toni's lips parted of their own accord. The tip of her tongue dipped out to moisten first her lower and then her top lip. But he didn't come any closer.

Matthews straightened but didn't back away from her. He blinked a couple of times, as though he was waking from a dream.

"I'm going to be leaving," he said. "I'll be deployed for six months."

The disappointment was bitter at the back of Toni's throat. Could this day get any worse? She'd lost her career. Had no place to go. And she'd made a fool of herself in front of the one man she wanted to see her as strong and brave.

"Maybe I'll just go back to the Purple Heart Ranch and marry some random soldier so I can live there."

Matthews's blue eyes iced over. His hands curled into fists.

When he'd been mistaken for her fiancé back at the hospital, he hadn't said anything. Neither had she. Toni had secretly liked the feel of having that title placed on him. She had liked the notion of having someone that was hers.

Topher Matthews was so strong. So confident. So cocky. He was the type of man that would save a damsel in distress. He'd saved her more than once. He hadn't left her behind. Not on the battlefield. Not in her rehabilitation. She could stay with him. She could—

"Topher Matthews, is that you?"

Matthews glanced to the side without turning his head. His brows went down in concentration, as though he was trying to place the owner of the voice who'd called out to him.

"Up to your old tricks, seducing some poor woman on the street?"

Toni saw his dilemma in placing the voice. It wasn't just one voice. It was a group of girls. Or rather women, if their shapely figures in sundresses and heeled sandals were anything to go by. In turn, each one of them lifted a brow as they looked at Toni. Those brows lowered almost instantly in what looked like dismissal.

"Everyone's taken a ride on that train," said one. "Enjoy it while it lasts, sweetie."

She hadn't even had the chance to get on the ride. Because she wasn't the type of girl who he rode around with. She wasn't the type of woman men stayed around for.

CHAPTER TWENTY

opher watched the guest house until the light went off. The drive home had been a tense and silent one. He wasn't sure what he'd done wrong, but he knew it was something.

It was probably that almost kiss. Whenever he kissed a woman, it was inevitably the beginning of the end of their time together. He wasn't ready for his time with Toni Solis to be over. Which is why he'd pulled away from her before he could mess things up.

Unfortunately, it hadn't worked. He'd still messed things up without even tasting those lush lips that had tilted up to meet his. He should've at least done the crime now that he was forced to serve this silent time out.

The silence he could handle. But only if it was temporary. He did not want her to go. At least not without fixing whatever he'd done wrong.

No, that wasn't right. Even after he fixed it, he still wanted her here. Still wanted her to stay on the ranch. He couldn't stand the idea of her going to an empty home with an absentee father. She needed someone to care for her.

It wouldn't be him. He would be gone soon. But his family would care for her. His father would take her in as one of his own. His brothers would ensure no harm came to her. His sisters-in-law would keep her company. He...?

He could what?

He didn't know what?

He just knew he didn't want her to be out in the world and he not know where she was, how she was doing. What if she tried to walk too far and re-injured herself? What if she tried to ride another horse and pushed herself so hard she was thrown? What if she went back for another doctor's visit and she neglected to tell him all the medicinals she was taking and something went wrong?

No. He couldn't let her go. She had to stay here where there would be people to look after her. People he trusted to keep her healing and happy. Until he could return to her. And… what?

He still didn't know the answer to that when the guest house light went out. Topher had been half paralyzed with fear that she'd sneak away in the middle of the night and he would never see her again. Never hold her. Never touch her.

He'd almost kissed her. If he'd kissed her, he knew he'd never see her again. That's how it went with him. He never stayed with a woman. His lovers always wound up getting their hearts broken, even though he never meant to handle that organ.

Dating was meant to be fun. He didn't know why women took it so seriously. Why they expected forever. He wasn't the forever guy. Not unless they were family.

He wanted Toni to be a part of this family and stay forever. If he'd kissed her, like he wanted to do, then she would have her heart broken. And he didn't want either of those things to happen.

A creak on the floorboard put him on alert. Topher knew it wasn't one of his brothers. They'd learned the art of stealth when they were boys. No, that creak was deliberate. The person wanted to be heard.

"Hey, Tricks."

"What'd you do to her?"

The hair at the nape of his neck stiffened. "I didn't do anything."

Tricksy stood with her arms crossed over her chest looking for all the world like the young girl he used to be friends with. His gaze went unfocused as he tried to reconcile the two. The bright-eyed girl with a big voice along with this creature who always wore a sour expression as she shouted into a microphone about being done wrong.

Despite it all, Topher missed being friends with her. He missed her playfulness and laughter. He even missed the sound of her singing voice. He just didn't want to hear another note from that song about their breakup. Though maybe he should listen to the anthem before he saw Solis again. To remind him how, after he'd kissed his friend, things had changed, and they'd never been the same again.

"She can't go back into the military," Topher admitted.

"I'm sorry to hear that."

"She's going to leave."

"Why?" Tricksy's gaze narrowed, and her lips curled. "What did you do?"

Topher sighed. The evening breeze brought a dull awareness to his body. This was a pointless conversation.

"She's in love with you."

He doubted that. But he couldn't be sure. It wasn't something he looked for in the women he dated. It wasn't something he was interested in knowing.

"Do you care about her at all?"

"Of course, I do. I want to help her get better, to help her keep healing. I want her to stay here and be with people who care about her. I don't want her to go out into the world alone where I can't be sure she'll be looked after."

He hadn't realized he'd started pacing the length of the porch until the sound of his boots stomping out a staccato rhythm broke his attention. He looked again to the darkened guest house.

"She's so strong, but she's vulnerable. She has a talent for thinking of every possibility, of every eventuality in a battle, but she still has blind spots. What if she misses a blind spot and I—" He cleared his throat and began again. "What if she doesn't have someone there to watch her back?"

Tricksy was silent as she regarded him. Topher held still under her scrutiny. He could only stand it for so long before he took up his pacing again.

"Why am I even telling you this? I'm the villain in your story. I'll always be the villain. And that's fine."

He reached the end of the porch and was confronted again with the darkened guest house. He wanted to go over there, to knock on the door and... And what?

Instead, he rounded on Tricksy. "You know what, no it's not. You continuing to cast me as the villain is not fine. I cared about you back then. I've never stopped caring about you. But just because I didn't feel the same way as you did doesn't make me the bad guy forever."

Tricksy's arms remained crossed over her shoulders as she took slow, careful steps toward him. "No, it doesn't."

Topher braced himself for an attack. But no blow came. Still, he remained on his guard. Those James sisters had grown up alongside the Matthewses. They knew how to throw a punch, especially when a guy was down.

"I saw it," she said. "I saw it the moment she stepped onto this ranch."

"You saw what?"

"That she was different. That you were different with her. You don't look at her like you do other girls."

"How do I look at her?"

"Like you care."

"I cared about you, Tricks. I care about you."

"Yeah, like family."

Topher didn't see how that was a bad thing. She was family. But she also wasn't hitting him and was having a conversation with him at normal volume. So he stayed quiet and let her continue.

"I watched you look at other girls back then. You would look through them like they were all the same. You always looked at me and saw me, just not in the way I wanted you to see me."

Topher had no idea what she meant. He mostly tried to avoid her gazes when she came over for dinner, or there was a holiday gathering, or they were out at a town event with their families. But he couldn't entirely avoid watching out for her. Especially when he knew a few guys had been after her, thinking to take advantage of her broken heart. He'd used his fists to set them straight each time.

"Even though you stopped looking at me, I knew that you saw me," Tricksy was saying. "When you look at Toni, it's like you see into her. It's like she's all you see."

That's because Solis was easy to read. She was an open book, if you knew how to read the signs. Or better yet, like reading a radar screen.

She was all blips and lines to others. But to his eyes, it was a perfect map. And he knew what her charted course would be.

"She's going to leave," he said.

"Tell her you want her to stay."

"I did. She thinks she's imposing. That woman is violently independent."

"Then use your charm on her."

"Then she would definitely leave. It always goes south after I date a woman. I don't want things to go south with her. I don't want her to go anywhere."

"Then use your charm on her."

"Then she would definitely leave. It always goes south after I date a woman. I don't want things to go south with her. I don't want her to go anywhere. I want her to stay here for as long as she wants."

Topher knew he was repeating himself. But he was very clear on what he wanted and what he didn't want. No other words were necessary.

"Wow." Tricksy rested a hand on his shoulder. "You've got it bad."

Topher didn't want to explain to Tricksy how he always lost interest in women after he'd kissed them. He didn't want to remind her that they always blew up at him when they realized their feelings for him were more than his feelings for them. He was sure that the reminder would unravel the fragile peace that had settled between them.

"Besides," he went on, "I have to leave soon."

"But you're coming back."

"I always come back."

"If you want her to be here when you do, then you'll need to give her a reason to stay. Or preferably more than one."

"Like a list? Like a checklist?"

"Sure, that—"

A blinding lightbulb went off in Topher's head. He bent down and smacked a kiss on Tricksy's cheek. "Thanks, Tricks. I think I know what to do."

Her gaze on him was one of pure bewilderment. She rubbed at the place where he'd kissed her and then looked quizzically at her fingertips.

"Tricks?"

"Yeah?"

"Are we really good this time?"

She punched him in the shoulder with the hand she'd used to wipe at the kiss. "We're getting there."

CHAPTER TWENTY-ONE

oni was up before the sun. She'd watched it go down last night. She'd kept the moon company while it did its nocturnal work. She'd been there to greet the sun after the moon went to bed.

She didn't have much time left. Her bags were packed and stacked by the door. She just needed to be sure of her direction.

Spying her phone sitting on the charger on the counter, Toni went to pick up the device to map out her new course. But when she reached for it, her hand skidded past the device and landed on a comb. It was the comb Latisha had used to part her hair a couple of days ago.

Toni's gaze went around the entire cabin. The James girls had made it cozy for her stay, adding a few personal touches that were slightly masculine, but still worked for Toni. She'd felt cozy here. But this was not her place.

She couldn't stay when Topher left on deployment. She couldn't stay while he was still here visiting with his family. She didn't want to feel like an outsider. She'd felt like that her whole life.

Turning her back on the interior of the cabin, she sat down the comb and picked up her phone. Then she dialed the number she'd known by heart since she was a child before she could talk herself out of it. The phone rang and rang. And then rang some more.

Just as she thought it would go to voice mail a deep male voice answered.

"Antonia?"

"Hi, Dad."

"Is there a problem with your recovery?"

Her heart quickened. There was a fluttery sensation in her stomach. "No, Daddy. I'm all right. I'm fine. I—"

"Good," he sighed.

The weight of that sigh landed like a stone in her gut, stilling the flutters. Her heartbeat slowed so abruptly, she felt the thud in her heels which caused her to rock back.

"I'm preparing for a lecture," he went on. "Can we reschedule this call? I have some time on Tuesday between 3:30 and 4:45. Will that work for you?"

Toni heard the click of his pen open. She envisioned him drawing a neat little column on the scheduler on his clipboard to write her in. Likely in a small corner, with a perfect square to check her off his list when the appointed time came.

Toni opened her mouth to respond, but she choked on the words she wanted to say. Because she wasn't sure what to say?

"Antonia, I have to get back to my notes. Why don't you send me an email with the dates and times that work best for you and I'll do my best to fit you in? Have a good day."

Cell phones no longer clicked when disconnected. The line simply went dead. She was left on her own by the one person in the world that was supposed to care for her. Again.

She needed fresh air. But the last thing she wanted to do was bump into Matthews. Looking outside, she saw that no one was about at the front of the house, and so she stepped outside.

She also needed a ride into town. But she didn't want to ask for help from anyone from this family. She didn't want them to know how alone she was. Not when there was so much togetherness here.

Maybe she could find Tricksy. That woman hated Matthews. Toni doubted Tricksy would be sad to see her go.

Out the window, she spotted her in the distance with those telltale dark curls. Tricksy was getting out of the car with two other men. One of them with skin a dark shade of brown like hers.

It was Matthews's father. He climbed out of the car and turned to her with a smile. That smile softened into a slight frown. His brows drew as he regarded her.

"Hey, Toni. Good morning," said the woman Toni had mistaken as Tricksy. It was her older sister Savy with her lush hair pulled back.

Savy looked bright and fresh and happy. Of course she did. She'd just come off her honeymoon.

"You coming in for breakfast? I can't wait to show everyone the pictures."

"I was just going for a walk," said Toni.

"Mind if I walk with you?" asked Father Matthews. "Been on a boat for days and then in that car for hours. I need to stretch my legs on solid earth."

Toni wasn't sure how to turn the man down. Standing under the soft glow of his kind smile, she wasn't sure she wanted to leave his warm light. And so she fell in step beside him.

The two walked in silence for a few moments. Toni kept a slow pace for him, but she somehow thought he was going slowly for her. Could he tell her injury was bothering her today?

"I'm sorry I haven't been here to help you," said Father Matthews. "I know that's what my son was hoping for. My boys seem to think I have a way of fixing their problems."

"I'm not your son's problem."

"No, my dear. You're not a problem at all. You're a solution for him, which is the problem." Father Matthews chuckled at his private joke.

"There's nothing between..."

Toni let the sentence die because it wasn't true. There was something between them. At least on her part. She might not have experience in relationships, but she knew a spark when she felt it. This spark was going to fizzle because it burned all by itself in a pit with no kindling.

"He was right to bring you here."

Toni shook her head. "I can't stay."

"I would be sad to see you go."

"You don't even know me."

"Exactly." His grin was wide. "I'd like a chance to get to know the woman who's stolen my son's heart."

"I don't have his heart. He hasn't even kissed me."

The moment the words were out, she blushed. Thankfully, her

cheeks wouldn't turn a telltale shade of red, but she was certain Father Matthews could feel the heat coming off them.

"Topher was the kind of kid who destroyed toys. Race cars with only three wheels. Toy soldiers missing arms and legs. But there was one he kept in a box and never played with because it was the most special to him."

"You're saying I'm a toy in a box?"

Father Matthews canted his head. "You could stay and find out."

"You're inviting me to stay even though your son is leaving?"

"I'm inviting you to stay because it's clear you need help. It's even clearer you don't know how to ask for it. So I'll make it easy for you—"

He didn't have a chance to finish his sentence. Not when a sob escaped from Toni. Quickly, she pressed her hand to her mouth. But the sob would not be held back.

She'd held it down for so long, but her shoulders were weary from the injury. The blow her own father had just dealt her had ripped at the bandages. Now she was standing before a stranger with her raw emotions exposed.

Father Matthews took hold of her shoulders. He turned her to face him, but she wouldn't raise her head. She didn't need to. He tucked her into his barrel chest and held her while the tears came.

He didn't make shushing noises. He didn't rub her back to hurry the tears out. He didn't tell her things would be okay with time. He didn't loosen his hold, signaling the end of his comfort. He simply stood there, lending his support for as long as she needed.

Toni didn't know how long they stood there like that. But slowly, her strength returned to her, and she felt strong enough to do what she knew needed to be done. She stepped out of Father Matthews's hold and put her shoulders straight. Her injury still ached, her heart was heavy with her own father's rejection, her spirit low from the knowledge that she wouldn't return to her career.

"I need help," she said.

Father Matthews held out his arm, like a gentleman caller would do. Toni took his arm as they walked back toward the guest house.

CHAPTER TWENTY-TWO

opher had seen her walk off with his father. He knew that was a good start. His father was good at making lost souls feel welcome. But Topher knew that he would have to be the one to convince Toni to stay.

He paced the length of the guest house porch, clipboard in hand. He patted the clipboard at his thigh; the nerves getting to him.

He always felt calm before a mission. He would rush into a sky full of danger and not break a sweat. Now his heart kept skipping beats. Sweat ran down his temple. His fingers cramped from the tight fists he kept clenching them into.

He couldn't fail at this task. It might be the most important of his life.

When he spied them in the distance, he knew the moment Toni caught sight of him. Her shoulders had been relaxed as she'd walked arm in arm with his father. There was a shy smile on her face as she nodded a bit, listened a lot, and spoke little.

Topher's dad had that effect on people. They instantly trusted him. Which was why he'd brought Toni home to him.

He'd wanted her trust. Somehow, he knew he couldn't gain it on his own. Not with his reputation. He needed to show her where he'd come from so that she might be willing to go with him where he wanted to journey next.

Topher hadn't truly understood the trajectory his life would take when he scooped Toni Solis into his arms that day after the crash. He'd just known that once he'd picked her up, he had not wanted to let her go.

Even now, he wanted to rush out to her. He wanted to peer down at the ground before she took any step to make sure no danger was set before her. He wanted to lift her and carry her in his arms so that nothing could touch her. He wanted to hold her close so that nothing could come between them.

He wanted to kiss her. Oh, how he wanted to kiss her. He cursed himself for not taking a shot at every chance that had come before when he'd turned away from her.

It hadn't been out of respect. It had been out of fear, fear of what she made him feel.

He had feelings for her. Were those feelings love? He supposed so.

The itching in his chest when he thought of her, the skipping of beats when she was near, the rapid-fire beats when she gave him a half smile, all those went beyond desire, beyond lust.

It was an ache that he felt. That ache was in every crevice of his body, and it never went away. Not when she was near. Not when she was away. Not when he was simply thinking of her. It was always there, had been since the day he'd first met her. He just hadn't understood it. He did now.

Those sensations, those feelings, were telling him to stay near this woman because she had found her way into his heart.

"Hey," she said, when she arrived at the steps to the porch.

"We need to talk."

Those were words Topher Matthews had always dreaded. Today, they were the beginning of the most important speech he'd make this far in his life. He'd made a plan of what to say. But his plan went out the window the moment she bit her lower lip.

He reached for her. The clipboard clattered to the ground as he brought her to him and crashed his mouth into hers.

She was at ease in his arms. He had her full attention. Her head tilted up to him in a salute and she presented her arms around his neck as he took another half step closer to her.

It was a kiss to end all kisses. It was a kiss that told him he ain't seen nothing yet. He didn't need to see anything more.

Toni's arms wove around his neck. Her fingers tangled in his hair. She made a soft mewling sound that ignited his hunger, and he pulled her even closer to deepen the kiss.

"Stay," he said.

"Okay," she whispered. Her eyes were dazed. Her lips parted as though she was expecting another assault and was ready for it.

"I was expecting a fight."

"It's the logical thing to do if I want to get better."

Logic. Right, she was a rational woman. And he must be losing his touch because that kiss should have made her completely irrational.

"And there's also the fact that I'm falling in love with you."

It wasn't the first time Topher had heard those words. In the past, it had always made him cut and run. He pulled Toni closer with one hand. With the other, he tugged one of her hands from around his neck and placed it over his heart.

"I'm pretty sure I'm falling in love with you, too." The smile that spread across her mouth had him hungering for another taste of her lips. "I've never felt this before. I'm not entirely sure what to do."

"We'll make a list."

"I already did." Topher bent and picked up the clipboard.

Toni grinned when she took it from him. Topher felt his heart skip a beat. That's when the last doubt of what he was feeling fled his mind. There was no falling involved. He was in the thick of it.

"Mission to be the Top Boyfriend."

Topher wanted to snatch the clipboard back so that he could scratch out that word boyfriend and replace it with something else. But all in due time.

"Does my plan meet your approval?" he asked.

"This is an excellent plan," she said.

"I remember you saying something about mindless repetition. We could practice item four, which covers dates and kisses."

She giggled at that, and Topher was certain it was the best sound he'd ever heard in his life.

"I figure we can go over it as much as we need before I deploy."

That word offered some levity to the situation.

"I'm coming back," he said.

"I don't doubt it," she said. "I'm gonna get better."

"I don't doubt it."

"Maybe not well enough for active duty, but I'm not finished with the military."

"We'll figure out our next steps together."

"That sounds like the perfect plan."

EPILOGUE

"*I* don't understand how we got stuck buying female supplies."

Mateo Matthews watched as his brother tossed a box of feminine products into the shopping cart. The cardboard box of supplies for a woman's time of the month landed with a dull splat at the bottom of the cart. Mateo lifted the box with a smiling woman on it who definitely did not look as though she were suffering from a feminine ailment and placed it back on the shelf. "That's not the right one."

"Oh, you're an expert in feminine hygiene now?" asked Aldo.

"No, I just know how to read instructions, and Savy specifically wrote down a different name brand."

Replacing the purple box, Mateo grabbed the pink brand of products from the shelf and placed them in the cart. With that last item on their shopping list checked off, they were down on the shopping excursion in town. They'd only been back home for a couple of days, and it was busier than usual on the ranch with all the Matthews boys home at once, a house full of foster kids, three James sisters, and Topher's new girlfriend who was living in the guest house.

With the rest of the adults having their hands full with ranch chores, repairs, and the general chaos that came with caring for foster kids, Mateo had offered to run errands in town for Savy. He hadn't expected his brother to come along on the domestic mission. But just like when they were kids, Aldo still suffered a bit from separation anxiety.

"The way you act sometimes, *hermano,* you'd think these were for you."

Mateo didn't think for a second that listening to the needs of another person meant that he was somehow feminine. In fact, he didn't think there was anything wrong with listening or with femininity.

"You need to knock it off," said Aldo. "It's ruining my rep."

"You do know that just because we're twins doesn't mean we share the same reputation."

Aldo scoffed at that.

Inwardly, Mateo scoffed, too.

For much of their lives, everyone around them linked the two with the other's behavior because of the way they looked. As identical twins, they looked exactly alike. Though their foster brothers and adoptive parents could always tell them apart. But to others, there was no distinction. So Mateo got blamed for a lot of the antics Aldo got up to, whether he agreed with what his brother got up to or not.

A lot of times, he did not agree.

Especially not the times when Aldo's mean streak made an appearance. Mateo was the lover where Aldo was the fighter. Not so much a fist fighter as a loud mouth.

Aldo had grown up a bully. Not because their biological parents had mistreated their kids. Their parents had wanted nothing but the best for their boys. They just hadn't been able to give it to them, and instead had lost everything when they'd tried.

The social workers and school counselors all said Aldo's bullying was all about self sabotaging. He didn't trust that he couldn't have anything good, so he tried to destroy any potential blessings before they could be taken away from him.

Mateo never had anything bad to say about anyone or anything. But because he looked like his brother, people didn't make the distinction between the two, especially not since Mateo often held his tongue and stood by when his brother went off at the mouth.

But for the first time in their lives, the Matthews twins' paths were about to diverge. Mateo was staying home after this last deployment, where Aldo was planned to go back into the service. While they were apart, Mateo hoped to settle down, build his own reputation apart from his twin, and perhaps even start to date. He wouldn't admit to his brother that he had one hometown girl in mind.

A certain red head with kind eyes and freckles dotting her cheeks.

Green eyes like a dense forest that Mateo got lost in when he daydreamed. And smiling pink lips that made him think of the heart-shaped hard candies he'd once left at her desk on Valentine's Day.

"Hey look, it's Raggedy Ann."

Mateo frowned. He didn't see a red haired doll with yarn for hair and a button nose anywhere in the shop. Belatedly, he remembered that that was the mean nickname his brother had given to the exact girl Mateo had just been daydreaming of. Then, looking up, he caught sight of that beauty.

Kailyn Jade stood in the produce section of the grocery store. There was a shopping basket on one arm, and she held a carrot in her hand. Her gaze was wide, like a deer in headlights, as she stared up at Mateo.

Just like when he was young, Mateo ached to go up to her. To reach out and offer his hand in friendship. To tell her a funny joke, to see her grin go wide and those freckles spread. To give her a heart shaped candy that said *Be Mine* on it.

But just like when they were young, Kailyn's cheeks went red when she was in his presence, making those freckles disappear in the blush. Those green eyes that he wanted to keep focused on him dropped to the ground. And her slender shoulders hunched forward, like she'd been dealt a blow.

"And, look," Aldo continued. "There's Andy."

"Oh, would you look at that," said a carbon copy of Kailyn, but with bone straight red hair devoid of curls and a pair of glasses set low on her nose. "It's a walking, talking feminine product. Too bad it won't fit down the toilet for a flush. It needs to be taken out with the garbage."

The malicious grin dropped from Aldo's face and he looked ready for war. Facing off against him, Elayne Jade looked ready to deal the first strike in a battle that had been started years ago, but ended in a bitter stalemate.

Mateo opened his mouth, ready at last to defuse this decades long feud between the town's two sets of twins. But it was Kailyn's soft voice that broke through the tension.

"We have somewhere to be Elayne." Kailyn glanced at Mateo and his closed mouth before turning away from him with a dismissive shake of her head. "They're not worth it."

And with that, the Jade twins walked away from the Matthews twins. Mateo was left standing beside his brother, looking for the world like a solitary *they* when he just wanted to be a *me.* It looked like his dream of asking Kailyn Jade to be a we with him would never come true.

———

Mateo's got his work cut out for him.
You'll have to grab the next book to see if he can find a way to sweep Kailyn off her feet despite their two warring siblings.
You don't want to miss the final two books and the last two Matthews brothers.
The family saga continues with
Vow to Respect,
Book Five in the Flying Cross Ranch romances.

VOW TO RESPECT

CHAPTER ONE

"Even though scissors are a part of the art program, I can't do my job if you keep cutting the funding."

Kailyn Jade resisted the urge to grab the sharp pair of scissors sitting in the organizer on the large oak desk. The office supply sat blade side up, far too dangerous to be in a classroom. But she wasn't in a classroom just now. She was in the assistant principal's office.

Owen Sharp's smirk was razor-edged, like his name and the unsafe display on his desk. His blond hair spiked up to the ceiling, likely in an effort to get away from whatever thoughts were going on in that delusional brain of his.

"Your funding hasn't been cut, sweetheart," he said.

Kailyn resisted the urge to go up onto her tiptoes as she faced off against her nemesis. He wasn't truly her nemesis. He was worse. He was her boss. And her ex-boyfriend. Kinda. Sorta. She didn't think their two dates counted, but he surely did.

"It hasn't grown," Kailyn said. "And don't call me sweetheart."

"You used to like it when I called you sweetheart."

That had been a major part of the reason she hadn't accepted a third date from him. Kailyn had never liked being called sweetheart. Just as she had never liked being called cutie. Or shortie. Or worse, red.

As if it heard itself being talked about, one of her red curls escaped her headband and bounced in front of her eyes. Kailyn reached up to swipe the lock away, but another vision of red danced in her eyes. This time, the color was on her index finger.

The red paint she'd been using in her art classroom to help guide Chad Martin through his feelings of anxiety over his parents separating was smeared from her fingertip to her knuckle. There were splashes of green and white from helping Lynnette Hardy find the perfect shade of green to express her feelings of her two best friends going on a shopping trip without her. And then, of course, there was the rainbow of colors on Kailyn's smock from her six periods of classes today. The smock was supposed to keep the paint off her clothes, but Kailyn had long since given up the battle to keep any of her wardrobe paint-free.

From the first moment she'd picked up a crayon as a toddler, Kailyn had found her calling. Even when she had been scolded by her foster parents for drawing on the walls, she hadn't been deterred. She had been terrified that they would send her and her sister back to the foster care home. Instead, they handed her a sponge to clean up her mess. By the time she was done, her foster dad had gone to the store and brought back an easel and a handful of canvases.

"You could let me call you sweetheart again," Owen was saying, "and I'll see what I can—"

Kailyn made a disgusted sound in the back of her throat. This was the other reason why they'd broken up. Everything was always tit for tat with him. And she was usually the one giving both and receiving little in return. That was not how relationships were meant to go.

Not that she believed things could ever truly be equal between two people. Someone would always give a little more than the other with such fluctuating math. Just the thought of an equation to try and balance out a healthy relationship made the left side of her brain hurt.

"You're sending more money to the sports program than others," she said.

Now there was math she could manage. Kailyn had had a look at the balance sheet for the supplies for the day as well as the after-school programs. When the spreadsheet was ordered from greatest to least, the art program was at the very bottom of the list. Unfortunately, that math hadn't changed in the three years she'd been working at the school.

"The sports programs bring in revenue," Owen countered.

"Art may not pay in dollars, but it does pay in sense. Kids are experiencing more and more mental health issues these days. Art is a proven way to deal with those emotions that they don't know how to process. An art therapy after school program is an investment in their futures."

"What future? You'd be a struggling artist if you weren't an art teacher."

Kailyn had long since given up counting to ten with Owen. On their first date, she'd counted to ten three times. On their second, she'd gotten as far as a hundred before the main course was finished. Trying for patience with Owen didn't work. Which made her wonder how a man who was in charge of hormone-riddled teenagers at the high school kept his job as the chief disciplinarian.

"I might be a struggling artist," she said, "but I'm a happy, well-adjusted and whole person because I'm in touch with my emotions."

A bell rang from overhead, causing Kailyn's shoulders to bunch. A second later, the sound of yelling and screaming bounced off the walls. The squeak of tennis shoes pounding against linoleum made her eye twitch. The change between periods was her least favorite time of day, topped only by the end of school when all of the children made a beeline for their lockers and milled around for longer than the five minutes of break between classes.

As an artist, Kailyn appreciated the artistry of chaos. But only on a canvas where it could be contained by a frame. Emotions were at their most effective when they could be captured by a pencil or paintbrush. Which was why she not only wanted more supplies for her classroom, but an after-school art therapy program for more kids to express themselves in a quiet and methodical way.

"These are teenagers," Owen was saying. "All they have are out-of-control feelings."

"Art therapy can help channel those feelings for a productive use."

"Look, sweet—"

The look on Kailyn's face made Owen begin again. He was still under the delusion that they were on a break and would get back together. That break would last until the end of time, as far as she was concerned.

"I would give you the funds if I could," he continued. "But the school board is in charge of after school funding."

That was new. The vice principals were usually in charge of recreational programming for schools.

"It's a new rule because they want to make sure things are done fairly," Owen said. "They're looking at two programs. Yours is one. You'll need to make a presentation to them next week."

This was great. She was great at presentations. It used her artistic skill to make beautiful posterboards and slides to bring her vision to life. The right side of her brain was eager to get to work. It was the left side of her brain that was held back with some anxiety.

She knew she could make a presentation pretty. However, when she spoke to people about the tenants of art therapy, few, if any, took to the idea. Just as many people had hang-ups about going to a mental health therapist, and they were even less willing to work out their issues with a paint brush and palette.

"I could put in a good word for you."

Kailyn wasn't interested in Owen's words, good or bad. There was only one person's advice she could rely on in a matter such as this. Leaving the administrative suite, she walked across the hall to the guidance counselors' office.

Passing by the first open door in the counselor's wing, she smiled at Mr. Fox, who had been counseling kids on career and college since she'd gone here. She avoided the shrewd gaze of Ms. Ayala, the academic counselor who had been hired in Kailyn's last year at the school when her grades had started to slip. At the third open door, Kailyn peered in and saw a mirror image of herself.

Elayne had the same deep, reddish-brown auburn hair as Kailyn. But where Kailyn let her curls bounce free, only confined by a headband to leave her eyes unobstructed, Elayne had her hair pulled back in a severe bun. Her twin sister held up her finger with one hand while she cradled the phone in the other.

"I'm looking forward to it, Dr. Patel," she said into the phone receiver. "I have no doubt your program on trauma in children is going to help me in working with students in our community."

Elayne was headed to a conference for school guidance counselors and social workers hosted by the Purple Heart Ranch, which was a rehabilitation ranch for soldiers. In the last few years, the ranch had also begun an after-school and summer program for the town's youth. They were doing remarkable work with children from disadvantaged and low-income homes.

Closing the door to her sister's office, Kailyn looked around at the pictures on the wall of her and her sister as kids, in college, with their foster parents, and at the camps where they'd worked. The twins were a dynamic duo. Where Kailyn got kids to express their feelings, Elayne was excellent at helping them to focus that released energy into something productive.

"Good news," Kailyn said when her sister hung up the phone.

"Bad news," Elayne said at the same time.

"You go first," said Kailyn.

"You'll never guess who's back in town."

Honor Valley was a small town. Not exactly a town where everyone knew everyone else. More of a town where everyone knew *of* everyone else. But even that distinction belonged to the older generation. Many of the second and third generations had left for bigger cities and broader opportunities.

"Who?" asked Kailyn.

"The Terrible Twins."

Kailyn's heart stopped. There were three sets of twins in the valley. The Silver sisters were bossy girls, but they had never been terrible to either Kailyn or Elayne. Besides, Tilly and Gunny had been back for months and were both happily married and settled. That left the other two.

"Maybe they're just visiting?" asked Kailyn, her voice sounding breathless.

"We can only hope. This town isn't big enough for Jades and Matthews."

The notion of Aldo and Mateo Matthews brought Kailyn mixed feelings. Both emotions resided in the pit of her stomach. The thought of Aldo made her feel sick. The thought of Mateo…

Kailyn was supposed to hate Mateo Matthews.

And she did.

Well, she disliked him.

Just not when she thought of his face. Because every time she saw his handsome face, he offered her a smile. It was a smile that stopped her heart each time. No man had ever done that since him.

Which was all the reason to hate him even more.

"They're both still enlisted. They're probably just on leave visiting their father." As soon as the words were out of Kailyn's mouth, she winced. She didn't want her sister to think she was keeping tabs on the twins.

"If they are visiting, hopefully it's just for a few days, and they'll be gone by the time I get back," Elayne huffed, brushing back a nonexistent wayward strand of hair. "What's your good news?"

It took Kailyn a moment to think before she remembered. "The art therapy program is as good as mine, but I'm going to need your help."

CHAPTER TWO

"*I*t's all but a done deal, son."

Mateo Matthews clasped hands with General Alan Jensen. Though the older man had a head full of white hair, it was clear he still kept up with his Basic Training regimen. His biceps were nearly as big as Mateo's head. In fact, Mateo had to stop himself from wincing at the strength of General Jensen's grip on his right hand.

The general had recruited most of Mateo's brothers. The man was as old as his father, but he still looked half his age. That's one thing military training did for you. If you kept up the regiments, it kept your body in top shape.

"Thank you, sir." Even if Mateo had not been a member of the Armed Forces for the last eight years, his parents had drilled manners and etiquette into him from a tender age.

"No, thank you, Captain Matthews."

General Jensen gave one more affirmative shake of Mateo's hand before letting go. Mateo's knuckles snapped, crackled, and popped back into place now that they'd regained their freedom. "Will I need to talk to anyone else from the school board? The principal, perhaps?"

"It's the board that makes these decisions. Something or other about fairness and equality of all programs." General Jensen shrugged.

Though the United States Military served an entirely democratic society, the organization itself had a strict hierarchal structure. A soldier always knew their place in a room according to the rank that they'd earned.

"What you're planning to do will be invaluable to this community," said General Jensen. "It will give the youth an outlet for their energy and a purpose for their future."

Mateo agreed. As a youth, he'd had more energy than could be contained in his small body. Growing up in the foster care system, it was prudent to be seen and not heard, and never seen to be doing anything too boisterous if you wanted to get adopted. Unfortunately, it was too much to ask for growing boys to sit still and keep quiet. It had taken a saint to adopt not only him, but his brother as well.

Haran Matthews and his wife Tessa had taken in six boys when they were already past their own childbearing years. The Matthews had made him into a good person, but it was the Air Force that had made Mateo into a man. Now Mateo wanted to provide other young boys and girls with the same opportunity. The JROTC program he'd proposed to General Jensen would provide the kids of Honor Valley a launch pad for that life.

Originally, when Mateo had made his plans to retire from the Air Force and come home to the valley, he'd planned to work with the Bright Horizons Foster Home, the place that had taken in him and his brother when they had nowhere to go. Now that place was situated on his foster dad's homestead. He would continue to lend a hand there, but he wanted a project that was all his own.

"I have the ear of the board," General Jensen was saying. "One word from me and the funding for an after-school JROTC program is yours. There isn't any viable competition."

The general held out his hand again. Mateo masked his face before he grimaced at another of the ultra-firm handshakes. If this was the only hardship he'd face on his way to his bright new future, then he had absolutely nothing to complain about.

He slipped his hand into Jensen's and took the brunt of the assault. The second wasn't so bad now that he was prepared for it. When the general let his hand go, Mateo felt a sense of peace wash over him. A handshake was as good as a man's word. First, his birth father had taught him that. Then his foster father had reinforced the lesson.

"The board meets next Monday," said the general. "We'll make it formal then."

With a nod, the man walked off. His gait was the powerful stride of a man who'd spent more than half his life in the military. Before General Jensen turned the corner, he nodded as another man saluted him. Once the general was out of sight, the other man strode purposefully to Mateo.

Looking the newcomer up and down, Mateo couldn't help but let out a long, low sigh. When he'd gotten up this morning, he'd done so as quietly as possible so as not to wake his sleeping brother. The two were sharing the pull-out couch in the family room at the Flying Cross Ranch. Their family home was overflowing with all of the Matthews boys home as well as the five foster kids taking up residence in the boys' old bunkhouse.

Mateo had offered to sleep at a hotel. None of his family would hear of it. The most vocal naysayer was his brother, who was walking toward him.

Even though Aldo had been fast asleep when Mateo had crept out of the family room before dawn, his twin had managed to pull on the same gray shirt and jeans that Mateo was wearing. The only differentiating visual between them was the shoes they wore. Mateo wore cowboy boots, where Aldo had pulled on black military boots.

"There you are," Aldo grumped. "I've been looking all over for you."

"I told you I had to come into town for a meeting."

"You should've woken me up so we could come together."

But that was just it. They weren't doing this project together. Mateo wouldn't mind if they stopped doing a lot of things together. Especially the dressing alike part.

Mateo had put up with it when his birth mother had dressed them alike. Though she'd done it mostly because she bought their discount clothing in bulk. Mateo would have done anything in the world to earn one of his mother's smiles. So when it came time to dress each morning, he dutifully put on what she laid out for her twin boys without any protest.

He still remembered the outfit she'd chosen for her sons as well as her husband on the day of their citizenship ceremony. He had been proud to dress like his father. Mateo still remembered the pride in his father's eyes as he peered back at his family as he recited his vows to the country of his heart. His mother had cried. It was the first time Mateo had understood happy tears and the word oxymoron.

Just a few months later, his parents would be taken away from them by someone breaking the rules. A drunk driver would take their precious lives and leave Mateo and his brother with no one. Into the foster system they'd went.

After they were adopted by the Matthews, Mateo wanted nothing more than his own individuality. He often tried to sneak out before Aldo woke and insisted they wore the same thing. All it would take was his younger brother's—younger by ten minutes—lip to start quivering and Mateo would give in. Now that the twins were no longer children, and no longer in the military, there was no good reason for them to dress alike. Or do much else alike either.

"You're really doing this?" said Aldo. "You're going to work with runts?"

"We used to be runts."

"That's the benefit of growing up. We don't have to deal with runts anymore."

Mateo not only wanted to deal with other people's runts, he wanted to deal with his own runts. The problem was there was only one girl he could see himself making runts with. He had an uphill battle where she was concerned.

"You don't have to deal with the JROTC program," said Mateo. "You can sign your contract and reenlist."

"Without you?" Aldo scrunched up his nose.

The scrunching was a familiar expression. When Aldo had decided he didn't like olives, he frowned, scrunching up his nose at Mateo every time he popped one into his mouth. He even went so far as to feign sickness whenever Mateo dared to enjoy the offensive fruit.

Aldo also insisted that they have the same friends. As well as the same enemies. That last one had been an anchor around Mateo's ankles for far too long.

"We're going to live our own lives from now," Mateo said. "My life is going to be here."

Aldo shrugged. "I'm not in a rush to sign a new contract. I can stay home. For a while."

Mateo pinched the bridge of his nose. His brother had selective hearing. At least their shoes were different today. It was a start. Now he just had to figure out how to ditch his brother long enough to go in search of a particular girl with dark red curls that made his heart skip a beat.

"Topher told me there are private military contractors visiting the Purple Heart Ranch this week," said Aldo. "With so many soldiers recuperating there, it's like fertile ground for the picking."

Well, that would be good. A few days on his own without his twin dogging his steps. A lot could happen in a few days.

CHAPTER THREE

Kailyn closed the door to her sister's office with a quiet snick. Checking in with her twin had been just the right idea to help her get started on the presentation for the board. Though she and Elayne had shared a womb, it might have been better if they'd burst into the world sharing a brain. Where Kailyn was clearly a right-brained person, artistic, creative, emotional, her sister's head listed to the left where logic resided.

Elayne was far more balanced than Kailyn. She could quickly analyze a situation and had the capacity to deal with both logistic and emotional fallout. It was a feat Kailyn both admired and begrudged.

Elayne always offered her more well-rounded brain to Kailyn whenever she asked. When it came to anything artistic, Elayne was all thumbs. They never attempted the switching places cliché everyone always thought twins got up to. Instead, they asked the other for help where they were weak. One weakness that Kailyn had never asked her sister's advice or guidance on was Mateo Matthews.

Walking the halls of the school, Kailyn saw the ghost of Mateo Matthews in Mrs. Cristobel's doorway, where he'd always leave with a smile. Mateo had been good at math. Whenever he raised his hand to give the answer, he always explained how he'd arrived at the solution. The lightbulb would go off over Kailyn's head each time he did, and she'd finally understand how to do that problem and then the next.

Next, she saw the ghost of his muscular teenage form bent over the water fountain after football practice. He was always there at that particular water fountain, which was right outside the art room, even though the boys' locker room and the football field were on the other side of the school. But she supposed it was the least crowded of drinking fountains, and that had to be why he always used it and ran the risk of running late to practice.

She also had a clear memory of Mateo sitting in the center of the cafeteria, where she would always sit on the fringe or take her meals in the art room. Like hers, Mateo's plate was always piled high with cafeteria food, even snagging the uneaten portions of their friends' before they could place the unopened cartoons of milk or fruit cups in the trash. She'd see him again at the end of the lunch period, placing his empty tray on the rack before leaving.

Kailyn understood that sentiment as a foster kid. Even though they both had been adopted by the time they were in high school, and they were in stable homes with good people, abandoned kids remembered the feeling of always being hungry. It never truly went away.

What was always a part of her memory, and never a ghost, was the vivid sparkle in his hazel eyes whenever he'd catch sight of her. Sometimes, when they were alone in the halls, he would smile at her. That smile always made her feet miss a step and her heart skip a beat.

It was cruel, that smile. Cruel because she could not return it. Not when he stood by as his brother, who never missed an opportunity to verbally assault her sister. Not when she walked side by side with her sister, who Kailyn was sure would claw out Aldo Matthew's eyes if given half the chance.

Kailyn never knew the reason Aldo had taken such a dislike to Elayne. Her sister had never been able to fully articulate why she hated Aldo so fiercely. They both must have sprung into the world this way and would go out swinging at each other in their elder years.

In the meantime, whenever they met, Elayne and Aldo would lay waste to everything in their path. They'd suck the color out of the day with their snips and snipes. If they remained too long in the same vicinity, the world would surely combust under their deep-seated hatred of one another.

Which was why it was such a blessing when the Matthews twins flew away to join the Air Force. There had been peace in the valley for eight years. There also hadn't been anyone else who had smiled at Kailyn in the way that made her miss a step or her heart skip a beat.

"Girls cook, not boys. So what does that make you?"

For a moment, Kailyn froze. It was more the tone than the actual words. There was the sound of a sneer in the speaker's tone. Whenever Aldo spoke to Elayne, he always wrinkled his nose, which made the pitch of his deep voice go an octave higher. To this day, if anyone spoke to Kailyn while wrinkling their nose, her shoulders would huddle in on herself and she'd go mute while her sister confronted her bully, making both her five-foot-four stature appear bigger and her light voice go gruffer.

Whomever was being sneered at didn't growl. They spoke in a friendly tone. "Actually, a majority of chefs are males. It's very sexist if you think about it, and I'm a feminist."

Kailyn picked up her steps again. Her light footfalls were the only thing that could be heard in the stunned silence. She peered around the corner, and standing in front of Mateo's water fountain was a group of four boys.

Though group was the wrong word. There was a pack of three who stood together. Those three faced off against one smaller boy. The smaller boy smiled up at the predators. Of all things, he held a cloche in his hands. He clearly didn't realize he was prey and would soon be served up.

"Oh look, guys, this little feminist made cookies in her Easy Bake Oven."

"The Easy Bake Oven packets are special formulas." The little chef shook his head in an admonishing factor, still not getting the fact that he was in danger. "I made these from scratch with—"

The chef didn't get to finish his recipe. One of the pack smacked the cloche from his hands. The dish fell to the floor. Some of the cupcakes fell into the inside of the cloche's dome. Others fell with a splat—icing side down—on the linoleum floor.

Kailyn hated confrontations. She hated any type of fighting. But even more, she hated watching anyone get picked on. So why had she chosen to work in a high school where bullying ran rampant? Well, it was the only job available to her at the time.

Most of the time, she preferred to stay inside her classroom with her peaceful art supplies. There were few arguments or fights here in this wing of the school where the theater and band department were housed. But every once in a while, something went down.

Usually, another teacher was nearby to stop it. Right now, Kailyn was the only adult in sight. She picked up her steps to get to the fray, but someone beat her to it.

"Knock it off before I make you eat that off the floor."

A tall, skinny kid placed himself at the center of the confrontation. He had an inch or two on the boys in the pack, but he was outnumbered. His thin body stood protectively in front of the little chef.

"Chill, Denny," said the kid that must have been the pack leader. "We're just joking."

"We gotta get home anyway," said his packmate to the left. "My mom baked us cookies."

The packmate on the right sneered, picking up the new line of insults. "I'm heading home to play catch with my dad."

The pack leader affected a false frown. "These two wouldn't know anything about that."

The words were a physical punch to Denny, to the little chef, and to Kailyn. She'd had mean girls pull the same kind of thing with her in school when they learned she was a foster child. Kids were cruel, and they were often cruelest to the poor and the parentless.

"You three are not going home," said the voice of an adult. Kailyn was surprised to find that adult had the same pitch as her own voice. She opened her mouth to continue. "Not until you go to the janitor's closet, clean this mess up, and then wait for me to call your parents to let them know what you did here."

The young wolves' jaws twitched. Their clawless fingers clenched. For a moment, Kailyn wasn't a teacher. She wasn't an adult. She was a little girl facing off against bullies again.

"If I repeat myself, it'll be a week of detention with the other Ms. Jade added on top."

That got the pack in motion. "Yes, Ms. Jade," they intoned.

Whereas Kailyn had a reputation for being soft, everyone knew Elayne was hardcore. Many students were seen leaving her office in tears. The threat of going into the guidance office and talking about their feelings was enough to turn most boys green.

Kailyn watched as the three walked down the hall to the janitor's closet. When she turned back to the other two, she wasn't met with thanks and praise. They weren't regarding her at all. They were in a tense argument.

"You can't be a pushover, Miguel. You have to fight back."

"I'm not a fighter. I offered them cupcakes. Here." Miguel picked up a cupcake that had rolled inside the cloche. "You can have this one."

Denny rolled his eyes and stormed off without the cupcake—or any acknowledgement of Kailyn.

Miguel looked up at Kailyn as she approached. He held the treat out to her. The cake bottom was a deep red. The icing was a creamy white. Sprinkles were artfully placed around the top like a starburst.

"Thank you, ma'am."

Kailyn winced at the ma'am. But it showed the kid had manners. Whoever was fostering this kid was doing right by him.

"This looks beautiful—Miguel, is it?"

He nodded. "I was trying to mimic Van Gogh's *Starry Night*."

"I see it." Kailyn grinned as she admired the artistic flair. "You're a foster kid?"

Shame spread across Miguel's cheeks, much like the pattern on his cupcake.

"I was, too."

"I used to horde food. Now I share." Miguel shrugged. "I thought I was evolving."

Kailyn liked this kid immensely. He was far more evolved than the pack animals lugging brooms and a mop down the hall. Those three would likely benefit from getting in touch with their feelings, but Miguel would blossom if he were a part of her after school art therapy program.

CHAPTER FOUR

"I don't understand how we got stuck buying female supplies."

Mateo Matthews watched as his brother tossed a box of feminine products into the shopping cart. The cardboard box of supplies for a woman's time of the month landed with a dull splat at the bottom of the cart. Mateo lifted the box with a smiling woman on it who definitely did not look as though she was suffering from a feminine ailment and placed it back on the shelf. "That's not the right one."

"Oh, you're an expert in feminine hygiene now?" asked Aldo.

"No, I just know how to read instructions, and Savy specifically wrote down a different name brand."

Replacing the purple box, Mateo grabbed the pink brand that his sister-in-law had shown him a picture of from the shelf and placed it in the cart. With that last item on their shopping list checked off, they were done with the shopping excursion in town. They'd been back home for less than a week, and it was busier than usual on the ranch with all the Matthews boys home at once, four of their significant others, and a house full of foster kids.

With the rest of the adults having their hands full with ranch chores, repairs, and the general chaos that came with caring for foster kids, Mateo had offered to run errands in town for Savy. He hadn't expected his brother to come along on the domestic mission. But just like when they were kids, Aldo still suffered a bit from separation anxiety.

"The way you act sometimes, *hermano*, you'd think these were for you."

Mateo didn't think for a second that listening to the needs of another person meant that he was somehow feminine. In fact, he didn't think there was anything wrong with the act of listening or with femininity.

"You need to knock it off," said Aldo. "It's ruining my rep."

"You do know that just because we're twins, it doesn't mean we share the same reputation."

Aldo scoffed at that.

Inwardly, Mateo scoffed, too.

For much of their lives, everyone around them had linked the two with the other's behavior because of the way they looked. As identical twins, they looked exactly alike. Though their foster brothers and adoptive parents could always tell them apart, to others, there was no distinction. So Mateo got blamed for a lot of the antics Aldo got up to, whether he agreed with what his brother did or not.

A lot of times, he did not agree.

Especially not the times when Aldo's mean streak made an appearance. Mateo was the lover where Aldo was the fighter. Not so much a fist fighter as a loudmouth.

Aldo had grown up a bully. Not because their biological parents had mistreated their kids. Their parents had wanted nothing but the best for their boys. They just hadn't been able to give it to them, and instead had lost everything when they'd tried.

The social workers and school counselors all said Aldo's bullying was all about self-sabotaging. He didn't trust that he could have anything good, so he tried to destroy any potential blessings before they could be taken away from him.

Mateo never had anything bad to say about anyone or anything. But because he looked like his brother, people didn't make the distinction between the two, especially not since Mateo often held his tongue and stood by when his brother went off at the mouth.

But for the first time in their lives, the Matthews twins' paths were about to diverge. Mateo was staying home after this last deployment, where Aldo planned to go back into the service. While they were apart, Mateo hoped to settle down, build his own reputation apart from his twin, and perhaps even start to date. He wouldn't admit to his brother that he had one hometown girl in mind: a certain redhead with kind eyes and freckles dotting her cheeks. Green eyes like a dense forest that Mateo got lost in when he daydreamed. And smiling pink lips that made him think of the heart-shaped hard candies he'd once left at her desk on Valentine's Day.

"Hey, look, it's Raggedy Ann."

Mateo frowned. He didn't see a red-haired doll with yarn for hair and a button nose anywhere in the shop. Belatedly, he remembered that that was the mean nickname his brother had given to the exact girl Mateo had just been daydreaming of. Then, looking up, he caught sight of that beauty.

Kailyn Jade stood in the produce section of the grocery store. There was a shopping basket on one arm, and she held a carrot in her hand. Her gaze was wide, like a deer in headlights, as she stared up at Mateo.

Just like when he was young, Mateo ached to go up to her. To reach out and offer his hand in friendship. To tell her a funny joke, to see her grin go wide and those freckles spread. To give her a heart-shaped candy that said *Be Mine* on it.

But just like when they were young, Kailyn's cheeks went red when she was in his presence, making those freckles disappear in the blush. Those green eyes that he wanted to keep focused on him dropped to the ground. And her slender shoulders hunched forward, like she'd been dealt a blow.

"And look," Aldo continued, "there's Andy."

"Oh, would you look at that," said a carbon copy of Kailyn, but with bone-straight red hair devoid of curls and a pair of glasses set low on her nose. "It's a walking, talking feminine product. Too bad it won't fit down the toilet for a flush. It needs to be taken out with the garbage."

The malicious grin dropped from Aldo's face, and he looked ready for war. Facing off against him, Elayne Jade looked ready to deal the first strike in a battle that had been started years ago but ended in a bitter stalemate.

Mateo opened his mouth, ready at last to defuse this decades-long feud between two of the town's sets of twins. But it was Kailyn's soft voice that broke through the tension.

"We have somewhere to be, Elayne." Kailyn glanced at Mateo and his closed mouth before turning away from him with a dismissive shake of her head. "They're not worth it."

And with that, the Jade twins walked away from the Matthews twins. Mateo was left standing beside his brother, looking for all the world like a solitary *they* when he just wanted to be a *me*. It looked like his dream of asking Kailyn Jade to be a *we* with him would never come true.

CHAPTER FIVE

nbelievable. A little kid had stood up for another kid that wasn't even his blood in the same halls that this grown man used to haunt. But today, all these years later, the adult-sized Mateo Matthews still couldn't—still wouldn't—stand up to his brother.

When Kailyn had initially spotted him, and their gazes had connected for the first time in years, her traitorous heart had gone skipping down the grocery store aisle. Her feet had nearly followed suit. The way his hazel eyes had gone wide with what looked like delight, the way his nostrils had flared with what might have been desire, the way his lips had quirked in what had seemed a welcoming smile had given her the crazy idea that she could run into his arms and he'd catch her right out of thin air.

The first sight of Mateo Matthews standing in the feminine aisle had been a shock to her senses. He'd grown. He'd grown a lot. He'd filled out in places where she didn't think his body had more space to grow. But it did, and it had grown spectacularly.

He had the kind of chest that was made for a woman to curl up against. His strong arms where he'd looped a basket of feminine products over his left biceps looked like it'd be the perfect thing to lean on during that time of the month. Kailyn envied his girlfriend for having a man that had no issues buying intimate products for her. Except for the fact that he still allowed his brother to bully women.

Because then Aldo had opened his mouth. And Mateo hadn't.

Frog-marching her sister away from Aldo Matthews was Kailyn's number one priority. Now that she was closer to getting funding for her after school art therapy program, she had even less desire to witness Armageddon. She and her sister could hop in their car and go shopping in the next town over if it meant avoiding the Matthews twins and world destruction.

"Why do you always stop me from fighting with that cretin?" said Elayne.

"Why do you always let him get to you?" demanded Kailyn. "You know, name-calling never does any good."

The automatic doors of the grocery store closed behind them. Since they were still standing on the welcome mat, the doors swung back open. Kailyn gave Elayne another tug until they were no longer setting off the sensor, and the doors remained closed.

Elayne opened and closed her fists as she visibly began to calm down. There was still red in her cheeks, and her eyes flashed back to the closed doors of the grocery store. "I don't know why he gets to me like that. I've had people say far worse, but when it comes out of his mouth, I just..."

She turned with a huff to face the other direction. Elayne's hands went on her hips. She even stomped her foot. She reminded Kailyn of the dance a stallion and mare engaged in when they were deciding whether or not to mate.

Kailyn knew that mating with Aldo Matthews was the last thing on her sister's mind. The better M word would be mar, or better yet, murder. She didn't remember Aldo dating much back in their high school days, though plenty of girls were interested. The only girl who he appeared to pay any attention to was Elayne, and that attention was always negative.

Yeah, the origin of the feud between those two was a mystery—a mystery the whole world wanted unsolved and just buried to never be discovered again.

"Kailyn?"

Kailyn didn't need to turn to know it was Mateo Matthews speaking to her. The softness in his deep voice was in opposition to the hard body she'd witnessed standing in the feminine aisle. She didn't want to turn around, but she didn't have a choice. It was as though magnets pulled her to face him.

Mateo wasn't smiling that almost smile he'd always had reserved for her when they caught each other in the halls or about town without their siblings tagging along. His brows were drawn, not wide with delight at seeing her. His shoulders slumped as though facing her now was a burden. He looked just as stressed by the encounter as she felt.

In his hands, he held a paper bag. A peak over the top of the bag's opening showed that it contained the items that had been in Kailyn's cart before she'd abandoned them to stop World War III. On top sat a pastry bag, food dye, icing, and sprinkles for pastry design.

As the art teacher, Kailyn got a small budget to pay for classroom supplies each year. Those monies were always gone before the first day of school began. After that, Kailyn, like most teachers, came out of pocket to pay for the things necessary for her students' education.

"I didn't pay for those," she said.

"I did."

Mateo held the handle of the paper bag out to her. Instinct and manners had Kailyn reaching for it. Just before the exchange, their fingers touched. The sparks shooting between the two of them made her gasp.

Instinct fired again, warning her to snatch her hand away lest she get burned. She ignored the impulse. Because Mateo's heat felt so good.

His nostrils flared. His throat worked. But once again, Mateo said nothing as a battle waged between them. It was that silence that snapped her out of her stupor and caused her to snatch the bag from his grasp.

"What do I owe you?" she asked.

"I owe you an apology for my brother's behavior."

A profound sense of relief washed over Kailyn's shoulders. These were the words she had been waiting years to hear from this man. She lifted her free hand toward him.

Mateo watched that hand as it rose. They both did. Kailyn had no clue what the hand was planning to do once it reached its destination. She wasn't entirely sure of its destination.

Was her hand planning to pat him on the shoulder in a *there-there* motion?

Perhaps her hand meant to reach out to shake his, to solidify this truce between them.

Or maybe her hand had the crazy idea to smooth the worry creasing his brow, then slide down to cup that strong chin of his.

In the end, the motion and the moment were snatched away as the automatic doors opened again to let loose the raging bull that was Aldo.

"I didn't do anything wrong." Aldo's voice boomed into the cool air, turning it humid.

"Of course that's what he thinks," hissed Elayne.

"Aldo!" Mateo's voice boomed.

"Elayne!" Kailyn's voice joined his.

"Car," they both commanded their siblings.

The power of their voices combined must have worked. Both Aldo and Elayne came to a stunned stop. In unison, they both picked up their feet, marching left-right-left, storming off to their respective cars. When Kailyn turned back to Mateo, he was staring at her.

Slowly, the stress seeped from his face to be replaced by a thoughtful look. His gaze roamed over her. She held still for his perusal, her heart in her throat.

"I'm sorry," he said.

That apology was heavy. It weighed too much to just mean this moment.

"I want there to be peace between us," Mateo continued. "I'm home to stay. We're going to be neighbors and... I'd like... I'd like for us to be friends."

He reached his hand out to her. His didn't pat her on the shoulder. Nor did it reach up to straighten the crease of her brow. His hand aimed at her torso, the exact height for a handshake.

Disappointment coursed through Kailyn. She shook it off and let her manners take over. When Kailyn reached out to meet his fingers, sparks fluttered across her palm, up her wrists, and settled in the crook of her elbows.

Meeting his eyes, she saw that she wasn't the only one affected. Mateo's Adam's apple bobbed as he regarded her. His eyes were bright again, a mixture of delight and desire. This was not a friendly handshake. It felt like the start of more.

Kailyn's heart beat wildly. Sometimes skipping beats. Sometimes beating twice. With her thumb on Mateo's pulse, she felt the same erratic rhythm coming from him. She was thrilled to know that she wasn't alone in this.

"You two have met. That's good."

For the second time today, Kailyn cringed at the sound of a man's voice who she dreaded interacting with. Aldo huffed inside the passenger seat of a car off in the distance. On the other side of the parking lot, Elayne sat in the driver's seat of her car, glaring up at the sky. Coming up to Kailyn and Mateo at the store front was Owen.

"I guess this handshake means you two are working it out." Owen stepped between Mateo and Kailyn's clasped hands, causing them to break apart. Stepping around Kailyn, much like a dog eying a fire hydrant, he placed an arm around Kailyn's shoulders.

Mateo's warm gaze darkened.

Kailyn stepped away from Owen's unwanted embrace. "What do you mean? Working what out?"

"Captain Matthews is in line for the after school funding, too."

CHAPTER SIX

Mateo could only concentrate on the hand around Kailyn's waist. His fingers clenched into fists, mostly to keep from reaching out and wrenching the guy away from her. But once they were in fists, he realized that he could do more damage. Taking a deep breath, he forced his hands to relax.

He relaxed even more when Kailyn stepped away from the man, as though his touch offended her. The interloper made to move closer, to regain his hold on her. Mateo clenched his hands into fists again, prepared to disabuse him of the notion.

He wouldn't need to. Kailyn took another step away from the guy. Her step brought her between the two of them. Mateo got the clear notion that she wasn't interested in breaking up any possible fight between the two unevenly matched males. Her attention wasn't even on the other guy. It rested solely on him.

"You're my competition for the after school funding?" she asked, pointing an accusing finger at him.

There were specks of paint on that finger. She must have been painting recently. He wanted to know what she'd created. Kailyn appeared to want an answer to his question because she spoke up again, her finger jabbing at him once more.

"Let me guess; you want to create some sort of military program? Like an RTOC?"

"JROTC," Mateo corrected. "Junior Reserve Officers' Training Corps."

Kailyn's eyes were bright with—what was that? Betrayal? Shock? Disbelief? Whatever it was, his fingers now ached to smooth furrowed line between her brows. Maybe not with his hands. It would be best to do those with his lips.

"You want to make child soldiers?"

That was disgust in her voice. He knew that tone too well. It sounded exactly like her sister's voice whenever Elayne engaged Aldo.

"Officers," Mateo said.

"Officers who fight in wars as soldiers."

"The program teaches kids to become leaders and managers. It could even pay for their college career."

Kailyn huffed, crossing her arms over her chest. She looked away from him, toward the other guy. The other guy smirked at Mateo, but when he made a move to swoop his tentacles around Kailyn again, she moved away. The fact that she had no desire to be touched by this man pleased Mateo to no end. But he still couldn't wrap his head around why she was so angry.

"You want to start an after school art program?" he asked.

Mateo was surprised there wasn't already one. He knew Kailyn was the art teacher at the high school. He'd kept tabs on her, casually bringing up her name whenever he'd call to chat with one of the James or Silver sisters. Between the nine of them, they knew everything and everyone in Honor Valley.

Having the JROTC program run through the school had been Mateo's first step in getting closer to Kailyn. He figured if they were colleagues, it would be easier to bump into her and strike up a conversation, a friendship, a relationship.

Had Mateo known that she was angling to teach art after school, he would've been the first in line to take her class. He remembered watching her paint in the high school art studio when he was supposed to be doing drills on the football fields. She always looked so peaceful as she swiped the brush across the canvas. He'd always sneak in afterwards to see what she'd created. He wasn't much for art or interpretation, but looking at her paintings always made something warm bloom in his chest.

"Of course I want to teach kids art." Kailyn took another step away from the man who stupidly still had his arm outstretched to her, though it was clear she'd forgotten he was even there.

Kailyn stepped up toe to toe with Mateo. That finger still hung between them. If he leaned forward, Mateo was the one in danger of being knocked out. A simple touch from her would've floored him. His knees shook when he inhaled Kailyn's fresh floral scent. There was a hint of paint chemicals coming off her pale skin.

"Art therapy has the capacity to heal so many children's inner wounds," she went on. "It allows children, and adults, to express themselves without having to verbalize past traumas and hurts."

Mateo liked the sound of that. He especially liked the idea of healing under this woman's capable hands and caring guidance. Her index finger had stopped pointing. The other four fingers of her hands came to stand by that lone soldier. For a moment, Mateo thought she'd touch his heart.

"I want to teach them how to manage their feelings." Kailyn balled her open hand into a fist and placed it over her chest. "You want to teach them how to shut them down and hurt someone else?"

"No," Mateo said softly. "I want to show them how to fight for what they believe in."

"Why do they have to fight at all? Isn't fighting and violence and strife the cause of all problems?"

"No," he said again, his voice remaining soft. "Art and combat are different sides of the same coin. One is used to protect the other. The other gives you something to fight for."

There was confusion on her brow, but it outweighed the anger and indignation.

"I don't see why we can't have both," Mateo continued. "We could run both programs together."

Kailyn's lips parted. She chewed at her lower lip, unsure. Mateo reached for her, and that's when the other guy stepped back into the scene.

"There's only enough funding for one program." His hand went around her waist again. "As vice principal and the administrator in charge of recreational programs for the high school, you have my full support, Kailyn."

Kailyn flinched at his touch, but she didn't pull away this time. Her lips remained pursed as she regarded Mateo. Unfortunately, she didn't have any more words for him.

Mateo knew the funding was as good as his. The vice principal might be in charge of the recreational program for the school, but he couldn't grant the funding. If he could, he would've already handed it over to Kailyn—and Mateo wouldn't blame him. He would've done the same. But right now, it was the VP who had his hands on the thing Mateo wanted most in this world. His fighting instincts wanted to kick in. But he knew that wouldn't work with a gentle soul like Kailyn.

She hated fighting. She craved peace. But Mateo knew that he was right; art and combat were often two sides of the same coin. He would simply have to fight to get her to see the other side.

CHAPTER SEVEN

Kailyn rubbed at her eyes. Her hands came away wet. Not wet from tears. It was a thicker wetness, with a good deal of viscosity. Looking down at the red streak on her palm, she knew she had smeared paint across her forehead.

It wouldn't be the first time. At least she'd caught it. Not that anyone was around to see.

It was the end of a long school day. The end of an even longer week. On Monday, she had assigned self-portraits in many of her art classes. She'd given students the leeway to use any materials they saw fit. Self-portraits were more of a window into a person's soul than the eyes were. Because the portrait didn't show what was in the mirror, it showed what was in their mind's eye.

Kailyn sighed as she flipped through the turned-in presentations. Kameron Harris, the quarterback and homecoming king, had drawn a football in green grass with a crown. He was finished on the first day of the assignment and spent the rest of the class chatting with the other jocks at his table thinking he'd gotten over and had gotten an easy A. Little did he know that Kailyn saw the clear cry for help in his portrait. The kid thought that this was all he could ever be, but he clearly yearned for more. If not, then why would he have painstakingly drawn each blade of grass getting greener the further away from the football the blades got?

Mika Devin, who was the uncontested frontrunner for class valedictorian, drew herself with full regalia befitting that honor. Also around her neck was a stethoscope. Instead of the royal blue and regal purple school colors, she wore a white lab coat. Aside from blue eyes, there was no other facial feature on her drawing. And unlike Kameron's creation, the rest of her canvas was blank. The poor girl was clearly under so much pressure.

The rest of the portraits were much the same. Black and white portraits that spoke loudly of depression. Neon-colored paintings that made Kailyn wonder about oversensitivity. The kids were all crying out for help. The question was, would any of them take the solution Kailyn wanted to offer?

Kailyn set the children's canvases aside and turned back to her own. While they had worked on depicting themselves, she had done a different painting exercise, one where she let the brush do what it wanted. Kind of a stream of consciousness painting. What her rational mind saw emerging from the canvas was a certain tall, dark, and handsome soldier.

She had never drawn him before. Not exactly. His eyes had a appeared a few times in drawings. That small smile that had always felt so big to her was reflected in more paintings than she cared to admit. But she'd never drawn a full-figured depiction of Mateo Matthews before.

And she'd drawn the warmonger in a pastoral scene, no less. Daisies and tulips dotted the green background, while he stood tall and proud in—were those fatigues? Yes, she'd drawn him in fatigues, though she wasn't even sure if a pilot wore fatigues.

It didn't matter. He was the enemy. He'd allowed his brother to be mean to her sister without any interference. And now he wanted to turn troubled youths into violent aggressors.

Kailyn jabbed at the canvas. The angry brush strokes ruined her pastoral scene. They muted the fatigues. But not a single bristle so much as smudged his smile.

"Wow, that's cool. It's like two opposing artists working on the same painting."

Kailyn dropped the paintbrush as though it was a cookie stolen from the treats jar. The paint splattered on the floor, leaving behind a starburst pattern. Instead of facing her sister, she grabbed a wad of paper towels and dabbed at the mess.

"He looks familiar, but I can't place him. Who is he?"

"He's no one," Kailyn stammered as she straightened. "I was just messing around."

"Whoever he is, he's beautiful."

Kailyn wanted to chuck the brush and the canvas against the wall. The angry art couldn't be beautiful. But looking at it, she could see the appeal in the softness beneath the harsh strokes. Maybe she should tell her sister who her unconscious inspiration was? That would certainly get Elayne to stop admiring the piece.

"You, on the other hand, need a bit of prettying up." Elayne grabbed a rag and came at Kailyn.

Kailyn made a half-hearted dodge away from her sister. Older by twenty minutes, Elayne liked to play mom to her from time to time. Every single time she did, Kailyn ate it up.

Neither of them could remember receiving this kind of attention from their birth mother. From what they'd been told, she had been a teenager herself. She'd kept the girls for a few months, but without any support from her own parents or their birth father, who was not named on the birth certificate, she'd turned the twins over to the state. She died in a factory accident a few years later.

"Better?" asked Kailyn after her sister had caught and cleaned her face of any remaining streaks of paint.

"Eh, you'll do." Elayne tossed the rag in the sink. "Listen, I wanted to say I'm sorry."

"About what?"

"About yesterday with the Matthews. I'm a grown woman. I'm a counselor to kids. I need to stop letting Aldo Matthews get to me like that. Next time I see him, I'm going to be cordial."

"I'll believe that when I see it."

Elayne cut her a look.

Kailyn held up her hands in mock defense. "I mean, I would like to see that."

And she really would. She did want to see a truce between Elayne and Aldo. But there would be no easy truce between her and Mateo. Not while he stood in the way of her plans.

Kailyn opted not to tell that to Elayne. There was war, and then there was intergalactic destruction. If Elayne knew that any of the Matthews were going against her baby sister, she'd go nuclear. Best if Kailyn handled this battle herself.

She could beat Mateo Matthews. Her presentation skills would be top-notch. What Elayne had already added to the slides yesterday couldn't be beat. And she did have Owen's support. She had this in the bag.

"Well, I'm off," said Elayne. "Just wanted to say that and goodbye before I head out for my trip."

"I hope you enjoy your conference."

"Excuse me, Ms. Jade."

The little chef from yesterday, Miguel, stood in the doorway. Seeing that the visitor was for Kailyn, Elayne waved goodbye and stepped through the door.

"Hi, Miguel," said Kailyn, beckoning the kid inside.

"You said you had some decorating tools I could borrow?"

She did. They were the ones she'd gone to the grocery store for the other day. The ones she'd nearly left in the middle of the aisle to get her sister away from her nemesis. The same appliances that Mateo Matthews had purchased and given to her as a peace offering. Well, at least now they'd be put to good use.

"You're welcome to keep them," Kailyn said, handing over the bag of goods.

Miguel's eyes lit up.

"Hurry now. I don't want you to miss the after school bus."

"Someone from my family is coming to pick me up."

Oh? She'd thought the boy was a foster after that confrontation the other day? Maybe he was being raised by relatives?

"I'm going to be adopted," Miguel said proudly. "They start the paperwork this week. That's why I want to make a special dessert."

"Congratulations, Miguel. I was a foster kid and then adopted, too."

"I didn't know that," he said, sitting down in one of the plastic chairs. "Was it a big family?"

"No, just my mom and dad and my sister."

"I'm getting two sisters, three brothers, and a whole bunch of aunts and uncles. I'm even getting a grandpa."

"That sounds amazing."

"It's great. I didn't think I'd like my uncles. They're all soldiers, and I thought they would make me run drills or shoot guns."

"Soldiers?"

"Yup. But Uncle Will said a soldier's first weapon is his mind, not his gun. Uncle Topher said he'd take his girlfriend's mind over any of theirs. And then Aunt Foxy said Ms. Toni—that's Uncle Topher's girlfriend—wouldn't be his girlfriend for long. She's clairscent—clairscenty—clairsentient. Aunt Foxy is, not Ms. Toni. Do you know what that means?"

Kailyn did know what that meant. She knew most of those people and their names. They were kids who had been at the Bright Horizon's Foster Home when she and her sister had been there. The boys had been adopted by the Matthews couple. The James girls had gone with their mother for a time before the eldest, Savy, had come of age and was able to claim responsibility for her two sisters.

"I'm making a celebratory cake, and it's going to have my new name on it; Miguel Matthews."

Kailyn tried to smile for the boy, but her lips wouldn't stretch.

"Oh, there's my ride now."

Kailyn looked up to see Mateo Matthews standing in the door. She was transported back almost a decade ago when he'd leaned over the water fountain or gone around a corner headed to football practice, or catch her eye in the cafeteria. There was that small smile he gave her that set off something big inside of her. Like it always did, her heart skipped a beat at the sight of him, and the air rushed from her lungs with a longing sigh.

CHAPTER EIGHT

Walking down the halls of his alma mater didn't bring up strong emotions for Mateo. High school hadn't been a dark place for him like some students. He'd had his share of popularity, though he had never let it go to his head. With his athletic build, he had always been a first pick by all the sports coaches for any team he tried out for. Since his parents demanded the effort, his grades were up to par, though not exactly Principal's Honor Roll. Because girls seemed to find manners charming, he was never without attention. Still, he'd only ever cared about having one girl's attentions.

Each day in this place had been broken into BK and AK. Before he saw Kailyn Jade in the halls and after he saw her. Her grades were better than his, so he hadn't been in any of her classes. He'd only ever catch glimpses of her in the halls. Oftentimes he'd go out of his way to make sure their paths would cross.

In tenth grade, they'd shared a lunch period. She'd sat with her sister, which made his approach tricky. He'd been steadily maneuvering his friend group's seating closer and closer to the table she sat with her sister and friends each day. Unfortunately, a few weeks into the semester, Aldo had managed to get switched to his lunch period, and the lunchroom had been divided into a war zone he could never safely navigate across.

In eleventh grade, his third period math class was right next door to hers. After a few days, he'd noted that she always lingered behind to talk with the teacher. Math, apparently, wasn't her best subject, and she never left without asking for clarifications on the day's lessons. Mateo developed the habit of lingering behind, too. He'd almost timed it right when Aldo started popping up at the end of the hall to hurry him along to the next class, which they shared.

By twelfth grade, he was out of ideas. Not about crossing Kailyn's path, about keeping his brother off his trail. But Mateo did have one failsafe.

The one place he would always see the object of his affection was the art room. Before school, after school, and sometimes during the lunch period. He knew every route that would lead him past the art room, and he braved many late passes to go that way.

Nearly a decade later, Mateo still knew the way by heart. Instead of waiting for Miguel in the pickup line, he made his way into the building. Got a visitor's pass. Then made his way down the winding hall.

When he came up to the door, his teenage heart pounded at the front of his chest, just like it had every time he'd catch a glimpse of her eight years ago. Kailyn stood in front of the windows, the sunlight streaming in to curl around her strawberry-colored hair.

"Kailyn."

Mateo didn't so much as say her name as he breathed it. It was both the prayer and the answer. It was both a plea and an expression of gratitude.

All the years he'd been gone fell away. All of the strife between their siblings evaporated as they stood gazing at one another. She was surrounded by color, and he felt like he'd been walking around in a monotone world.

There would be no more Aldo to block his path. There would be no more staying quiet in the face of any fights or arguments that didn't involve the two of them. Mateo was done with it. He was done holding his tongue and redirecting his steps to the one thing he'd ever wanted all to himself.

Mateo wasn't waiting any longer for the life he wanted to begin. He took a step across the threshold of the art room. Each step brought him closer and closer to where he had always dreamed of being.

When he reached her, Mateo's instinct was to wrap his arms around Kailyn and pull her to him. Because finally he could. There was nothing to stop him. Nothing except the single finger she held between them—that same finger she'd held up yesterday when she'd learned that he was her competition for the after-school program funding.

"What are you doing here?" she asked.

There was no bite to her words, only a breathless quality. It sounded close to surrender. With her finger as her only weapon, she was otherwise defenseless. As deterrents went, that single digit wasn't much. Her fingers were weapons he wanted to gently dismantle one by one with a kiss to each of her finger pads.

"I knew you'd be here." He spoke the truth he'd wanted to say the four years they'd inhabited these halls together.

"Me?" she asked.

"He means me, Ms. Jade."

Both Kailyn and Mateo frowned at the voice that came from the side. From the corner of his eyes, Mateo saw Miguel standing there watching the two of them. Miguel wasn't watching them closely in the way that Denny or LaTisha would. Those two kids would've immediately seen what was between Mateo and Kailyn. Miguel was still at that stage of adolescence where he didn't notice, or simply wasn't interested, in the attraction between men and women.

Miguel held up a bag. Mateo belatedly recognized it as the bag of groceries and appliances he'd purchased for Kailyn the other day.

"I got what I needed," said Miguel. "Now we can go home so I can decorate my cake."

"You bought those for Miguel?" Mateo asked Kailyn.

"You're his foster brother?" Kailyn asked Mateo.

"Foster uncle, I think." Mateo grinned. "Charlie and Savy are adopting him and all the kids that were at Bright Horizons. Didn't you know? The foster house got moved onto my family's ranch."

Kailyn shook her head, but she smiled as she did so. And wonder of wonders, that finger lowered. She was no longer on the attack.

"I had heard the home was moving," she said. "That's good. That's great."

Her smile spread. First while she was looking at Miguel. Then it spread to Mateo.

Mateo took the opportunity to move in closer. He wasn't cornering her, per se. She wasn't his enemy. But he had no intention of letting his target get away. "You should invite Ms. Jade to your celebration dinner, Miguel."

Kailyn's green gaze flared at the suggestion. She took a step back. Too late, she realized she had nowhere to go. "You don't have to—"

"Please come," said Miguel. "I'm still having trouble with pairing the right colors."

Kailyn swallowed. Her gaze went first to the intent warrior towering over her whom she couldn't possibly hope to get around. Then at the child, who gazed up at her with pleading, innocent eyes. She was well and truly cornered and trapped.

She took a deep breath and nodded. It wasn't a white flag, but it was a laying down of arms. A surrender.

Mateo had won this battle. He would be ruthless to win every battle he could until the war between them was over. Until he showed this woman that there was a lifetime of peace to be found in his arms.

CHAPTER NINE

The click of the passenger door closing should have felt like the slam of a jail cell. No, not a jail cell. The padded wall of an insane asylum. What normal person would willingly climb into the car of their nemesis and then allow said nemesis to shut them inside? Apparently, that abnormal person was Kailyn.

Because to Kailyn, that quiet snick didn't feel like a trap. It didn't feel like an end. It felt like something that had been wide open for far too long, clicking right into place.

"Seatbelt," said Mateo.

Of her own free will, Kailyn reached for the leather belt and pulled it across her middle, effectively strapping herself in. There was a phenomenon when a hostage stopped fighting their captor and began welcoming their captivity. Stockholm syndrome, it was called.

That had to be what she was experiencing as she sat calmly in the passenger seat as Mateo Matthews drove her away from the high school. She caught a brief sight of Owen thumbing the fob to his sports car. He frowned in their direction. It was that kind of look where you think you might know someone, but you didn't get a close enough look to be sure.

Kailyn was sure Owen hadn't placed her. The light of recognition didn't brighten his gaze. More importantly, that misplaced look of possession never crossed his features.

When she had climbed into Owen's car on the first date, she had felt something prickle at the back of her neck. Not danger. Just a feeling that she was in the wrong place with the wrong person.

The sensations running across her skin right now weren't prickles. They were tingles. Kailyn felt the fine hairs on her body stand at attention. Not out of fear. There was a sense of excitement that urged her to sit forward, to lean toward Mateo and his heat.

Kailyn kept her back pressed firmly into the passenger seat. She folded her hands in her lap, twining her fingers together until they were on lockdown. She pressed her lips together so that no words could escape and concentrated on making her breaths deep and steady.

Neither of the adults in the car said much on the drive. There wasn't much silence to fill in. Miguel kept up a steady stream of conversation about the ingredients he was going to use in his cake. Once those details were outlined, he started in on the makings of the icing.

Mateo smiled indulgently at the kid from the rearview mirror. He'd *hmm* and *ahh* at the appropriate intervals to show he was paying attention, but Kailyn knew Mateo wasn't engaged in Miguel's recipe. Just as much as she wasn't invested in his choice of food coloring combinations for the icing.

She was focused on how little space there was on the middle console where Mateo rested his right hand. Her fingers dangled over the arm rest so close to his. A bump in the road or a pothole and they'd be holding hands. She should remind him that the proper position for road driving was hands at ten and two.

Kailyn kept her lips sealed. There was too much danger of something else entirely escaping her mouth about what Mateo Matthews could do with his hands.

The scent of his cologne was like one of those visible cartoon clouds. It was doing something funny to her brain. Maybe he was drugging her? Because all she could think was how much she wanted to lean over, bury her nose in his neck, and take a good strong whiff.

Those rumbling assents Mateo gave to Miguel had her crossing her legs toward him. Only to uncross and turn away from him. Which would then expose the back of her neck to him. Those *hmms* and *ahhs* then tickled the space behind her ear, causing her to shudder and then turn back toward him.

Not to mention that her heart was skipping every other beat now that he was a constant in her presence. Before, she'd only had glimpses of him in the hall. She'd been in his presence for a half an hour at this point, and she wasn't sure her body, her entire being, could take much more.

Finally, the torture was over. They turned off the main streets of the town and began down a long drive. To the left was the Silver Star Ranch, a place Kailyn had been a couple of times over the years. She'd been casual friends with Tilly and Gunny, the Silver twins. Those two had gotten married recently, and both Kailyn and Elayne had been invited to their weddings. Mateo had still been in his last deployment at that time.

Instead of turning left, they turned right. It was a direction Kailyn had never taken in this town. In the space of a breath, the sprawling lands of the Flying Cross Ranch came into view.

The scene looked like it had been painted by Van Gogh. The shades of blue sky meeting and mingling with the gradations of green pasture were simply breathtaking. The landscape looked unreal, yet so detailed that she had the thought that if she reached out, she could smear the vivid paint.

The passenger car door opened, and another work of art stepped into her view. Mateo looked like he'd walked off the canvas. A flawless creation from the Crayola Colors of the World collection. When he reached out his Medium Almond colored palm to her, Kailyn placed her Light Rose fingers in his, eager to be pulled into the mural.

"Charlie and Savy spruced up the bunkhouse where we used to sleep," Mateo said, pointing to what looked like an overlarge, long and narrow barn. "And they're adding prefab houses for my brothers and their wives. The Silver sisters are helping with that project. Other than that, it hasn't changed much since we were kids."

"I've never been here before," said Kailyn.

The reason why she had never been to his home before was left unspoken.

"Aldo's out of town for a couple of days," he said.

"So's Elayne."

The air around them changed. It had been heavy with things left unsaid. It lightened considerably under the absence of their siblings.

A cool breeze blew between them as Miguel shot past them and into the house. A little blonde girl eyed them curiously from the porch. There was a broom in her hand as she swept the wood slats. Below the porch, a brown-skinned girl was down on her knees as she dug her hands into the rich earth. Off to the side, Kailyn saw two other young boys fussing over a bale of hay. Both boys were pale skin with fair hair. One had his hair done in silky cornrows. The other boy Kailyn recognized as Denny.

"It looks like you're running a child labor farm," she said.

"You're just determined to think the worst of us, aren't you?" said Mateo.

There was no bite to his words. Just patience. Along with a vulnerability. His hand twitched. She half expected him to let her go, but his hold didn't loosen. Instead, he jerked his head in the direction of the children, indicating that she should follow.

"This is a working ranch, so everyone pulls their weight. Kids sleep in during school year, but they have chores after school and on the weekend."

"You could hire ranch hands."

"Or we could use this to teach them responsibility, how to care for the land and the animals. Equally, it's a lesson in how families work together and take pride in their home."

Looking closer at the kids, she saw that they weren't frowning or angry. They were a bit sweaty. But the occasional laugh sounded, along with good-natured joking. The two boys with the hay weren't alone. The tall figure of Charlie Matthews came up behind them and patted them both on the back.

"Kailyn Jade, is that you?"

Savy James squinted at her from the open door of the house. Her eyes went wide with recognition, and she let the porch door slam behind her as she came toward Kailyn, arms outstretched.

"I'm covered in paint," said Kailyn.

"I'm covered in ranch," said Savy. "Girl, get in here."

Even when they were both scared foster kids, Savy had always given the best hugs. Her hugs and her singing voice were the only thing Kailyn missed about being in the Bright Horizon's Foster Home.

"You don't seem surprised to see me here," said Kailyn.

"Why would I? Mateo's had a crush on you since we were all in foster care."

"He has not."

Behind her, Mateo said nothing. He didn't look embarrassed. He didn't deny it either. He just held her gaze. Kailyn's palms warmed from where he had held her hand only seconds ago. It felt like they were still connected.

"And Aldo's always had a thing for Elayne."

That brought an expression and a grunt of dissent from Mateo. Kailyn echoed both his loud facial expression as well as his vocal protest.

"They can't stand each other," said Kailyn.

Savy shrugged. "Boys tug the pigtails of girls they like until they know how to behave better."

Just then, Charlie came up and tugged at one of his wife's wayward curls. She swatted at him good-naturedly before turning back to Kailyn. Charlie Matthews had never tugged at Savy's pigtails when they were kids. He'd professed his feelings for her clearly. Aldo had gone in on Elayne from day one, clearly stating his dislike. Whereas Mateo had said nothing.

Savy was right about her particular Matthews. But Kailyn wasn't so sure her insight was clear on the other two Matthews boys.

CHAPTER TEN

"Miguel, you outdid yourself. We are the luckiest family in the world to be getting a son like you."

Miguel's eyes sparkled under Savy's praise. Around the table, heads nodded in assent. Well, the adult heads all did. The pride and love in Savy's and Charlie's eyes was brighter than the overhead dining room light. Foxy winked at Miguel, and her husband, Joe, gave the kid a thumbs-up. At the head of the table, Father Matthews rubbed at his belly as a satisfied grin stretched across his brown face.

Denny, the tallest kid, rolled his eyes, but he couldn't hide the small uptilt of his lips as he took another bite of the dessert Miguel had prepared. The two girls grinned broadly, and the third boy with blond braids in his hair nodded his head once.

While he'd been away, Mateo's family had grown. But in so many ways, it had remained the same.

Just as it was when he'd first sat down at this table as a scared and confused adolescent. He looked up to see that he wasn't alone. He was sitting with a family. A real tight-knit family. With rules and rituals and discipline and deep affection. The Matthews homestead was bursting at the seams at the moment. But Mateo knew they would always make space for more.

Mateo watched Kailyn as she used her dinner napkin to dab first at the corner of her mouth and second at the corner of her eye. When she raised her head, she met his gaze. She lowered her eyes, but only for a second. Looking up at him from beneath her lashes, she offered Mateo a shy grin.

Mateo sat his knife and fork down on his plate. Then he placed his hands below the table. It wasn't enough. He lifted and sat on his hands. He had no other choice. More than anything in this world, he wanted to launch across the table and taste that grin.

But there were rules and rituals in this family. Chief amongst them was no mauling the girl you had been in love with since childhood at the dinner table. That one had come courtesy of Charlie and Savy about a decade or so ago.

Mateo wanted to strip the shyness away from her grin. He wanted Kailyn to open up to him fully, to show him her emotions. He wanted her to know it was okay to be vulnerable in front of him. He wanted to capture each one of the tears that had threatened her eyes and let them know it was safe to fall because he would catch them. He would catch her. He wanted to taste the smiles that came to her lips. He wanted to hold that hand that made the world so much more beautiful.

He wanted her. Always had. Always would.

Looking down at the calluses on his hands from his time in battle, he wondered if she would ever let him. Kailyn was a gentle soul. She had always gravitated toward the beauty in the world. Where the underbelly of society always showed itself to him.

"I didn't know that the foster home had moved to the ranch," Kailyn said.

"It was Charlie's idea," said Savy.

"It was my only option to finally get this woman to marry me." Charlie planted a kiss atop his wife's head. Savy's hand snaked around to stroke his cheek. A secret smile was on both their faces.

"In some ways these kids brought us all together," said Foxy. "Joe and I finally admitted our feelings when we went to look in on Daria when she was in state custody."

"*You* admitted your feelings." Joe held up a finger. "*I* never made any secret of how I felt about you."

"Ash brought the two of us together," Tricksy said with her gaze on Will.

"I did make a secret of how I felt about her," said Will.

It was a poorly kept secret in this house. All of the Matthews boys had known that Will was head over heels in love with Tricksy. Well, all of them except Topher. But Topher rarely noticed anything outside of a mirror.

"From what I understand, that was your fault." Toni Solis raised an eyebrow at Topher.

For once, Topher wasn't trying to catch a glimpse of himself. His attention was entirely focused on the woman at his side. His arm was casually draped behind her chair, but his fingers kept playing in the braided ends of her hair.

"We all know I don't keep secrets. I told you exactly how I felt…" Topher frowned, looking off into the distance. "As soon as I understood what it was that I felt."

A chorus of laughter went around the table. Mateo had missed this during his time in the service. Sure, he had a family of soldiers in his unit. But nothing could ever replace the years and the scraps and the scars and the love of his family.

"Everyone's married or engaged except the twins," said Savy, her gaze falling not on Mateo, but on Kailyn.

Mateo got the urge to wave frantically in front of Savy. He wanted to make every signal to stop, slow down, and caution that he knew. Not because he didn't want to go down that path. Because he didn't want to scare Kailyn away. But maybe keeping secret how he felt about her was doing him a disservice. It certainly hadn't worked for any of his brothers.

"Oh, that won't be for long," said Foxy as casually as she would announce the weather forecast for the next day. "Aldo's getting married this weekend."

Silence zinged around the table. Foxy fancied herself a psychic—clairsentient, to be exact. But she was only right fifty percent of the time. This would definitely be one of the times she got it wrong. Aldo was off discussing a private military contract job.

"Whether or not the marriage will last, I can't see." Foxy rubbed at her eyelids.

"On that note," said Charlie, "it's time for bed."

There was only a cursory protest from the kids. They'd had a long day at school, followed by chores, and now their bellies were overfull. Even if they didn't think they'd fall asleep soon, they'd be proven wrong pretty quickly. They all got up and marched to the bunkhouse like good little soldiers.

Mateo used the distraction of the kids going off to bed to get Kailyn all to himself. She had had a long day of school herself. Her plate was cleared, and Savy had packed her some leftovers in Tupperware. It was the perfect time for the two of them to escape.

Kailyn said her good nights to everyone with promises not to be a stranger. Father Matthews gave his son a knowing look, which Mateo returned with a sly grin before handing Kailyn into the car. No, this woman was not going to be a stranger for long.

"I always expected you to go into the art field," said Mateo as they turned out of the long drive. "I'm surprised you're not selling your art."

"I do. But I find it more rewarding to use art to help those in pain or distress."

"I've heard about that—art therapy? Some of the soldiers with PTSD did that on base."

Kailyn tilted her head to one side, looking out at the starry sky. "I usually work with kids. I never thought of working with soldiers."

"I think it helped. I think any program where you can get someone to face their issues head-on helps. Especially if it leaves the world a better place. That's why many men and women go into the armed services to begin with: to make the world a better place."

She seemed to think about that, but she didn't offer any commentary. All too soon, he had pulled up to her house. He remembered it from when he was young. He'd heard that her parents had passed away a few years ago.

Like his family, Kailyn and her sister had kept the house mostly the same. It was still painted white, likely a fresh coat sometime in the last five years. The trim was a deep green that he could make out under the streetlights. But the dormers were painted in a colorful array. Those were new. They had to be Kailyn's artistic touches.

Parking on the street, Mateo walked around the car in time to hand her out. Her hand in his was a jolt to his system. It was the third time he'd touched her today. Each time had been at the passenger car door. Mateo had half a mind to ask her to go on a joy ride with him just so that he could hand her in and then out of the car again.

A wind blew, shifting a strand of vibrant red hair into her face. Kailyn brushed the strand away, but one tuft of hair refused to stay out of her eyes. Mateo could't blame it. Without thinking it through, he reached and tugged the hair from her eyes and tucked it behind her ear. When his gaze met hers, she was staring at him.

There was something in her gaze. He'd seen it before. H"d seen it each time he came upon her in the halls. He knew it all too well because it was what he felt when he looked at her during those brief stolen moments. It was hesitancy.

A hesitancy before she decided whether or not to acknowledge his presence. A hesitancy before she confirmed it was safe to smile. A hesitancy before taking a step toward the something more that had always lingered between them before either or both of their siblings burst onto the scene.

Kailyn didn't look quite so hesitant now. Mateo stepped closer. She tilted up her head. Her lips parted. His nostrils flared. Her gaze dipped to his lips. Mateo leaned in, but a call from a man's voice jerked them apart.

CHAPTER ELEVEN

When Mateo Matthews tugged at Kailyn's hair, she knew it wasn't an act of misbehavior. The way the pad of his forefinger lightly brushed her temple before seizing the runaway strands spoke volumes that this was a man in command. The way he wound the tendril of hair around the length of his finger loudly proclaimed that he was a man of strategy. He had her cornered, trapped, and as his captive, her body would go anywhere he directed her to go.

Forget Stockholm syndrome. Kailyn wasn't in some foreign land kidnapped by a twirly mustached villain she didn't know. She was in the familiar surroundings of Honor Valley, walking straight into the well-lit embrace of the man she had always secretly yearned to be near.

With his index finger trapped by her hair, Kailyn's head dipped to brush against the tips of Mateo's three other fingers. His thumb caught her cheek, and his hand opened to welcome the side of her face into the palm of his hand. The heat she'd felt from his fingertips was nothing compared to the full force furnace of his entire hand.

From somewhere deep inside her, a voice shouted *Home*. Something in her chest sighed in that way where, after a long journey in a car, she looked out the window and spotted her street. Mateo Matthews was more than her street. He was the safe place she'd been looking for her whole life.

As a foster kid, Kailyn had been without a home for a relatively short period of time. But the fear and uncertainty in that brief time period had taken root at the back of her mind and made a permanent home. She'd always been the quintessential good girl to her foster parents because, though that feeling never went away, she never wanted it to become her reality again. She never wanted to be without a home of her own again.

Resting in the relatively small space of Mateo's hand, her breathing came easily. The perpetually tight muscles of her back went slack, and her shoulders loosened. There wasn't a single tendon of tension inside her body. She would've equated the feeling to that of nothingness, except she felt everything, everywhere, all at once.

Kailyn got the sense that no matter where she went, or how far she traveled, as long as Mateo was with her, she would never be far from home.

She opened her eyes, having just realized that she had closed them when she'd given her head over to his capable hand, and looked up into his gaze. Kailyn might not have had a lot of experience with men, but she knew desire when she saw it. It was shining brightly in Mateo's dark gaze.

Savy was right. Boys might tug at a girl's hair to get her attention until he knew how to behave better. Mateo was behaving in exactly the way a woman would want.

He was behaving in exactly the way she wanted. There was no friction between them. Everything was easy and peaceful. Kailyn could've stayed just like this for the rest of the night. For the rest of her life.

"There you are."

Owen's voice was like a record scratch on a classical piece of music. It wasn't the first time he'd shown up at her house unannounced. It had been a long time since he'd tried it. Kailyn was sure the only reason he'd tried now was because Elayne was out of town.

"I've been waiting for you to get home." Owen's narrowed gaze was focused on Mateo, not Kailyn. The corners of his mouth and eyes twitched, much in the same way Kailyn's would when she was faced with a particularly daunting math problem that didn't add up.

"Why would you be waiting for me to get home?" Kailyn twinned her fingers with Mateo's. She brought their hands down between them as they both stepped toward the latched gate that led to her front door.

Owen's confusion shifted. It darkened a bit as he glared at Kailyn and Mateo's laced fingers. "Your car was still at school. I was concerned."

"Thank you for your concern, Vice Principal Sharp. But as you can see, I'm perfectly okay."

Mateo's hand had dropped from hers. For a brief second, Kailyn panicked. She slipped into that dark hopelessness she'd felt when she realized that she wasn't like other kids, she didn't have a mom and dad or a home to call her own. That feeling when she realized she didn't have much protection in this world aside from her sister.

She wanted to grab for Mateo. For his hand. For his arms. For any part of him and bring it back around her.

She didn't need to.

Barely a fraction of a second passed before Mateo's free hand came to rest at her low back. Those same fingers that had twined around her hair, that had laced with her own, dug just a little bit into her hip. It was a clear sign of possession, and Kailyn was here for it.

Mateo's possession felt more secure than her adoption papers. More secure than her name on the deed her parents had left her and her sister. Her parents had passed from this world. The house could be blown away by a crazy act of nature, like a tornado or earthquake. But Mateo's hand, that felt like it would never leave her side.

"Why don't I walk you inside?" said Owen, still oblivious to the status of their non-existent, never-had-existed relationship.

Kailyn felt Mateo bristle. She tensed in his hold. The last thing she wanted was a confrontation between these men.

It wasn't that she feared for Mateo's well-being. No one with eyes would look at these two men and worry for the dark-haired one. With the touch of his pinky finger, Mateo would flatten Owen onto the sidewalk. That show of violence was something Kailyn never wanted to witness. Not from the person she had decided to trust her heart to.

"No need," she said, lifting the latch to the gate. "Mateo's got it."

Mateo's fingers relaxed at her back as he followed behind her. His palm pressed against her spine as he turned to latch the gate behind them, shutting Owen out on the other side. It was all done without the two men so much as addressing each other with words.

Kailyn was sure if it had been Aldo, there would have been a scuffle on the street. Just the thought of any kind of violence made her shiver. Mateo brought his arm from her low back to wrap around her shoulder. Kailyn stopped walking at the steps to the porch, with her back to the front door. She turned to face Mateo.

"Do you want to come in?" she asked.

Mateo looked over her shoulder at the front door to her house. Then his gaze dipped as he studied her. "No."

Kailyn's stomach clenched. Her chest tightened and her limbs went heavy even as her body deflated.

"I want to ask you *out*," he said.

"Out?"

Kailyn lifted her head. The light from the moon cast Mateo in an otherworldly glow. Stars coalesced in a pretty pattern around his dark head. Despite her whirlwind of emotions, her hands itched to reach for a set of paint and brushes.

"Out on a date," Mateo was saying. "To see if we could have a future together because…"

And here he paused and dipped his head. Mateo took both her hands in his and took a deep breath. The breath reached so far down that Kailyn thought he might have stolen some of hers away.

"Because, Kailyn, I've been in love with you for all of my past."

Yes, he had stolen some of her breath because she couldn't breathe. Kailyn's heart did that fluttery thing it only ever did for him. But it was doing that stuttery skip and not beating as it should. The effect was dizzying, and she wasn't sure she wouldn't pass out.

"What do you say?" he asked.

Kailyn said the only thing she could. She reached up onto her tippy toes and pressed her lips to his. The kiss was brief. But only because she was seriously in danger of fainting for lack of breath.

When she broke off the kiss, they both took a heaving gasp. Kailyn still had nothing to say. Mateo didn't offer up any words of his own, just a satisfied smile. It was enough. She'd made herself clear, and he understood her perfectly.

CHAPTER TWELVE

ateo couldn't stop touching his lower lip. It still blazed from the soft, cool touch of Kailyn's mouth. Her kiss had been fleeting, but it had left an impact.

As a soldier, Mateo had been on a plane during a storm. He'd been on a battlefield with gunfire. He'd faced hand-to-hand combat where he was outnumbered.

None of those harrowing ordeals had rocked him the way that Kailyn's kiss had.

He felt dizzy for the rest of the night. When he got up the next morning, he had to look down repeatedly to ensure his feet were touching the ground. All through the afternoon, he had to concentrate on taking deep breaths, but still the air didn't completely fill his lungs.

It hadn't bothered him this morning that the bathroom hadn't been free until well after breakfast. Mateo had debated for hours whether or not to brush his teeth last night and decided not to. He wasn't so sure he'd change his mind this morning. He was seriously contemplating never washing his face again. Or at least not until kissing Kailyn Jade became a part of his everyday routine.

He could see that future with the two of them together. It was so clear as he stood looking out at the sprawling pastures of the Flying Cross Ranch. Mateo knew this land like he knew the back of his hand.

He'd spend days when he got here as an adolescent roaming free. He knew the bend of every tree branch. He could judge the distance h"d gone by the color of the wildflowers growing beneath his feet. He could tell the time of day by which animal sounds were the loudest in his surroundings.

As he'd come to know the ranch as a kid, he'd always imagined having one person by his side on his explorations. Very soon, he'd bring Kailyn to the two trees that had grown so close together it looked as though they were hugging. He'd pick a bouquet of white, blue and yellow wildflowers for her and sit by and watch her bring the flowers to life on one of her canvases. He'd tune out the world when he cupped his hand to her cheek and brought their mouths together in a kiss that would last the entire day and into the night.

The idea of a bright and colorful and kiss-filled future thrilled Mateo so much he heard a ringing in his head. Then he realized it was his phone. The thought of Kailyn calling him had him diving to accept the call.

He put the device to his ear with a breathy, "Hello."

"Hey, bro."

Mateo realized he was still pressing his fingers to his Kailyn-kissed lips. He dropped his hand from his mouth at the sound of Aldo's voice.

"Were you eating or drinking something sweet right now? I swear I just got a sugar rush"

Mateo balled his hands into fists. This was another of those times where Aldo took their twin sense too far. If Mateo truly thought his twin could feel what it was like to kiss Kailyn, then Mateo would have to punch his brother in the mouth.

"Oh wait, it was Miguel's party last night. He made cake?"

"Yeah," Mateo confirmed. "Yeah, we all had cake." Mateo was still loathed to be singled out by his brother and their twin-sense. Sharing basic necessities with Aldo had never bothered him. It was his own experiences that Mateo wanted to keep to himself.

"You better have saved me some. From our bond, I can taste it was really sweet. Mmmm."

Mateo pursed his lips, trying to rein in his temper. He felt cold all over and wanted his brother to feel that through their twin-sense bond. Anything but the idea, the thought, even the inkling of his time with Kailyn.

"These meetings are going great. I think you'd be interested in a couple of these contracts."

"Aldo, I've already told you. I'm out. I'm staying here in Honor Valley. I'm doing the JROTC. I'm putting down roots."

Mateo didn't mention that those roots would be securely dug in around Kailyn Jade. He knew he'd have to tell his brother eventually. But not while things were new and fresh and so sweet with Kailyn. He knew Aldo would ruin it if Mateo didn't figure out how to deliver the news in a way that didn't make Aldo feel he was being cut out.

Even though Aldo was definitely being cut out of this aspect of Mateo's life.

But maybe the distance would be the best thing for announcing Mateo's new trajectory. Aldo was gone for another two days. If Mateo told him now, it would give him time to stew out of sight, and maybe he'd be calm—or at least be calmer—when he got back.

"Listen, Aldo, you should know I'm dating—"

"Andy."

Andy? Mateo didn't remember any friends they shared named Andy. Maybe Aldo had made a new friend there at the event. But Aldo wasn't the best at making new friends, especially when Mateo wasn't around.

A cloud moved overhead, and realization dawned. Aldo had used that name a lot. He'd used it as an ugly reference when they were kids. He'd pinned it on one of the two redheaded twins in their town.

"Elayne? What are you doing with Elayne Jade?"

"She's here. She's at the conference hall."

Mateo's hackles went up. The last thing he needed was for Aldo and Elayne to go nuclear when neither he nor Kailyn were around.

"Just stay away from her," Mateo said, his fingers curling around the phone.

"How can I stay away from her when she's coming right at me?"

"Look, Aldo, just—"

"Gotta go, bro. Save me some cake."

And with that, his twin cut their connection.

CHAPTER THIRTEEN

Kailyn wasn't sure how she made it through the school day. In third period, Al Morris spilled a tub of red paint on one of the worktables. The paint narrowly missed Becca Green's white jeans. Her patent leather shoes weren't so lucky, and World War III broke out. In the fifth period special needs art class, Erik Spader got hold of the glitter and… well, Kailyn made a note to give the school custodians a healthy Christmas bonus.

By some miracle of all the angels smiling down upon her, the final bell rang. Kailyn made her way around the red ravages of war on the floor on her left, hopped across a sparkling bit of linoleum on her right, and was out the door of the classroom. The trying events of the day brushed off her shoulders and her body tensed for what was to come next. That tension was a welcome weight as she thought about what she would wear on her date with Mateo Matthews.

Unfortunately, before she got to the main doors to exit the high school, she was stopped by a low voice with high self-importance.

"I take it you won't be using school grounds as your private parking lot tonight, Ms. Jade?"

She wouldn't have turned around, except her parents had impressed upon her the need to always be kind and courteous when someone in the community spoke. Even though her parents were gone, she still wanted to curry their good will and be the best representative of the couple that had taken her and her sister in.

Kailyn put her shoulders back, plastered on a fake smile, and turned to face Owen. Before she could spew any niceties, he spoke over her. Which was typical of their time together on their two ill-fated dates.

"I don't know what's gotten into you going out in the dead of night with strange men."

Of course, this is what this would be about. Owen didn't like competition. There should be two assistant principals in the high school. The last one had barely lasted two years, and rumors were that was because of Owen. Principal Barrow didn't complain too much, as Owen did the work of two people. But it was only because he didn't share well.

"I wasn't with a strange man. I was with Mateo Matthews. We all went to school together, remember."

"Those Matthews boys are no good. None of them know who their parents are."

Kailyn's back muscles tensed. She rolled her right shoulder as a bead of sweat trickled down her spine. Her chin lifted and her nostrils flared as she took one step toward Owen. "Is that a crack about him being a foster kid?"

For the first time since their acquaintance, Owen got a clue. His teeth pressed together as his lips twisted. He swallowed, but that didn't help whatever he'd tried to suppress from coming out of his mouth. "I'm just saying you were raised by two good Christian people. And he—"

"He was raised by a preacher who is also a decorated soldier."

Owen bit his lip. His eyes darted as he searched for another tact. "He's using you, Kailyn. Can't you see that?"

"Using me for what? The only thing he wants that I have to give is my time and attention. And I want to give both to him."

"He's been seen with the board members. Did you know that? He's playing you."

Board members? Was this about the after school funding? Kailyn knew that both she and Mateo were still in contention for the funds. Though she hadn't thought much about that particular rivalry—especially not after that kiss last night. One of them would get the funding and the other wouldn't. She had to hope that when the board saw her amazing presentation and awarded her with their decision, that Mateo would be man enough to take it gracefully.

Kailyn had the feeling that a tall drink of water like Mateo, with muscles for days, would be strong enough to handle the rejection. And she couldn't wait to kiss it better.

"You can't be that naïve, Kailyn," Owen was saying.

"I'm seen every school day with you. You said out loud to others, including Mateo, that you were siding with me and my project."

Owen opened his mouth for more protests, but nothing came out. Kailyn didn't wait for him to think of more. She was done with the conversation. She was done with him. No more trying to remain friendly with the man. He clearly didn't understand that or the true meaning of camaraderie.

Twenty minutes later, she was standing in her bedroom, looking into her closet. She wasn't sure she had anything to wear. Nothing seemed special enough for this date with Mateo. Not that he'd seen her in any of the outfits before. And she didn't have time to go shopping.

Kailyn left her room and marched into her sisters. Running her fingers through Elayne's color-coordinated offerings was as close as going to shopping for something new that she had time for. She snatched a pale cocktail dress, along with a belt to cinch her waist and a pair of strappy heels to complete the outfit.

Even though the two were twins, Elayne had a few more curves than Kailyn. She had to fluff the dress over the belt in order to accentuate what assets she had. She might not look like Marilyn Monroe in the dress, but she didn't look like a twelve-year-old flat-chested girl either. The dress made her legs look long and what curves she had stood out. It did nicely.

By the time the doorbell rang, Kailyn was putting on the final touches of makeup. She pulled a wrap out of the closet, slipped her keys in her bag, and went to the door. A cool breeze blew into the foyer, but barely touched her because in the doorway Mateo stood broad and tall, blocking the night wind.

His gaze swept over her, leaving her heated. His lips were parted, making her hungry. His nostrils flared, causing her heart to thud against her chest. There was a spark in his eyes that made her see stars.

"Hello, Kailyn."

"Hi, Mateo."

"You are…breathtaking."

She felt breathtaking. She couldn't inhale enough to fill her lungs.

Mateo reached out his arm, crooked in an old fashion way of a

Victorian gentleman. Kailyn placed her fingers on his biceps. The two of them fell into step as they walked down the path to lead to his car.

She hesitated to let him go when he opened the passenger door for her. She had to remind herself that they would be together for the rest of the night. She had to tamp down on the whisper in her heart that said she never wanted the night to end.

As they walked into the restaurant, her hand was back on his biceps. He was a sight. He wore dark slacks and a crisp white shirt and a gray jacket. It all accented his strong body and handsome face.

She saw a few women she knew. Mostly parents who were a decade older and a few familiar faces of her generation. The women's eyes roamed over Mateo as he strode confidently through the tables. When he pulled out her chair, Kailyn didn't want to let his arm go. She wanted all these women to know that this man was taken.

For his part, Mateo only had eyes for her. He only looked at her. He only smiled at her. He only seemed to notice her.

"I have to tell you again how beautiful you look in that dress," Mateo said as he refilled her wine glass.

"It's Elayne's. I don't know why I just told you that. And don't tell her. She hates when I borrow things without asking first."

Kailyn smoothed her hands down the dress as she watched Mateo fill her glass. A tremor went through his steady hands. A *clink* sounded as the wine bottle tapped the edge of the wine glass. There was a *plop* as a healthy dollop of liquid splashed into the glass before Mateo righted the bottle and set it back on the table between them.

"You haven't talked to your sister?" Mateo's gaze had been on her all night. He lowered his lids now as he reached for his own wine glass.

"Not since she left, no."

Mateo nodded. He opened his mouth and then closed it.

Kailyn got the sense that something between them had shifted. It had to be the mention of their warring siblings. This wasn't a topic they could hide from. If they were going to be together—which this night was proving to her that she wanted—then all four of them would have to find some common ground.

"It's nice to talk with another twin," Kailyn said. "I'm sure that growing up with someone who looks and sounds just like you made you yearn for and seek out your own individuality."

He glanced up then, his eyes alight with the spark that had burned when he stood gazing at her on her doorstep. In that moment, Kailyn felt the connection between them restored and stronger than before.

"Aldo wanted us to dress alike all through high school." Mateo let out a gust of air through his nose. "Going into the military was partly to soothe that side of him."

Kailyn giggled. Her adoptive parents had loved dressing her and Elayne alike, but the two of them hated it. They held their tongues because they were so grateful for the loving home, but they would strip off their matching sets once they got to school. They'd long been in the habit of stashing clothes in their lockers so they could change and be their own individual selves.

Kailyn told Mateo as much. He bemoaned the loss that he'd never thought of that idea, which made Kailyn toss her head back and laugh even more.

"That's just as beautiful as I remembered it," he said, his gaze holding hers once more.

"What is?" she asked.

"The sound of your laugh. I used to hang near the art class window to hear you laugh. I would go out of my way to pass you in the halls just for a glimpse of your smile and the possibility to hear you laugh."

"Why didn't you just come and talk to me, tell me a joke?"

"You know why."

She did. They both did. But neither of them brought up their siblings in this moment that was solely theirs.

"The main reason I came back was to see you." Mateo reached for her hand, and she gave it to him. "I want to see a lot more of you, Kailyn."

"I'd like that."

Mateo's fingers curled around hers. His fingers jerked but didn't pull from hers. A shadow moved across his face as he looked passed her shoulder. Kailyn thought it must be his brother walking toward them. But when she glanced over her shoulder, she saw an older man.

"I thought that was you, Captain Matthews."

Mateo let go of her hand and stood. He came to attention in that rigid way soldiers did when they met with someone of a higher rank. "General Jensen."

"I didn't mean to interrupt your dinner." The general gave Kailyn a friendly but dismissive smile. Then he turned back to the pudgy man in a business suit at his side. "I wanted to take a moment to introduce you to one of the investors interested in your program. Matthews is starting a JRTOC program here in the valley. He has my full support, and I think you should look at his plan to consider coming on with us."

And that's when it hit her. There was a general on the board of education. Kailyn had never met him, but she supposed she just did.

General Jensen was talking about the JROTC program like it was decided. Mateo was shaking the hand of the businessman like it was a done deal. When Mateo turned to introduce her, Kailyn didn't give him a chance. She was already out of her seat, heading for the door.

CHAPTER FOURTEEN

$\mathcal{E}$ven though Mateo had been taught manners by all of his parents, even though the military had pounded the deference of rank into him, he marched past the general and the investor, who could potentially fund his entire business endeavor, without another glance or word. Though manners did insist that Mateo throw his credit card down onto the table before he dashed off. Disrespectful he could stand to be called, but a thief or a cheat, he could never abide.

With the bill taken care of, Mateo promptly forgot about credit security or how he'd retrieve his card. He didn't give the other guests, many of them he knew and those who knew his family, even so much as an excuse me as he whizzed past them in pursuit of his sole objective. There was only one thing he needed to retrieve this night, and it was getting away from him. If he lost Kailyn, his whole world was crashing down around him, and he would not let that happen.

Mateo was thankful for his military training in that instance. Kailyn was no match when it came to physical fitness. He would have run miles over days to catch up to her. Luckily, it only took a few strides after exiting the restaurant's door to catch up to her.

Once he had her, he had to ball his hands into fists not to grab her to him. He kept in stride with her, but she wouldn't slow down. She teetered once in her heels, and he had to grit his teeth to keep from picking her up bodily and slinging her over his shoulder.

"Kailyn, wait."

She didn't, and she teetered again.

Mateo had had enough. He reached for her, but she wrenched her arm from his hold. She looked like an avenging angel under the streetlight in that yellow dress that looked golden under the moonlight. For a second, Mateo could only stop and marvel at her beauty.

The flaring nostrils. The bright eyes. But it was the hurt in those eyes that cooled his ardor.

"He was right," she said. "He was right."

"Who was right? Kailyn, stop."

"Owen was right."

Owen? The vice principal? Mateo did not like hearing that name come from Kailyn's mouth. She had told him they'd dated during their dinner conversation, but they'd been incompatible. Mateo got the sense from the two run-ins the two men had had that Owen hadn't taken the hint about incompatibility. If Kailyn thought Owen was right about something, it would appear they'd talked again since last night.

"I can't believe I fell for it. You were playing me this whole time."

"No, I—"

"I'm so stupid. I let myself trust you."

"You can trust me."

"Really?" Finally, she stopped. She whirled on him, a finger pointing at the center of his chest.

Mateo was certain Kailyn meant that finger to be an accusatory assault. Inside his chest, his heart pounded to get to that finger and wrap itself around it. He placated the organ by taking a step closer to her so that the tip of her finger rested against his pounding chest.

"How can I trust you when you never stopped your brother from hurting my sister?"

That brought Mateo up short. His heart stopped as his mind tried to work out the implications of that statement.

"That's right. You kept quiet. Just like you're doing now, because that's what you do. You stand by quietly and let others get taken advantage of."

Kailyn's index finger curled into a ball, her other fingers surrounding it until her hand became a fist. That fist lifted an inch away from him and then came to rest against his chest. The movement was soft, but inside he felt like she'd punched right through him.

Mateo knew she was speaking of both matters at hand: the explosive history between their siblings and the after school program, which she had to think he'd stolen from her. He could let her think the worst of him about the program. But he couldn't let her thoughts about their families stand a moment longer.

"I did keep quiet," he admitted as one of his hands snaked up between them to capture her fist. "Whenever my brother and your sister went off on each other, I kept my mouth shut. My only concern was to protect you."

Kailyn opened her mouth, but Mateo rushed on to fill the silence with his truth.

"As long as the two of them fought each other, they kept you out of it."

"Your brother called me Raggedy Ann."

"No, that wasn't him." Mateo crushed her hand to his heart. With his other hand, he dared to finger the red locks that had fascinated him since the first time he'd seen her walk into the foster home. "That was me."

The betrayal on her face made his knees buckle. She turned to walk away, but he wouldn't let her go. He was never letting this woman go, not now that he finally knew what her fingers felt like wrapped up in his. Not now that he knew the texture of her hair in his palm. Not now that he knew the honey-sweet taste of her mouth against his.

"My mother had that doll. It's one of the things she brought with her when she crossed the border. It's the only thing I have left of her now, and it's my most cherished possession."

Kailyn's futile tugs against him weakened, and she gazed up into his solemn face.

"That doll had a triangle nose, pert and proud. She had button eyes, with a sparkle at the center. And her hair was made of this vibrant, red yarn."

"Your mother had a Raggedy Ann doll, and I reminded you of it?"

Mateo nodded. He watched as Kailyn struggled with this new information. On the one hand, he'd told her that she reminded him of a cherished possession. On the other hand, most didn't consider the Raggedy Ann doll to be the most attractive of toys.

"Aldo thought I was making fun of you, but I wasn't. I was a kid. I hadn't seen anything more beautiful. I didn't have anything else that I cherished more."

Kailyn swallowed. Her features softened as she regarded him. Her fist unballed. Slowly, she rotated her wrist until her fingers twined with his. Before their hands were clasped together all the way down to the webbing, she pulled back.

"The after school program?"

And now they were back around to that.

Mateo nodded. Gently, he pressed their hands together until their palms touched and they were locked in. His knuckles brushed against hers, hard calluses meeting soft skin.

"They weren't talking about the after school program in there," he said. "I withdrew my application to the board. I'm investing in commercial property to build a private program for my JROTC program."

"Wait—" She closed her eyes as though it was too much information to hear all at once. When she opened them again, her green eyes were dark with incomprehension. Yet there was also the tiny spark of hope. "We're not competing against one another?"

"No." Mateo smiled, brushing his fingertips across her brow in an effort to smooth the worry there. Like butter, it melted under his touch. "As soon as I knew you wanted the after school program, I stepped back. It's yours. You just need to make the presentation."

Her body went slack in his hold. Not as though she fainted or passed out. More like she gave up control of her body and gave it to him, like a doll that was ready to be picked up and played with.

Her chest became flush with his. Her head came to rest in the palm of his hand. Her hands slid around his neck like he was her anchor.

"I'd like to be yours, too," he said. "I don't want to fight anymore, Kailyn. I want to be at peace. With you. But I'll fight for you if you—"

The body that had gone slack against his burst with life. Kailyn snaked her hands into his hair. With a tug that didn't take much of her strength, she pulled him down until his lips were against hers.

Now it was Mateo's body that gave up control and gave everything to her. He wrapped his arms around this woman. He picked her up off her feet and held her to him as he deepened the kiss. She was as pliant as a doll in his arms, but she was warmer and filled with life. A life that Mateo planned to spend all of his playtime in.

CHAPTER FIFTEEN

ailyn tilted her face up to the sun. The warmth of the rays was nice. The full force of the daytime star was nowhere near as nice as what it felt like to be inside Mateo's embrace. Its penetrating rays had nothing on the sensation of his lips brushing hers.

She had occupied that piece of heaven for a few hours last night after the dinner disaster. The quick goodnight kiss on Kailyn's porch steps had lingered longer and longer until the Petersons next door flicked their porch lights at the amorous couple. Too happy to be embarrassed, Kailyn finally said good night and slipped inside the front door.

She'd barely slept before the sun was up. The new day promised more embraces and sweet kisses from Mateo. The short hands of the clock moved slowly around the dial until it was time to drive over to the Flying Cross Ranch to meet him.

A family lunch was moving fast for a second date. But she'd already been introduced, and her presence had been requested for a family day of activities this Saturday. Kailyn was spared from doing any manual chores, but the Matthews did put her to work when she arrived.

Mateo was seated next to a blonde. The girl leaned into him, looking up at him with complete adoration. Kailyn felt a spike of jealousy. Not because she thought the adolescent was going to steal her man. She just wanted to switch places with the little girl, whose name she'd learned was Daria.

Mateo gave the precocious adolescent a wink, along with an affectionate smile. Then he looked up and caught Kailyn's gaze. His grin morphed into something private, something secret, something hotter than the sun's rays.

"What's next, Ms. Jade?"

It took Kailyn a moment to focus on that voice and orient herself. She was on the porch of the Flying Cross Ranch. The five foster children were seated around her with art supplies. Some of the adults had joined too at Mateo's insistence. They were helping her prepare examples of therapeutic artwork for her presentation to the board of education.

Daria had chosen the task of drawing mandalas. Sketching the repeating patterns was very useful in regulating a person's emotions and their nervous system. The child had been a wiggly little something until Kailyn had given her instruction on how to begin. Now Daria was calm and focused on the patterns she created. Except for her glances at Mateo.

LaTisha squinted at her canvas as a caricature of herself emerged. Drawing a self-portrait was meant to mirror how a person saw themselves from the inside out. It often revealed insecurities and doubts a child, or an adult, might harbor in their souls. The petite form of that particular child didn't showcase any self-esteem issues in her broad, confident strokes. The brown-skinned girl drew herself standing in front of the White House. In the portrait, everyone around her looked much smaller, and most of them were males. LaTisha knew who she was, where she was going, and she even had a small pathway in the background indicating that she knew exactly how she was going to get there.

The little girl certainly had one of the best role models around. Savy sat leaning forward as she worked on a self-portrait of her own. The drawing was full of people. Even without a headcount, it was clear she drew her increasing family with a doting Charlie at her side.

Charlie wasn't at her side in real life. The doting husband sat on the ground leaning against Savy's legs as he glued pieces onto a mask. The pieces were all heart shapes made from the leftover scraps from the others. The making of a mask was another endeavor to reveal hard-to-express feelings. Charlie's feelings were clear about himself and about his family. He was surrounded by love, both inside and out.

"What should I do now, Ms. Jade?" asked Miguel.

Kailyn had asked Miguel and Denny to draw pictures of their emotions on a blank sheet of paper. Miguel had used every color in the crayon box to draw sunshine and rainbows. Denny hadn't drawn much, but he'd chosen blacks and grays and browns to scratch across the paper. Little did he know that said a lot about him.

"Now I want you to tear it up," said Kailyn.

That lit surprise on Denny's face. It brought a frown to Miguel's.

"Go on," Kailyn encouraged.

The boys did as instructed. Miguel tore the paper once, carefully down the middle. Then he collected the two pieces together and tore again, taking care to keep the tear as straight as possible. He likely thought he could manage to glue the pieces back together again. But once torn, things never quite fit the same way. Denny ripped his sheet to shreds.

"Now you're going to take the pieces and make something new," Kailyn went on. "Something beautiful that you plan to give to the person who means the most to you."

Miguel's smile returned, and he got to work. Denny eyed her suspiciously. He glanced at his sister and reached for the glue.

"I suppose this means our ugly emotions can be made pretty?" said Denny.

"Something like that," Kailyn agreed.

The kid gave her another suspicious side-eye, but he got to work.

That gave Kailyn a moment to make her way over to Mateo. She'd given him the family portrait assignment. Glancing at his drawing, she saw that he'd drawn himself. He was hard to mistake with that dark hair and proud chin. Two sets of gray-haired adults flanked him: one couple with light brown skin and the second with a darker Crayola shade of brown. Those must be his birth parents standing next to the Matthews. More people dotted the background: his brothers, their partners, and the children. Kailyn noted that Mateo's twin was far away from him, tucked in the corner, and without color.

The meaning was clear. Mateo no longer wanted to be identified with his twin. Kailyn's hands reached for his shoulder. Before she rested a single fingertip at his back, his pencil's movement caught her eye.

Mateo wasn't done with his artwork.

Looking closer, she saw the beginnings of a female form standing next to Mateo. When he reached for the red-colored pencil, her breath caught.

"What do you think?" he asked, holding up two red pencils. "Raspberry red? Or red orange?"

Kailyn's heart was racing too fast to let her brain form words. She was part of his portrait. She was in the picture of his life. He'd said as much last night, but seeing it on parchment somehow made it real to her.

"This is exactly the kind of activity that my wife would've loved," said Father Matthews from his rocking chair. "But she would've never gotten the boys to hold still and do much crafting."

The family's patriarch had shaken his head good-naturedly when Kailyn offered him a pad and colored pencils. Instead, he sat watching everyone with unadulterated joy on his face.

"Art can be very therapeutic if given the right conditions," Kailyn said. "They say the right brain is analytical and logical, while the left brain is where art and emotion lie. When you use art, it helps to balance the two. Especially if you're someone who tries to suppress your emotions, like a lot of kids with trauma tend to do."

Father Matthews nodded. "Seems that's something that adults could use, too. Especially soldiers back from deployment."

This wasn't the first time Kailyn had heard the idea. But she wasn't sold on it. "I'm not sure hardened soldiers and veterans would take what I do seriously."

"This one does," said Mateo. He pointed around the porch to his brothers. "So do those ones."

Charlie flashed a smile. Joe, who worked on a creation with Foxy, gave her a nod. Will hadn't picked up any craft supplies. Instead, he watched Tricksy work on a mandala. His breathing was deep and easy as his gaze tracked the motions of her colored pencil on the parchment. Topher and his girlfriend Toni hung by. Neither of them had chosen to participate, but they didn't scoff or outright disagree with their brother and father.

All in all, it wasn't an entirely glowing review of Kailyn's offerings. But it wasn't a full-on rejection. The idea of working with soldiers had some merit. Maybe someday in the future. Right now, her focus was on kids.

The Matthews kids, even with the trauma of foster homes and the later trauma of being in combat as adults, were all just fine. Mostly. They had their quirks and their tempers, but even more than that, they all had love. They had a home big enough to fit all of them. And even when the home started to burst at the seams, they made more room.

They were enjoying her art projects. It was revealing parts of themselves they might not have vocalized. But deep down, this large family, by choice if not blood, knew that no matter what, they were going to be okay.

Standing amongst them, Kailyn let the feeling wash over her. She'd had love in her life. The love of her sister was ever present, if sometimes annoying. The love of her adoptive parents was still a warm shawl over her shoulders. But this big love... well, this was something that a girl could get used to.

A big arm came around her waist. That arm said she was included. That arm said she was wanted. Just as Kailyn made up her mind to burrow into that embrace and take the owner of the arm up on his offer, Mateo stiffened and let her go.

When she looked up into his face, gone was the welcoming light in his eyes. Gone was the open gaze that offered her a future. Following the line of Mateo's gaze, Kailyn saw a car ambling down the drive. When it came to a stop, an identical replica of Mateo climbed out.

Except this Mateo was frowning. Because that wasn't her Mateo. Aldo had come home early.

"What's Raggedy Ann doing here?"

CHAPTER SIXTEEN

Mateo's hand on Kailyn's back felt like the start of something. No, not the start. He had always had a foot over the starting line where it came to this particular girl. He had just been waiting for his chance to take off at a sprinting pace. The moment she smiled at him a couple of days ago, Mateo had heard the resounding blast from a starting pistol—and he was off.

He felt like he was running the ace of his life, and it was all moving too slowly for him. His heart had been pounding out a fast-paced rhythm the last few days, but Mateo barely felt the impact of his feet on the ground. Now Kailyn was finally catching up with him. His head was so far in the clouds with the plans he was making for a future with this woman that he could see clear into the next year, the next decade, and beyond. With his hand at Kailyn's back, Mateo planned to run with her for the rest of his life.

For now, he held still as his family took in the two of them. His father's looks were approving. His sisters-in-law wore those calculating expressions as though they were sizing Kailyn up for a bridal gown. His brothers, on the other hand, had taken one look at the two of them together, then commenced with giving each other those speaking glances that annoyed Mateo so much.

Once upon a time, Mateo had been on the other end of those glances. He would look over at his twin and roll his eyes when Charlie and Savy snuck off together. Both he and Aldo would lift a brow whenever Joe snuck a glance at Foxy. The twins would frown in tandem whenever Will took a step back from Tricksy in order to let Topher step forward. Now those lovestruck men all traded smirks as they watched Mateo stake his claim on Kailyn.

This time, when Mateo caught his brother's eye after Aldo hopped out of his car, they frowned at each other. But it was Aldo who rolled his eyes while frowning and then completed his repertoire of facial expressions with a raised eyebrow.

"What's Raggedy Ann doing here?"

Mateo had been so focused on Kailyn that he hadn't heard the sound of tires kicking up dirt coming toward them. He'd been too fixated on the strands of gold nestled in her red locks to hear the tires screech when Aldo put the car in park. Not even the slam of the car door called to him. Not even the call of his twin's name by the young kids getting up off the porch to launch themselves at the newcomer.

But those five words did.

Not for the first time, Mateo realized how much Kailyn Jade reminded him of his mother's prized possession. Kailyn's hair was that same bright, vibrant red as the doll's. Her nose was lifted into the air with the same perky tilt. The round buttons of her eyes had the same sparkle.

Except the spark was slowing going out of Kailyn's eyes. His redhaired beauty's cheeks were flaming with a blush. Her lips were pinched. Her body was tense.

Mateo looked again at his reflection. Aldo was glaring at him. In his brother's eyes, Mateo saw that there was no fascination with the antique doll. Aldo didn't see the beauty of his mother's treasure, nor the woman that Mateo treasured. When Aldo said the name, it was an insult, not an endearment.

"You don't get to call her that," said Mateo.

Aldo's gaze narrowed on his brother. Just as there had been wordless communication between the other Matthews boys moments ago, the twins engaged in a silent conversation. The corner of Aldo's eye twitched in a belligerent question. Mateo's answer was broadcast loudly in the compression of his lips into a thin, implacable line.

Mateo knew the silence would be short-lived. Aldo, who could rarely keep his mouth shut during a confrontation, would retaliate with words that would likely hurt Kailyn. And then Mateo would have to knock his brother's teeth loose.

True to form, Aldo parted his lips.

Mateo tensed. The hand that rested at Kailyn's back opened and closed. He wanted to keep his hold on her, but he had to be prepared to launch at his brother. His knuckles cracked with indecision.

Aldo's gaze flicked to Kailyn, and then he spewed words that Mateo could never imagine hearing him say. "I'm sorry, Kailyn."

The silence on the ranch was so complete. Mateo couldn't even hear his own heartbeat because he'd gone so still. He couldn't have heard what he thought he just did.

Kailyn blinked hard. Then she blinked again. She rubbed her ear for good measure. She wasn't the only one. All around, his brothers and sisters tugged their earlobes or rubbed at their foreheads as though trying to reset a phone or computer screen.

"I've had a trying couple of days," Aldo continued. "I shouldn't have taken it out on you."

Mateo's instinct was to go to his brother and ask what was wrong, because he knew something was wrong. He didn't need his twin-sense to know. It wasn't just the unexpected apology, nor the fact that Aldo had backed down from a fight.

There were bags under his eyes. His hair was out of place, like he'd run his hands through it one too many times. His shirt was wrinkled, and there were a couple of scuffs on his shoes. Not normal behavior for a man who had just left the military and come from a military contract interview. Not normal behavior from one of Captain Haran Matthews' sons.

"You okay, Al?" Charlie spoke the words that had caught in Mateo's throat.

Aldo shrugged. His gaze didn't meet anybody's. Instead, he leaned back and looked up at the sky.

"Things work out with any of the military contractors?"

"Yeah, but I'm no longer interested in that work," Aldo said, his gaze still unfocused and not landing on anyone in particular. "I'm gonna stay home."

"That's good news, son," said Father Matthews. "What will you do instead?"

Aldo looked to Mateo. Mateo held his breath.

This was not the plan. The plan was for Aldo to go and give Mateo a break to be his own man and not a twin. If Aldo stayed and tried to work in the JROTC program, that would interfere with his social and professional life.

"I don't know," Aldo said finally. He looked lost. "I need to figure some stuff out."

"You should get Ms. Jade's help," said Miguel. "She's really good at helping you figure out your insides and your outsides."

"I don't need Elayne Jade's help," Aldo snapped.

The absolute silence track made a repeat appearance. Only this time, Mateo heard a low hiss from the woman standing next to him.

"If you ask me, she's the one that needs therapy to deal with all that baggage she carries around."

"Hey, that's my sister you're talking about," said Kailyn, taking a step forward. "And if she has any baggage, it's because you put it there."

"Me? What have I ever done to her?" Aldo put his foot on the first step up the porch.

"Are you serious?" Kailyn took one step down the porch.

Mateo rushed down a couple of steps to stand between the two of them. It was a position he never wanted to be in—his hands outstretched between his brother and the woman he wanted to spend the rest of his life with.

"Mateo, tell your brother to back off my sister," said Kailyn. Mateo's fingertips brushed the cotton of her shirt over the spot where her heart beat out a rapid pace.

Aldo stepped right up to Mateo's other hand, his chest heaving with passion. "Mateo tell your... Wait? What is she to you?"

"She's my..." And there Mateo faltered.

He couldn't say *She's my everything*. She was more than a girlfriend. With his arms outstretched, trying to hold off World War III and his heart in his throat, that left his tongue tied. His hesitancy made both Aldo's and Kailyn's gazes narrow on him.

CHAPTER SEVENTEEN

Kailyn had never had the occasion to hate anyone or anything. Aldo Matthews had always been the closest thing to that line that she never crossed. Today, that childish man had taken enough steps for her to cross it.

She had never found a single thing to like about Aldo other than his face. His face which was so like his brother's. But now, upon closer inspection, the identical twins looked absolutely nothing alike. There were frown lines at the corners of Aldo's eyes. Mateo had the same lines at the corners of his eyes, but they were from perpetually smiling.

Aldo's nose was long and proud. But his nose looked slightly crooked. Likely because it had been punched a few times when his mouth got him into trouble.

The brothers had the same mouth. Kailyn was sure that if she took a measuring stick to their lips, she'd find the exact same proportions across both males. The difference would likely be slight, but the visual sight was clear enough for her to see the stark differences. Aldo's lips rested in a grimace where Mateo's, even when he wasn't actively smiling, curled slightly, ready to grin at any moment.

No, the Matthews twins couldn't have looked more different to her. But the biggest tell was that Aldo, for some reason, spewed hatred whenever it came to her sister. Even when she wasn't there to defend herself. Well, too bad for Aldo that Kailyn was there to defend her sister, if no one else would.

Kailyn was not a fighter. She hated fighting. But enough was enough.

She had one last card to play. She looked to Mateo. He had been her silent champion when it came to Owen. Silent and steady. Without raising a fist, he'd run Owen out of her life—her personal life, at any rate. If anyone could get his brother to ease up on her sister, then he could. He had to.

Mateo had proven himself level-headed. He would smooth this out by talking to his brother. Every time Aldo and Elayne had clashed in the past, Mateo may have stood off to the side without a word, but if Kailyn asked him to say something, to step in, she knew that he would. She just needed to ask him.

"Mateo, tell your brother to back off my sister," said Kailyn, her voice filled with the calm she reached for. The calm that always came over her when Mateo was near.

"Mateo, tell your..." And there Aldo paused. His cruel face contorted into confusion as he looked between her and his twin. "What is she to you?"

"She's my..."

There were so many words Mateo could have used to fill the end of that sentence. He could've said *friend*. Kailyn would've been disappointed at that low-rung categorization. But in reality, the two of them had only been on two dates. Technically, only one, as she wasn't sure this counted as an actual date since his family had put her to work.

If he had said *girlfriend*, that would've made her heart skip a beat, sure. But it was only a couple of rungs higher up on the relationship ladder. For Kailyn, their relationship felt like it had reached higher ground. She knew in her heart that she wanted to go all the way to the top with Mateo.

But then he paused... and she felt herself slip on the ladder that they'd begun to climb together.

Mateo didn't know what she was to him? She knew exactly what he was to her. He was the man that stole her breath. He was the man that had her heart skip beats. He was the man she was falling in love with.

No, falling was the wrong tense. She had fallen for him a long time ago. Likely when they were kids, and he'd smiled at her that first time.

She had been free falling for years now. Right now, she felt the thud of the impact. It wasn't gentle.

"I think they're going to get married."

All adults turned sharp gazes back to the porch. They all faced toward Foxy. But the self-proclaimed psychic hadn't been the one to voice that opinion. It had been Miguel.

"Isn't that right, Ms. Foxy?" said Miguel. "Can't you see it?"

Foxy cocked her head to the side and regarded Mateo and Kailyn. A slow smile broke across her face, but she neither confirmed nor denied Miguel's claim.

There was a fluttering in Kailyn's belly as she took in the exchange between Miguel, with his vociferous claim, and Foxy, with her silent acknowledgment. Her knees felt weak as she stood on the porch steps with the realization that she wasn't the only one who saw the steep climb up the relationship ladder that was laid out for her and Mateo.

The question was, would Mateo take that climb with her?

Kailyn bit at her bottom lip. When she looked up, Mateo's gaze tracked the motion. Slowly, his hands lowered until they rested at his side. He turned his back on his brother and faced her fully. He lifted one foot, placing it on the porch step just below hers. His hand reached for her, palm up this time instead of outstretched in a stop-in-the-name-of-love motion. His open palm asked her to come to him in the name of love. Kailyn lifted her hand to meet his, but that's when Aldo interrupted them again.

"That would be the biggest mistake of your life," said Aldo.

Mateo dropped his hand as though it had been scalded by fire. His face morphed until it looked like his brother's. Gone were the soft lines at the corners of his eyes. Gone were the groves at the corner of his mouth that always formed his smile.

Anger lit Mateo's face. His hand balled into a fist. Kailyn reached for him, but it was too late. He swung, adding another dent to that crooked nose and making him and his twin brother look even more different.

The sound of bone meeting bone turned Kailyn's stomach. The sight of blood when Aldo's head snapped back made her recoil. The two men were a blur as they continued to trade blows. Kailyn could no longer tell Mateo from Aldo as they went down to the ground in grunts and groans.

The sight of the violence was more than she could handle. She took a step back as the brothers tussled in front of her. When the other

Matthewses dove into the fray, she stepped to the side. Kailyn kept walking until she was on the other side of the fight. She kept going until she'd reached her car in the drive. She placed her keys in the ignition and then she was driving away until the sound of angry shouts and the sight of brutality was no longer in her rearview mirror.

CHAPTER EIGHTEEN

Mateo let his arm swing. The defensive move was wide—wide enough that an opponent a mile away would see it coming. Aldo could've blocked it. He had plenty of time to step out of Mateo's path. Instead of moving or deflecting the punch, Aldo closed his eyes and tilted up his chin.

That action sent a shockwave through Mateo. It shook him as fiercely as an uppercut would have. Why wasn't Aldo fighting back? The man never backed down from a fight. Especially when it involved Elayne Jade.

But this fight wasn't about Elayne. It was about Kailyn.

No, scratch that. This fight was about Aldo and how he would need to mind his tongue and respect boundaries if he was going to have any hope of maintaining a place in Mateo's life. Because Kailyn was his number one priority right now.

In the space of Mateo coming to that realization, his other brothers had the time to catch his wayward punch before it could connect. Joe and Charlie each grabbed one of Mateo's arms, while Will and Topher did the same to an eerily compliant Aldo.

It took Aldo another second and a long sigh before he opened his eyes. Mateo wasn't sure what to do with the turmoil of emotion he saw reflected back at him in eyes that were a mirror image of his. He didn't have time to unravel what was going on with his brother. He had to clean up the mess Aldo had made in front of Kailyn.

Mateo tried to turn around, but Charlie and Joe had him on lockdown. Glancing over his shoulder, he didn't see Kailyn where he'd left her. He jerked his head to the right, expecting to see her huddled with Savy and her sisters. But Kailyn wasn't there either.

The children were all huddled together at the end of the porch. Denny stood protectively in front of the wide-eyed bunch. The protective stance of the teenager, along with the look of betrayal in his gaze, colored Mateo's cheeks with shame. He'd have to fix that, but first he had to fix things with Kailyn.

Mateo turned back to face the front… and that's when he saw her.

Dirt kicked up from her tires as she drove out of the gates to the Flying Cross Ranch. Mateo lifted his foot to catch up the distance between them. His legs assured him he could keep pace with her car as it pulled out onto the two-lane street. The steel traps around his arms and shoulders and biceps begged to differ.

"Not until you calm down, bro."

Charlie's voice and his hold could only deter Mateo so much. With Joe's added strength, Mateo knew he was grounded. He could only watch as Kailyn and her car faded from his view. When next he looked over his shoulder, he found his father's gaze.

Father Matthews didn't look angry. He didn't even look at Mateo. His gaze was on the cloud of dust left by the car retreating from his home.

Haran Matthews did not condone fighting. He preferred his sons to talk matters out. But he also knew that boys would be boys, and if they hurt each other, he expected them to patch each other up.

His father reached into his pocket and pulled out a pristine white handkerchief. He handed the cloth to Mateo. "Clean your brother up."

The white cloth acted like a flag of surrender. Joe and Charlie let go of Mateo's arms. Topher and Will did the same to Aldo. Aldo still didn't raise his head to look at his twin. He didn't need to for Mateo to see the trickle of blood from where his fist had connected.

"With all due respect, Father, I think I should go after Kailyn. She's the one that was hurt the worst."

"You shouldn't go after her in this state," said his father, waving his hand at Mateo's chest.

Looking down, Mateo saw that there were a few spots of blood on his shirt. Not only that, but his pants had collected dirt. He looked like he'd rolled in mud with a pig. In reality, he just had.

"Uncle Mateo," said Miguel, "Ms. Jade doesn't like fist fighting. You should've used your words."

Here he was being chastised like a child, by a child, when it was Aldo who started it. It was always Aldo who started things. And always Mateo, who had to pay the price. Well, he was done.

Aldo sat on the bottom of the porch stairs. Savy snatched the cloth from Mateo and knelt beside him to fuss over his bloody lip. He didn't wince when Savy put the cloth to his mouth. Aldo didn't budge when Mateo stepped in front of him. Aldo hadn't even thrown a punch back at Mateo in that fight. He hadn't even defended himself. It was very unlike him.

"I'm fine," Mateo said, shrugging off Charlie's hand when he went to hold him back. "I just want to talk to him."

His brothers gave him a doubtful look as they crowded around the twins. For his part, Aldo ignored his brothers and reached for a piece of paper that had fallen down the steps of the porch. It was Mateo's drawing. A drop of blood splattered on the edge. Mateo yanked the artwork from his brother's hands. His thumb smudged the blood, pressing the unwanted coloration into the corner of his handiwork. He blotted at the blood, but he doubted it would come out.

Aldo kept his gaze forward. There definitely was something off with his brother. But Mateo's first concern had to be Kailyn.

"You owe her an apology," said Mateo.

Aldo blew through his nose. His lip curled into something that looked like a smile, but it had no joy in it.

"She's in my life now."

"I can see that." Aldo motioned to the painting. "Meanwhile, I've been put in the shadows."

Red was the most vibrant color in the painting. It was vivid in the loops and curls that were Kailyn's hair. It was true that Aldo was placed in the back. But he was just as colorless as the other people in Mateo's life. Because for Mateo, it was Kailyn that shone brightest.

"We were born together," Mateo began. "You're close to me. But it's time to let others get closer to us. It's time for us to be individuals."

Aldo lifted his head. Mateo saw dark circles under his eyes. It not only looked like his brother hadn't rested in a while; it looked like a light inside of him had gone out.

"You think I can't be by myself?" said Aldo. "You think I can't make my own decisions?"

"I think you like having me there. But I want to be with her."

"Well"—Aldo stood and brushed his hands down his pants—"you can't be with her."

Aldo turned to head up the steps, but Mateo grabbed his shoulder. From the corner of his eye, he saw his brothers move in. Mateo let his twin go and held up his hands.

"I'm still using my words," said Mateo. "But he needs to shake out of this—whatever this is."

"You're the one that needs to shake it off, bro." Aldo jabbed his finger at Mateo's chest. "You can't be with Kailyn because she's your sister."

For the third time that afternoon, a total silence descended upon the Flying Cross Ranch. There definitely was something very wrong here. Mateo and Aldo didn't have any other biological siblings. Their parents had wanted more, but they hadn't been blessed before they had graduated to glory.

Aldo scrubbed his hands through his hair and down his face. When he got to his mouth, he winced as his callused fingers brushed against his busted lip. "Yesterday, I… I kinda got married."

Mateo took a step back. He bumped into the broad chest of Charlie as his brothers all moved in closer.

"Married?" asked Joe.

"To who?" asked Charlie.

Mateo felt like he knew the answer to this question, but it seemed impossible. It was unimaginable. By the looks on all the adult faces surrounding them, it was clear they'd all come to the same conclusion. So no one was surprised when Aldo said the name.

"To Elayne Jade."

In this fourth silence, even the insects hushed. Not a cricket chirped. Not a bird tweeted.

"We got drunk and… and it just happen"d."

As the silence continued, the ants halted their march beneath the porch steps at the shocking news. The squirrels stood at attention, clutching their acorns and nuts against their chests as though they were clutching their pearl".

"That doesn't make me and Kailyn blood relations."

It was the only thing Mateo could think to say. It was the only piece of logic that he could grasp on to. Except… there was one other undeniable, irrefutable truth in this situation.

"Aldo, you don't drink."

CHAPTER NINETEEN

"Oh, I can totally believe every word you just said. Aldo Matthews is a conniving, lying, trickster and I can't wait for him to leave this town and leave us in peace."

Kailyn hadn't said any of those things to her sister. In fact, she had been very judicious in her description of the events of earlier that afternoon once she'd arrived home and found her sister pacing the living room. Elayne was still pacing the length of the living room floor now as she got herself worked up.

Elayne was barefoot, but the impact of her heels striking the floor brought to mind a booted army storming the capitol. Her rigid shoulders brought to mind a general preparing to give the final order to decimate the opposition. Her curled lip looked like a devil who would enjoy glaring down at all the carnage he'd been a party in creating.

Elayne did not look like herself.

"That family is nothing but a bunch of brutes," Elayne went on. She punched her fist in the air and pointed her finger to punctuate her statements. It was a pretty brief statement, but her hand gestures continued long after she'd stopped talking. She did not stop pacing.

"I don't think you're being fair," said Kailyn. "The Matthews are decent people as a whole. There's only really one bad apple in that bunch."

Elayne came to an abrupt halt in her pacing and rounded on Kailyn. "I thought you said Mateo threw the first punch."

Kailyn recoiled at the accusation hurled at her. "Only because Aldo insulted me."

One by one, Elayne curled her fingers into her palm until they were a tight fist. "I just wish I could have been there to see him go down. No —no, I wish I could've been the one to punch him in that proud nose of his. He thinks he's so handsome."

Elayne had stopped her forward march. Now she stood with her legs braced. The pounding continued as she punched her closed fist into her open palm. Her gaze went wistful, as though she was picturing that proud nose on that handsome face as she continued to punch into the center of her hand.

"Wait a minute." Elayne's attention came back to Kailyn. "What were you doing behind enemy lines in the first place?"

"They're not our enemy."

"Oh, you naïve girl. He's finally gotten to you, hasn't he?"

"What? Who?"

"Don't play dumb, Kailyn. I've seen the way Mateo Matthews used to look at you when we were kids. He was all puppy dog eyes while his brother was a pit bull."

Kailyn pressed her lips together because that was the truth of it. Mateo had gotten to her. He'd gotten inside her head. He'd gotten inside her heart.

She did not condone violence. It made her beyond uncomfortable. But maybe she should have stayed and talked it out with Mateo instead of coming home to Elayne.

"They're playing some kind of game with us," said Elayne.

"Who?"

Elayne threw back her head and let out an annoyed huff. "The Matthews twins."

"Mateo isn't playing with me. He has feelings for me. He said he has for a long time."

For a moment, Elayne simply stared at her sister. Even though they had the same eyes, Kailyn couldn't decipher exactly what was in her sister's green gaze. When Elayne finally spoke, her voice was a snarl.

"Aldo said the same thing to me."

"Aldo? You had a conversation with Aldo?"

Elayne's face softened for one whole second. And then it iced over. She turned away from Kailyn and began to pace again.

"Elayne?"

"I hate him." She flounced down into a chair and turned away, but not before she dabbed at her eyes. "I just hate him so much. I wish the earth would just open up and swallow him whole. But then it probably would spit him back out because the man is so distasteful."

Elayne's last words were barely intelligible because they were said on the tail end of a sob. That sob became a hiccup. Once the hiccup cleared, Elayne began to cry in earnest.

Kailyn felt the sharp pain in her chest before her sister began to rub there. She felt a tightness in her throat as Elayne sobbed uncontrollably. Even as she rushed over to her twin to wrap her arms around the shaking form, Kailyn felt the weight of the world descend on her shoulders.

She tried to squeeze her sister tight and take on some of the burden. Kailyn just wasn't sure what she was lifting from her sister's heart.

"He tricked me, Kailyn."

"Who tricked you? Aldo?"

Elayne sniffled as she nodded her head. "And I fell for it."

"What did you fall for? What did he do?"

"Aldo Matthews tricked me into marrying him."

The weight Kailyn had been trying to take from Elayne forced Kailyn back on her haunches. Her world spun around. Up was down. Right was left. In was out.

Elayne had married Aldo Matthews?

"I told him I wanted to annul it immediately." Elayne shrugged off Kailyn's touch and straightened her shoulders. "He said no."

Kailyn wanted to speak. To ask questions. To get answers. To make her world stop spinning. But she was having difficulty swallowing due to the lump in her throat.

"He thinks he's got me cornered for..." Elayne swiped angrily at the tears falling down her cheeks. "For whatever game he's trying to play. But I'm going to make his life miserable until he does give me that annulment and end this sham of a marriage."

CHAPTER TWENTY

Mateo's wrist worked as he polished his shoes. It didn't take a healthy amount of elbow grease before he could see himself in the shine. From the gleam of his shoe, a stranger looked back at him dressed in uniform.

All his life he'd done nothing but love this country. From his birth parents' reverence of it, to his adoptive parents' devotion to it. He had been proud to enlist to serve this union, which had given him so much. Though he had retired from service, he intended to continue to serve.

Straightening to his full height, Mateo saw his mirror image, though there was no reflective glass in the family room. Aldo wore the same uniform, the same medals, but he and his twin did not look the same this morning.

Aldo looked old and tired. He also looked determined. That determination was the only other thing besides their uniform that the brothers had in common today. Unfortunately for Aldo, this was one battle he was going to lose.

"You're not coming," said Mateo as he bent down to put on his shoes.

"Yes, I am."

Mateo gave a decisive shake of his head. Aldo said nothing. Nor did Mateo see his brother walk away in his polished shoes. When he straightened, Aldo put up his hands.

"I owe her an apology," said Aldo. "Kailyn, I mean. She's important to you."

Mateo opened his mouth to deny his brother, but as he took in the sight of his twin, he paused. Aldo's shoulders should have been straight. Instead, they drooped. His gaze should have been direct and his chin high at attention. Yet his jaw was visibly clenched, and bags weighed his eyes.

"What if Elayne's there?" asked Mateo.

Aldo turned away until his face was in profile. But he couldn't hide the turmoil that pinched the corner of his mouth and lowered his eyelids to half mast. He opened his mouth, but nothing came out except a weary sigh.

Mateo knew that sigh. It had come from his chest all night long as he waited for the sun to rise on this day—this day where he could finally do what he did best and take action. Aldo had been tightlipped about what happened between him and Elayne and their impromptu marriage. But his brother had sighed a great deal since returning home from his adventure.

"Just promise not to cause a scene," said Mateo.

"When do I ever cause a scene?"

Instead of answering that rhetorical question, Mateo marched past his brother. He was certain there would be a scene. There always was whenever Aldo and Elayne were in the same room together. But no one could have ever written the drama that had unfolded when none of them were looking at those two. Mateo had a strong notion that Aldo didn't want the curtain to fall on whatever they were playing at.

"I'm glad the two of you made up," said Father Matthews. Their father looked up at his two sons with pride in his eyes as they stepped out onto the porch.

It was a warm day on the ranch. A slight breeze blew through the trees. The children milled about doing their chores as it was a teacher workday and they were out of school. Being out of school did not mean a day off for the Matthews brood.

Denny and LaTisha lugged a bale of hay into the horse stalls. The two chatted amiably as they got to work. Miguel and Daria laughed as Ashton wiggled his thin body in a dance move over in the garden.

"You thought that was a fight?" Aldo was saying. "We caused more damage to each other on the playground as kids."

Father Matthews sighed, but there was a grin touching his lips as he did so.

"We're good, Dad," said Mateo. "This knucklehead is just coming along to give moral support."

"And to class up the place," said Aldo. "Everyone knows I look good in my uniform."

"We have the same face, you know," said Mateo.

"I've been thinking about wearing another uniform," Aldo said. "I know the town police force is hiring."

That statement lifted the weight off of Mateo's heart. It looked like Aldo was feeling the need for some space of his own. His twin was finally coming to terms with his need to be an individual. Perhaps that was due to whatever was going on between him and Elayne. Mateo knew he wanted his own space to make room for Kailyn. Because he was determined that she would be in his life. And he had just the plan to make that happen.

With all of his investors lined up in under a week, Mateo had already secured the space for the new JROTC program. They were set to move into the place in just a matter of weeks. Mateo tucked the plans in his bag and climbed into the car to head to the Board of Education meeting.

He'd given Kailyn time to cool off. Today was the day of her presentation. He wasn't entirely sure if she wanted him there, but he wouldn't miss it for the world. Besides, he had a very important question he needed to ask her. One that would change both of their lives if she said yes.

When he walked into the small conference room appointed for school board meetings, she was the first thing he saw. She had always been a beacon for him, from her brief time at the foster care home to their years in school together. Even when he had enlisted and she'd stayed local, he'd kept tabs on her. Now he wanted to get and keep his arms around this woman.

He especially wanted to hold her now as she wrung her hands. Was she nervous? He couldn't imagine why. She had this in the bag. He'd eliminated all competition so that she could have exactly what she wanted. Mateo planned to pull that particular move for the rest of their lives, which he hoped they would spend together.

Kailyn gave her fingers a shake. She rolled her shoulders back, taking in a deep breath. When her gaze lifted, it fixed on him.

Mateo's heart stopped. His whole body held still as she regarded him. She wasn't frowning. She looked bewildered, as if his presence was unexpected.

His heartbeat picked up again when her gaze softened and she breathed a visible sigh of relief. She didn't take a step toward him. She couldn't as she was standing at the presentation podium. But she did hold his gaze for a few seconds.

Mateo smiled brightly at her. In that smile, he tried to communicate encouragement. He wanted to remind her of how strong she was. How deserving she was for this program of hers to get funded. He wanted to mouth the words *I love you*. But he didn't dare go that far. At best, it would throw her off her game.

The meeting was called to order. Kailyn turned to face the board, who were all gathered in a semicircle at the front of the room. General Jensen sat just off to the right. He gave Mateo a nod before turning his attention to the presentation screen.

There were a few stammers as Kailyn began. But each time she looked up and caught his gaze, she found her way again. The presentation ended with polite applause. The vote was taken immediately. The ayes were unanimous. The funding was hers.

Kailyn stood at the podium, stunned. In front of her, the board members rose from their seats to come down and congratulate her. Around the room in the audience, town members and concerned parents lined up behind the podium, prepared to discuss the issues they felt with the school curriculum, testing procedures, and accommodations for their children.

Before long, Kailyn stood by herself. Her lips were still parted in that O of surprise that things had gone her way. Had she truly expected that she would have to fight for anything she wanted? Not while he was around. He would fight this woman's every battle so that she could spend all her time spreading her peaceful art over the ugliness of the world.

"Hi," Mateo said after she stepped out of the door to the conference room.

"Hello," she said as she let the door close behind her.

"I'm sorry about the other day. I should've handled that better."

"I should have stayed and discussed my feelings with you."

Mateo half smiled, half grimaced. If any other woman, or any other person, had mentioned the need to discuss feelings with him, he would have run for the hills. For this woman, he wanted to know her every thought and emotion.

"Congratulations," he said, motioning to the now blank presentation board.

"I feel like I just added a lot more work to my plate without much compensation. But I know it'll be worth it."

"About that—I have a proposal I want to run by you."

"A... a proposal." Her lower lip trembled as she sounded out the second word.

"It's one that would have us spending a lot of time together for the near future."

"It would?" Kailyn pressed her right hand to her heart.

Mateo took a step closer to her. He reached up with trembling fingers of his own and placed them over hers. "But I think it's the right decision, and there's no one else I would dream of asking."

"Ask me."

For a moment, Mateo forgot the question he had planned to ask her. His heart was demanding he ask her a very different question. Mateo pulled the paperwork from his bag. He didn't present it to her just yet. Instead, he held it between them.

"Kailyn Jade""

"Yes, Mateo?"

"Would you be my..."

"Would I be your...? What?"

"Would you come work at my program and be my art therapist?"

CHAPTER TWENTY-ONE

Kailyn had lost her breath. Her heart was racing so fast as Mateo posed his question to her. He was going to ask her The Question.

Could this day get any better? No, she didn't think it was possible.

Her presentation had gone off without a hitch. Well, no, that wasn't entirely true either. Her voice had hitched more times than she cared to admit. Each time she got nervous and lost her way in her prepared remarks, she'd only needed to glance over at Mateo, and she'd felt a surge of confidence. A surge of certainty. It was what she was feeling now as he prepared to pose his question to her.

She knew it was too soon for that particular question. Her life was about to change with added work. She was taking on more responsibility now that her after school program was being fully funded by the school board. There would be supplies to buy and lessons to plan and advertising to get kids interested in what art therapy could offer them.

It would be an uphill battle. But she wanted to take the trek. And taking a trek with a ring on her finger and this man at her back sounded like the smartest thing she could do.

They'd barely gotten past their first fight. But the mere fact that they were standing face to face after he'd gotten physical and she'd run away had to mean that they could work out anything that came their way.

He'd come for her today. He'd come and stood by her, lending his silent strength even after she'd run away from the problem.

Kailyn realized that Mateo's silence all the years that they were children hadn't been complacence. He'd been protecting her even then. So long as their siblings were focused on battling one another, none of their ire could reach the two of them. The only time Mateo had ever spoken up was when the verbal battle had come too close to her. Like the other day.

This man would fight for her if she needed him to. He would do it with silence, with words, or with his fists. Kailyn didn't want Mateo to fight. Not for her. Not with her.

Kailyn loved Mateo. She loved him deeply. Likely had since the first time she'd laid eyes on him. That feeling, that knowledge, brought her peace. Peace was the only thing she wanted from him. So when he asked his question, she knew she was going to say yes. Almost before he got the words out of his mouth, she was saying it.

"Yes. Yes! Wait. What?"

Mateo hadn't said the word *wife.* He'd asked her to be his *art therapist.* To come and work for him? To be his employee?

"You made me see the value of what you do," said Mateo. "Savy usually has to threaten the kids to get them to sit still or get up and do something. You had them all in line with the art. You made it okay for them to uncover and focus on their emotions. I think this could be really valuable to those about to go into the military, as well as those currently in the armed forces, or those who have finished their service. I think you could make a real difference with them, like you have with me."

It wasn't what Kailyn was expecting to hear from him. But it was exactly what she needed to hear. It was exactly what she wanted to do. She did want to help those warriors who were prepared to fight or who came home battered and bruised on the inside or out to find the peace that she found in Mateo's silent embrace.

"Yes," she said again, a bit more sedately this time.

"Also—" Mateo stepped forward, his voice going quiet so that only she could hear. "I'd like to take you out again on another date."

"Yes," she said.

"Not just one date. I'd like to monopolize as much of your time as I can manage."

"Yes."

"And then, sometime in the near future, at a more appropriate time, I'd like to ask you another big question."

"Yes."

Kailyn took a deep breath in. As she breathed out, Mateo inhaled. He inhaled her relief. He inhaled her joy. He inhaled the beginnings of their future together.

With his hand still over hers and her hand on her heart, Mateo leaned in. Kailyn tilted her head back to receive his kiss. Before his lips could connect with hers, yelling interrupted them. Those raised voices were all too familiar.

"I don't know what game you're playing at, Aldo Matthews, but I'm going to make you regret it."

"You think I could regret anything more than finding myself hitched to you?"

"Well, there's an easy fix to that." Elayne shoved a paper clipped stack of documents against Aldo's chest. "Just sign the annulment papers."

Aldo stepped back from the papers as though they'd burned his chest. His nose scrunched as though he smelled something foul.

"Well? What are you waiting for?" Elayne demanded. "You want to be rid of me, don't you? Sign the papers."

Elayne let go of the pages. Aldo reached for them too late. A number of pagers slipped free of the paperclip and wafted to the floor. Somehow the paperclip had gotten wrapped around Elayne's red hair, which had come loose from her bun.

Aldo reached up to snag the metallic clip. When he did so, his fingertips brushed against Elayne's check. Her inhale of breath was audible from across the hall.

Elayne's lips parted. Aldo's did the same. He gave a tug, and the paperclip came loose. He held it between them as they stood in a puddle of divorce papers.

The sound of arguing wafted from the closed door of the conference room, likely some parent unhappy with the board's decision and how it was affecting their child. The raised voice snapped Elayne from her stupor. Without another word, she stepped away from Aldo and stormed past him to the exterior doors.

Aldo stood watching her go, paperclip still in hand and annulment pages in disarray at his feet.

"Those two need to get that annulment," said Mateo. "And fast."

"They're not going to get an annulment," Kailyn said.

"They can't stand each other."

"I don't know." There was certainty in her voice. But her tone was still tinged with worry. "Your brother seems to like tugging my sister's hair."

"Isn't that a bad thing?"

Aldo and Elayne clearly had a whirlwind around them. It was a weather system Kailyn wasn't interested in. She much preferred the warm sunshine of Mateo's embrace. Though they had already proven that a little stormy weather wasn't enough to tear them apart.

"I don't know," she said, twining her arms around his neck. "Try it and see."

Mateo's grin spread across his handsome face as he reached up and gave one of her curls a tug. The tug only served to make Kailyn giggle. When she threw her head back in laughter at the second tug, Mateo captured her lips. The world tilted off its axis as he pulled her close, deepened the kiss, and caused the temperature between them both to rise a few degrees.

EPILOGUE

$\mathcal{M}$ost people had favorite colors. His birth mother's favorite color had been red on account of a doll. His adoptive mother's favorite had been mahogany, which was reddish brown.

For years, Aldo had thought Tessa Matthews loved that color because of a film starring her favorite actress which she'd watch at least once a month on the old television in the family room. At her funeral, he'd learned that his second mother had fallen in love with the color after her husband planted a hibiscus shrub as a border around her garden.

The bush still thrived there today. Its reddish-brown foliage had never held Aldo's attention like it did for his twin brother Mateo. Whenever Mateo encountered anything with red, he usually treated it like a stoplight and came to a halt and stared at it with a stupid grin on his face.

Aldo didn't have a favorite color. But he did have a favorite letter. It was the letter M. The beginning of his new last name, which had given him a fresh start in life.

He liked the curves that made up the top of the letter. The symmetry of the form was pleasing to his eyes. Maybe another reason Aldo liked the shape of the M because there were two curves in the letter—twin peaks.

Just as he reached the summit of one side, he would arrive in a valley and look up to see another mountain to climb. Though sometimes the twin mountains would flatten out, compressing into a thin line. He didn't like it when that happened. Other times, the mountains would smoosh together, making the distance between them closer and the valley non-existent. In his mind, he thought of stretching his body out across the twin peaks. Maybe even tasting both summits at the same time.

"Are you even listening to me?"

Aldo blinked. He jerked his attention up. Way up past the purse of her top lip. Up beyond the flare of her nostrils. Higher to the blaze of those bright green eyes.

There, he had to pause. It always took him at least two seconds before he could orient himself in her gaze. Having Elayne Jade's full attention on him always made Aldo feel hot under his collar. The steam from that heat would fog up his brain.

He had to be careful because in those few moments, she could get the better of him. And if she got the better of him, he would be the one to lose in the game they had played since they were children. They game of who could make the other pop their top.

Aldo was the reigning champion of the game. With just a few well-placed words, he could rile Elayne up enough that those perfectly shaped lips would part, forming the most exquisite M shape he could ever imagine.

"I don't know what game you're playing at, Aldo Matthews, but I'm going to make you regret it."

Her lips parted slightly. But the shape was all wrong. The right side of her mouth lifted higher than the left side, making the shape off balance. He needed to find the right words to irritate her enough to get them back in alignment.

"You think I could regret anything more than finding myself hitched to you?" He hurled the words at her. And bingo! Her lips parted, but only briefly, before she huffed out an angry breath that made them bow a bit.

"Well, there's an easy fix to that."

Aldo felt something thump against his chest. At first, he didn't react to it. His heart often beat rapidly around Elayne Jade. It was the thrill of the game they played, and he knew he was winning.

"Just sign the annulment papers."

Her mouth compressed into a flat line as she breathed through her nose. Uh-oh. He was losing. The mountains were disappearing in the horizon of her face.

Victory had been so close. Where had he gone wrong?

Aldo looked down at the papers she had thrust at him. In bold black letters, he saw words across the top. One word stood out to him.

Annulment.

Aldo recoiled at the word as though it were a snake weaving through his tranquil valley. That word had no place here. It did not belong between them.

"Well? What are you waiting for?" Elayne was saying. "You want to be rid of me, don't you? Sign the papers."

She flung the pages at him, but Aldo refused to catch them. Why would he? This was not what he wanted. This was not how he wanted to play the game. He had been so close to winning. Now it felt like he was not just losing this match, it felt like he might never win with her again.

The pages slipped free and cascaded down to the floor with abandon. Aldo saw why. The paperclip that had held them came loose and was now caught in Elayne's hair.

Without thinking, he reached up to snag the metallic clip. When he did so, his fingertips brushed against Elayne's cheek. Her lips parted on a sharp inhale. His gaze was immediately drawn to her mouth, where he saw it—two perfect twin peaks.

Climbing was the last thing on his mind. Conquering was what he wanted to do. Aldo wanted to take that perfectly shaped M and capture it in his mouth. He wanted to plunge into the valley between her top lip to find the treasure buried there. For the first time, he realized that was the prize in this game that they played.

If he won, which he had every intention of doing, then he could kiss Elayne Jade's perfect mouth.

A sound from across the hall jerked her attention away from him. Elayne blew out a long, low breath that she must have been holding. The exhalation compressed her lips, flattening the mountain Aldo had been about to conquer.

She pulled away from his hold before he could close his hands around her nape. The papers swished and crumpled under her feet as she stormed off. His first instinct was to give chase, but there was no need. He already had her cornered. He just needed to bide his time before he came out the inevitable victor.

Oh boy!
I think you can see the writing on the wall with Elayne and Aldo.
Are you ready for an enemies to lovers romance?
But I don't think these two are true enemies...
Get caught up in the whirlwind of their unexpected romance in
"His Vow to Defend,"
the final book in the Flying Cross Ranch Romances!

VOW TO DEFEND

CHAPTER ONE

"Your mama is so old, she took her driving test on a triceratops."

A chorus of oohs rang up in the backyard of the Bright Horizon's Foster Home. The sun was setting on the horizon as Aldo Gonzalez jutted out his chin and peered down at his domain as all the foster kids, young and older, cheered his opening entry in the game of Dirty Dozens.

Aldo was faced off against the new kid. Christopher, or Topher as he told everyone to call him, was bigger than Aldo. Which was why Aldo had immediately challenged him. He'd known better than to use his fists, too. With those steak-sized hands, Topher could pound him into the ground. But no one could best Aldo's mouth.

"Your mama is so fat..." Topher fidgeted, those meat-sized hands grinding one into the other like he was pounding pizza dough.

The thought of pizza made Aldo's belly grumble. They'd already had a cold breakfast of runny oatmeal and a lunch of crunchy chicken nuggets and oily fries. Dinner wouldn't be for another four hours. During the summer months, Aldo wished for school because then at least he could sneak into the cafeteria at a different lunch period and grab seconds, and sometimes thirds.

"No, your mama is ugly..."

The kids around them were already snickering and pointing. Topher hadn't even gotten out a full sentence, and he'd already lost this game. This was the only game that mattered in the foster system. Even at the young age of twelve, Aldo had learned this lesson quickly. If you're not high up on the food chain, you might not eat.

Because Aldo was at the top, kids gave him an extra cookie, or an extra juice box in order to get favors from him. Or to keep him from challenging them to a game of the Dirty Dozens where Aldo would humiliate them.

"Your mama… your mama is…"

Aldo began to snicker. You might be the biggest or meanest on the playground, but laughing at a kid would always point out that they were the loser. All around, the other kids began to laugh. A few pointed at Topher. The bear cub of a boy pursed his lips. They began to tremble. Aldo knew that if the boy cried, he would never live it down, and Aldo would retain his place as king of the backyard of foster care.

"Yeah, well, you don't have a mother," Topher said. "At least I do."

It was never silent in a foster home. There was always someone shouting, be it child or adult. There was always someone crying, either in pain or from hunger. There was always some sound of human misery. But there was never silence.

Every mouth shut at Topher's words. Even the birds in the trees hushed in anticipation of what Aldo would do. Even the insects on the ground stopped the search of scraps to see what would happen next.

It had been a long time since Aldo had had an actual challenge. The comeback blindsided him. Over Topher's shoulder, Aldo saw his reflection.

A kid just his height, with his same coloring and facial expressions, broke off from the crowd. Aldo's mirror image was calm and unassuming. His double kept his hands in his pockets, his shoulders hunched as though telling Aldo that he should concede the fight.

Aldo ignored his twin brother. Instead of lifting his fists, Aldo opened his mouth. "Yeah, but you were so ugly your mom put you here so she didn't have to look at you anymore."

Topher's head snapped back. If Aldo had actually struck the boy, the crack of the muscles in his neck wouldn't have been so loud. Those meat fists stopped grinding and formed two huge cleavers. The cleavers rose and flew.

Aldo saw the blow coming. He was fast enough to duck away.

Topher's knuckles only grazed his ear. But when Aldo blinked, he saw red.

Not blood. He saw red hair. He saw the biggest green eyes he'd ever seen. The contrast was so striking to him that he didn't immediately put up his guard, and Topher got in a free punch.

When the ringing in Aldo's head stopped and he blinked, he was seeing double. Two heads of red hair. They looked similar, much like he and his brother looked similar. But Aldo could tell the two girls apart.

Another set of twins. Someone else like him and Mateo. He wondered if they had lost their parents like he had. Or if their parents had given them up like a lot of kids here had.

Aldo opened his mouth to ask her, but the redhead cringed and turned away from him. Confusion was Aldo's first reaction. Pain was his second as Topher's fist landed in his gut, nearly forcing Aldo to give back the nuggets and fries from lunch.

"That's enough." Mateo stepped in between Aldo and the blond bear cub.

There was a part of Aldo that knew he had to get up and deal with Topher. He'd taken two blows with no retaliation. His street cred had taken a hit along with his body. But his eyes went again to the redhead.

She was looking at him again. Her arm was around her twin. The other girl had her face buried in her neck. His twin, the one with the fire in her green eyes, looked down her nose at Aldo.

A few of the girls at school looked at Aldo with stupid grins on their faces, and he hated it. If he tried to play the Dirty Dozens with any of them, they'd tear up. He doubted this girl would. She looked like the type that would challenge him right back.

Aldo climbed to his feet. He started toward the redhead, but a hand held him back.

"I said that's enough."

Aldo blinked at Mateo. His brother stood with both his hands outstretched. One was on Aldo's heaving chest. The other was on Topher's.

But Aldo had completely forgotten about the other kid. He didn't care what the other kids might think of him now that Topher had gotten in two blows, and Mateo had to step in to help Aldo. The only opinion he cared about was the redhead's.

His redhead's attention was still on her twin. When the other girl lifted her head and chanced a glance over at him, Aldo heard Mateo exhale. His hand dropped from Aldo's chest as he turned and stared at the newcomers.

Aldo knew what Mateo was experiencing. They had that twin sense, after all. Neither of them had ever seen a girl with red hair before. It was like their mother's favorite doll. The doll Mateo sometimes took out of their garbage bag of belongings and held close to his chest when Aldo felt that hollow ache in his chest from missing his mother.

Aldo had never needed to do that. He wouldn't be caught dead with a doll. But he had fought when another kid had tried to steal it from Mateo. Both he and Mateo had gotten punished for that. But now he was seeing a living and breathing Raggedy Ann and Andy dolls. She wasn't ugly like his mother's dolls. Probably because her eyes weren't made of buttons. They were as green as the fields he liked to run in.

The girls turned and were walking away from the clearing in the yard, along with the other foster kids. In wordless agreement, Aldo and Mateo took a step to follow them.

"You two stay out of my way," snarled Topher from behind them.

Neither Aldo nor Mateo turned to acknowledge him. Together, they could've taken the kid. Mateo definitely could've, but Mateo preferred to keep both his words and his fists to himself. But it was Mateo who spoke first.

"Hello," Mateo called out.

Neither girl stopped walking, though Aldo was certain they'd heard Mateo's greeting. The first one, Aldo's twin, turned back, flashing green fire at him.

The heat in her gaze made something flutter in his belly. His heart did a weird skip, like it fell down. When it got back up and he gulped down air to fill his lungs, Aldo said the first thing that came to his mind.

"Hey... red," he said.

They both stopped. The smaller one cowered away from him. They were both the same height. But Aldo's twin seemed somehow bigger. Once again, she flashed those green eyes at him.

Aldo's heart did that same weird skip. His belly made the sound of being empty and in need. But looking at her, he didn't feel in the least bit hungry. He felt like he could get his fill just by staring at her.

"That's offensive," she said.

Aldo liked the way her lips moved when she formed words. English hadn't been his first language. He'd learned by watching people form the words. Her voice, her words, were smooth and clear.

"We're not interested in playing your childish game," she said. "We might be new here, but we don't need you making fun of us."

But he wasn't making fun. He hadn't mentioned her mother at all. He'd only said hello. And mentioned the color of her hair. Because he didn't know what else to say to her.

"You're nothing but a bully, and I don't want anything to do with you."

And with that, she turned. Those green eyes flashed again. Those lips moved in a way that made his chest tighten. And that hair flung around.

Mateo sighed and watched the girls walk off without any objection. Aldo made to follow, but Mateo held him back.

"Leave them alone," said his brother.

Aldo didn't follow them, but he had no intention of leaving her alone. He wanted to see her eyes flash that green fire again. He wanted to watch her lips move in that precise way. He wanted his belly to feel full, like it did when he had her attention. He'd just have to wait another day to get his fill of her.

CHAPTER TWO

*E*layne Jade had suffered from migraines since puberty. The headaches came on when she was stressed. Or when she ate too much sugar. And also during the rare times when she'd had one too many drinks.

She was stressed. She remembered that much. Her job as a school guidance counselor had been her dream since her first Career Day in middle school. Now that she was in the counseling suite in the halls of her alma mater, the politics of the position had been tying her in knots for the last few years.

That stress had driven her to keep chocolate candies in her purse. She'd filled up the belly of her bag for the weekend she'd spent at a counseling conference. She had the distinct memory of reaching for one of the foil-wrapped stressbusters at the end of the conference yesterday, and she'd come away empty-handed.

So two out of three of her nemesis had tackled her. Or was it nemeses? Nemesi?

It hurt her brain to try to be smart this morning. Not when it was doing karate kicks against her cranium. Wait? Was the cranium at the front or the back?

The devil if she knew. When she tried to sit up, it felt like a devil was sitting on her chest. Elayne winced, causing her brows to press together, her nose to wrinkle, and her tongue to press against the roof of her mouth. That's when she tasted it.

Last night she'd sat at the bar. She distinctly remembered the curly-haired blond handing her a drink. But the drink hadn't been clear liquid. It had been darker. But not quite amber.

Elayne forced her brain to pull up a coherent picture of last night, but it was all hazy. The dark drink was the only thing she could make out. It hadn't reflected the light like a normal dark-colored liquor. It had been thicker. And sugary. With a hint of bitterness. Kinda like...

Had she had a chocolate drink? The bittersweet remnants in her mouth confirmed her suspicions.

Wait? Had she ordered a second? And then... was that a third drink she was remembering?

The pounding on the right side of her head suggested she had finished all three. The throbbing on the left side of her face felt like it had rested against an anvil. The pins pricking at the back of her skull felt like the hammer was still pounding. The silence was so loud it made her ears ring.

Was she outside? She swore she heard running water. And was that singing? Was the radio on?

It had to be the radio because her sister's voice was not that low. But wait? Kailyn liked instrumental music and not vocalists. Also, Kailyn's bedroom was down the hall with her own private en suite. Elayne shouldn't be hearing her twin's voice or radio.

And why were her curtains closed? Elayne's room was at the back of their house. She always slept with the curtains opened and the windows cracked. The sunrise and birds chirping had been her natural alarm clock since she and her sister had moved into their adoptive parents' home.

There was no birdsong this morning. There was only that loud, ringing silence. And the man's voice coming from the bathroom.

But wait. Had she left the conference hotel yet? She had no memory of it. Just as she had no memory of what had happened after that third drink.

She wasn't home. She was still in the hotel. That much helped her get a bearing on her whereabouts and ground her in space and time.

Her blurry weekend started to come into focus. She'd arrived at the Purple Heart Ranch on Friday for a workshop for school counselors to learn more about how the veterans on the ranch were working with disadvantaged youth. Elayne remembered the wizened face of Dr. Patel, a leading psychologist who worked with wounded veterans. Those vets had brought kids onto their rehabilitation ranch and begun using the same healing techniques prized for healing their battle wounds with adolescents and teenagers to great effect.

Elayne had taken many notes, which was why her hands were sore. She had ridden a horse, which was why her legs ached a bit. That didn't explain why she had gone and had not one, not two, but three drinks at the bar two nights later.

Saturday was a bit clearer. She'd taken a seat at the front of the conference room, eager to share her ideas with the other guidance counselors from around the state. At every turn, she'd been silenced, talked over, or outright ignored by the gray-haired men and diamond ring-wearing women.

Elayne's hair was a vibrant red. Her fingers were bare of jewels. She was the youngest person in the room and unmarried. For that reason, the counselors made no secret that they thought she should sit quietly at the back and let them steer the guiding.

The ageism of it all curled her hands into fists. The notion that vows trumped her degrees and experience made her lip curl. But it was the sound of the water in the bathroom stopping that made her stomach drop.

Shifting on the bed, trying not to make a sound, Elayne had a moment of gratification when she saw that beneath the covers she was still clothed. Mostly.

Her shoes were off. Her blouse hung over the back of a chair. There was a cotton cami covering her chest and belly. Her skirt, though wrinkled, was still on and zipped up.

Relief swam through Elayne to know that nothing had happened under the sheets last night. But still there was a man in her bathroom.

Elayne was not the type of girl that got caught up in a one-night stand. She'd only had two boyfriends in her entire life, and neither relationship had progressed to weekends away in hotel rooms. Definitely not with her high school boyfriend Darius Cox, which had only lasted a couple of weeks before he'd broken up with her over text. Elayne had no idea, no memory, no inkling of who could be behind that door.

Rolling over, she saw that there was a head imprint on the pillow beside her. The sheets next to her were ruffled. Had he slept here? In her room? In her bed?

The mystery man shuffled behind the closed bathroom door. Were those the sounds of a strange man getting dressed? Was he on his way out? Elayne had to get away from here.

Her feet slapped down onto the thick carpet. Her head protested the shift from horizontal to vertical. The ringing started up in her ears again. So too did the singing.

Elayne stopped moving. Her head cleared. Not enough that she remembered every detail of last night. No, her head remembered the first time she'd heard that song.

The man in the bathroom was singing Bruce Springsteen's "Red-Headed Woman."

The lines of that song had been explicit for a twelve-year-old kid to know. They were even more racy coming from that same foul mouth in his late twenties. What was she doing in the same hotel room as Aldo Matthews?

Not just the same room but the same bed? What possible reason would she have had to let Aldo into her room? If that was his head indent on the pillow, had the world outside come to an end with pigs flying around on angel's wings?

A look out the window showed a bright, sunny day. Cars zoomed by in the distance. The only thing in the sky was a Boeing 747 taking off in the distance.

Elayne ran a hand down her face. Something cold touched her forehead, giving her a moment of relief. Her eyes locked on the ring on her lefthand finger. Her head stopped pounding for a second as shock took over her system.

What was that ring doing on her finger?

The door to the bathroom opened. Aldo was framed in the doorway. And he was... smiling.

Elayne had never seen the man smile. Definitely not at her. The look scrambled her brain even more. And then he opened his mouth, and her world tilted off its axis.

"There's my beautiful bride," he said. "How'd you sleep?"

CHAPTER THREE

*A*ldo joined the chorus of feet tapping on the sticky linoleum flooring of the history class. All eyes weren't on Mr. Merchant, who droned on at the head of the class. The middle schoolers' gazes were on the clock on the wall, watching the seconds tick by. Just a few more rotations and they'd all be set free for recess.

Recess and lunch were the only reasons Aldo enjoyed school. He was good at math, but bored by it. He was bored by history, but good at memorizing all the facts. Studying any subject seemed like a waste of time to him, since he knew exactly what he'd be doing when he turned eighteen.

Like his adoptive father, Aldo would be enlisting and joining the United States Air Force. The military had made a fine man of his father. Aldo's only goal in the world was to be exactly like Haran Matthews when he grew up. School was just a way to pass the time until his real life could begin.

Aldo would much rather be back at the Flying Cross Ranch doing his chores and taking care of the animals. Father Matthews gave him and his brothers a lot of responsibilities. Aldo now had four other brothers. One of them was Topher, who had gotten a lot better at the Dozens now that he and Aldo shared the same last name.

Unlike his actual blood brother, Topher liked to get into scraps and fights. While Mateo always had Aldo's back, Topher was usually the one to actually back Aldo up in any skirmish. Mateo was always looking far off in the distance, like he was waiting for someone to show up.

Finally, the fifth period bell rang. Aldo held fast to his seat. His knuckles were white from gripping the underside of the chair. His adoptive mother had drilled manners into him. Aldo knew he wasn't actually dismissed until the adult in the room said so.

"Enjoy your recess, children."

Aldo hated being called a child. He'd had to do more things than most grownups before he was ten years old. He'd buried both his parents. Had to take care of himself and his brother in the foster care system. And now he had grown man chores on the farm at the ranch. Because he loved his adopted parents and knew you never talked back to adults, he held his tongue as he rose from his desk.

"Let's head to the basketball court before the others get there," he said to Mateo.

The middle school administrators had originally put Aldo and Mateo in separate classes their first month of sixth grade. Something or other about how the research proved that twins did better when they had separate experiences. People were always saying that about him and his brother. But none of the people talking were twins themselves.

Aldo had originally been in Ms. Frances's history class. After raising his hand every three minutes and asking question after question, Ms. Frances's patience visibly began to wear thin. Apparently, there was such a thing as a stupid question, and Aldo knew how to ask them all with a straight, inquiring face. Mateo had been staring out the window on the day Aldo had surprised him in Mr. Merchant's class. For some reason, his twin hadn't been pleased to see him. Then Aldo glanced at the seats near the window and saw the reason why. Kailyn Jade was in the class.

There were three sets of twins in the town. The Silver twins, Gunny and Tilly, who were a couple of years younger than Aldo and Mateo. And the Jade twins, who were the same age as the Matthews twins.

Elayne Jade had made it known that Aldo was her nemesis. He'd had to look that word up in the dictionary. A nemesis was the agent of someone's downfall. Like the villain in a superhero movie. Except there was a secondary definition beneath the first. The second definition said the nemesis was a goddess.

That was Elayne Jade: a red-haired goddess. It was her mission to bring Aldo to his knees. Well, all he had to say to that was bring it on.

Which meant that having Kailyn Jade, the nemesis' sister, in their history class might prove a problem. So of course, Mateo was worried about any recon the sidekick could bring back to her sister. But Kailyn mostly kept quiet, often doodling in her book. She didn't even look up at Aldo when he came into the room.

"I have an extra credit assignment to do," Mateo was saying in response to Aldo's recess plans.

Aldo wracked his brains to figure out what assignment they had that they hadn't finished. He and his brother were in almost every class together. Except art class. No matter how hard he tried, Aldo couldn't talk Mateo into ditching the crayon class and taking another gym class with him.

"Do it later," said Aldo.

"I won't have time. We have soccer practice later."

"Fine," Aldo huffed. "I'll come with you."

"No!" Mateo held up his hands. "If you don't meet Topher on the court, he'll be outnumbered and will lose the game. And"—Mateo pursed his lips, his gaze darting to the window again—"you might lose your cred if that happens."

Aldo nodded. His brother was always looking out for him and his reputation. "Well, try to finish up quick so you can join us. Just scribble down some lines."

"Yeah, I'll do that." Mateo turned and hurried away.

Aldo didn't understand his brother's need to get a good grade in art. He didn't understand his brother's need to take an art class. He supposed it was for the easy A. But it seemed more trouble than it was worth if he was always doing extra credit.

Mateo had a reputation to protect outside. Turning on his heel, he started for the doors that would lead him to the courtyard when he collided with another person. His harsh tongue was all set to light into the guy who wasn't watching where he was going until he realized it was a girl.

Manners immediately engaged, he reached out to steady the soft form. He knew better than to grab too low or too high. With perfect, gentlemanly aim, he caught hold of a bony elbow. That's when a strand of red hair fell into his face.

The wisp of hair was like fire as it brushed his cheeks. That tendril of fire swiped at the corner of his mouth, blazing a trail across his lower lip. Aldo inhaled and smelled warm cinnamon. He didn't need to pull back to know that he was holding his nemesis in his arms. The sensation of falling down told him it was her.

Was this it? Had she won the game they'd been playing all these years? Was this moment his downfall?

"Get your hands off me, Aldo Matthews."

Elayne Jade had a heart-shaped mouth. Much like a mountain. Aldo loved watching it compress into twin peaks. It always did that when she said his name.

"You need to watch where you're going," she said. "You could hurt someone."

"You were the one looking down, not me."

"You could've moved around me."

Why would he do that? If he did, he wouldn't get to see her lips do that thing he liked. He wouldn't get to smell that hot cinnamon of Christmas that was on her skin year-round.

And then there was her hair. The color had lightened over the years. It was a softer shade of red. More like the carrots in his mother's garden.

"What are you staring at?" she demanded.

"Carrots."

"What?"

"Your hair looks like carrots."

Those carrots were sweet. Aldo always snacked on them when it was his chore to harvest. They were one of the only vegetables he didn't balk at eating when they were set before him on the dinner table.

"Ouch." Aldo rubbed at his chest where Elayne had slammed her algebra book.

"You are the meanest boy in the whole school. No, the whole town, Aldo Matthews."

And with that, she stormed off. But Aldo had gotten to see her lips make the M shape again. They remained pursed in the two peaks as she stormed off.

She left him standing on his own two feet. So this wasn't the scene of his downfall. The game was still on.

CHAPTER FOUR

$\mathcal{A}$ldo Matthews smiled at her from the open bathroom door. That uptilt of his mouth scrambled Elayne's brains, and she had to look away. When her gaze dipped, she was confronted by something far worse: Aldo's bare torso.

He wore dark slacks that hugged his thick thighs so indecently that Elayne thought it might be best to call Social Services. The tails of a crisp white dress shirt hung open around the pants, like they were happy to enjoy the show. The curtain was open on the main stage, which was a six—no, make that an eight-pack of toned abdominal muscles. Who had an eight-pack?

Aldo Matthews did, that's who. Try as she might, Elayne couldn't wrest her eyes away from the glistening, sculpted indecency of it all. Until she caught sight of that perpetual smirk on his face.

He always wore that expression. Like he knew he was God's gift to women. Physically, she couldn't argue with that notion. Aldo clearly broke the mold. The problem was always when he parted those lips and spoke that made the record scratch.

"There's my beautiful bride," he said. "How'd you sleep?"

Those words made no sense to Elayne. So she didn't address them. She addressed the far more pressing manner.

"What are you doing in my room?"

"My room," he said, chucking a thumb at his chest.

His still very bare chest. He'd lifted that thumb from the bottom of his shirt where he'd begun the slow task of slipping each button into its hole. He stopped to clarify the room's ownership. His hand now made the trek back to the shirttails to resume the job.

Elayne tore her gaze away and took another glance around the hotel room. That's when she noticed the bed was on the opposite side. The window had been reversed, too. And the television was in a different place. It was a mirror image of the room she had been staying in the last two nights.

"What am I doing in your room?" She asked the question out loud but more to herself. "And what is this ring doing on my finger?"

With her right hand, Elayne clutched the sheets to her cami-covered chest. She raised her left hand and stared at the gold band with a modest diamond at its center. It was beautifully made. Understated but still elegant. Like the jewel at the center had no need to boast. Like it knew its purpose: to show that it was a sign of devotion.

Aldo raised an eyebrow at her. "That's what happens when a man vows to love and cherish a woman for the rest of his days. He gives her a ring as a symbol."

Elayne opened her mouth. Then closed it. She opened it again because she needed air, but her brain had gone offline, so there was no mechanism to remind her how to breathe.

Had Aldo always been that big? Had his shoulders always been that broad? Had that cruel mouth always looked so ripe with the threat of pleasure?

He strode across the room. His shirt was buttoned. Not all the way. There was still a peekaboo of that broad chest with the last two buttons hanging open.

He reached for Elayne's left hand. It was still held out in front of her. He wrapped his large fingers around hers in a warm, firm grip. And wonder of wonders, Elayne let him. Because it felt…

Never mind what it felt like. It was wrong. It was all wrong.

"Vows?" she managed.

"Hmm," he hummed as he sat on the bed, bringing her hand to his mouth like a duke in a regency romance novel.

Elayne didn't snatch her hand back. She didn't have the energy to. Her head was spinning. From lack of oxygen? From the impossibility of this situation? From the hangover migraine? Though that last one was slowly ebbing away ever since he'd taken her hand.

Feeling exhausted, Elayne pressed her back against the headboard. Aldo leaned closer, as though he belonged in her personal space. The scent of minty soap and clean male assaulted her nose and made her brain scramble.

Aldo reached up his hand and tugged at one of her curls. He'd never been this close to her. Heat radiated off him like he was a furnace. She suddenly felt too hot to keep the sheets around her. But she didn't dare let them drop. They were her only defense.

"The ring tells everyone else that you're off limits." He turned her hand over and pressed warm kisses into her palm.

"Is that what this is?" she asked.

"Is that what what is?"

Aldo rested his cheek in her palm and gazed at her. The stretch of his lips made her stupid. She'd watched him grin at other girls, and they had tittered. Elayne was on the verge of tittering. She snatched her hand back. This whole scenario was finally beginning to make sense.

"You tricked me into marrying you so that other guys would stay away from me?"

"Well, yeah, that is kind of the idea of holy matrimony."

Aldo leaned closer, aiming that grin at her. Was he about to kiss her? It was just too much. Even more because a part of her was curious as to what his lips would feel like against hers. What his mouth would taste like first thing in the morning... later in the evening...

But no. This was Aldo Matthews. Her mortal enemy. Her nemesis.

"I would never marry you." Her voice was hoarse. Likely because her statement lacked conviction.

Aldo blinked, a hard blink as though she'd slapped him in the face. He recovered quickly, though, and the smirk came back full force. "Your actions from last night would call you a liar."

He rubbed his thumb over the diamond on her left hand. Elayne shook her head. She snatched her hand away and slipped out of the bed. Then immediately grabbed for her shirt when she remembered she only wore a cami.

"This is a cruel joke, Aldo Matthews."

He was staring at her. At her lips. He always did that whenever she said his name. Like he detested the fact that she had to put his name in her mouth.

"I know you hate me but—" Elayne had to take a breath and turn from him when her lip trembled ever so slightly. "But I never thought..."

"I don't hate you. I never have."

His voice was soft. So soft that she was tempted to turn around. Aldo Matthews didn't do anything softly. But there was still a quiver in her lower lip.

"Of course you do," she said to the wall. "You've tormented me since the first day I met you."

His silence had Elayne peeking over her shoulder. There was no smirk on Aldo's face. He stared at her, dumbfounded.

"You've called me names. Raggedy Andy and carrot."

Again, the dumbfounded look remained as he sat on the bed. He looked at her like he had no idea what she was talking about. Like they'd had two different versions of their childhood.

"It was a game," he said finally. "It was all a part of the game we played."

"What game?" Elayne turned to face him fully. "The game where you hurt my feelings and laugh about it?"

"I… hurt your feelings?"

He stood, rising impossibly tall. But the way he looked down at her made Elayne feel small. She couldn't maintain eye contact with him. That mischievous hazel gaze looked off. Like, literally off. Like a light had gone out.

"I don't know what happened last night," she said, tugging her shirt over her head. "We both must have gotten drunk."

"You don't remember anything?"

"No." She bent down to pull on one and then the other shoe. "Do you?"

He didn't answer. He must have forgotten, too. But he was surprisingly steady for a guy waking up with a hangover.

"Luckily, we didn't take things too far," Elayne continued. "We can get this annulled, and it'll be like it never happened. No one needs to know."

More silence from the other side of the room. At least the smirk was gone. His lips were a thin line, as though he was chewing on the inside. It was the longest Elayne had known him to be silent.

Good, that had to mean he was finally seeing this conundrum for what it was.

"Aldo?" Elayne approached him carefully, tentatively. Like she would an unknown, injured dog on the street. The mutt might lick at the hand extended to it. Or the mongrel might lash out and take a bite out of her.

It was a fifty-fifty chance with Aldo Matthews. "It's time we grew up and put this childish feud behind us. I don't want to fight with you anymore."

"I like fighting with you."

There was no bite behind his words. His expression was confused, as though Elayne was taking away his favorite chew toy. This man would never change. What had they put in that drink last night to make her consider for even a second that this was a good idea?

"I can't walk out of this room with you. It'll ruin my reputation as a counselor to impressionable kids."

Something shifted in his posture. A stiffness that she'd never seen before. Elayne realized she was looking at the disciplined soldier.

"Fine," he said. "I'll leave."

He strode forward to the door. Each step measured. His features were set in an unreadable mask. The sound of his shoes impacting the carpet was like the staccato of a drumbeat. When he reached for the door handle, Elayne stopped him with a last request.

"You won't tell anyone?"

He looked over his shoulder at her. The smirk was firmly back in place. A quizzical brow raised as he took her in. "Me and Elayne Jade? Who would believe me?"

The light in his eyes was still out, but there was vulnerability there. Elayne had the urge to smooth his brow. But she quickly shut that down. This was Aldo Matthews. Even though they'd just made a truce, he was the same bully from her childhood.

Breaking the gaze, Elayne reached down to pull the ring off her finger. It wouldn't budge.

"Keep it," he said, opening and closing the door behind him.

When he was gone, she felt the emptiness of the room all the way down to her toes. Her chest hurt, like her heart had slipped and fallen down on something hard. What had happened last night?

CHAPTER FIVE

"Hey bro, I forgot something at my locker." Mateo chucked a thumb over his shoulder as he twisted his upper body to move in the opposite direction without breaking his stride.

It was a move that caught more than many of the passes Aldo had thrown at him during their first year on the varsity football team. Seeing the move performed in the senior class hallway and not on the field had Aldo twisting his lips. That and the direction Mateo was headed.

"Bro, your locker is the other way," Aldo called after his twin's retreating form.

But Mateo was too busy dodging bodies as though he was indeed on the football field and headed to the end zone. He made a left turn that would lead him straight into the Creative Arts hallway where the theater, band, and art rooms were housed.

A crease formed on Aldo's brow, and he scratched his head at the empty hole his brother left in the crowd of upperclassmen. Mateo's behavior had been weirder and weirder as they approached their eighteenth birthday. It would soon be time to enlist, but his twin seemed to be dragging his feet.

"Hey, what's up, Al?"

Aldo didn't like his name being cut in half. Darius Cox, a third string tight end, often called his twin Matt. Aldo was proud of his Hispanic heritage. But he'd corrected Darius one too many times. The kid couldn't seem to learn—which was likely why he stayed on the bench all last season and it looked like he'd be keeping his spot warm this season as well. Aldo didn't want to waste his breath on the kid. Besides, he saw someone else he'd much rather talk to.

It had been over a week since he'd talked to Elayne Jade. She'd gone on a leadership summit Friday afternoon before the Homecoming game. He had no idea whose bright idea it was to have a conference during his big game. They'd won with Aldo launching the ball into his brother's hands twice and getting past a blitz himself that scored the winning touchdown.

It had been epic. They were still talking about it. Would be talking about that game for years to come. But Elayne hadn't seen a moment of it.

Someone had to have told her about it, though. The leadership conference had only been a few towns away. He wondered if she'd gasped as they described his fancy footwork around the defensive players who'd tried to take him down. Maybe her eyes had lit up when she learned how he ran thirty-three yards to score. If she had, he bet her forehead did that wrinkly thing when she was surprised.

The last time he'd seen her forehead wrinkle was when she'd worn a yellow headband. The yellow made her hair look an even brighter red than usual. The band had also pulled on her forehead, making her eyes look wide. It had reminded him of the great owl that stood in a tree in the woods bordering the Flying Cross and Silver Star ranches. The bird had the softest looking feathers that begged a boy to climb a tree and touch it. But the bird was fierce and proud. Aldo had gotten pecked before he felt a single feather.

Unfortunately, when he'd made the comparison out loud, Elayne had snapped at him. Much like the owl. She'd called him a rat that deserved to be swept up by a winged predator, then stormed off.

She'd been doing that more and more lately in their epic battles. Instead of engaging him and trying to take him down like a nemesis should, she'd sigh, roll her eyes, and retreat. Each time she did, Aldo's chest would tighten, and any words would get locked in his throat.

"Here comes your sworn enemy."

The creases deepened beneath Aldo's brow. He wasn't sure where the voice had come from. He turned to see Darius standing shoulder to shoulder with him as though they were friends. They were not friends. And he needed to know that.

"Been running a little interference on that front for you, bro."

Aldo took a split second to try to figure out what Darius could possibly mean. But that fraction of a second was too long to waste on the kid. With a shake of his head, Aldo turned from Darius and took a step toward Elayne. It was her bright smile that stopped him in his tracks.

He'd seen her smile from afar plenty of times over the years. Just like the first time he'd seen her, it made something flutter in his belly. His heart was like a stone skipping across the water. He had to swallow a few times before he could get his lips to part to let air down his lungs.

"Her knees are still knotted, but I think I'm pretty close to working out that particular kink and then—"

Aldo loved action films. His favorite part of any action film was always the slow-motion stride. Especially if things slowed down to a hard rock anthem. Those were the best.

Things didn't happen like that in real life. They sped up. In one second, Darius was smirking at him. His lips were moving as his gaze slid past Aldo to leer at Elayne.

In the next second, Darius wasn't there. He was flat on the ground and there was blood seeping out of his cracked lip. It was an improvement as there were no longer foul words coming out of his mouth and his eyes were closed and not on Elayne.

Behind him, Aldo heard a feminine scream. He knew it was Elayne without turning around. That's when the slow motion started.

Time slowed as Aldo glanced over his shoulder at the firebrand storming toward him. In that fraction of a second, Aldo knew that he would do anything—*anything*—to scoop Elayne up in his arms and protect her from anything and anyone who would make her scream in hurt, in fear, or in outrage.

The second thing he knew was that he was the cause of her outrage at this moment. Whatever game Darius was running on her, his smart, beautiful, no-nonsense girl had fallen for it. She'd fallen for Darius' game and not his. Well, that wasn't going to fly. She was his nemesis and no one else's.

As time continued its slow-motion action roll, Aldo leaned down to whisper into Darius' ear. It was only a few words. By the look on Darius' bruised face, Aldo knew the message was received loud and clear.

Then he was being wrenched off Darius by surprisingly strong hands. He backed off, helpless not to do anything Elayne commanded of him. The slap across his face stung but not more than the words she spat at him.

"Aldo Matthews, you are the worst," she said. "Absolutely rotten to the core. I knew it the first time I laid eyes on you, and you haven't changed an iota."

Aldo knew what an iota was. It was the ninth letter in the Greek alphabet. So it didn't mean exactly what she thought it meant. But his attention wasn't focused on her misuse of the word.

As always, Aldo was fixated on Elayne's mouth. The way it moved and formed words. But today, the words penetrated. His heart stilled from those skips. His belly clenched like it was empty.

"You can't date him," said Aldo.

"You cannot tell me who to date or not. You cannot believe that I would listen to anything you say."

"You don't know him."

"You don't know me. You don't know anything about me."

Aldo looked at her, dumbfounded. He knew everything about her. He knew she loved a good cup of tea, but she liked it weak. He watched her from across the cafeteria and saw her dunk the tea bag exactly three times before taking it out of her cup and sitting it aside.

He knew that her favorite pens were the Paper Mate Ink Joys. She preferred to write with the purple one when she was making any corrections instead of the red. She hadn't said it out loud, but he guessed it was to do with her hair color. Whenever she opened a package of new pens, she always left the red ones in the library. Aldo had a collection in his sock drawer at home.

A drop of red blood smeared on her thumb as she cradled Darius' face. The kid winced at her touch. He outright recoiled when he caught sight of Aldo's murderous glare.

Proving he wasn't as dumb as he looked, Darius shook Elayne's help off. He crab-walked backwards until he was on his feet. Then he took off down the hall without so much as a word to her.

Elayne watched him go, her wide eyes slowly casting downward to the linoleum floor of the senior class hallway. She looked devastated at the rejection. She turned that anger on Aldo.

"From now on, don't look my way. Go in the other direction if you see me. I don't want to see your face. I don't want to hear your voice. I don't want anything to do with you ever, Aldo Matthews."

CHAPTER SIX

Elayne slammed the hotel room door behind her. She walked away with quick steps, terrified Aldo was lurking behind some corner. She needn't have worried. The hall remained silent.

When she found her room, she double-checked the number before sliding the keycard out of her skirt pocket and opening the door. Once inside, she leaned back against the frame. She barely made it to the bed before her body sagged.

What in the heck had just happened?

Flicking on the bedside lamp, the low light provided no answers. The ring on her finger shimmered at her as though beckoning her to lean forward so that it could tell her its secrets.

Elayne didn't fall for it. She didn't want to know any secrets from this ring. She wanted it off her finger. But another few tugs and the piece of jewelry refused to budge.

She glared at it. Then she gave in. Raising her left hand, she leaned her ear to the ring. And… nothing. Flopping down on the bed, Elayne covered her face with her hands and moaned.

Married? To her worst enemy? This could not be happening to her.

Needing to take something off, Elayne stripped out of her clothes. Padding to the bathroom on bare feet, she hopped in the shower. At first, she let the cold water run. She needed the shock to her system.

Unfortunately, the cold didn't wash away her reality. The diamond continued to sparkle at her under the chilly sprinkles.

Turning the dial over to the red markings for hot, Elayne waited for the temperature to rise. It took a good three minutes, which served her right. In those three minutes, she swore that she would never drink again—going so far as to consider giving up chocolate.

By the time the hot water came out of the shower head, Elayne decided there was no need to be that harsh. She was going to need some cocoa courage to deal with the fact that she was now Mrs. Aldo Matthews.

The thought sent a shiver through her. Though unlike when she was a young girl thinking about Aldo, that shiver wasn't cold. It didn't make her belly grumble in disgust. Not with the vision of those eight-pack abs etched forever on her brain.

And then there was that kiss he'd laid on her knuckles, in the center of her palm. Her hand still felt hot from where he'd laid his mouth. It felt like the impression might still be there.

Elayne pressed her lips to the center of her palm. All she tasted was cool water.

Giving herself a shake, she scrubbed at her flesh and washed her hair to get all memories and any evidence of him off her. When she climbed out of the stall and patted herself dry, she could still smell him on her.

Despite the hot water and soap, that scent of strong male lingered. Where had he touched her? Probably all over her back if he'd been lying beside her all night. Had they… cuddled?

The thought should have twisted her gut. In a way, it did. But the writhing was warm and pleasurable, like being bundled up in a thick, heavy blanket set before a cozy fire.

And that was enough of that!

Elayne pulled on clean clothes. Then she doused herself in perfume, spritzing her wrists and the air around her a couple times more than was decent. But she had no plans to be sniffed by anyone. She still had one more session of the conference to go to before she was out of here. She would just sit in the back of the room, like the older and married attendees wanted her to, and for once, she wouldn't complain about it.

Peering out into the hall, she looked left and right. But she didn't see him. Was she expecting to see him?

Yeah, she was. Elayne was expecting—hoping—Aldo would jump

out of from a hiding space with a camera crew in tow and shout *Psych!* Or maybe he'd hit her over the head with something and she'd wake up from this nightmare.

But the halls were empty, and her eyes were wide open. The headache had dulled at least. If she got a cup of tea in her with some toast, she just might be able to fake normal.

The elevator ride down, which was just three floors, let her know normal was not in the cards for her today. The fluorescent lights in the main lobby made her doubt normal would be available tomorrow, either. Rubbing at her temple and squinting, the bar area came into view, and so did a few flashes from her time there last night.

The amber liquid in a crystal glass. A male's face getting in her space. But that wasn't Aldo's. Had someone hit on her?

She could remember seeing Aldo appear in the mirror, his face stony as he glared at the guy. What was the guy's name?

Elayne couldn't remember the guy's name. She wasn't sure if she'd learned it. He was there and gone so quickly. And then there was just Aldo.

Aldo had smiled, and it had dazzled her. Even in her memory, his smile stopped her in her tracks. Elayne stood staring at the barstool where they'd sat and… talked.

They'd talked for a long time. But for the life of her, she couldn't remember a single thing that had been said. She also couldn't remember how they'd gone from the bar to the City Hall for a marriage license and holy matrimony.

A chorus of laughter came from a private dining area off to the side of the bar. Elayne recognized the first couple that came out of the room. With the doors slowly closing, she recognized even more of her colleagues seated at tables in pairs.

More memories from last night started coming back to her, though this time, they had nothing to do with a broad-chested soldier. The face that came to Elayne's mind was a woman's.

Elayne had been speaking to Shirley Moss after dinner. She'd tried to corner the head counselor for the county after the meal about incorporating more mindfulness techniques in the curriculum. Dr. Moss had only given Elayne a perfunctory smile as she'd looked over her shoulder at the couples gathering at the exit. With a promise to discuss it later, she'd extracted herself from the lone single woman at the conference and made her way out the door with the other married couples.

She wondered what had been decided in that breakfast meeting that she hadn't been a part of. That she hadn't been invited to because she didn't have a ring on her finger.

Elayne glanced down at the ring on her finger. She'd forgotten it was there. She tugged at it. It still wouldn't come off. Maybe Aldo had put super glue on it? Maybe that was the joke.

"Ms. Jade? Is that...? Are you...?"

Dr. Moss' gaze and index finger were pointed at Elayne's hand. Like a kid with their hand in a cookie jar, Elayne's first instinct was to put it behind her back. She was too slow, and Dr. Moss grabbed at it, holding it high.

"Oh, my dear, why didn't you tell us? When did this happen? You have to come into breakfast and tell us all about it."

"It?"

"Your engagement." Dr. Moss let out a delighted giggle.

Her engagement? Of course, Dr. Moss would think she was engaged because she had been ringless less than twenty-four hours ago. What irresponsible guider and counselor of children would be fool enough to elope in the middle of the night?

"But..." Elayne searched her addled brain desperately for a solution, or at least a stalling tactic. "But there's the last session."

Dr. Moss waved the notion away. "We're not missing anything. Besides, we can talk about curriculum at the luncheon before we depart."

There was a luncheon? Elayne hadn't seen that on the schedule of events.

"That's where the real movers and shakers on the curriculum committee will be. But first, we need to discuss that darling ring and your new fiancé."

CHAPTER SEVEN

"You're just the kind of soldier we could use in an operation like Manned Power, son."

Aldo's right eye twitched. He'd learned not to go on wincing when a superior called him *son* during Basic Training. It still rankled him. The word rang like a gong between his ears. There were only two men who had earned the right to call him that.

It was just another factor that soured his notion of joining the military contractor outfit. Manned Power specialized in providing escort and protection for high-risk figures. The notion caused Aldo's left eye to twitch. He'd spent his entire career in service to everyday people who oftentimes couldn't fend for themselves. Not those who'd become wealthy putting others' lives in danger.

Still, Aldo pocketed the card before heading out of the conference room. The day had pretty much been a bust. He hadn't vibed with a single contractor outfit at the event. Vibing was important to Aldo. He hadn't liked all the men and women he'd served with. But he had respected each and every one of them.

The glossy sales pitches and obvious lies from the suits at the conference left Aldo feeling cold. He knew there were reputable military contracting outfits. None of them had shown up this week.

Maybe he'd just reenlist. But the thought of serving without his twin —without any of his brothers—didn't warm him. All of the Matthews brothers were at home now, all married or soon to be. Except for him and Mateo. Maybe he could join his brother on his new JROTC venture.

"Matthews? Aldo Matthews, is that you, son?"

Aldo winced. Not at being called *son*. It was because of who had called him that. "Officer Moss, how are you, sir?"

Moss had gotten to know Aldo well as a foster kid. He'd been more than rough around the edges, having just lost his parents and having English as a second language. He'd lashed out on more than one occasion. Officer Moss had had the dubious job of reining him in.

"It's Captain now." Captain Moss grasped Aldo's hand for a firm shake. There might be gray at his temples, but the man was still as strong as an ox. "Look at how you filled out. And a soldier too, if I heard right."

"Yes, sir, a pilot."

"Well, I'll be. I always knew you'd make something of yourself if you just kept your nose clean."

Aldo sniffed at that.

"You looking for contract work?" Moss asked, glancing over Aldo's shoulder at the hiring convention banners.

Moss didn't wait for Aldo to answer. He pulled a card out of his wallet and handed it to him. It was on cheap card stock, but it proudly proclaimed the officer's rank and name.

"We need help on the force, if you're interested in staying in your hometown."

"Me? On the police force?" Aldo would've laughed if not for the serious expression on Moss' face.

"You never were a criminal mastermind, but you always had that mischievous streak in you. I need a man who thinks like you on my side. Help keep our town and its residents safe. Think about it?"

With a nod and firm clap on his shoulder, Moss took off, leaving Aldo thinking about it. Every thought that flitted through his head, he liked. He liked the notion of staying home and being close to his family. He liked the idea that he could protect the place and the people whose faces he knew.

Each thought left a pleasant sensation, leaving a sweet taste in his mouth. Either this was the best idea he'd ever had, or it was his twin-sense activated. Still holding the card in his left hand, Aldo reached his other hand into his pocket and dialed his brother.

"Hello."

"Hey, bro."

"Were you eating or drinking something sweet right now? I swear I just got a sugar rush. Oh wait, it was Miguel's party last night. He made cake?"

"Yeah," Mateo confirmed. "Yeah, we all had cake."

"You better have saved me some. From our bond, I can taste it was really sweet. Mmmm."

There was silence on the other end of the line. The sweet taste in Aldo's mouth soured. Was his brother that loath to share their new foster nephew's cake?

"These meetings are going great. I think you'd be interested in a couple of these contracts."

There was one contractor who had been hired to help build a school in a third-world country. That kind of job was right up Mateo's alley. If Mateo gave an inkling that he'd take that kind of job, Aldo would go along. Looking down at the card in his hand, Aldo decided not to give him any of those details.

Not that Mateo would listen. He was still talking. Going on and on about the JROTC program, which essentially was Mateo building a school on their home turf. The idea wasn't looking so bad to Aldo anymore. Especially if he made the police force and could stop by and hang with his brother.

Staying in town had its other benefits. It wasn't just his family he could see on a regular basis. There were other people Aldo wouldn't mind catching sight of. Like a particular redheaded woman who Aldo had never been able to get out of his mind. She was so much in his mind that he swore he saw her seated at the bar.

"Listen, Aldo, you should know I'm dating—"

"Andy!"

Aldo's feet were moving before he was conscious of making the command. The closer he got to the woman, the more he knew he was right. It was her.

"Elayne?" asked Mateo in his ear. "What are you doing with Elayne Jade?"

"She's here. She's at the conference hall."

"Just stay away from her."

"How can I stay away from her when she's coming right at me?"

"Look, Aldo, just—"

"Gotta go, bro. Save me some cake."

And with that, he cut his connection with his twin. But once he got within two strides of the bar, he came to a dead stop. Aldo's last interaction with this woman hadn't been the best. Their siblings had to separate them and send them to opposite ends of a parking lot.

Aldo had stewed, sitting in his car while not being able to catch another sight of Elayne. He'd glared at his brother and her red-haired sister. Again, he wondered how people insisted they looked alike when the differences were so clear to him.

Kailyn's red hair was at least two shades lighter than Elayne's. Kailyn's face was round where Elayne's was clearly heart-shaped. And there was something too quiet and meek about Kailyn where Elayne was nothing but fire.

"What can I get you, son?" asked the bartender.

The man couldn't have had more than a couple of years on Aldo. Was Aldo just inspiring men who wanted to be father figures to speak to him today? Before he could wince, Elayne did it for him. She tossed back a brown liquid that looked thicker than whisky and her facial features scrunched in on themselves.

It was the most adorable thing Aldo had ever seen in his life. The two strides of distance were a thing of the past, and he was standing in front of her.

"Excuse me," came a gruff voice behind him.

Aldo hadn't even realized there was another person sitting with her. It didn't matter who he was. With a menacing look tossed over his shoulder, the man squeaked off the bar and scurried out of sight, leaving Aldo alone with Elayne.

She opened her eyes from the wince and blinked at him. Then she blinked a few more times. "Am I having a nightmare?"

Aldo watched her lips move. They rounded to make the vowel sounds and compressed on the consonants. He took a step closer, unable to help himself. That rumble in his belly he'd always felt as a kid at the sight of her, that skip of his heartbeat. He knew what those meant now.

"Must be a nightmare because this day can't get any worse."

He wanted to reach out to her brow and smooth the creases there. He wanted to take her chin in his hand and tilt her head high where it should be. He wanted to kiss that mouth. Dear God did he want that kiss.

But he couldn't do any of those things. Not yet. Maybe he could if he put a hurting on whoever made her unhappy.

"Tell me about it," he coaxed.

Maybe it was the chocolate glop of alcohol that loosened her tongue. Because she did. She told him. Elayne Jade confided in Aldo Matthews.

"I'm getting shut out at work because I don't have a ring on my finger. Can you believe that? A piece of jewelry is stopping me from getting any promotions or more responsibilities that could lead to career advancement."

"I have a ring."

Mateo had their mother's prized Raggedy Ann and Andy dolls, but Aldo had inherited her ring. He pulled it out from the necklace he wore around his neck. The one that also held his dog tags.

Sliding it off the chain and presenting it to Elayne felt right. Like when he officially became a Matthews. Like when he received his wings. That's what it felt like to hold the modest diamond out to this woman.

"Will this solve your problem?" he asked.

Elayne stared at the offering, unfocused. She was drunk, meaning she could not consent. So that kiss would have to wait.

"Why would you give me a ring? You hate me."

"I've never hated you."

"You call me names. You call me Raggedy Andy."

Aldo recognized the woman was drunk, but he knew for a fact that he wasn't a saint. And so he did it. He reached up and grabbed a strand of that vibrant red hair that was so like his mother's prized dolls. He ran his finger through it the way he'd always wanted to.

"We're always fighting," Elayne continued, completely oblivious to his rapture in her hair.

"Yeah," Aldo agreed. "It's the only way you'll talk to me. You decided you didn't like me. But I like you, Elayne Jade."

"You like me?"

There went that crease between her brows. Reluctant to loosen his hold of her hair, Aldo used his free hand to smooth the furrows in her forehead. Her skin was the softest texture he'd ever touched.

"You're the smartest girl I know."

"You think I'm smart?"

"And beautiful."

Elayne reared back, but she didn't get far. Aldo cupped her cheeks in both hands. Her green gaze went wide. "I think I'm drunk."

"I think so too."

"Or maybe I'm drugged." Her eyes dipped to his lips and then back to his eyes and then flitted away to the bar where her drink sat empty. "Did you slip something into my drink?"

"I would never do anything to hurt you, Elayne. Let me prove it. Take my ring."

"Are you asking me to marry you?" she said.

"Yes."

"You think I'll say yes?"

"No. Not yet. But maybe one day. Until that day, I'm going to prove I'm the one for you."

CHAPTER EIGHT

"Oh, I can totally believe every word you just said. Aldo Matthews is a conniving, lying trickster, and I can't wait for him to leave this town and leave us in peace."

In fairness, Kailyn hadn't said any of those things to Elayne. But she hadn't needed to. These were the facts about the man she loathed. The man she was now married to. The gold band burned her hip inside her pocket.

Elayne had finally gotten the wedding ring off her finger after much soap and oil and prayer. She paced the length of the living room floor, getting herself worked up all over again. The impact of her heels striking the floor brought to mind a booted army storming the capitol. Her rigid shoulders were like a general preparing to give the final order to decimate the opposition. Her curled lip looked like a devil who would enjoy glaring down at all the carnage he'd been a party in creating.

"That family is nothing but a bunch of brutes," Elayne went on. She punched her fist in the air and pointed her finger to punctuate her statement. It was a pretty brief statement, but her hand gestures continued long after she'd stopped talking. She did not stop pacing.

"I don't think you're being fair," said Kailyn. "The Matthews are decent people as a whole. There's only really one bad apple in that bunch."

Elayne came to an abrupt halt in her pacing and rounded on Kailyn. "I thought you said Mateo threw the first punch."

While Elayne had been gone and getting tricked into marrying one Matthews twin, the other had begun seducing her sister. Mateo Matthews had taken Kailyn out on a couple of dates and likely would've pulled the same marriage stunt if Elayne hadn't come back home early. The two Matthews twins were clearly up to something.

But what? What could marrying her and her sister be all about? When Elayne turned her attention back to her sister, she saw her recoil. Was it at the memory of the fight between brothers? The notion of Mateo and Aldo coming to blows made even less sense than this sham of a marriage. If the twin brothers were working in cahoots, why trade blows?

"Only because Aldo insulted me," Kailyn was saying.

One by one, Elayne curled her fingers into her palm until they were a tight fist. "I just wish I could have been there to see him go down. No —no, I wish I could've been the one to punch him in that proud nose of his. He thinks he's so handsome."

Elayne had stopped her forward march. Now she stood with her legs braced. The pounding continued as she punched her closed fist into her open palm. Her gaze went wistful, as though she was picturing that proud nose on that handsome face as she continued to punch into the center of her hand.

"Wait a minute." Elayne's attention came back to Kailyn. "What were you doing behind enemy lines in the first place?"

"They're not our enemy."

"Oh, you naïve girl. He's finally gotten to you, hasn't he?"

"What? Who?"

"Don't play dumb, Kailyn. I've seen the way Mateo Matthews used to look at you when we were kids. He was all puppy dog eyes while his brother was a pit bull."

Elayne knew her sister did not condone violence. But they were under attack. Why couldn't she see that? Likely because Elayne had Aldo's ring hidden in her pocket and she hadn't told her twin about the marriage.

"They're playing some kind of game with us," said Elayne.

"Who?"

Elayne threw back her head and let out an annoyed huff. "The Matthews twins."

"Mateo isn't playing with me. He has feelings for me. He said he has for a long time."

For a moment, Elayne simply stared at her sister. When Elayne finally spoke, her voice was a snarl. "Aldo said the same thing to me."

"Aldo? You had a conversation with Aldo?"

Elayne turned away from Kailyn and began to pace again. She wasn't ready to share her news with her sister. She wanted to solve the problem before she spoke of it with anyone.

Aldo Matthews had humiliated her one too many times. With her first high school boyfriend, who'd dumped her over text message after that nasty brawl in the hallway. All those times he called her that awful nickname Raggedy Andy.

"Elayne?"

"I hate him." Elayne flounced down into a chair and turned away, but not before she dabbed at her eyes. "I just hate him so much. I wish the earth would just open up and swallow him whole. But then it probably would spit him back out because the man is so distasteful."

Elayne's last words were barely intelligible because they were said on the tail end of a sob. That sob became a hiccup. Once the hiccup cleared, Elayne began to cry in earnest.

Kailyn rushed over to her twin to wrap her arms around the shaking form. She tried to squeeze her sister tightly and take on some of the burden. Elayne couldn't tell her that it wouldn't work this time. This was a burden her sister couldn't share with her.

"He tricked me, Kailyn."

"Who tricked you? Aldo?"

Elayne sniffled as she nodded her head. "And I fell for it."

"What did you fall for? What did he do?"

"Aldo Matthews tricked me into marrying him."

The weight Kailyn had been trying to take from Elayne forced Kailyn back on her haunches. When Elayne's vision unblurred and became clear, she saw her sister staring at her with wide, disbelieving eyes.

"I told him I wanted to annul it immediately." Elayne shrugged off Kailyn's touch and straightened her shoulders. "He said no. He thinks he's got me cornered for..." Elayne swiped angrily at the tears falling down her cheeks. "For whatever game he's trying to play. But I'm going to make his life miserable until he does give me that annulment and ends this sham of a marriage."

On Monday morning, she would get this taken care of. Then she would never have to see or think of Aldo Matthews again.

CHAPTER NINE

On Monday morning, Aldo got up and dressed in his uniform. He looked in the mirror and saw a carbon copy of himself. Though it wasn't an exact replica. For the first time, he started to notice how different he and his brother were.

There were worry lines at Aldo's eyes where Mateo's looked upbeat and happy. There was a sag to Aldo's shoulders where Mateo's were straight, ready to take on the world.

Aldo felt tired. He looked tired.

Mateo looked energized and happy. The man was in love. And the woman he loved returned his feelings. That much was evident in how Kailyn Matthews threw herself into Mateo's arms after she won the bid for the after-school program the two of them had been vying for for the past few days that Aldo had been out of town.

True, Mateo had eliminated any competition for her, including himself, so that the bid would be hers. When Aldo had tried to eliminate any competition between him and Elayne, he'd gotten an earful. That's where the wariness came in. But still, he couldn't stop himself from going into the fire that was Elayne Jade.

Most people had favorite colors. His birth mother's favorite color had been red on account of a doll. His adoptive mother's favorite had been mahogany, which was reddish brown.

For years, Aldo had thought Tessa Matthews loved that color

because of a film starring her favorite actress, which she'd watched at least once a month on the old television in the family room. At her funeral, he'd learned that his second mother had fallen in love with the color after her husband planted a hibiscus shrub as a border around her garden.

The bush still thrived there today. Its reddish-brown foliage had never held Aldo's attention like it did for his twin brother. Whenever Mateo encountered anything with red, he usually treated it like a stoplight and came to a halt and stared at it with a stupid grin on his face.

Aldo didn't have a favorite color. But he did have a favorite letter. It was the letter M. The beginning of his new last name, which had given him a fresh start in life.

He liked the curves that made up the top of the letter. The symmetry of the form was pleasing to his eyes. Maybe another reason Aldo liked the shape of the M was because there were two curves in the letter—twin peaks.

Just as he reached the summit of one side, he would arrive in a valley and look up to see another mountain to climb. Though sometimes the twin mountains would flatten out, compressing into a thin line. He didn't like it when that happened.

Other times, the mountains would smoosh together, making the distance between them closer and the valley non-existent. In his mind, he thought of stretching his body out across the twin peaks. Maybe even tasting both summits at the same time.

"Are you even listening to me?"

Aldo blinked. He jerked his attention up. Way up past the purse of her top lip. Up beyond the flare of her nostrils. Higher to the blaze of those bright green eyes.

There, he had to pause. It always took him at least two seconds before he could orient himself in her gaze. Having Elayne Jade's full attention on him always made Aldo feel hot under his collar. The steam from that heat would fog up his brain.

He had to be careful because in those few moments, she could get the better of him. And if she got the better of him, he would be the one to lose in the game they had played since they were children. The game of who could make the other pop their top.

Aldo was the reigning champion of the game. With just a few well-placed words, he could rile Elayne up enough that those perfectly shaped lips would part, forming the most exquisite M shape he could ever imagine.

"I don't know what game you're playing at, Aldo Matthews, but I'm going to make you regret it."

Aldo had come to Kailyn's presentation with his brother. It wasn't so much that he wanted to support his brother's new girlfriend as he wanted to catch sight of his brother's girlfriend's sister. As soon as the meeting was over, Elayne stormed up to him, that red hair blazing a trail of fire, those green eyes igniting.

Her lips parted slightly. But the shape was all wrong. The right side of her mouth lifted higher than the left side, making the shape off-balance. He needed to find the right words to irritate her enough to get them back in alignment.

"You think I could regret anything more than finding myself hitched to you?" He hurled the words at her. And bingo! Her lips parted, but only briefly, before she huffed out an angry breath that made them bow a bit.

"Well, there's an easy fix to that."

Aldo felt something thump against his chest. At first, he didn't react to it. His heart often beat rapidly around Elayne Jade. It was the thrill of the game they played, and he knew he was winning.

"Just sign the annulment papers."

Her mouth compressed into a flat line as she breathed through her nose. Uh-oh. He was losing. The mountains were disappearing in the horizon of her face.

Victory had been so close. Where had he gone wrong?

Aldo looked down at the papers she had thrust at him. In bold black letters, he saw words across the top. One word stood out to him.

Annulment.

Aldo recoiled at the word as though it were a snake weaving through his tranquil valley. That word had no place here. It did not belong between them.

"Well? What are you waiting for?" Elayne was saying. "You want to be rid of me, don't you? Sign the papers."

She flung the pages at him, but Aldo refused to catch them. Why would he? This was not what he wanted. This was not how he wanted to play the game. He had been so close to winning. Now it felt like he was not just losing this match, it felt like he might never win with her again.

The pages slipped free and cascaded down to the floor with abandon. Aldo saw why. The paperclip that had held them came loose and was now caught in Elayne's hair.

Without thinking, he reached up to snag the metallic clip. When he did so, his fingertips brushed against Elayne's cheek. Her lips parted on a sharp inhale. His gaze was immediately drawn to her mouth, where he saw it—two perfect twin peaks.

Climbing was the last thing on his mind. Conquering was what he wanted to do. Aldo wanted to take that perfectly shaped M and capture it in his mouth. He wanted to plunge into the valley between her top lip to find the treasure buried there. For the first time, he realized that was the prize in this game that they played.

If he won, which he had every intention of doing, then he could kiss Elayne Jade's perfect mouth.

A sound from across the hall jerked her attention away from him. Elayne blew out a long, low breath that she must have been holding. The exhalation compressed her lips, flattening the mountain Aldo had been about to conquer.

She pulled away from his hold before he could close his hands around her nape. The papers swished and crumpled under her feet as she stormed off. His first instinct was to give chase, but there was no need. He already had her cornered. He just needed to bide his time before he came out the inevitable victor.

He had no intentions of signing those annulment papers. Because they weren't married. At least not yet.

CHAPTER TEN

$\mathcal{E}$layne stormed into the front doors of the high school on the next morning after the school board meeting. She was dressed in full body armor. Boots with a thick stem that a military general would lift an appreciative brow at. A killer skirt that hugged her curves and ended just above the knee so that she had the mobility to kick down any door—or six-foot aviator.

Hmmm? That's what this outfit was missing: a pair of Aviator sunglasses would complete the look. But then no one would see the take-no-prisoners glare she wore. They also wouldn't see the bags under her eyes from the sleepless night.

Nightmares had plagued her dreams. Most of the visions behind her eyelids featured a dark-haired man grinning down at her. That grin was carnivorous. Like a shark. A shark licking its chops as it balled and unballed its fists. Or were those fins?

The shark's toothsome smirk came closer and closer. Elayne couldn't tell if he was going to kiss her silly or take a bite out of her. Worse than that, she didn't know which she wanted.

It didn't help that when she pulled open her front door this morning, she saw his face. Though it wasn't *his* face. It was his twin brother's face.

Mateo recognized her instantly in that way twins could always tell other twins apart. "Good morning, Elayne."

His warm smile took some of the fight out of her. But not all of it. She neither wanted to kiss Mateo nor carve him up. Unlike his obnoxious brother, Mateo was a decent human being. But he still shared a face with the enemy.

"Morning." She rushed past him. "I'm gonna be late. Don't make her late."

Elayne chucked her thumb at her sister, whose grin was so bright that Elayne once again wished she had that pair of Aviators. The heat bouncing off Kailyn and being absorbed by Mateo's adoring grin was enough to power a plane from here to Europe. It was making Elayne a little green—and not the sick kind of green. Envy poured from her veins.

"Wouldn't dream of it," Mateo was saying, though how he formed words through that grin was a mystery. "I just brought her a treat for her first day on her after-school job."

Sweet. Mateo Matthews was sweet. Why couldn't he have rubbed off on his bitter brother? Probably because Aldo had shouldered his way out of their mother's womb, leaving Mateo to nurse his wounds.

That's why probably why Mateo's features were often scrunched in a wince when he stood in a crowd. His mouth often twisted before he stood up to speak in class. His smile back then had always been a bit self-deprecating, as though he was apologizing before he opened his mouth. She'd watched him do that a lot in their youth. He'd often get blamed for his brother's antics.

Elayne decided right then and there that she wouldn't do that to him any longer. Mateo made her sister happier than she'd ever seen Kailyn. It wasn't his fault that he was attached to that foul beast of a brother.

Too bad Mateo couldn't extricate himself fully from Aldo. That was a feat Elayne had every intention of accomplishing for herself. She had been tipsy on that ill-fated night of their marriage.

Okay, she had been drunk. But she suspected Aldo hadn't been. So he'd done whatever it was that they'd done with a completely sober head.

What was he up to? What was his long game? She'd offered him a way out yesterday with those annulment papers. Why hadn't he taken them? And why had he stared at her mouth for so long, like he wanted to kiss her?

Or maybe take that bite out of her?

"You okay, Elayne?"

Mateo's voice was so like Aldo's that she jumped. If it hadn't been a half an octave deeper, she might've put that stem of her boot to good use. But she didn't want to start the workday by dropkicking her sister's new boyfriend. So she did an about face and made for her car.

"I gotta get to work," she said, moving farther away from the happy couple's glow.

"Have a good day," Mateo called after her. "And Elayne..."

Elayne halted her forward march. She was hesitant to do an about face. Only because she didn't want to look into Mateo's happy face. She also didn't want to go back on her word of all of a minute ago to treat him separately from his brother. She allowed her upper body to perform a corner turn but kept her boots pointed in the direction of her car.

"Let me know if you need anything." Mateo stood with an arm at Kailyn's back. His words were heavy, pregnant with the twin that stood between him and Elayne.

Elayne nodded, chewing at the inside of her cheek. She was ready for a truce with Mateo. She was unsure if she was ready to have a Matthews as an ally.

But there one was. Standing in her doorway. A protective arm around her sister. An open and friendly smile extended her way. A bit of their warm front melted the edges of the cold around her.

"There you are," came a new voice, followed by a blast of cold. "Still shining brightly at being a newly engaged woman."

Mrs. Moss beamed at Elayne from the head counselor's office doorway. Her bright smile fell along with her gaze. When Elayne realized the woman was looking at her left hand—her bare left hand—she shoved her arm behind her back.

"Did something happen between you and your man?"

Elayne pressed her hand to her pocket where the ring was safely stored. She could have left it on her dresser this morning, but for some reason she was loath to leave it out of her sight. She pulled it from her pocket now. She presented the ring to Mrs. Moss and prepared to come clean.

"Oh, good," Mrs. Moss breathed a sigh of relief. "For a moment, I thought I was about to make a mistake."

"What mistake?"

"There's a spot open on the counseling curriculum committee. I put your name in the hat."

"You did?" Elayne's voice was breathless. This was the promotion she'd wanted for the last two years, but she'd been passed over.

"The only thing holding the committee back before was our uncertainty that you would stay put. So many single people move around and change jobs these days."

But that wasn't Elayne. This was the only home she'd ever known. The year she and her sister had spent as foster kids was long enough to let her know that she never wanted to be uprooted again. She had no plans to ever leave Honor Valley.

"Now that we know you're getting married and you'll put down roots and be settled, we think that you're the perfect person for the job."

Elayne opened her mouth to argue, to rage at the unfairness of each and every one of those statements, but her thoughts went blank. No, not blank. They swirled around in her head so fast and chaotically that she couldn't catch hold on to any of them.

"Your young man is Aldo Matthews, isn't that right? My husband saw the two of you together at the hotel bar. I suppose that was the night he proposed."

The sound of his name settled the whirlwind in Elayne's head. But she kept her mouth shut. She had never been a good liar. Mrs. Moss and her husband thought she and Aldo were engaged. They didn't know that truth, that she'd gotten married while drunk and couldn't even remember saying her vows.

She would have to set her straight soon. Especially since Aldo would be deploying again at some point in the near future.

"My husband's the police chief, you know. He said your man was applying to be on the force."

CHAPTER ELEVEN

*A*ldo reached over the desk and clasped the callused hand of his new boss. It was the first time he'd shaken the man's hand. In his youth, he'd been given many a stern talking to by the town's police chief. Today, the two faced each other, not quite as equals, but with equal respect.

"You'll make a great addition to the force," said Chief Moss. "Not only with your military training and instincts but also with your history in this town."

"My history, sir?" Aldo stood erect, years of training showing him how to react in front of his superiors. Though in his youth, he hadn't looked at Officer Moss as his superior. He'd regarded the man as another adult who thought he knew best how Aldo should live his life. The joke was on Aldo, because Moss had been right.

Before his adoption, Moss had warned Aldo to straighten up if he wanted to make something of himself. He'd urged Aldo to follow the rules instead of break them. He'd challenged Aldo with making friends instead of enemies.

"You were a troublemaker in this town," Moss said now.

Aldo held his breath to hold in the retort that wanted to come out. That part of his personality hadn't been trained out of him quite so thoroughly. It would forever need reinforcements.

"I half expected you to be behind bars, not handing you a pair of handcuffs."

"Times have changed, and I grew up."

"That you have, son." Chief Moss nodded approvingly at Aldo, lessening the unpleasant sting of that last word. "You're still young enough to be in the service. Still a few medals to earn. Why leave now?"

A red-haired fire sprang into Aldo's vision. Green eyes that made him feel grounded stared back at him through his mind's eye. And then there were those lips, the only mountain Aldo wanted to summit, or get lost in, or even fall from. He couldn't imagine leaving the place where she made her home.

"I was thinking about contract work," is what he said to Chief Moss. It was the whole reason he'd gone to the Purple Heart Ranch that past weekend. But Aldo had found something else entirely that he wanted to dedicate his life to. "Now I want to settle down, start a family."

Chief Moss nodded again. The twinkle in his eye made Aldo think of his biological father, whose hazel gaze was often filled with laughter and pride as he looked down on his twin sons. Father Matthews had the same look of delight and honor when he looked at Aldo.

"I also want to be a part of the community I fought so hard for," Aldo continued. "Not just for the citizens of my country, but for the people in this very town. The residents of Honor Valley gave me a lot of second chances. I want to show them that I've earned them."

A broad smile spread across Moss's face. "When can you start your training?"

"As soon as you're ready for me."

"We'll start tomorrow."

Aldo left the chief's office and the police precinct with a pep in his step. Mission Win Himself a Wife was in full effect. He'd secured gainful employment. Now he just needed to locate his woman.

As though he'd conjured her out of the blue, Elayne Jade walked toward him on the street. More like stormed toward him. She was dressed to stop a man's heart in a skirt that embraced each and every one of her curves. The boots on her feet tapped out a battle cry. Aldo prepared for a complete surrender.

When she stood toe to toe with him, Aldo's instincts were to reach for her. To pull her close and kiss her silly. The expression on her face, that perfect-shaped M, told him that a smooch would not be welcome.

Her expression had been fierce. The corner of her mouth quavered when she tilted her head back and stared into his eyes. Her features didn't soften. She might have laid down one of the weapons she had brought to this battle against him.

"What are you doing?" she demanded.

Aldo's gaze tracked the movement of her mouth, trying to hold himself back from claiming what he swore would soon be his. "Deciding whether or not it's safe to kiss you right now."

Every weapon she'd loaded fell out of her hold. She swallowed hard, making a choked sound. It was all he needed. Her defenses were down, and he was a trained warrior.

He reached for her, wrapping both arms around her waist and pulling her close. Elayne stepped back, but there was nowhere for her to go. She was good and caught.

"You're supposed to be leaving." Her hands were on his chest, but the push she delivered was ineffectual. Or maybe it was hesitant.

"I'm not going anywhere."

"You were supposed to be headed back to the Army."

"Air Force," Aldo corrected. "My contract is up."

"Sign a new one."

"No."

"Glad to know it's not just my paperwork you won't sign."

He grinned down at her mouth. There was the M. He wanted to make Elayne Jade say more M words. Like *my* and *Matthews* and *mine*. She would be a Matthews soon, and he was going to kiss those lips that would belong to him.

"Look, Aldo…" she sighed, still pressing against his chest, but not enough to actually dislodge him. "I need you to do something for me."

Aldo pulled her tighter, pressing his chest to hers. His head came down another inch closer to her lips. Just a little closer. "I would do anything for you."

That won him another shocked glance. This time her lips parted, forming a perfectly shaped O. It was his new favorite look of hers. Aldo wondered what O words he could get her to say. He should start with a simple *ohhh* and go from there. He bet a kiss would elicit that sound from her perfect mouth.

It took her a moment to compose herself. Plenty of time for him to make another sneak attack. But he didn't want this to sneak up on her. He wanted her to come to him.

"I need you to come to dinner with me," she said finally.

"Done."

"It's with the police chief."

"My new boss."

"So you really are joining the police force? You're staying here? Why?"

Aldo didn't answer with words. Instead, he reached for a strand of her hair. Elayne watched him from the corner of her eye. They both stared at the hair he twined around his index finger.

Slowly, she backed away from him, letting the coil of hair unfurl from his finger. But she still looked caught. He let her go, secure in the fact that he'd won this first battle and was close to winning the war with his nemesis.

He'd fallen long ago for Elayne Jade. Now it was her turn.

"I'll pick you up for dinner," he said.

"Fine." She turned to go, but then turned back. "They think we're engaged, not married. Don't tell them the truth."

"I won't," he promised. "You have my word."

CHAPTER TWELVE

"You're going on a date?"

"It's not a date." Elayne tossed aside the skirt she'd picked up. It's what she wore when she wanted guys to buy her a drink. It never failed. It was far from the school guidance counselor look of skirts that went below the knee at the bottom and provided space for a prim blouse to be tucked into the top.

No, this skirt molded to her backside, leaving lots of space to take hold of the imagination. Meaning it made men hope, wonder, and pray. It also stopped way above her knees, just shy of mid-thigh. If she wore this, Aldo might think he had a prayer of a chance to…

To what? He'd already managed to get his ring on her finger. Was he expecting that to gain him access to full marital rights?

Elayne scoffed at the thought. Well, she opened her mouth to make a scoffing sound. That dismissive vibration started at the back of her throat. But when it rolled off her tongue, it was nothing but a breathy sigh that was a prayer of her own.

She needed patience. She needed strength. Most of all, Elayne needed understanding.

She needed to understand why Aldo had done this. And done it sober. She still couldn't figure out his angle in this farce.

Putting back the free-drinks dress, because Lord knew she wasn't drinking again anytime this century, Elayne pulled out a pale, prim dress that covered her collarbones and kissed her calves. For all intents and purposes, this dress would serve as armor. She had to be on her guard for anything Aldo Matthews might say or do tonight.

"If it's not a date, then what is it?" asked Kailyn.

"Dinner with some work colleagues."

"You don't work with Aldo."

"He was invited by my colleague, and he's picking me up to conserve gas."

"Hmmm," Kailyn hummed, bouncing one crossed leg over the other while she sat in a plush chair next to Elayne's closet. "Your husband is taking you out to dinner with some friends from work. It sounds like a date."

Elayne threw up her hands, exasperated. She was done trying to explain this to her sister. With her hands up in the air, she let go of the armor dress. It fell into a heap on the floor.

From her short stint in the foster system, Elayne had learned it was her responsibility to clean up after herself and not to rely on adults. She carried that lesson over and into her adoptive parents' house. Dishes were never left out overnight and typically were washed and cleaned right after the meal. The counters were always spotless, the floors always gleamed. So technically, her closet floor should have been clean enough to not transfer any dirt or dust to the dress.

But Elayne decided it was better to be cautious. So back on the hanger the pale, conservative armor dress went. Which left her looking again at the free-drinks dress. Maybe she could pare it with a cardigan to dampen its power?

"You're wearing that?" said Kailyn.

"What's wrong with this?" Elayne asked, holding up the black dress to her form. She'd been wrong. The dress was a little higher on her thigh than she remembered.

"Nothing." Kailyn grinned. "It's just that I borrowed it a few nights ago for a date with Mateo, and he couldn't keep his eyes—or his hands—off me."

Elayne stepped into the garment and pulled the fabric up her body. The zipper glided smoothly up her side until the dress fit her like a second skin. She stepped in front of the mirror. Wow, that hem had risen even higher.

"If you want an annulment, I don't think that's the way to go."

"Of course I want an annulment. I still don't know what got into me agreeing to marry that man. Or what a pastor or judge must have been thinking when he saw the state I was in to think I was giving consent."

Elayne smoothed her hand down the dress. She definitely wouldn't have to buy a single drink the way she was looking tonight. Any man who caught sight of her might decide he was punch drunk based on the amount of cleavage she had on display.

"But I'm getting invited places I didn't have access to because of this." Elayne held up the ring she'd put back on her finger. "I'm just going to secure my place in the guidance office, secure my ideas with the head counselors. Aldo and I can still handle the annulment quietly. The Mosses just think we're engaged. After the paperwork is filed, we can call off our engagement, and by then I'll already have what I want."

Her twin nodded sagely, but Elayne knew better than to think Kailyn was agreeing with her—or letting her off the hook.

"Meaning you'll lie. Even though you hate liars."

That she did. And Aldo Matthews was a liar. "I'm not lying. I'm just not giving all the information."

Kailyn opened her mouth like she was going to say more, but that's when the doorbell rang.

Elayne snatched the pale cardigan from a hanger. She pulled it around her shoulders, knowing full well that it wouldn't dampen the power of the free-drinks dress. Not with her long legs still on display.

She slipped into shoes and went to open the door before Kailyn could get there. Elayne pulled open the door to see Aldo standing on the other side. She had intended to keep her forward motion going right out of the door and into his car, but she came to an abrupt halt. Her body might've stopped moving, but her heart slammed into her rib cage and kept moving as though it were racing to him.

Elayne had never let herself notice before just how devastatingly handsome Aldo was. Chiseled jaw. Lips lifted in a perpetual grin of mischief. Those eyes—they'd often held her in place when they were younger and fighting. But during those times, she'd been fuming, seeing red. Now she was caught in the golden flecks of hazel sparkling down on her.

"Wow," Aldo breathed. "You just took my breath away."

And he had just stolen hers. The thief. He was a liar and a thief. A devastatingly handsome thief who stole any response. A liar whose approving gaze dared her to blink first.

"You've always been a knockout, Elayne, but tonight..." Aldo let the sentence trail off as his gaze took the slow route down her body. The cardigan could have been a flimsy piece of lace the way he looked through it.

"Don't do that," she demanded.

"Do what?"

"You don't have to be nice to me right now. No one's watching."

"How should I behave when no one's watching us, Elayne?"

The way he said her name, it came out husky. Had he ever called her by her name before? Or had it always been Andy?

Andy, like his mother's favorite doll. Mateo had admitted to Kailyn that those dolls were his prized possession, just as she was to him. It should have changed the context for Elayne, but Aldo had never divulged that particular fact. For all she knew, he could've hated the dolls.

"You said you wanted there to be peace between us." Aldo took a step toward her, crowding her space. If there was a line in the sand, he'd definitely crossed it. "This is me being friendly. Can you do the same?"

"I'm not sure how to be nice to you."

"Just don't bite my head off, and we'll call that a start."

"Me?" Elayne pointed at her chest. "Bite your head off?" She turned her index finger on him. "You always start it."

"Because you're cute when I ruffle your feathers."

Once again, she had the wind knocked out of her. She wasn't sure how to deal with this man like this when he was being… Was he being charming? Was he flirting? Elayne felt drunk, and she hadn't touched any alcohol since that night at the hotel.

"Can we just go?"

"Yes, dear."

"Don't call me that."

"Okay, sweetheart."

She glared at him as he walked her to the car. The man was impossible. And she wasn't sure how she was going to survive this night.

CHAPTER THIRTEEN

"*R*emember, they just think we're engaged and not married yet."

"Okay, babe."

"So don't let it slip that we're actually married."

"Sure, dumpling."

"Or that we're getting an annulment."

"Whatever you want, angel."

"Because we *are* getting an annulment."

"If you think so, love."

Yeah, Aldo liked that last one. Calling Elayne Jade *love* rolled off his tongue effortlessly. *Babe* had sounded a bit too smarmy. He'd almost chuckled as he'd said *dumpling. Angel* was definitely not the one, as the woman had proven time and again that she had the devil firmly planted on one shoulder. But Aldo liked that side of Elayne.

Love? Yeah, that one would stick. That would be his endearment for the woman who would one day be his wife.

"Will you take this seriously, Aldo?"

"I take the two of us very seriously, Elayne."

She blinked, her eyes fluttering like a bird's. Then she swallowed hard, like she'd tasted something bitter. Right, she didn't want him calling her by her name.

"Sorry, love."

"Don't call me that either. I'm not someone you love."

Aldo wanted to dispute that. He had loved Elayne Jade since the first time he'd seen her when they were in foster care together. He hadn't understood what those sensations of his heart skipping a beat, him losing his breath, that grumble in his belly, and feeling hot all over, meant.

As a grown man, he understood it now. He'd seen it happen to each of his brothers when they were in the same space as the women they loved. That same dummy look that coated their features when they spoke about their girlfriends or wives. He'd worn that same look every single time he'd come face to face with Elayne.

He'd thought that, as his nemesis, she would be his downfall. Now he knew he'd fallen that first day, and he'd be at her feet for the rest of their lives.

But she didn't look at him that way. Not exactly. She was still fighting. She hadn't noticed that he had surrendered in their game.

"We're supposed to be in love," he said. "It would make sense to other people, especially other couples, that I have an endearment that I call you."

Elayne chewed at her lip. Aldo turned green. Jealousy rose in his throat and coated his tongue. He wanted to take over and bite that plump lip himself.

"Would you rather me call you Andy?"

She let go of her bottom lip. Her top lip slammed down, like a jail cell shutting him out. Aldo only barely stopped himself from leaning down and kissing those lips apart. *Soon,* he told himself.

Soon.

But why not now? They were playing the role of smitten newlyweds. It would make sense for him to touch her, and kiss her, and whisper in her ear. As if he were a green light incarnate, Chief Moss and his wife appeared at the door to the restaurant.

It was the perfect opportunity to show affection for his bride. Aldo, who had always been told he had poor impulse control, decided to take advantage.

His hand circled around Elayne's back. She bristled as he got close. Then froze as he got even closer. Her lips parted, but he knew that particular move of hers. She wasn't about to encourage him. She was about to admonish him, to start an argument.

There was a part of Aldo that wanted to watch her mouth move this close as she ripped into him. But the desire to taste those lips that had always fascinated him was too great.

"Careful," he soothed. "The Mosses are right in front of us."

He caught Elayne's intake of breath. It was as close to a green light as he needed. Aldo brushed his lips against Elayne's, ensuring that she would take in the air he breathed. Turnabout was fair play. Now maybe she'd feel some of the lightheadedness he endured whenever she was in his presence.

Aldo kept the kiss light. He had to. His instincts were to gorge himself on her. Just this slight sweet taste was already heating his blood to dangerous levels.

Elayne's lips quivered beneath his. Aldo touched his tongue to the summit of her mouth. Her sigh sounded to his ears like surrender, and he fell.

Or at least he felt like he was falling. Aldo plummeted down the twin peaks he'd dreamed about for nearly two decades. That divot in Elayne Jade's upper lip was where he found heaven.

Elayne leaned in, seeking more of him without realizing it. He gave himself to her. Showing her that there wasn't a single iota of resistance to him, to them, inside of him. She had always been the inescapable agent of his downfall: his nemesis.

Aldo deepened the kiss. Just enough to give them both a taste of the bliss he knew they would create when she finally accepted what was between them. He nibbled at the center of her upper lip, and it nearly brought him to his knees. The sound of a throat clearing, and then two throats clearing, and then a loud *ahem* brought him back from the brink.

"Do you remember us at that age, Jim?"

"I remember you couldn't keep your hands off me."

Mrs. Moss smacked her husband on the chest with the back of her hand. Captain Moss caught and held that hand, pressing his wife's fingertips to his lips.

Desire shot through Aldo. That's what he wanted with Elayne. To be gray and wizened and to capture her hand when she lashed out at him.

Because he knew she would lash out at him. It was their thing. It was his favorite thing about her. The way Elayne would get fired up, all of her attention focused on him and how to take him down.

"Seems like you didn't tell the little lady about taking the job at the force," said Chief.

"No, I wanted to surprise her." Aldo looked down at Elayne. She looked dazed and unsteady. Her gaze darted as though she was ready to bolt. Aldo's hold tightened.

"Sorry, I ruined that," said Mrs. Moss, a sheepish grin on her face as she took in the two of them.

"It was a happy surprise, wasn't it, my love?" Aldo kissed the cone of Elayne's ear.

She shuddered and had to swallow a few times before she could answer. "It was a shock to learn you wouldn't be going back into a war zone."

Aldo nearly laughed. He loved that she could still rib him even while trying to play nice. He would never get bored with this woman as his wife.

"You proposed the night of the conference?" said Mrs. Moss. "I didn't even know you were there."

"I was attending a military contractor event hosted by the Purple Heart Ranch. I would've married Elayne that night. There were two pastors at the ranch."

"Pastors Patel and Vance." Captain Moss nodded. "Those are two good men. Married most of the men and women on the Purple Heart Ranch. Crazy about that zoning law."

Aldo played with Elayne's hair, running his fingers through it like he'd always wanted to. He'd go on couples' date after couples' date if it meant he had this kind of access to her. She was a captive right now, and he wasn't going to stop until she waved the white flag of surrender.

CHAPTER FOURTEEN

He was a convincing liar. Elayne would give him that. He almost had her fooled. The way he looked at her with those adoring eyes. The way his hand rested over the back of her chair, his thumb running lazy circles on her shoulders. She was half tempted to take the cardigan off to cool her heated skin.

But it was difficult to break away from his touch. From his gaze. From those kisses.

He kept sneaking in kisses. In her hair. At her temple. On her shoulder. On the back of her neck Now on each of the fingertips of her left hand. And she couldn't pull away.

Not if she wanted to keep up this farce. Because it was a farce.

Aldo was playing a game. He was always playing some form of the Dirty Dozens with her. Only this time she couldn't be sure if she was losing or he was winning. What was the difference?

"It was love at first sight for me."

That statement should have infuriated her. It was all lies from the first word to the emphatic period. Aldo had hated her the first time he'd set eyes on her.

Hadn't he?

"I never knew how to talk to her," he continued. "She was so smart and so pretty. She reminded me of a doll."

Her breath caught. *Don't say it.* If he said the name Andy, she was going to lose it.

Hazel eyes met hers. That smirk lifted at one corner, as though he knew exactly what she was thinking. That single word was between them. But even though he smirked, it didn't look like he was joking or being mean.

Elayne knew Aldo's mean face. Or at least she thought she did. How could he be saying such kind, romantic words with that mouth that had always caused her pain?

His hand lifted to her neck. His thumb rubbed at the spot just behind her ear. It was soothing, caring. The kind of move that a loved one would use to tend to a wound. Instead of making Elayne feel better, it muddled her mind.

"You were both in the foster care system?" Dr. Moss asked.

Elayne couldn't answer. She forgot how to form words with Aldo making those pacifying circles behind her ear. Aldo nodded and spoke for them both.

"We both got adopted by the best couples in this town. We both want to give back to it. That's why, after years of military service, I'm joining the police force. And Elayne has great ideas for helping the kids in Honor Valley. Don't you, love?"

That was her cue. They hadn't discussed the need to highlight Elayne's professional traits at this dinner. But somehow he knew, and he'd served her up on a platter to her boss. But Elayne was still stuck on the endearment he'd chosen for her.

Love.

She had to remind herself that she wasn't his love. That he wasn't in love with her. It was all a farce. Just like their marriage.

But why? Why had he done it? What was he doing now? Besides making her feel ooey and gooey inside.

"Elayne?" asked Dr. Moss.

Elayne cleared her throat. She'd rehearsed what she was going to say during this dinner. She'd written reports about the counseling programs and protocols she wanted to implement in the high school to help this new generation, who seemed more stressed-out and anxious than any that had come before.

She leaned forward and presented her ideas. All the while, she felt Aldo's hand resting at the back of her chair. He wasn't rubbing behind her ear anymore. Now his fingers played in her hair. Hair he'd made fun of as a kid. Why would he be gazing at it as though he couldn't take it in enough?

"These are really good ideas," said Dr. Moss. "We should bring them up at the next meeting."

Elayne had tried that. But she'd been shoved to the bottom of the agenda, then promised they would take it up at the next meeting, only to be shoved down again. She didn't remind Dr. Moss of any of this. She was being heard now, and it was all thanks to Aldo.

Aldo, the man who insisted on paying the bill for all of them. Aldo, the man who rested his hand at the small of her back as they said goodbye to the Mosses. Aldo, the man who handed her into the passenger seat of his car and waited for her to buckle up before climbing into the driver's side.

Elayne sat back in the passenger seat. She felt like a passenger in her own life. She wasn't sure which direction she was going in. Aldo had accepted another double date invitation with the Mosses for the weekend. She should have declined. Their marriage would be annulled by then. Already, tonight she had gotten what she wanted: She'd be placed on the counseling program's agenda and be heard. She didn't need to use Aldo anymore. So why was he still here?

"Why are you doing this?"

"Driving you home?"

"You know what I mean."

"Actually, I don't. There's more than one angle at work here, love."

"Stop calling me that. We're alone again."

"So when we're alone, you want me to call you Elayne."

"You're so frustrating."

Elayne slumped farther in the passenger seat, but when she did, her dress rode even higher up her thighs. A glance to her left told her that Aldo wasn't looking at her legs. He was grinning at her face.

"Your face goes red when you get frustrated. It's always fascinated me. When we were kids, I used to think that's why you had red hair, like a blush. I thought you had magic in you and that you could turn your whole person red if I just got you riled enough."

"Is that why you picked on me? To see if I'd change colors?"

He'd pulled onto the main street as he spoke. The light turned from green to yellow. Aldo had time to roll through the changing light before it turned red, but he slowed the car to a stop.

"Picking on you, as you call it, was the only way you'd talk to me."

"That's not..."

The red light changed to red. Across the street, the white pedestrian sign blinked, letting walkers know it was safe to cross.

"I tried to be nice to you a couple of times," he mused. "It never worked. You either ignored me or yelled at me. You never ignored me when I poked at you. So I kept poking."

The walking man changed to numbers in a countdown. Time was almost up for the people in the middle of the street to make their way across before vehicles once again claimed the open road.

Elayne opened her mouth and closed it again. She ran through scenario after scenario of her time going toe to toe with Aldo Matthews. Had he ever said a kind word to her? She honestly couldn't remember.

She was still sifting through her memories when the car pulled to another stop. They had arrived at her house, and she couldn't remember the ride. He hadn't said another word to her. It was the longest time she'd heard the man be quiet.

Elayne reached for the door handle. The look of displeasure Aldo gave her made her snatch her hand back from the handle. As he climbed out of the driver's side and walked around the front of the car, Elayne realized he'd never looked at her like that before. With dark displeasure.

Aldo had always had a slight smirk on his face. His eyes were always bright and excited as he gazed down. Had he? Did he? Did he enjoy fighting with her? Did he think of their relationship as an actual game? One that he played for fun and enjoyment? One that he looked forward to playing with her? Not with the dread she felt every time she rounded a corner and saw him lying in wait.

When Aldo opened the door, she took the hand he offered her. She had to. Elayne couldn't tell which way was up or down. Left or right. Right or wrong.

"Should I kiss you goodnight, Elayne?"

Elayne blinked. They were standing under the porch light, but she didn't need any added illumination to see the desire or the excitement in his eyes. Was this part of the game?

"Do you want me to kiss you again, love?"

Finally, a question she knew the answer to. Though the answer surprised her so much that she wouldn't let it pass her lips. So she bobbed her head instead.

As though he knew her struggles and reveled in them, he said, "Ask me to."

In the darkness, pride left her. Desire was the only thing keeping her warm. That and Aldo's hand resting lighting on her hip. "Kiss me."

"Ask me nicely."

That broke the spell—mostly. Elayne's eyes flashed up at him. All she saw was the bright glare of sharp, white teeth as Aldo chuckled at her.

That was him. That was the devilish boy from her childhood. The bully from her teen years. How could she think for a second that he—

Aldo's mouth crashed down on hers. Not just his mouth on her lips; his hands were on her too. One cupping her chin, fingers tangling in her hair. The other sat at her lower back, pulling her closer until there was no space between them. It was a full-on assault, and Elayne immediately threw up the flag of surrender.

How could she not? She had no other choice. He had knocked down every single one of her defenses, leaving her spinning in circles so he could perform this sneak attack.

Aldo didn't kiss her. He ate at her mouth. Like he hadn't eaten the meal on the table and some off her plate less than a half hour ago. He devoured her, deepening that kiss and taking more than she thought she had to give him. He left her breathless and starving for more.

"Go inside," he growled when he broke the kiss.

Elayne's head might be foggy, her defenses might be down, but she was very clear on what she wanted to happen next. "You know, we are married. So..."

She let that sentence dangle as she threaded her arms around his neck. Aldo took a deep breath, then a second before disentangling her.

"Go inside, Elayne."

The starvation she'd just experienced turned to an instant pain. There it was. That was his game. To get her riled up and leave her wanting more.

He hadn't changed. He would never change. And he'd won again. Elayne opened the door and slammed it in his face. The slam echoed inside the hollowness in her chest.

CHAPTER FIFTEEN

*S*houts and squeals roused Aldo from his sleep. The sounds disoriented him because they were high-pitched and youthful. Not the grunts and body sounds of grown men in close quarters. He wasn't on the base, but he wasn't some place unfamiliar to him.

"You're taking forever."

"Other people need to get ready for school."

Yes, those wails he remembered. For years, Aldo had risen late in the morning in the foster home to a smelly shared bathroom as boys got ready for the day. In the military, morning rituals had been more regimented, but the sounds and smells were much the same. There was nothing like the bickering of siblings to get a man to roll out of bed on the wrong side.

Aldo had spent his formative years in the bunkhouse with his five brothers as they got ready each morning for school, chores, or church. Those same sounds and smells could be heard and sniffed every morning on the Flying Cross Ranch, which only had three bathrooms and at least seven male bodies who had to get ready at the crack of dawn.

Father Matthews was always the first up, and his sons would never hear a peep from him as he went about his morning rituals. He was always at the breakfast table or out on the ranch working by the time the boys wiped the crust from the corners of their eyes. Aldo was usually the last of his brothers to rise and was often met with a cold shower, nearly depleted toiletries, and no clean towels.

In that moment, he preferred the sounds and smells of the base.

"I need this bathroom to get ready," said the deepest male voice. It was Denny, the eldest of the new foster kids inhabiting the bunkhouse where there was only one bathroom and limited hot water.

Denny's voice mingled with a high-pitched feminine voice, who could've been his sassy little sister Daria or the wise-beyond-her-years LaTisha. Aldo would put his money on the voice of contention being Daria. LaTisha would've been like his dad and risen at an optimal time to not have to deal with any bickering.

The bickering was coming from across the hall in the main house where Aldo was bundled up on the pull-out couch in the family room. The space was Aldo's until he decided if he was going to build a place of his own on the land or find a place in town.

Mateo had found and leased an apartment the day after Aldo returned from his trip. It was the first time they'd lived apart outside of the military. It was also the first time that Aldo didn't feel like a piece of himself was missing.

He didn't want Mateo's sharp eyes on him right now, questioning and judging him. No, Aldo wanted Elayne Jade's green gaze to do that.

This morning, while World War III waged across the hall, Aldo wished he'd taken Elayne up on her offer to come inside her house. He wouldn't be hearing adolescent bombs going off right now. He'd be hearing those little moans she made at the back of her throat when he kissed her.

Aldo groaned just thinking about it. He threw his hand over his head. And there it was. He caught just a hint of that spicy scent of hers: hot cinnamon on a cold evening.

He inhaled deeply, wishing his nose was buried in the crook of her neck. Wishing his fingers were tangled in those red strands. Wishing his teeth were nibbling on the divot at her upper lip.

Soon, he promised himself. He'd done so much wrong in their relationship over the years. This time, he was going to do everything right. That started with not taking her offering last night. Not when there was a big, fat lie between them.

True, Aldo was harboring a lie about his relationship with Elayne. But if he played his cards right, that lie about them being married could become a reality. With that wishful prayer, Aldo rose for the day and promptly fell back on his behind.

A quart of cologne wafted out of the bathroom before Denny did. Aldo teared up, looking with desperation at the window latch on the other side of the family room.

"What?" asked Denny.

"Did you spill the bottle on yourself?"

"Too much?" Denny asked, raising his forearm to his nose. In true teenager fashion, with a young nose that was immune to most noxious fumes, the kid didn't even flinch.

"You trying to impress a girl or something?" Aldo asked.

He flinched at that, his broadening shoulders huddling in on himself. "Yeah."

Aldo nodded slowly, considering his words. "Girls like subtly. When it comes to cologne, anyway. You want to give them just a hint and then make them lean in."

Denny nodded slowly, considering Aldo's words. He reached back into the bathroom and rubbed a washcloth over his neck and wrists. "What else do they like?"

"Shouldn't you be talking to Charlie about this?"

Denny rolled his eyes. The movement caused another waft of cologne to singe Aldo's nose hairs. But Aldo could understand the eye roll.

Charlie had only loved one girl all his life. Any dating advice he might come up with in his total lack of game would be to follow the object of affection around until she threw up her hands and gave in. That method had taken Charlie nearly twenty years to finally get a ring on Savy's finger.

There had only been one girl for Aldo too. He'd gotten his ring on Elayne's finger in a very different manner. "Have you told her you like her?"

Denny shrugged. "I haven't even talked to her. Savy says I should compliment her."

"Compliments don't always work." Aldo had tried to compliment Elayne, and she would always turn it around on him. Or worse, she'd ignore him completely. "You gotta say something to get under her skin. Make her stop and take notice of you. That's not always the nice thing."

"You're telling me to be mean?"

"Not mean exactly. I—"

"I heard about that tactic on a YouTube Channel. It was called Chad Bro. This guy Chad talked about how he got a lot of women's numbers."

"I don't think you should listen to a guy who calls himself Chad Bro."

"I hear you. Why would I want a girl's number when I can just DM her social media handle?"

"Wait? What?"

"Thanks, Uncle Aldo. I knew you were the best guy to talk to about this. You're the only one who isn't married or engaged."

"No, I am…" He was what? Not married. Not exactly engaged.

"I thought Uncle Mateo said you were getting an annulment."

"No one's getting anything annulled."

"I don't see your wife here with you."

"Yet."

Denny looked doubtful, but he nodded, hands up as he walked backward down the hall toward the front door.

Aldo dressed quickly, preparing to go in for his first day of training for the police academy. His father was rocking on the porch when he came out. Aldo rested a hand on the old man's shoulder. Father Matthews didn't need to turn to see which of his sons was at his back. Even though he'd raised six boys, two of them twins, he could be resting with his eyes closed and know who had approached him.

"Denny has a point. I would like to meet this wife of yours."

"You heard that from all the way out here?"

"I have the hearing of an elephant, son."

"I thought elephants had long memories."

"And big ears." Father Matthews grinned.

"She's not my wife," Aldo admitted. "Not yet."

Father Matthews turned a surprised gaze to his son. It was hard to catch the man off guard. It was usually Aldo who accomplished it.

"I proposed to her. But she was…" He didn't want to say that Elayne was drunk. That wouldn't make a good impression. "She didn't entirely agree at the moment. But you're going to meet her soon, and you're going to love her."

Father Matthews chuckled. "Never thought that it would take a heart attack to make all my boys come home and find love."

"Yeah, don't do that again."

"Don't worry, son. I won't. My heart is too full to skip a beat again."

CHAPTER SIXTEEN

"Have I told you how beautiful you are this morning?" said Mateo.

"Yes, but only about three times so far," said Kailyn.

Elayne made a face in her oatmeal. Mateo had come over for breakfast before seeing Kailyn off to work. This was after he'd brought her twin sister home late last night. It had barely been seven hours that they'd been apart. And here they were, back together again, making gooey eyes at each other.

It was too early for this.

Elayne needed her sister's attention. They hadn't had a chance to talk about Elayne's disastrous, confusing, pulse-pounding, heart-stopping, not quite a *date*, but definitely *something* with Aldo Matthews. And then there was that soul-stirring kiss. Followed by the bucket of ice water dumped over her head in the form of a rejection.

Glaring at Mateo, who had the misfortune of sharing facial features with Aldo, Elayne thought of what she wanted to do to Aldo. She wanted to slam the door in his face again. Preferably while his perfect nose was in the way.

"What did my brother do?"

Elayne blinked, looking up at Mateo. Though his features were similar to Aldo's, she had to admit that the two men looked entirely different. There were smile lines at the corner of Mateo's eyes. His hazel eyes were a softer shade too, with less sparks of gold around the edges. Mateo also held on to her sister's hand, twining their fingers and stroking Kailyn's bare ring finger.

Elayne ran her thumb over her left ring finger. Aldo's ring was there. She had no idea why she was still wearing it. She should have flung it across the room last night. But she'd spent too long staring at it in the moonlight.

She still didn't remember accepting it. Not entirely. There was the hazy memory of Aldo grinning at her as he held up the sparkling gem.

He hadn't gotten down on one knee. That she knew she would definitely remember. Seeing her greatest foe fall to his knees was a dream her brain would never let go of. He'd been standing toe to toe with her when he'd asked the question, Elayne was sure of it.

"It was our mother's ring," said Mateo, nodding to the band on Elayne's finger. "I took the dolls. He kept the ring."

Aldo had told her that. Hadn't he? She vaguely remembered him talking about his mother.

"Your eyes were throwing daggers at me a moment ago," said Mateo. "But I'm not my brother."

"I know that," Elayne sighed. But she wasn't about to explain to her sister or Aldo's brother that she was upset about being turned down by him last night. "I don't blame you for your brother's actions. I never have. You've always been decent."

"Even if silent?" Mateo said with a wince.

Kailyn's fingers tightened around his. He looked up at her through his long lashes. Kailyn had often remarked that Mateo had stood by when Aldo and Elayne got into it. The fact that Mateo would never step into their arguments always bothered Kailyn. It looked like Mateo had resolved not to hold his tongue any longer.

"My brother's been obsessed with you since we were kids," he said, turning his attention back to Elayne.

"Obsessed?" Elayne's hand rose to her mouth as the word left her lips. Her breath blew through her fingers as though she could capture that one word and examine it. It was such a farfetched notion.

"Well, what would you call it? He would always seek you out. Every day in school, he would find a way to talk to you. What else would you call it?"

That made no sense. If he actually liked Elayne, he would've found something nice to say to her at least once.

I tried to be nice to you a couple of times. It never worked. You either ignored me or you yelled at me. You never ignored me when I poked at you. So I kept poking.

Aldo had kept poking. And she'd kept arguing with him—talking to him.

"He tricked me into marrying him." Elayne held up her left hand in evidence. The gems winked back at her, twinkling in the early sunlight like they were dancing on her finger.

"I know I don't know you well, Elayne," Mateo was saying, "but I have never seen you do anything you don't want to do. Especially where my brother is concerned."

Elayne glared, but Mateo was unperturbed. Right then, he looked exactly like his twin. The corner of his mouth was raised in a smirk. The light in his gaze challenged her to disagree with him.

"Savy said something interesting the other week," said Kailyn, but she was turned to Mateo as she spoke. "She said boys tug on the hair of girls until they know how to behave."

Mateo nodded with a grin. "Sounds about right." He reached up and tugged on Kailyn's hair.

"You don't have to do that anymore," she giggled. "Now you know exactly what to say to me."

"I do," he said. "I'm so hopelessly in love with you, Kailyn Jade. You're going to have to save me."

"Don't worry, I've got your back." Kailyn leaned in for a kiss. For a moment—make that two minutes—the two lovebirds completely forgot Elayne was standing there.

"I'm headed out," Elayne said, dumping her half-eaten oatmeal into the trash. "You can get a ride from your hopeless love."

"Say hi to your husband for me," called Kailyn, arms still wrapped around Mateo's neck.

"He's not going to be my husband much longer. Besides, I'm not seeing him today."

"You saw him last night."

Elayne nodded.

"And the day before."

Elayne exhaled sharply from her nose, not liking where this was headed.

"And you spent the weekend together right before you got married."

"This marriage won't last," said Elayne, checking in her bag for the annulment papers.

"I hope it does," said Mateo. "You're a really good influence on my brother. I've seen changes in him I never expected."

There was a part of Elayne that wanted to ask what changes. But the more vocal part, the part that was still reeling from Aldo's rejection after that scorching kiss, was louder. It responded to the hopelessly devoted couple by storming out the front door.

The smell of teen spirit, which was a mix of too-sweet perfumes and noxious cologne, hit her the moment she walked into the school's front entrance. The buzzing sound of adolescents all speaking excitedly over one another dulled her own thoughts as she walked down the hall. But the ghosts of times past decided it would visit her today.

Near the sophomore hall of lockers, Elayne remembered an encounter with Aldo when he'd told her her hair looked like carrots. Moving beyond that, she turned the corner near the junior hall when he'd witness her first boyfriend dump her.

The dumping had happened after Aldo had punched Darius Cox in the face. Months later, Elayne had counted her blessings after a couple of girls got in a fight over who was really Darius' girlfriend. As she'd listened into the catfight, she'd noted that at least one of them had been dating Darius at the same time he'd been hitting on her.

Had Aldo known what Darius was up to? Had that been the reason he'd told her that she couldn't date Darius?

My brother's been obsessed with you since we were kids.

Elayne still couldn't wrap her brain around Mateo's words. She couldn't wrap her brain around Aldo's proposal. She couldn't get her brain to function very much at all these days.

"Anybody ever tell you that your hair looks like Medusa's snakes?"

Elayne's gasps mingled with the lanky girl who the insult was aimed at. Standing between the lockers, Elayne spied a brown-skinned girl—Keisha, she thought the girl's name was. The glistening coils of her dreadlocks hung down her back and across her shoulders. She pushed them all behind her neck as she averted her gaze from the bully.

Elaine recognized that kid, too. It was one of the new generations of Matthews. Denny.

Denny's grin dropped as he watched Keisha turn away from him with a brush of her index finger at the corner of her eyes. He held up his hands as though to stop her, but immediately dropped them when he saw Elayne.

"I don't understand," he said to Elayne as though he was the affronted party. "Why did she get upset?""

"What made you say those things? In what world would you think that's okay?"

Denny looked truly confused. He crossed his arms and chewed at his lower lip, his gaze still down the hall where Keisha was ducking into the girl's bathroom. "I just wanted her to talk to me. My uncle said sometimes the only way girls will talk to you is if you're mean to them."

"Which uncle?"

"Your husband."

CHAPTER SEVENTEEN

ldo loved nothing more than a day of hard work, clear instructions, and a job well done. He'd accomplished all three of those things on his first day of training at the police academy.

He'd been worried that police work wouldn't give him the same thrill, the same feeling of service and satisfaction as his military career had. There was an adrenaline rush to being in the air, to sleeping close to a combat area, to rushing into a battle zone with your fellow soldiers at your side. But learning the protocols and procedures of how to protect the people in his small community felt even bigger than protecting all the citizens in his country. This was more personal.

"Good work today, Matthews," said his new boss.

Being that it was a small town, his training was being held at the local community college. There were only three other cadets at the desks with Aldo. At first Aldo had balked at being put back in a class-room. But the lessons on how to handle domestic violence calls and child abuse cases made him sit forward.

Back during his time in foster care, he had witnessed the aftermath of those two things combined, but he'd been too young to do anything about it. Overseas in war zones, he'd witnessed them happening before his eyes, but his hands had been diplomatically tied then. Today, he was being given the skills to make a difference.

"Thank you, sir," Aldo said to Chief Moss. "I'm eager to get started.

Even more, I feel this is what I'm supposed to be doing in this next phase of my life."

The chief grinned at him with a satisfied head bob. "I had a good time last night. Shirley and I would love to see you and the missus again." Moss held up his hand in apology. "Sorry, I mean your fiancée. Though you two sure act like an old married couple."

It was on the tip of Aldo's tongue to come clean, tell his new superior that Elayne was neither his wife nor his fiancée. His lips wouldn't form the words. Not when his heart flatly refused the notion that Elayne wasn't his.

So Aldo said nothing. All he could do was force a weak smile and nod. Chief Moss didn't appear to notice anything out of order. He gave Aldo a slap on his back and sent him out into the early evening with a grin on his face.

Aldo's grin widened when he saw Elayne leaning against his car. His mouth opened, ready to tell her every feeling that raged to the surface. Each and every one of them was about her.

His heart sped up. Skipped a beat. Only to race forward again. It didn't bother him in the slightest to know that this was how he was going to die: from a cardiac arrest over his devotion to this woman.

His head swiveled left and right, bobbing up and down, trying to take her all in at once. She wore a prim skirt, colorless blouse, and pale cardigan. She looked every bit the matronly guidance counselor preparing to shepherd the wayward youth of his generation. Aldo knew exactly where he wanted to be guided.

"Hey, love," he drawled as he came within earshot of her. "Ready for me to come home?"

Elayne had been looking down at the ground. Her lips had been moving, her features fierce. Much as she'd looked when he seen her rehearsing for a debate in English class. She'd won every argument during that lesson. Now she looked up at him, startled.

Aldo's gaze was latched onto her mouth. Her lips had parted when she looked up, making a perfect O shape. Her lips were usually compressed in that exaggerated M shape that he loved so much.

The O was stunning. It was also the perfect shape for kissing.

Elayne backed up from him. When her back came flush to his car, she startled again, realizing she had nowhere to go. The O shape returned briefly before her lips pursed into an M.

"You made it perfectly clear you didn't want to go home with me," she said.

Aldo crowded her into the car, boxing her in with his big body. Every warrior instinct in him told him to pounce. His prey was weak, and she had no escape. But he didn't want Elayne as docile prey. He wanted her to be the passionate predator alongside him.

"Didn't you?" she demanded.

Her eyes flicked down to the ground. They took a full breath before they rose back to meet his. Elayne backed down from a staring contest with him. Aldo didn't like the uncertainty he saw on her face. So he leaned in and kissed the corner of her eyelid.

Hot cinnamon heated him under his collar as her breath of surprise blasted against his neck. Her hands came up in front of his chest. They fluttered between them, like a bird uncertain of where to land.

"You think I don't want to come home with you?"

When he looked down, her eyes were dazed, unfocused. Her cheeks were flushed a beautiful shade of pink. But the uncertainty was still there in her features.

"I drove around your block for two hours last night. I have calluses on my calluses from gripping the steering wheel so tightly so that I wouldn't bang on your door."

Slowly, the uncertainty began to melt away. Her throat, which still was that warm shade of pink, worked as she swallowed a few times. Her eyes narrowed, but not in the defiant way she always looked at him. Confusion tipped her lashes.

"I'm not coming into your house until you stop believing I'm the big bad wolf."

Her gaze widened. The determined M came back to her lips. She leaned away from him, pressing herself back into the car. "Well, then you need to stop terrorizing little kids."

The woman always caught him off guard, and he loved every second of being knocked off-kilter. "What are you talking about?"

"Did you tell Denny to be mean to a little girl?"

"Why?" Aldo tempted fate by brushing his thumb just under her lower lip. Surprisingly, his digit remained intact. "Did it work?"

"No." Elayne's lower lip trembled slightly. "She got upset."

"But she noticed him." Aldo rubbed just at the edge of the plumpest part of her bottom lip. "She talked to him."

Elayne had to swallow before she spoke, but she still didn't pull away from his touch. "He hurt her feelings."

"He'll make it better." Aldo kissed the right corner of her mouth. Then again on the left side.

"So it's true?"

Her lips were barely a breath from his. He could've claimed her mouth, but he liked the position they were in too much. This was where he wanted to spend most of his time: right on the edge of having her.

"What's true, my love?"

When she spoke, her voice was barely a whisper and she wouldn't meet his gaze. "You've been mean to me all these years because... you liked me?"

Aldo waited in that space. He waited until she looked up at him so that she could see the truth rather than hear it.

Elayne swallowed a couple of times. Each compression of her lips brought their mouths closer and closer together, but Aldo refused to claim her. Not until she looked up.

Then she did. And she shoved him away.

Aldo stumbled back. Not from the force of the blow. From the shock of her rejection.

"That's the stupidest thing I've ever heard," she said, her voice back at full volume.

"Now who's name calling?"

"Why didn't you just try to talk to me, to be civil when we first met?"

"Because you ignored me. You looked at me like I was trash."

"I was a scared little girl. And you were fighting on that first day."

"I wouldn't have hurt you."

"Physically, no. My feelings, yes."

Aldo nodded, hanging his head. "I'll never do it again."

"Yes, you will."

Fair point. "I'll always kiss it better."

He took a step closer, his hands raised. She pursed her lips in that combative M. Aldo knew he had her. Sad, uncertain Elayne, he wasn't sure how to deal with. This Elayne who was ready for war, he knew exactly how to get past her defenses.

"Want me to kiss it better now, love?"

He wasn't even the slightest bit surprised when she sighed and admitted defeat with a weary "Yes."

Aldo pulled her close, but before his lips could descend and take the kiss his entire body was so hungry for, Elayne punched him in the chest. Right over his heart. The organ took it as a love tap and pressed harder against his chest to get at her.

"Ow, what was that for?"

"Don't tell any more boys to be mean to girls. It doesn't work."

"It worked for me."

"I'm still not sure I actually like you."

"Then come on a date with me. No other couples. No brothers or sisters or kids. Just you and me."

"That sounds dangerous."

"I'll protect you."

"From yourself?"

Aldo grinned, and then he claimed Elayne's mouth. All the while in his brain, he was mounting a defense to claim her heart so that his ring would stay on her finger permanently.

CHAPTER EIGHTEEN

*E*layne entered the school building the next morning on Cloud Nine. She knew her head was in the clouds when she couldn't hear her heels clacking against the sticky linoleum floor. Her sister bounced beside her on an adjacent cloud.

"The Matthews boys," said Kailyn, her voice hushed in wonder.

"Who knew?" Elayne's voice held the same note of stunned awe.

"I did." Kailyn's look turned smug as they passed the cafeteria, where the breakfast rush was in full swing. "I felt something the first time I saw Mateo. We probably would've been together back in high school if it wasn't for you and Aldo's feud coming between us."

"It came between us too," Elayne admitted.

The sisters passed by the scene of Elayne's great breakup with Darius Cox. She saw Aldo standing over her ill-fated love with menace etched into his handsome face. She'd thought him the villain back then. Now she realized he was protecting her in the only way he knew how.

"But now that's over?" asked Kailyn. "The feud between you and Aldo, I mean."

"Yeah." Elayne blinked, the vision of Aldo from the past morphing to the man who had kissed her breathless outside the police precinct yesterday. "Yeah, I think it is."

Kailyn linked her arm through Elayne's. Elayne leaned into her sister. The two shared a secret smile that didn't hide that they were both falling stupidly in love.

The notion of love had Elayne tripping. Her heel came down hard on the linoleum. The sound was like a record scratch. But instead of coming to a halt, the music in her mind simply changed. It switched from a battle march to a love sonnet. Because Elayne wasn't storming forward any longer. She was falling in love.

"Hey, Keisha, wait up!"

"I don't want to talk to you, Denny. What you said to me the other day was inappropriate and offensive."

Both Kailyn and Elayne came to a halt at the far end of the hall where Denny was carefully, yet urgently, trailing behind the object of his affection. Keisha's long locks were hidden under a colorfully wrapped scarf piled on top of her head. Though one coiled tendril escaped on the side. She quickly tucked it behind her ear.

"I wasn't trying to be offensive," Denny was saying. "Well, I was, but I realize that was bad advice."

"I'm going to be late for class."

"I always thought Medusa was beautiful."

Keisha halted, her head whipping around to glare at him.

"In the Greek myths, it says Athena cursed her because she was so beautiful. Then in the Percy Jackson film, Medusa was played by Uma Thurman, who is crazy hot."

Keisha twirled the lock behind her ear as she regarded him.

"Then there's the actress who's going to play the new Little Mermaid. What's her name?"

"Halle Bailey."

"Yeah, her. She has locks, and she's really pretty."

Keisha's smile was tentative. Her gaze lowered and then rose to meet Denny's hopeful grimace.

"I just wanted to say I'm sorry," Denny said. "I didn't mean to hurt your feelings. I went about things the wrong way. Friends?"

Denny extended his hand, palm up. Keisha let go of her lock and placed her hand in his. The two stood there, gazing at each other with puppy dog eyes.

"Can I walk you to your class?" Denny asked.

Keisha nodded. He took her bag and walked side by side with her, stealing sheepish glances along the way. He still hadn't let go of her hand as they walked by Kailyn and Elayne.

"What was that?" asked Kailyn.

Elayne tilted her head to the side as she watched the two young people turn the corner. "That was history correcting itself."

"What?"

But Elayne only shook her head. She bussed her sister on the cheek and then headed right at the fork in the road that would take her to her office in the guidance suite. She plopped down in her chair, and the motion made the office chair spin halfway around. As her head spun, Elayne couldn't help thinking to herself how different her life might have been if she had behaved differently that first time she'd met Aldo.

The sound of her purse falling on the floor brought Elayne back around. Reaching for the spilled contents of her bag, she spied the annulment paperwork. She had forgotten the document was in there. Holding the pages in her hands, she was unsure what to do with them.

She could admit to herself that she was developing feelings for Aldo Matthews. But were they a lifetime's worth of feelings? A knock at her door brought her head up. The person standing in the door had Elayne's fingers fumbling to flip over the pages of the decree facedown on her desk.

"There you are," said Dr. Moss. "I wanted to tell you the good news myself. The committee took a look at your proposals—"

"What proposals?"

"The proposals you submitted."

Elayne opened her mouth and promptly shut it. The proposals she'd submitted months ago had been entirely ignored by the committee. She kept getting empty promise after empty promise that they would be placed on the agenda. At least the committee was making good on their word.

"The committee is interested in formally posting a position for a Mental Health and Wellness Counselor."

Elayne gasped, sitting up straight in her chair. This was the main proposal she'd been trying to impress upon the guidance committee for years. Her suggestion had always fallen on deaf ears, with members insisting that mental health wasn't the arena for school guidance.

"We think you're the right person for it, and we would like you to consider applying for the position."

"Thank you. Thank you." Elayne stood to shake Dr. Moss' hand. She kept saying the words on repeat. Even when she walked the woman to the door, she kept expressing her gratitude. This was the position she'd dreamed of having since college when she first realized the impact of stress and anxiety was growing not just in her generation, but in the one coming up after her. "I don't know how I could ever thank you enough for… for all of this."

"Just give me and Jim an invitation to your wedding. I hear the Silver sisters and Matthews brothers' weddings have been the talk of the town over the last few years."

"Wedding. Right."

"You probably have so much on your mind. A wedding to plan. Now a new job. And pretty soon..."

Dr. Moss patted Elayne's very flat belly. There was a hollow feeling there. But Elayne said nothing as she watched her boss leave the room.

She looked again at the turned-over annulment papers. She might not be ready for a wedding, and definitely not children of her own, but she also didn't care to sign the documents any longer. So Elayne tore them in half and let them fall into the wastebasket. The rest she would talk over with her husband.

Her husband? Elayne reached for the chair, letting her body slump into it. The more she thought about the H word, the more it felt right.

CHAPTER NINETEEN

$\mathcal{A}$ldo rested his hip against the gate of the Jade home. He'd never been inside the ranch-style house that was painted a vibrant shade of blue. He'd only been past the white picket fence once. This afternoon he'd been invited.

The text from Elayne had come at the end of his training. She'd simply said *Come over.* It wasn't the first time Aldo had received a text like this from a woman. It was the first time it had been from the woman he wanted to come to. Now that he was here, exactly where he wanted to be, he wasn't sure how to get over the obstacle of the closed gate.

As if she heard his distress, the front door flung open. Elayne stood in the entryway. She wore an apron over her outfit. In bold block letters, the words on the apron read *Your opinion wasn't in the recipe.* Aldo chuckled at the phrase that was so her—at least when she was face to face with him.

His gaze continued down her lush body. The apron hung lower than her skirt, making her legs look bare. She wore no shoes, putting her purple-painted toes on display for him.

The sight of a nearly bare Elayne had Aldo clutching at the passenger side door. He was certain that if he let go, he'd launch himself at her. And where would that get him on his slow and steady campaign to win her over?

Elayne had been grinning at him, but her smile faltered. "You're not coming in?"

Aldo nodded and tried to swallow.

Elayne's features fell even more.

"No, no, I am coming in. I just—you just—" Aldo took a deep breath, let go of the passenger side door handle, and started again. "Elayne gotta warn a man before you do something like that."

He waved a hand in her general vicinity. Elayne looked down at her apron. Her bare toes flexed upwards. When she lifted her head, her features were colored with confusion.

"Something like what?"

Aldo couldn't answer. He'd gotten his wits back, and he knew exactly what to do. His addled brain remembered how to unlatch a gate. His military training kicked in, reminding him how to sneak up on an adversary.

But Elayne Jade was an adversary no longer. He prowled to her on sure steps, not hiding his intentions. Unlike him, Elayne didn't step back to grab at the front door handle. She stood still, waiting for him. The confusion morphed into certainty as she reached out a hand to him.

It was the first time she'd ever done anything like that. It was almost too much for Aldo to process. Almost.

Aldo launched himself at her. Or she flew into his arms. Either way, they met in the middle. He captured her upper lip and devoured it. She tugged his bottom lip into her mouth. He ate at that divot in the middle of her top lip. The taste was so sweet, so savory, so her. She made a sound at the back of her throat that suggested his opinion just might be welcome in the recipe they would make together.

He could've stood there in the doorway gorging himself on this woman, but a throat cleared behind him. Aldo didn't need to turn to know who had made the sound. It was exactly the sound his throat would've made if he'd had a death wish.

Aldo growled as he looked over Elayne's shoulder and saw his brother grinning at them in the foyer.

"Never thought I'd see this day," said Mateo as he walked up to his brother.

His brother's arm was slung around Kailyn. A face so similar to Elayne's but at the same time so very different grinned up. Then Kailyn turned that smile to Mateo, and the brightness went from one hundred to a one thousand-watt smile filled with love and adoration.

"What day is that?" asked Aldo.

"The day when I didn't have to step between you and Elayne Jade to counteract World War III."

"You'd be a fool to try to get between us right now." Aldo's fingers dug into Elayne's hip.

She'd turned around in his embrace, but she hadn't stepped out of it. Nor did she complain as his possessive fingers kept hold of her. She still looked dazed from the hungry kiss they'd just shared. She looked happy as she rested the back of her head against his shoulder.

"Are you going to feed me or what?" Aldo growled as he kissed the top of her nose, then her cheek.

Elayne's lips spread into something soft and private just between them. With a sigh, she pushed off him. With a grunt, he let her go. Elayne reached for her sister. The two bent their heads together and giggled.

Mateo and Aldo stood watching after them. There was a dumfounded expression on Mateo's face. Normally, Aldo would've made fun of his brother. He didn't because he knew they wore twin expressions.

After their whisper session, Kailyn disentangled herself from her sister. She came up to Aldo and stood with her hands on her hips as she regarded him. He could tell when she'd made a decision and her head bobbed in a nod. Then she stepped closer to him, came up on her tiptoes, and pressed a light kiss to his cheek.

It startled him, but Aldo decided he liked it. Nowhere near as much as he liked kissing her sister. But he'd let Kailyn buss him on the cheek anytime she'd like.

"Hurt her again, and I'll paint your chest hairs with turpentine. Mkay?"

Aldo could only grin at the girl he'd always seen as the quiet, docile twin. Kailyn reached behind her for Mateo's hand. Mateo had clearly heard her threat because he grinned his approval before walking out the front door with her.

Aldo followed Elayne into the kitchen. He had to make himself take a seat at the island and not stand behind her as she worked over the pots and pans. He constantly had to talk himself down from leaping over the island, snatching her around the waist, and taking her lips as dessert before dinner even finished cooking.

No one was more surprised than him when his resolve lasted long enough for Elayne to put the meal on serving plates. The roasted chicken with garlic potatoes and steamed broccoli made his mouth water. But nowhere near as much as the cook did.

"I have news," said Elayne as she sipped at her glass of wine. "I got offered a new position in the guidance office."

Aldo set down his knife and fork and reached for her hand. He mirrored Elayne's posture, pushing his shoulders back and lifting his chin high. He couldn't be prouder of her.

"We're probably going to have to fake our wedding now."

Aldo's hold on her fingers went lax. His chin dipped. She must have read the question in his eyes.

"Because only our family knows our wedding has already happened, and how. It's not a good look if the townsfolk know that the woman in charge of their children's mental health and career guidance eloped on a drunken bender. Everyone will expect a wedding."

"You want to marry me?"

"Not... I mean... Not, like, this weekend or anything. I thought we could just keep dating for now and tell people we're planning for a ceremony next year or something."

"Next year?"

"I mean, unless we kill each other." She winked at him. "Besides, I would like to actually remember my wedding."

Aldo opened his mouth, then immediately closed it. The truth was on the tip of his tongue. He knew he'd have to tell her, eventually. Otherwise, she was going to find out and be blindsided.

A blindside would hurt her, and he swore he'd never allow any hurt to come to her. This was going to sting, but he had to believe they'd get through it. The worst she could do was yell at him. And that had never bothered him before.

"We're not married."

Elayne threw her head back and laughed. Oh, did that laugh rain down over his heart and soothe him? Though she wasn't taking his words seriously, she still hadn't let go of his hand. Not until she sobered and saw that he hadn't cracked a smile.

Her fingers stiffened in his hand. Then she began to pull them away. It was the fight of his life to loosen his hold.

CHAPTER TWENTY

The day called for rain. At least that's what the meteorologist had said when Elayne had turned the television on as she'd gotten dressed in the morning. It had been overcast for just the first fifteen minutes after she'd stepped outside before work. The sun had shone bright all afternoon, but the rain clouds remained in view in the distance all day long.

"Say that again?" Elayne's voice was calm, as gentle as water lapping on a sandy beach.

She heard the sound of Aldo's throat working. The throaty swallow, was that a nervous gulp? She'd never known the man to be uneasy a day in his life.

Definitely not with her. But there it was—a quiver at the corner of his lips. A twitch in his right eye.

"When I came over to you at the bar that night, you were drunk and sad. You thought no one wanted to marry you."

The first patter of rain fell against the windowpane. It obscured Elayne's view of the patch of flowers her mother had planted on the day their adoption was made final. She lifted her gaze to Aldo's face and had to blink once to bring him into focus.

"I said I did. I wanted to marry you, and then I gave you my mother's ring. But you never agreed to marry me."

Elayne blinked a few more times, but it did nothing to bring the vision of that night into focus. What was clear was the sound of Aldo's voice. Elayne remembered him saying the words, but she didn't remember the expression he'd worn on his face while doing so.

Aldo Matthews had a special talent for delivering stinging putdowns, all with a straight face. Or worse, his words would rip someone to shreds while wearing that devilishly handsome smirk. His lips were forever lifted in that impish grin that would silently cut Elayne to shreds when he bullied her.

Had he been smirking when he'd said those words to her when she had been at a low point?

"So it was all a joke?" Elayne's voice was still a quiet storm, even as the rain outside picked up. Droplets tapped at the window like they wanted to be let inside.

"It wasn't a joke."

The ferocity in his voice made Elayne blink a few more times, but she couldn't bring him into focus. Somehow the rain had made its way inside and was trailing down her face. Aldo opened his arms and aimed his big, warm body at her.

There was no triumphant smirk on his face. His features fell like he knew his defeat was imminent. But like the stubborn fool that he was, he wasn't giving up.

"You were drunk."

"So you took advantage of me."

"I took you to my room and stayed there with you. I didn't want to leave…" He closed his eyes and inhaled, lines formed in the grooves of his forehead as though the memory was painful. "I couldn't leave. So I stayed and watched you sleep."

"You lied."

It was the only thing Elayne could see clearly. She certainly couldn't trust her ears. The sincerity and contrition she heard in his voice had to be false. Especially not with her eyes watering the way they were. She swiped at her cheeks before continuing.

"I still can't understand the point of it. What do you get out of pretending to be my husband? Just…" She hiccuped. "Just to ridicule me?"

Arms came around her then and Elayne felt too tired to fight it. She wanted to push him away, to punch him in the chest. But if she did that, he would definitely stop holding her. And she needed to be held, just for a minute, while the world was so blurry.

"What I got out of it was you," he said. "What I wanted out of it was you. I've only ever wanted you."

Elayne shook her head. She couldn't believe those words. Not when she'd seen the exact opposite.

"For more than half my life, you've made fun of me, called me names, and tormented me." When she squirmed, Aldo held on tighter.

"Because it was the only way you would talk to me." His voice was low in her ear. "I tried to be nice to you that first day we met when we were kids. You turned your nose up at me like I was trash."

That wasn't how Elayne remembered it. Aldo had been making fun of another kid, his soon-to-be-brother Topher. Then he'd turned that attention on her and made fun of her hair. Once again, she couldn't believe what he was telling her, not when she had the memories to back up the truth of it.

"I was fascinated by your hair," he said, using one hand to stroke his fingers through her strands. "I called you *Red,* and you shot daggers at me."

No. No, that wasn't how it happened at all. Was it?

"After that, you became my nemesis, and I fell for you."

Elayne pulled away from him. "That's not what that word means."

"You're the goddess who brought me to my knees."

It was an utter downpour outside. A crackle of thunder split the silence between the two of them. Elayne loved a good thunderstorm. She would curl up in a comfy chair with a blanket, a warm cup of tea, and a book. She wanted to forgo the book and tea and use Aldo as a blanket.

But she couldn't.

"You still lied to me about being married."

"No, I didn't. I asked you to marry me. I put a ring on your finger. You and everyone else assumed—"

"You"—Elayne pointed an accusing finger at him—"lied."

He inhaled, holding her gaze. There was so much in that gaze. Defiance, resignation, hope. But she wouldn't be swayed by it.

Elayne couldn't abide liars. She needed all the information to make a decision. The counseling team had kept her in the dark and not included her in on decisions that would affect her job and her livelihood. And now Aldo, the man who had snuck in and stolen her heart, had bald-face lied to her. With him not telling her the information she needed, that would definitely put her job and her livelihood in jeopardy.

"Let's do it," he said.

"Do what?"

"Let's get married."

"Are you insane?"

"Of course I'm insane. I've been in love with a woman who can't stand me since I was a kid. You would never talk to me or look at me without ripping into me, and I came back for more each and every day that I could lay my eyes on you."

Another rumble of thunder crackled between them. The sound of the rain changed. The droplets were no longer banging against the window. The storm was moving on.

Elayne turned away from Aldo. She crossed her arms and hugged herself tightly. She needed to lean on something because her head was spinning around and around. She pressed her lips together to keep herself from screaming or crying.

"Don't do that," he said. "Don't turn away from me. Don't stop talking to me."

She would not let her lip tremble. She would not cry in front of him. "I need to think."

"Think out loud. Talk to me."

"I can't do that. Not when I can't trust that you'll tell me the truth."

"I have never once in my life lied to you."

"But you also didn't tell me everything, did you?"

Not the truth about their relationship status. Not the truth about his feelings.

Aldo inhaled again, but no words came out. There was a part of Elayne that wanted him to fight. Wanted him to get in her face, to shout her down and argue every point that she made with that devil may care smirk in tow. Except this time, she wanted him to care.

Instead, those massive shoulders that had offered her comfort in the storm slumped. He hung his head as though the thunder had struck him in the back. The light in his eyes went out now that the rain had moved on. He looked past her at the back door.

Elayne's heart pounded in her chest. She was angry, but not enough for him to leave. But she couldn't open her mouth to say so. The man she never had any trouble arguing with. She couldn't say anything to him.

It appeared he couldn't say anything to her. Slowly, he turned on his heel and walked to the door.

Her heart thudded when he put his hand on the knob. Her gut wrenched when he turned it with a flick of his wrist. She felt the cold of the rainstorm seep into her bones when he closed the door behind him.

CHAPTER TWENTY-ONE

"You haven't said anything all day."

Aldo got the impression that his brother had been speaking to him for a long time. That beginning of his sentence sounded like it had come in the middle of a longer discussion. But Aldo hadn't been in the mood to have any kind of discussions when he got home last night. He was even less inclined this morning. Why would he talk when the one person he wanted to talk to had stopped talking to him?

If they'd still been kids, Aldo would've marched over to the school and lain in wait until Elayne rounded the corner of the study hall and pounced. Or he could've gone up to the student government offices and casually bumped into her when she came out with her index cards all in order. The time he'd done that, the cards had gone all over the place and were out of order. They'd argued a good ten minutes while he'd helped her gather them up and put them back in order.

If he could go back, he'd toss those note cards aside and pull her to him. He would take a handful of that red hair and tug her closer to him. She would be shocked and indignant, but he would have her full attention.

And that's all he wanted: her attention, her closeness. To feel her mouth pressed against his, whether she made words or not. He knew the exact shape her lips would make. He knew exactly how he would press his mouth against her and taste the shape of her, the texture of her, everything about her.

"Al?"

Aldo looked up at his brother. Into the face that was so like his. There was concern etched on Mateo's features. Beneath that concern was joy.

Mateo had won the heart of the woman he loved. He hadn't proposed to Kailyn, not yet. But when he did, there was no doubt that she would say yes. And it wouldn't take a disgusting mix of chocolate and alcohol for her to do it. It was clear in the way that Mateo and Kailyn looked at each other. In how she always reached for him. In how he was always waiting to receive her touch.

Was that where Aldo had gone wrong? Should he have been gentler with Elayne? Maybe he shouldn't have tugged on her hair. Maybe he should've whispered soft words to her all these years.

But no. He'd tried that and failed. Arguing was the only thing that kept her close to him. He was just too tired to do that with her anymore.

"I don't know what to do," Aldo finally admitted.

Mateo didn't ask the obvious question. *About what?* Even if the two of them didn't have the twinsense between them, it was clear to anyone looking at Aldo that he was heartsick.

"I just want to be with her," he admitted. "When I'm not… everything hurts."

Aldo scratched at his chest, but it didn't lessen the ache inside. His head throbbed from trying to work out the best angle to approach her and coming up empty. His eyes stung from being wide open all night long. His fingertips were numb from being clenched into fists at his side as he tried to hold himself still and not race back to her house and bang on the door to be let in, to be let close to her.

"Have you told her that?" asked Mateo. "She might like to know you're in pain."

The laugh hurt his throat as it pushed out of raw lungs. But it felt good. Sitting out on the back patio with his brothers felt good. Charlie sat in their dad's creaky rocking chair, rubbing his thumb and index finger on his chin in the same way their father had done when they asked him for advice.

"Don't give up, bro," said Charlie. "It took me and Savy two decades before we finally got our forever."

"Until you got your forever?" Topher scoffed from his place, sitting on the steps. "You sound just like her. What's next? You'll be singing show tunes while you sweep the kitchen floor."

Charlie took off his hat and tossed it down the stairs. The assault only got a chuckle out of Topher as he snatched the hat out of the air and flung it back at Charlie.

"I wasn't going to give up," Aldo said. "I just don't know how to fight this battle."

"Statistically, you shouldn't fight," said Joe as he leaned against the railing. "With each of our relationships, we chased after the women, but it wasn't until they stopped running and marched up to us that the battle was over."

"Are you telling him to give up?" Will asked from his cross-legged position on the ground. There was a pen in his hand, a pad of paper in his lap. Mateo couldn't see the words, but he was certain Will was working on a poem that his wife Tricksy would take to the studio and turn into another hit song.

"I'm not saying give up," said Joe. "Just stop fighting. She'll come back to you when she's ready."

"Did Foxy say something to you?" Aldo asked hopefully. Joe's psychic wife had seen each of their relationships unfolding before they got underway. But Foxy's visions, or rather her clairsentience, weren't perfect. She was only right half the time.

"She saw that you two were married when you got back home from your trip," said Joe.

"But they weren't married," said Mateo.

Foxy had gotten that part wrong. Aldo had proposed, and he'd meant it. He wanted to spend the rest of his life with Elayne. Fighting with her, making up with her, doing all manner of things to that expressive mouth of hers.

"You need to march over there and let her know what's what," Topher said as he rose from his place on the steps. "Demand to see her. Demand that she listen."

"And how would Toni react to that?" Charlie asked as he rocked back in the chair, his mouth quirked in the same way as when their father decided to let one of his sons touch the fire to see how hot it was. Metaphorically speaking—mostly.

"She'd take my head off." Topher grinned as he scratched the back of his head. "But at least I'd have her hands on me."

Aldo liked Topher's idea the best. He'd let Elayne pound on him, yell at him, do anything she wanted to him. Just so long as he had her with him.

Her wrath he could stand. He'd been doing that for years. It was her silence, her absence, that would break him.

In the end, Aldo decided to compromise. He would give Elayne some space for the rest of the day while he was at the police academy training. Then he would go and pound on her door.

When he took his seat in class, he was gratified to know that they had added a new cadet to the program. The town was growing, and it would need a lot more officers to ensure its citizens were safe. Aldo would help with recruiting once he got himself situated on the force. Any and everything to keep Elayne safe, especially if he couldn't be with her all the time.

For the next four hours, Aldo managed to keep Elayne off his mind. Mostly. The knowledge that everything he was learning would be put in use to protect her and keep her safe allowed him to focus on the lessons at hand. As they were packing up to leave for the day, Chief Moss poked his head in the door.

He shook hands with the other cadets and asked after their health and their progress. When he got to Aldo, he placed a strong grip on Aldo's shoulder. The older man's smile broadened, reminding Aldo of his biological father's grin.

Aldo had been a bit of a hellion growing up. But both of his fathers had each seen past that to the man he would become. Standing in front of Chief Moss, a man who had been at the crossroads when Aldo could've gone down the wrong path, that approving head nod was confirmation that Aldo had made all the right choices in his life, and the chief recognized it.

"The missus and I are having some friends over for dinner tonight," said Chief. "I know it's short notice, but I'd love for you and your fiancée to join us."

Aldo opened his mouth, but the words stuck in his throat. He was that snot-nosed kid staring down two potential paths. Except this time, he wasn't the only one his decisions would affect. He knew exactly which road he was supposed to take. He just didn't know how his decision would affect the woman he loved.

"Elayne isn't my fiancée, sir."

"No?"

"She didn't say yes when I proposed."

"She's been wearing your ring."

"She couldn't get it off her finger at first."

"Well, that's a sign if ever I saw one," Chief Moss chuckled.

"I misled her. Not when I proposed, but…"

Aldo let the sentence die. He couldn't see a way to explain that he'd proposed to Elayne when she was drunk, and then spent a platonic night with her, only to wake up in the morning and not correct her when she thought they'd actually gotten married. Hearing it that way made him see why Elayne was a bit miffed.

"The problem is, I'd do it again." Aldo tilted his head back and looked out the window at the cloudless sky. "All I've ever wanted was to be close to that woman."

"Then you should come with me. There's something I think you should see."

CHAPTER TWENTY-TWO

*E*layne sat in the meeting room at the school board. It was supposed to be her day, the one she'd been working toward for years. She felt nothing but a hollow ache in her chest.

"Tell us about yourself, Mrs...." Ted Heath, who had been hired a year after Elayne, looked down again at the stack of papers set before. "I beg your pardon, *Miss* Jade."

Elayne couldn't even muster a single huff of anger at the man. She was all tapped out of the emotion. Even if she could get upset, she wouldn't waste it on the likes of the tall, thin man whose wedding ring kept slipping up and down his boney left ring finger.

He knew her. All of the men and women sitting across the table knew her. This was the first time they'd actually paid attention to her. And it was all because of the ring on her finger.

Elayne glanced down at the ring. She'd tried to tug it off again last night. The ring held fast. She had to admit that her attempts had been halfhearted. The ring had become a comfort sitting on her finger instead of a vise.

"I'm not married," she said in answer to Ted's question.

All around the table, pencils stopped waggling around on paper. Gazes came up and looked at her. But not really seeing her.

Dr. Moss was the first to recover her smile. She poked the eraser tip of her pencil at Elayne's left hand. "Not yet, but I hope you're planning for a spring wedding. I do love spring weddings."

"I don't know if there's going to be a wedding. I didn't agree to the proposal." Elayne rolled the band around her finger. It was looser than it had been. Using her thumb, she tucked the ring snuggly down toward her knuckles. "But I want to marry him."

Around the table, the other counselors shuffled and fidgeted. Once again, Dr. Moss was the first to speak up.

"None of this matters, Elayne. Whether you accepted Mr. Matthews' proposal at first or later—"

"But it does matter. Because none of you took me or my ideas seriously until he put this ring on my finger."

Elayne held her hand up as evidence. The diamond twinkled at her. It reminded her of the look in Aldo's eyes, the look when he'd asked her to marry him under the dim lights of a bar.

"I would never do anything to hurt you, Elayne," he'd said. "Let me prove it. Take my ring."

He had asked her to marry him. He hadn't smirked or scoffed. There had been vulnerability in those hazel eyes of his. There had been hope and desire. Because he wanted her.

"I didn't say yes," Elayne said to the room of confused peers. "He said he'd spend his days proving he's the one for me."

A few sighs from the women in the room brought Elayne back to the present moment. Dr. Moss had a soft smile on her face. Ted looked on the verge of annoyed. Elayne didn't care. She rose from the seat.

"Where are you going? We're not done here." Ted pointed to his list of questions.

"I proved I'm the one for this job on my first day. If you all need more proof than that, then I'm not the one. But I need to go and find my one."

"What?" said Ted, his gaze connecting to the two other men in the room, only one of who wore a similarly baffled expression.

The women dabbed at their eyes. One of the women who had been here since Elayne was in school gave Elayne a discreet pump of her fist.

"She's right," said Dr. Moss. "The creation of this new position is based on a report Ms. Jade wrote. She knows the role inside and out. This interview is just a formality. The job is yours."

Dr. Moss rose and reached across the table, extending her hand.

Elayne hesitated. Not because she wasn't sure if she wanted the job or not. She did. But she wanted to get out of this room and find Aldo to tell him how she truly felt. But there was no reason she couldn't have both her man and the promotion. Elayne took Dr. Moss' hand.

"The job is yours regardless of your marital status," said Dr. Moss. "But if you're a smart woman, you'll lock that Matthews boy down. I've seen the way he looks at you."

Elayne let herself see the things she'd never seen in Aldo's eyes as she replayed the words he'd said to her over the last few days.

I've never hated you. You decided you didn't like me.

I like you, Elayne Jade. You're the smartest girl I know.

If she was so smart, how come she was so dumb? How could she not see that none of the words out of his mouth had been said in hatred? How had she not seen that quirk in his smile when he faced off with her? It was all so obvious now.

Are you asking me to marry you?

Yes.

You think I'll say yes?

No. Not yet. But maybe one day. Until that day, I'm going to prove I'm the one for you.

That was it. That's when it happened. She'd fallen for Aldo Matthews, and it had taken a cocktail of alcohol and chocolate to make her see the truth.

"I'm gonna go and lock that down. I'm going to marry that man. But I have to propose to him first."

CHAPTER TWENTY-THREE

"Come sit with your family, son."

Sitting was the last thing Aldo wanted to do. He was itching to go find Elayne. When he and Captain Moss had arrived at the Board of Education where they were holding her interview, the room had been empty. Aldo hadn't waited for Moss to call his wife to see where they might've taken Elayne for a celebratory meal or drink. He'd started his hunt.

She wasn't at her house. She wasn't at the school. Kailyn, who sat in the cradle of Mateo's arms, didn't know where she was either. She wasn't picking up any calls or answering texts. Aldo was starting to worry.

"I need to find her, Dad."

"I understand, son. Just nourish yourself first. It's the first time we've all been together under the same roof for years."

By all, Father Matthews didn't just mean all six of his sons. All wives, fiancées, and girlfriends were here as well. So was the other half of their family. The six Silver sisters and their husbands were also gathered in the yard, filling out two picnic tables. And then there were the five foster kids who were all officially adopted and now proper Matthewses.

But his father's words weren't exactly true. They weren't all together. One person was missing.

Aldo stood up to defy his father and leave when the sound of a car kicking up dirt down the drive had him turning. He knew it was her before his body came completely around. There was no one else unaccounted for.

He ran down the lane to meet her to a chorus of cheers from his brothers, sisters-in-law, Silver sisters, and fellow brothers-in-love. Aldo barely waited for the car to come to a stop before yanking the driver's side door open, lifting her out, and pulling her into his arms.

He had no clue whether she was there for him or not. He had no idea if she'd deck him for being so forward, and he didn't care. She was right where she belonged: in his arms.

"Where have you been?" he shouted as he pulled back.

"I was looking for you," she shouted right back at him.

"I was looking for you." Aldo hadn't let her go. They were still pressed together from their knees to their chests. But they glared into each other's faces. "Why didn't you answer your phone?"

"Because I was driving around looking for you." Elayne's cheeks were flushed and red as she pursed her lips and gave Aldo her death stare.

"Well, that was smart." His hands clenched into the back of her dress. "It's not safe to text and drive."

"I know." Her nostrils flared as she shoved her hand against his chest, right over his heart.

The organ gave a kick, like it was a puppy who'd just gotten its first scratch behind the ears. "I love you."

Elayne threw her arms around his neck and locked down. "I love you, too."

She hadn't cold-cocked him in the jaw, but it was enough to knock him backward. He was done with the shouting and fighting. He had a better plan for those expressive lips of hers. Like the warrior he'd been trained to be, Aldo stormed in and captured Elayne's mouth.

She didn't put up any protest. She hugged him tighter than he knew she had the strength to do. She pressed herself into him, giving herself fully to him. Her fingers tugged at the strands of his hair, and he knew exactly what that meant.

"I'm sorry," he said when he let her up for breath.

At the same time as she said, "I'm sorry."

"What did you do?"

"The same thing I've always done to you: I didn't listen. I misjudged you. I walked away instead of talking it out. And I'm sorry."

Aldo shrugged, burying his nose in those red strands that had always fascinated him. "I don't care, as long as I've got your attention."

"I'm going to be nice to you from now on."

"Why?" He pulled back, staring down at her in utter disbelief. "I mean, sure, if you want to."

"I'm trying to give a grand gesture." She smacked him on the shoulder.

Aldo captured her hand and kissed her fingers. "You're doing it beautifully, love."

Elayne curled her fingers. She looked down, chewing at the inside of her mouth. She looked vulnerable, uncertain. Aldo tightened his hold.

"I have something to ask you," she said finally.

"The answer is yes."

Her small smile was only half amused, and then the uncertainty came back. "Listen to me."

Aldo made a show of sobering his expression. But she had to know that he was telling her the truth. Whatever she asked him, the answer would be yes.

From the picnic tables, there was silence in the peanut gallery. Forks were abandoned. Even the kids were quiet as they watched the final soap opera across the Silver Star and Flying Cross ranches play out.

"You asked me a question," Elayne said. "I couldn't remember it before. Until today."

He nodded, holding his breath. Had she remembered the night he'd proposed to her? He wanted to know exactly what she remembered. But it looked like she'd gotten the highlights.

"I called you a nightmare."

Aldo shrugged again. "Close enough to an endearment for me, my love."

"You're not a nightmare. You're my hero."

"Well, you are my nemesis. It's the least I can do."

She shook her head, but the uncertainty was gone. Aldo decided he'd spend the rest of his life trying to replicate that smile. When her lips stretched broad, it was so much better than the M of upset. Much easier access for kissing, too.

"Aldo, I came here to propose to you."

"You know that's the man's job."

"Hey!" She smacked his shoulder.

"But I'm an evolved man. So ask me."

"Quit bossing me around, Matthews."

"You think I'll say yes?"

"Oh, please! You are so into me."

"It's true. I am."

Elayne opened her mouth to say more, but Aldo had already heard everything he needed to hear. Her lips were stretched in another smile, and it was past time he knew what that expression on Elayne Jade tasted like. So he dove in.

ALSO BY SHANAE JOHNSON

Shanae Johnson was raised by Saturday Morning cartoons and After School Specials. She still doesn't understand why there isn't a life lesson that ties the issues of the day together just before bedtime. While she's still waiting for the meaning of it all, she writes stories to try and figure it all out. Her books are wholesome and sweet, but her are heroes are hot and heroines are full of sass!

And by the way, the E elongates the A. So it's pronounced Shan-aaaaaaaa. Perfect for a hero to call out across the moors, or up to a balcony, or to blare outside her window on a boombox. If you hear him calling her name, please send him her way!

You can sign up for Shanae's Reader Group and receive a FREE NOVELLA in this world at

https://shanaejohnson.com/ReaderGroup

ALSO BY SHANAE JOHNSON

a Flying Cross Ranch Romance

His Vow to Love

His Vow to Treasure

His Vow to Adore

His Vow to Trust

His Vow to Respect

His Vow to Defend

The Silver Star Ranch Romances

His Pledge to Honor

His Pledge to Cherish

His Pledge to Protect

His Pledge to Obey

His Pledge to Have

His Pledge to Hold

The Brides of Purple Heart

On His Bended Knee

Hand Over His Heart

Offering His Arm

His Permanent Scar

Having His Back

In Over His Head

Always On His Mind

Every Step He Takes

In His Good Hands

Light Up His Life

Strength to Stand

His Grace Under Pressure

The Rangers of Purple Heart

The Rancher takes his Convenient Bride

The Rancher takes his Best Friend's Sister

The Rancher takes his Runaway Bride

The Rancher takes his Star Crossed Love

The Rancher takes his Love at First Sight

The Rancher takes his Last Chance at Love

www.ingramcontent.com/pod-product-compliance
Lightning Source LLC
Chambersburg PA
CBHW070226200726
48293CB00005B/1490